ORCONOMICS

A Satire

ORCONOMICS

A SATIRE

BOOK ONE OF THE DARK PROFIT SAGA

J. Zachary Pike

Edited by Karin Cox

Cover design by James T. Egan of Bookfly Design
Published by Gnomish Press, November 2014

Version 3.0.6

Gnomish Press, LLC
P.O. Box 64
Greenland, NH 03840
GnomishPress@gmail.com

GNOMISH
– P R E S S –

Acknowledgements

There are a number of reasons I prefer the term "independent publishing" to "self-publishing," but first and foremost is the fact that this book took the time and effort of many people to become what it is today. I am indebted to all of them.

Karin Cox has been a wonderful editor. She's a pleasure to work with, and her gentle corrections make me a better writer.

John Corsi is a remarkably talented art director and graphic designer, and I'm lucky to have worked with him on the print edition of this book.

Thoughtful feedback and encouragement from my beta readers has made this a better story, and I'm indebted to them. Thank you to Nate Bates, Elizabeth Bushnell, Josh Cole, Richard DiPippo, Christopher Kellen, Ariele Sieling, Glen Westerberg, and Talley Westerberg. A special thank you to my friend Kristin Boucher and sister Erin Wallace, who have been reading this story years at the time of publishing, and still provided amazing feedback. I must also make special mention of the work of Mike Tibbals, who not only read the book, but also constructed a wiki, drew maps, and made an excellent attempt at translating Shadowtongue. His work was invaluable, and I dream of one day having fans with that much enthusiasm.

Over the years, many friends have read my work and offered critique and encouragement. Thank you to Eric, Nick, Warren, Ryan, and Al.

Thank you to my parents for the love and guidance, and for always projecting absolute certainty of my eventual success.

Finally, I must extend my deepest gratitude to my wife, Becky, who was my most encouraging beta reader, and whose support and patience make my writing possible.

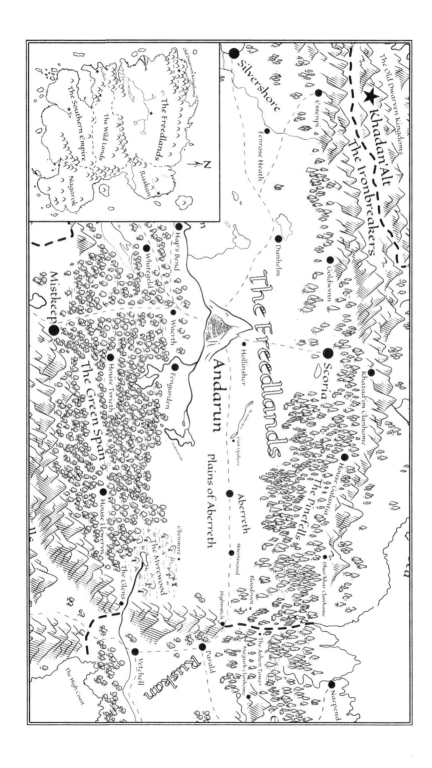

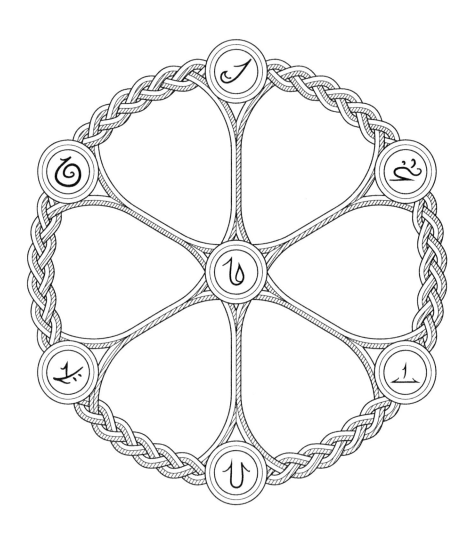

To
Grace & Madelyn

Prologue

As a general rule, signs are too subjective a topic for polite company. Where one man sees a sign of blessings to come, another sees bad tidings, and a third is puzzled by the animated discussion his companions are having about an oddly shaped piece of toast. With so much disagreement regarding the meaning of portents, let alone whether there is a meaning at all, it's seldom wise to discuss them. All things considered, however, it's probably safe to say, without fear of controversy, that a crying bride is a bad sign.

Naturally, there's nothing foreboding about a gently weeping bride, her glistening tears only highlighting the joy of her radiant countenance, nor even a nervous bride softly weeping as the stress of anticipation and uncertainty and an overbearing mother-in-law-to-be leaks out before the vows; such things may or may not be taken as signs, embraced or dismissed by reassuring friends and family with equal ease.

A bride whose entire body shakes with wracking sobs, however, a bride whose choking wails send streams of spittle and snot to join the tears running down her face, is almost unquestionably an ill omen.

Just such an unfortunate woman, if she was old enough to be called a woman, stood in a dimly lit stone room, her long white dress soaked in sweat and tears, her dark curls tangled and mussed from a night that should have left her without any tears to cry. Yet, standing in the cold, damp chambers next to a pathetic sliver of a groom—a milk-white, scrawny boy in an oversized suit with a mop of greasy hair that did too little to cover his pocked, ratty face—the bride found a sudden reserve of tears, and she heaved them forth with all the grief she had left.

"Enough, Princess," said the man officiating the ceremony. He wore royal purple robes bearing a silver skull motif that announced he was a wizard. A neatly trimmed beard implied he was meticulous, and his hard expression suggested the ceremony should continue with all haste, lest things become much more unpleasant. "Now, do you swear to stand by your husband, through good times and bad …"

The groom gave his bride a clumsy smile and fumbled for her hand. She swatted his clammy paw away. "No!" she screamed, bursting into a renewed fit of sobs. "No! I won't!"

"Marja, you will marry my son," the wizard said coldly. "The ceremony will be completed, you will take him back to the royal palaces, and he will be third in line to the throne. Quiet, boy!" he snapped, cutting off a comment from the groom. The boy nodded dumbly and looked at the floor.

"He was supposed to come." Marja sobbed quietly. "He was supposed to save me."

"What are you babbling about?" barked the wizard. "Nobody is saving anyone!"

"Detarr Ur'Mayan!" called a voice like a trumpet. An armored foot kicked in the great oak doors of the chamber. A knight in shining armor followed.

"Johan!" The princess shrieked in delight.

"Oh, by the gods," said the wizard with a sigh.

Johan was the kind of physical specimen that inspires sculptors, clad in the kind of cutting-edge gear that inspires bankruptcy. Faint, sorcerous lights flickered in the runic etchings of magical armor that would cost a king's ransom. A magical flame danced along the edge of a blade that would cost a king's fortune. The torchlight gleamed from a perfect smile that would win it all back again.

"Detarr Ur'Mayan!" he shouted again, crimson cape and golden hair streaming behind him as he strode into the room. "You have been declared a foe of the people of light. I come for the princess, and for your head."

Detarr's lip curled into a condescending smile. "Have I? Well, I think you'll find that I'm not so easily — "

He was cut off by a sudden wail.

All eyes turned to the young groom, who lurched for the back stairs and fled the room in an ungainly, knock-kneed sprint.

"Did he just wet himself?" asked Princess Marja.

The wizard rubbed his temples. "He's been having trouble with … he just gets nervous," he said, his voice heavy with paternal exasperation. "No matter! It's a setback. Just a setback."

"It's your last one." Johan hefted his sword. "Come, sorcerer. To battle. To death."

Detarr made no reply; instead, he pulled his hands into an intricate pose. Thin strands of sorcerous light spread from his palms, and his fingers deftly wove them into an incandescent sphere of dark magic and malice. With a guttural cry, the wizard hurled the spell at the knight with all the force of a lightning bolt.

He missed.

One moment Johan was standing in the doorway, grinning confidently at Detarr, and the next, he was standing several paces to the left of where he should have been, smirking at the passing spell. A heartbeat later, he was directly in front of the wizard, moving with the fluid grace and speed of a shadow.

"You —" gasped the startled wizard.

"Me," said Johan with a swift swipe of his sword. The air whispered like steel on silk, and Detarr's head bounced on the floorboards. His body slumped to the floor a moment later.

"Ha haaa!" Johan's laugh was musical and resounding.

"Johan!" The princess threw her arms around him. "You came!"

"Indeed, Milady." He gently lifted her into his muscular arms. "And now, I shall return you to your father's palace."

Princess Marja gave a little laugh and tossed her curly auburn locks. "Oh, no rush."

"And you shall be married to your good prince!"

"Or not," said Marja suggestively.

"Ha haaa!" Johan trumpeted once more. He strode triumphantly over the corpse of the fallen wizard and out the door, ending a very well known story and setting the stage for an even greater one.

Chapter 1

"And that's how Johan saved the Princess Marja from the evil wizard," said the old farmer.

"Uh-huh," said the warrior, without looking up from the long scroll of parchment in his hand.

"And she married good Prince Handor, who's King Handor now, long live his majesty!" The farmer was as gnarled and leathery as the turnips strewn around his field. He was the sort of rural soul who had more fingers than teeth — and he was missing several fingers.

"I think we're all familiar with the story of Johan," said the warrior, marking his document with a weathered quill. He was a pot-bellied man, covered in furs and scraps of armor.

"Didn't ask for nothing in return, neither," said the farmer.

"He got a rather large estate in Andarun, as I recall."

The farmer got a sly look in his good eye. "Ah, but he didn't ask for it, see? 'Cause he was a true hero."

"Well, I'm a professional one. Just pay your bill, sir."

The farmer snorted and gestured to the turnips haphazardly scattered around him. "You an' yer so-called professionals tore up half my fields!"

"In pursuit of the reported Goblin threat," said the hero. He made another mark on the document.

"You burned down my barn flushin' the varmints out!" The farmer pointed his three-fingered hand at a pile of smoldering beams and charred hay. "Where's the sense in that?"

"I'm afraid it doesn't matter if it makes sense," said the warrior. "It's standard procedure."

"But you broke all my barrels!"

"Standard procedure."

The farmer was aghast. "You looted my basement!"

The hero shrugged. "Standard procedure."

"But … but …" The farmer grasped the hero's arm and spoke in a low whisper. "But you and … and my daughter." The nervous tittering of an infatuated young woman rang out from within the ramshackle farmhouse.

A hint of a smile twitched at the warrior's mouth. "Standard procedure," he quipped.

"But … you can't … you …" The farmer reeled uncertainly.

"Sir, you put out a contract to exterminate a nest of Goblins," said the warrior, brandishing his document. The contract was written in exquisite script, and near the bottom of the page, the hero had checked off and initialed a number of tasks; below that, the farmer's signature was scrawled among several others, surrounded by official seals and stamps. "The good people at Adventure Capital Incorporated accepted your contact and hired me and my associates to kill said Goblins, and outfitted us with the gear necessary to do so. And now that the Goblins are dead, I'm afraid it's a little late to decide you don't like the terms of your contract."

"I …" The farmer shook his head and stared out at his ravaged fields. The ground was littered with green corpses and ruined crops. "I thought the loot would pay your fee. Thought there'd be some left over for me, too. Heard that's how a man can get rich nowadays. Find some foes, claim the contract, get a cut of the loot. Barten Mander had a griffin take his cow, and he bought hisself three acres with his cut of the hoard."

He turned back to the hero, his eyes filling with tears and futile rage. "And then you come in, you ruin my farm, you take all the food in my stores and you tell me that's the loot! You rob me, give me half my stuff back, and charge me for it!"

"No, the Goblins in your basement robbed you," corrected the warrior. "We took it from them. That's what loot is."

"It came from my house!"

"Where else do you think loot comes from?" hollered the hero, finally losing patience with the old man.

The farmer didn't have a ready answer, but he was spared the trouble of finding one by a high-pitched scream.

A lone Goblin, presumably startled by the warrior's shout, burst from its hiding place in the charred ruins of the barn. Once the creature's huge, panicked eyes caught sight of the warrior, it took off, sprinting in the opposite direction, clouds of soot billowing in its trail.

"Bones!" swore the warrior.

"Oh!" The farmer pointed to the hero and then to the fleeing Goblin, and then back to the hero again. "You ain't done! You ain't got 'em all! I ain't payin'!"

"Sir," the hero tried, "the Goblins are all dead or dispersed. One or two stragglers—"

"Contract says exterminate!" said the farmer, practically dancing. "Ye ain't done!"

"It doesn't make sense to chase down every single Goblin," protested the warrior. "They're harmless alone."

The old farmer's malicious grin displayed his limited collection of teeth. "Don't have to make sense, do it?" he cackled. "It's standard procedure."

There was no recourse for the hero. Fuming and sputtering curses, he hiked his belt up, tucked the contract into his rucksack, adjusted a couple of armor plates, and set off at a brisk trot after the Goblin.

Goblins do not excel at much, but they are masters at tactical retreat. This particular Goblin was talented enough at fleeing that it took the hero more than an hour of tracking before he even had the creature in his sights. The Goblin led him off the old man's farm, down a stream, through some scrubwood, and to the main road from Mistkeep to Andarun. The warrior had to chase it for a further mile down the road, until both were well past the point of stumbling exhaustion.

Finally, the warrior was close enough to make a desperate swipe with his sword; the Goblin made an equally desperate attempt to dodge it. The maneuver sent the creature tumbling into a muddy ditch on the roadside, the warrior barreling after it. The hero raised his sword for the final blow. The Goblin fell backward onto a pile of mud and leaves—which immediately startled both combatants by sitting bolt upright and roaring like a demon.

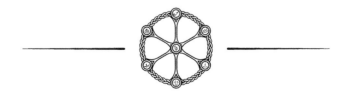

Goblins are famously unsavory creatures. A Goblin's skin is pale green and oily, and reeks even when it's clean, which is almost never. Their large yellow eyes constantly run, their mouths bristle with serrated teeth, and their stunted, piggy noses are always dribbling something disgusting. Like a bad hangover, a Goblin can make any experience much more unpleasant.

Gorm Ingerson had the misfortune to discover new depths of displeasure when he awoke to a Goblin and a bad hangover combined. The creature was clambering over his face, and the dull, throbbing sobriety thundered in his skull with such fury that he sat up with a start and screamed. His shout startled the Goblin into screaming, too, which scared the fat Human enough to cause him to fall on his rear. Consequently, for a time, the three of them sat shrieking at each other in confusion.

"What are you doing here?" hollered the fat man, pointing his sword at Gorm and the Goblin in turn.

"Keep it down," growled Gorm, gripping his forehead. "I was sleepin' it off, before it jumped back on again." His initial surprise was receding, but a dull pain was washing in to replace it. Gorm stood with slow, labored movements and tried to remember how much he had drunk. Last night was a blur; this morning was a smear.

"You're a Dwarf!" exclaimed the fat man.

"What tipped ye off? The beard?"

"Oh, I couldn't see that under all the leaves and muck," said the man, pointing at detritus that covered the Dwarf from head to toe. "It's just that you're really …" The warrior trailed off.

Gorm and the warrior stared at the warrior's hand, held level with the Dwarf's head at about chest height. "Aye?" Gorm said softly.

Some would say Dwarves are sensitive about their height, but not when Dwarves are within earshot. It would be more accurate, and much safer, to say that they enjoy vigorously defying stereotypes about height and prowess.

"… speaking with a thick accent," finished the warrior.

"Ha. Right," said Gorm, realizing that the Human looked like a professional hero. His mismatched armor had clearly been scavenged from a variety of foes, and his sword showed a faint glimmer of magic around its edges. Probably somewhere around the third rank. "Ye on a run?"

The rank-three warrior's demeanor warmed at Gorm's use of heroic jargon. "That I am," he said. "You a hero, then?"

"Oh, I've done my fair share of quests and grinds. Used to be a big name in the guild. Still am, in some circles." This was true, strictly speaking. Specifically, the Heroes' Guild's Internal Affairs and Enforcement departments maintained a keen interest in Gorm. "What's the job?"

"I'm harvesting greenskins for the points."

Gorm gave a short laugh and pulled a clump of leaves from his long rusty beard. "Well, ye don't take 'em for the loot, right?"

"Right," guffawed Rank Three. "Not the best job I've had."

"Well, you take what comes."

Opportunism was the mark of a professional adventurer. When a potential payout passed a hero's way, he was either ready or missed out. Gorm had spent too many nights clutching an empty belly to let a chance for a quick bit of gold pass him by—even if he was hungover and covered in mud.

"Quite right. If you'll excuse me, there's just one left," said Rank Three with a nod to the Goblin. The wretched creature was lame with exhaustion, crawling on its belly away from the two men. When it realized it was being watched, it squealed piteously and doubled its futile effort at escape.

"This won't take but a moment," said the hero, cleaning his sword. It was a nice-looking sword, at least twice enchanted. Valuable.

"But here's a thought," said Gorm pointedly, pulling another clump of filth from his beard. "Why not let the little blighter live, an' just say ye killed it? All of the benefits, none o' the risk. Very economical, see?"

"It's the nature of being a professional hero." Rank Three shrugged. Gorm could hear the warrior's purse jingling.

"Fight, kill, loot, get credit. Repeat until you're dead," said the hero.

"See, I just skip the fightin' and killin', and forego the credit," said Gorm. "Instead, I give the target a chance to hand over the loot."

Rank Three took off his helmet, which was easily worth forty giltin, to scratch his head. "I don't see how that benefits you."

Gorm smiled. "I'd say ye'll benefit more'n I will."

"Eh?"

"This here's your chance."

Realization spread over Rank Three's face, quickly giving way to anger. "That sounded like a threat," he growled.

"More of an offer." Gorm pulled his old axe from the mud. It was a simple wedge of iron on a solid oak shaft wrapped in grimy leather grips. Old and plain and not the least bit magical, it was, however, Dwarven-made, which meant it was balanced and sharp. Gorm didn't need much else. "I got a feelin' I'm about to find a stash of loot.

Don't make a difference to me if I find it on the ground or on your corpse."

"*Suggich?*" asked the Goblin.

The warrior's eyes narrowed. "Dwarf, I don't want to fight you."

"No, ye don't," agreed Gorm. He could see the warrior sizing him up, trying to gauge his rank.

On the whole, professional heroes are remarkably prone to violence, and this is by necessity; a hero's work consists almost exclusively of forcibly separating deadly monsters and nefarious villains from their valuables. A long history of armed conflict had shaped the Heroes' Guild into a group that was remarkably effective at killing and remarkably poor at conflict resolution. Professional-versus-professional combat remained an ever-present threat to up-and-coming adventurers, especially those who couldn't quickly determine whether or not they were outmatched.

"Do yourself a favor, lad," Gorm said, nudging the warrior in the right direction. "Lose the gear and gold. Specifically, where I can find it."

Instead, Rank Three opted to call the bluff Gorm wasn't making. Red-faced and spraying spittle, he charged forward with an angry bellow.

A good charge is a hard thing to appreciate. Most people assume anyone can grab a weapon and run straight at an enemy, pointy-end forward, and for the most part, they're correct. The tricky part of a frontal assault, Gorm knew, was surviving it. But if you had the finesse, timing, and skill, a good charge could be unexpectedly effective.

A sloppy charge, on the other hand, is easily countered. A feint to the left, a quick knee to the gut, perhaps an elbow to the nose for emphasis, and a swift uppercut could leave an inexperienced assailant flying through the air with blood and surprise all over his face—theoretically, anyway. In practice, it took a second uppercut.

Gorm took a moment to retrieve Rank Three's fallen sword before strolling over to where the warrior had landed.

"You're no hero." The wounded warrior gasped, struggling for as much breath as a broken nose and bruised sternum would allow. "You're … you're a common thief."

"I still ain't found the difference," said Gorm. "Second chance, lad. Ye won't get a third."

As luck would have it, Rank Three had found time to reconsider the attachment to material possessions that had overtaken his life and had recently threatened to end it. He departed shortly thereafter, with a renewed appreciation for existence, his undergarments, and little else, leaving Gorm to take inventory of his recent "find."

The warrior's purse contained over forty giltin in loose coin, plus another eighty in bank notes and guild cheques. Much of the armor was worthless: leathers so old and furs so thin that a tanner wouldn't buy them for scrap. Still, the iron helmet was sturdy enough to fetch a decent price, as were a steel pauldron and a pair of chain greaves, and the sword alone was worth at least a hundred. Bundled with a couple of rings, some hard provisions, and a sturdy belt of Elven make, Gorm estimated the hero had been carrying well over four hundred giltin worth of goods and gear and, perhaps best of all, a salt-pork sandwich for lunch.

He was cleaning crumbs of crusty bread and bits of grease from his whiskers when a small voice piped up from the edge of the woods. "Gleebek?" it chirruped.

Gorm looked up from his recent haul. The Goblin was crouched at the edge of the woods, eyeing him with optimistic caution.

"Gleebek?" it said, tapping its ribcage with a bony fist. "Gleebek."

Gorm snorted. "Oh. Thought ye'd run off. Probably should have." He turned back to organizing his new armor by weight and value.

"Gleebek. Da gub Tib'rin. Ra lubbinz da poot." The Goblin tapped its chest.

"Look, Gleebek—"

"Gleebek!"

"Aye, or whatever ye call yourself," Gorm said without looking up. "I know it must have looked like I saved your hide, but really I was just liberatin' these here valuables. It's your lucky day that I ain't got no reason to kill ye, but I ain't got a reason not to either. So ye'd best leave before my mood changes."

The threat in Gorm's voice was strong enough to leap over the language barrier. The Goblin's face flashed with panic, and it swiftly retreated back into the woods.

But it didn't leave.

Gorm caught glimpses of a nervous green face peering at him from the trees as he bundled up the goods. When he took a bath in a nearby brook, he could hear something splashing around downstream. Something small and furtive had darted through the woods and startled the wandering tinker who bought the stolen weapons and armor. And Gorm heard a few people claim they saw a Goblin skulking outside the roadside tavern where he spent most of the day's earnings on enough alcohol to drown his memories and give them a proper burial at sea.

The next morning, he awoke in a different part of the Freedlands, lying facedown in a different ditch, with different mud smeared through his beard, and the same Goblin crouched a few yards away, staring at him with big amber eyes.

The wretched creature even followed Gorm after breakfast, as he wandered the road from Mistkeep to Whitegeld, and hid in the trees a hundred yards behind him. It got closer when Gorm settled down for lunch, and it was following within a couple of arms' length by the afternoon. No amount of hollering or threats would keep it away for long.

For a while, Gorm thought about putting the Goblin out of his misery — Gorm's not the Goblin's — but the idea didn't settle well in his gut. There was no money in it, and gods knew the points wouldn't do Gorm any good.

Mostly, he didn't like the taste of killing someone, or something, just for being too friendly. He'd have much preferred to scare it off.

Later that evening, sitting by a makeshift fire and swigging cheap rum, Gorm realized it would be difficult to scare off a Goblin when he was probably the least threatening thing the Goblin could encounter.

Heroics was an increasingly popular profession. Despite the low base pay, poor benefits, and a mortality rate that made working in a Gnomish foundry look like an office job, there was no shortage of men and women lining up to wield a blade and delve into some ancient dungeon in search of fame and fortune (not necessarily in that order). To get into an ancient dungeon, however, a hero needed to be of sufficient rank. Rank-ten heroes regularly struck down eldritch horrors for bags of gold, but a rank-one hero was lucky to clean a basement of uncommonly nasty rats for a handful of giltin.

The only way to gain ranks was to get points on your Hero's license. The fastest way to get points on a license was to kill things that the Heroes' Guild had designated as foes, or more accurately F.O.E.s — Forces Of Evil. To any of the multitude of young, up-and-coming professional heroes wandering the Freedlands, a wild Goblin was a walking professional advancement, just waiting to be skewered.

The Goblin had to choose between a forest full of professional Goblin killers and a surly Dwarf whom he had seen fighting one of them. The fact that Gorm was even thinking about the Goblin, instead of cleaning it off his axe, put him leagues ahead of any other choice. Gorm was the best of bad options.

"More the pity for you," slurred Gorm, raising his bottle to the Goblin crouched opposite the fire pit. "It don't go well for folks who pin their hopes on me."

"*Nub gugginz?*"

"Better off on your own," said Gorm, but even in the depths of his inebriation, he knew that wasn't true.

It would be an understatement to say that Goblins are family-oriented; they have breeding habits that would make a rabbit blush, enshrined in a culture that valued a large family over any other virtue. The Anthropological Society of Scoria theorized that Goblin culture was steeped in procreation because they were bred to be the shock troops of the armies of evil in ages long past. To this day, strength in numbers remains a Goblin tribe's most viable defense. Goblins don't live alone — at least not for very long.

This particular Goblin had undoubtedly been blessed with a large family before a group of adventurers made short work of them, leaving it alone and frightened. It reminded Gorm of when he'd heard the sentence handed down, and the great gates of Khazad'im had closed to him forever, leaving him standing in the cold damp of the Pinefells wondering how he would live without his brothers and uncles and clansmen. Where he would live. How he could work. How he could eat …

Gorm took a swig of rum as the unwelcome memory surfaced. It didn't work. "Gleebek."

"*Gleebek?*"

"Here." Gorm tossed a hard biscuit to the Goblin. Then he bundled up his provisions and lay down, using his pack for a pillow. He was sick of drinking, and sick of being sober, and regretting that those were essentially the only two options he, and everyone else, ever had.

Above him, sparks from the fire danced up toward the leaves of oaks and birches, cavorting in a summer breeze that smelled sweet and smoky. Beyond the trees, the stars glimmered around a gibbous moon. He listened to the crickets, and the breeze, and the frenetic scarfing sounds of a Goblin attempting to inhale a hard biscuit.

Gorm didn't see any good options. He could leave the Goblin to its fate, but this had proved more difficult than anticipated in the past, and he knew what the fates held for a lone Goblin in the Span. Or he could take the Goblin with him, but if the little blighter wanted to avoid trouble with the Heroes' Guild, it would be best not to be within a wide radius of Gorm.

The only option left was to take the Goblin to Andarun to get its noncombatant papers. With those in hand, a Goblin could walk the streets in relative safety, provided it kept its head down. Gorm was a proponent of keeping one's head down; unfortunately, that was why he usually avoided Andarun.

Still, the Freedlands' capital was a big city, and he'd been there before without any trouble he hadn't been looking for. And a set of papers could be acquired within a day. If he timed it right, he wouldn't even need to spend a night in the city.

It was a small thing, really, Gorm thought. A tiny kindness for a Goblin nobody would give a second thought to. Totally inconsequential. He'd have forgotten he'd even done it by this time next year, if not next month.

Gorm made his decision.

History pivoted on it.

Deshmin Scroot enjoyed his job. He saw interesting things at work. He met interesting people. Most importantly, he was the big man in the room, and not just because he was the only man in his department who wasn't some variety of Gnome. "That will go on lot A, Mr. Muggens," he said to a Halfling who was struggling under the weight of a massive claymore.

"Yes, Mr. Scroot."

"And tell the Tinderkin I want to see the half plate properly polished."

"Yes, sir."

Scroot walked through the airy warehouse festooned with long cerulean banners that featured a sword crossed by a flaming comet—sword and sorcery being the ancient crest of the Heroes' Guild. The room was divided into lots, each rapidly filling with weapons, armor, jewelry, gems, and sacks of gold.

Any professional hero will tell you that the most important step of any quest, big or small, is dividing the loot. The hero's business model is based on the principle that ancient and powerful evils also tend to be wealthy ones, due to the fact that the FOE have spent so long pillaging the countryside and slaying well-equipped heroes. Thus the old axiom, "The bigger they are, the richer we'll be."

Of course, a monster's killers aren't the only ones with claims on its loot. A quest-giver, be it a simple shepherd or an entire city, could lay claim to nine-tenths of a hoard, minus the heroes' fee. And quest-givers could often capitalize on those claims by selling shares of the hoard, even before the foe in possession of the loot had been slain. The speculators who bought those shares often bundled them into plunder funds, which were then divided up and sold to other companies, who were owned by other companies, and beyond that … well, it hurt Scroot's head to think about who owned what.

Fortunately, the shares owned by each interested party were always written down for him. Scroot glanced at his clipboard as he made his way up the stairs to the catwalk. The city of Scoria, twenty-six percent. Adventure Capital, thirteen percent. The heroes, led by one Arthan the Brightblade, got ten percent plus a six thousand giltin fee. The Whitegeld Bannermen Pension Fund, eight percent. Relic Investment Group, three percent. Goldson Baggs High Risk Adventuring Fund, one percent. Goldson Baggs Ironbreakers Hoard

Fund, half a percent. Scroot stopped reading. The rest of the list was all plunder funds.

As far as Scroot was concerned, percentages were the easy part. Dividing loot always boiled down to the same question: who gets what? After all, a ring of safeguarding and a conch of the sea were technically worth the same amount, but it was a lot easier to sell warriors a ring that surrounded a wearer in a magical shield than a big shell that could summon fish. Larger hoards often had so much treasure and so many interested parties that the loot couldn't be divided without guild intervention. That was where Scroot stepped in.

Scroot stepped into the warehouse office.

"Arbiter Scroot! Arbiter Scroot! Sir, I must insist—"

Scroot walked calmly through the crowd of shouting representatives and heroes, all clamoring for his attention. He didn't hurry as he made his way around the long oak table in the middle of the room to the great windows at the rear of the office. Folding his hands behind his back, he wordlessly stared out the window at the work below.

It looked like a good hoard. Heaps of treasure and gear filled every lot from A to H. Most of the gold wasn't even giltin, but old solid gold coins from before the turn of the age. You didn't find those often anymore, not even amid the peaks of the Ironbreakers.

Apparently, it had been an ancient wyvern; Scroot could see a team of Hill Gnomes hauling the long reptilian carcass in. The head would wind up on the wall of some tavern, the talons and venom sac would be sold to the Elves for medicinal purposes, the hide would be valuable to high-end armorsmiths, and the meat could be fed to dogs or orphans.

By the time the wyvern was on the butcher's block, silence had fallen in the room behind him. Scroot turned to find a cadre of indistinguishable businesspeople, representing various companies, seated around the table, all forcing polite smiles. The full party of five guild heroes was also present, including a diminutive Scribkin wizard and a rather fetching cleric of Musana. Scroot smoothed his mustache and sat at the table. "Now then," he said. "Let's begin."

One by one, treasures were carried in by the attendants and placed on a dais near the door, along with an initial appraisal. More often than not, the men and women around the table agreed to the estimates without comment, each noting the items that they would most like to procure.

Some finds, however, were more contentious, such as a small black statue of a puma. "This sculpture will apparently summon a celestial war cat from the metaphysical planes," Scroot read from a card.

"What can you make the cat do?" asked the party's warrior, a burly man in a horned helm.

"Let me see ..." said Scroot, checking a scrawled note in the margin. "Ah, nothing. It is, after all, a cat. Still, it is valued at ten thousand giltin."

The sum prompted protests from the warrior, but was defended by the representatives from Adventure Capital.

They bickered and argued and debated for a while, until Mr. Scroot weighed in with a suggested price of nine thousand giltin, and all agreed. The next item was brought in.

The process could take days. Scroot surmised the treasure from this hoard would take a week just to assess; actually dividing and distributing the loot would likely take another month. The cleric and the wizard were eyeing the same amulet.

Just after Scroot returned from his lunch break, the marble busts were wheeled in. There were five of them in the display case, each about a hand's length to a foot in height, milky white with orange stains running down their surface. They were carved into heads with angled, exaggerated features. Time and weather had worn away much of the detail, but one could still make out tiny eyes, sloped brows, and square jaws with tusked underbites.

Scroot didn't have time to glance at the stones' card before one of the businessmen spoke up. "Excuse me, Arbiter Scroot. These will be sent to Relic Investments in Andarun."

"That remains to be seen, I believe," said Scroot.

"No, it does not." The speaker was a thin Human with a dark suit and a pair of silver spectacles. His name plaque identified him as Mr. Boggert. He looked almost exactly like Scroot, with perhaps a little more gray in his hair. An uncanny resemblance, really. "Relic Investments will forfeit any other claim on this hoard," Mr. Boggert added.

The other stakeholders seemed more confused than upset by the proclamation. Aside from being unorthodox, it was just bad business. They'd seen over three hundred thousand giltin in treasures so far today, and there was coin worth over half a million. Whatever secret the stones held, it wasn't worth a three percent stake in such a hoard.

Still, whether or not it was good business was someone else's problem. Scroot's concern was procedural. "It is my job to arbitrate and decide how this loot is divided, Mr. Boggert. And I shall do so only after it is all accounted for."

Mr. Boggert's companion leaned forward. He was an exceptionally unattractive specimen, with a face like a gnarled oak and a single bulging eye. His neatly cropped hair, rumpled suit, and conspicuous eyepatch were all the same shade of gray. He had no name plaque. "That won't be necessary," he said, pointing to the card in Mr. Scroot's hand.

Scroot glanced down. The card read, in large type:

LOT B, ITEMS 782–786.
THESE ITEMS SHALL BE THE PROPERTIE OF RELIC INVESTMENT GROUP INCORPORATED, HEREAFTER RELIC INVESTMENTS. ANY OTHER CLAIM OWN'D BY RELIC INVESTMENTS TO THE HOARDE OF THE WYVERN OF DARKCRAGGE MTN. IS HEREBY FORFEIT.

Aside from that, there was nothing on the card except for the seal of the Office of the High Arbiter. It was unorthodox and unprecedented, but the high arbiter wasn't constrained by orthodoxy or precedence.

"Ah," said Scroot. "It seems the matter is settled, then."

"Yes," agreed Mr. Boggert, standing. "Thank you and good day."

"A pleasure," added the one-eyed man.

They walked out of the room. The case of stones was wheeled out after them. A double-headed great axe was carried in. The assessment resumed.

Later, Scroot stood in the office window, observing the floor during a coffee break. He watched the team of Hill Gnomes load five small crates onto a carriage bearing the Heroes' Guild crest while Mr. Boggert climbed aboard it.

Scroot saw the carriage leave the loading bay and take a turn on the road south.

Then he turned back to the meeting, and he didn't give the stones or the carriage another thought until a week later, when Guild Investigators told him that both the carriage and the cart had disappeared somewhere along the road to Andarun.

Chapter 2

The Freedlands' eastern regions were dominated by great forests, from the chilly Pinefells in the northeast to the verdant Green Span in the southeast. The northwest was renowned for harsh mountain ranges with names like the Ironbreakers and the Black Cliffs, jutting from the mainland into the frothing waves of the Greencurrent Sea. The southwest of the mainland was splintered into tiny islands and peninsulas, with swift, salty rivers and stagnant swamps running between them. In the middle of the Freedlands, the great Plains of Bahn spread for leagues. From the plains' center, Mount Wynspar thrust upward like the gnarled toenail of some long-buried titan, and all along its southern slope sprawled Andarun, the highest city, the gleaming gem of the Freedlands.

Legend held that Andarun had once been the greatest city on Arth, in the early ages when it was the high seat of the kingdoms of the Sten. Then the Sten betrayed the rest of mankind and were subsequently wiped out in retaliation. The armies of Man were quickly driven away by a dragon, which was followed by hordes of Lizardmen, who fell to the Gremlins, who were slain by an Ogre tribe, and so on and so forth. By the time the Freedmen liberated the city from the rule of Ogmar the Mad, one could barely walk down Central Avenue without tripping over a priceless relic from a long-faded conflict. Of course, no one could even venture near a sewer grate for fear of giant spiders or Venomous Scargs or any of the other monstrous denizens that had never fully been expunged from the city.

Ironically, these ancient threats were key to Andarun's rapid gentrification. Dangerous monsters and abundant treasure attract heroes. Wealthy heroes in need of gear attract merchants. Well-to-do merchants attract industry. Industry needs workers, who need developers for housing, who need builders and laborers, who need services. The ancient ruins beneath Mount Wynspar fertilized a blooming economy on its surface. Within an age, Andarun was again the greatest city on Arth, this time built atop the most deadly dungeon on Arth.

In Andarun, one could wake a nameless fear or two just by digging a wine cellar.

"The city's built on big steps carved into the mountain back when the Sten were around," Gorm told Gleebek as they made their way through Andarun's crowded streets. "The lowest step is called the Base, and the top is the Pinnacle. Every step starts in the Ridge," he said, pointing to the rough cliff face that cast the western side of the city in shadow, "and ends at the Wall." He turned and pointed to the giant stone edifice that made up the eastern mirror of the Ridge.

"A zabba," Gleebek said with a low whistle.

"Aye. The Wall and the Ridge cast long shadows down here on the lower steps. But Andarun rises to their tops, so up near the Pinnacle, where the uppity-ups live, the Wall ain't much taller than a hedge. Good views, I'm told."

"Da grongo?"

"Everything's better by the Wall—the view, the light, the smells. Course, everything's more expensive too. Makes Andarun almost like a map of society, ye see. The higher up the mountain ye go, the higher your status. The closer to the Wall ye are, the more money ye have."

"Grong, da nub'root Hupsit—"

"So if we get separated, head down toward the Base and west to the Ridge. Eventually, ye'll come here." Gorm rounded a bend and gestured down an alley that was deeper and darker than most swamps.

"Ga'pab?"

"Welcome to the Underdim," grinned Gorm. "They don't get any more Ridgeward or Baseward."

Gleebek shivered and peered into the gloom. "Guz pabbo."

"It's one of the worst neighborhoods in Andarun, and that says something." Gorm started to trundle down the alley and into the Underdim. "Course, that means it's where ye'll be most welcome."

When he'd been on the road to Andarun, walking with Gleebek had earned Gorm withering stares, whispers, and more than a few unwelcome offers from aspiring heroes to eliminate his Goblin problem. Here in the Underdim, nobody looked twice at him for walking alongside a Goblin. Shadowkin, as the cursed races were collectively known, were common down in Andarun's Baseward tiers. There were few people in the narrow streets, but a large part of them were Orcs, Gnolls, Kobolds, Goblins, and Gremlins.

Between the Ridge's shadow and the walls and other buildings rising above it, it was never really day in the Underdim. Even at midmorning, a handful of crude torches illuminated haphazard rows of shacks. A few of the older hovels had been built atop rooms hewn from the granite side of the Ridge, but most were cobbled together wherever building materials could be scavenged. The streets were surprisingly clean, save for a few bleached skeletons lying in the gutters. Nothing edible lasted a night on the Underdim's gravel roads.

This was where you dropped a body that would never be found. This was where you sent a man you didn't want to hear from again. This was where you holed up when you needed to be unseen for a while. Or, Gorm thought, this was where you came to find someone who had done all of those things.

There were few bars around, and all of them were private venues. Those denizens of the Underdim who could afford to drink didn't like doing so in the company of strangers. If you passed out in the wrong company or the wrong place, you weren't going to wake up. It took Gorm some searching to finally find a flimsy shanty with dim light leaking through holes in the wall and the clinking of tin tankards sounding from within.

A peephole slid open as Gorm and Gleebek approached. "Password?" barked a gruff voice.

Gorm punched through the frail door, grabbed the lookout, and slammed him against the doorframe three times. "That work?" he said.

He heard the hurried sounds of a lock working, and then a battered-looking Gnoll opened the door. He stood a head shorter than Gorm and wore a thick, crimson coat below a hound's face that looked like it had been banged into a doorjamb even before Gorm had banged it into a doorjamb. His hackles were up, but his tail was between his legs as he muttered, "I've got papers, hero. I'm not a foe anymore."

"And I ain't a hero anymore," said Gorm cheerfully, brushing past the Gnoll. Gleebek scampered after him.

"Bar" would have been too generous a term for the establishment. A few wagon wheels and broken axles had been fashioned into makeshift tables. Lonely figures huddled on large rocks placed around the tables. Behind a bar constructed from an old door stood the barkeep: a thin, bespectacled man above the counter but a tremendous serpent beneath it. A sign hanging from the decrepit rafters proclaimed the establishment as "Angusss's."

"Ye must be Angusss," said Gorm, stamping up to the bar.

"Anguss," corrected the serpentine barkeep, polishing a glass. "The middle 's' is silent."

Gorm tried not to scowl, but failed. Naga were very particular about their mispronunciation. "I'm looking for the Mask. Any idea where it is?"

"Maybe I know sssomething; maybe I don't," said Angusss.

"Maybe this'll help." Gorm plunked a single giltin on the table.

The Naga eyed the thin golden coin, unimpressed. "You made quite a ssstir on your way in," he said, nodding to the Gnoll sulking by the door.

"It's all relative. Compared to how I'll leave if'n ye don't help me out, that was downright chummy."

"Big talk for a man with only one ssovereign to ssspare."

"Fine," said Gorm, fishing a second coin from his belt pouch. "Two giltin. Who is he these days?"

"Three."

"Two and a complete set of internal organs."

"I've got enough internal organs."

Gorm patted his axe a couple of times. "And ye'll answer me if ye care to keep it that way."

The Naga flicked a forked tongue over his teeth, considering; then he snatched the coins from the bar with the tip of his tail. "I hear he just got back from a job up in Ssscoria with Damrod the Eye." He resumed his work with the dishes. "On an unrelated note, I hear a Dwarven blacksmith by the name of Foblerson up in Lowly Heights is away on business."

"And the Eye?"

"Away on more business, they sssay."

Gorm thanked Angusss, left the bar, and made for the stairs on Mycen Avenue. The stairway up the mountain passed through a small arch in the wall at the edge of the Base, guarded by a couple of bannermen. Gorm kept his eyes firmly on the timber and iron steps as he passed them.

It was only one tier up and a couple of blocks Wallward to Lowly Heights, but the residents clearly thought they were halfway up the mountain. They were the sort of folk who believed in hard work and clean living. The houses were just as slapdash as those in the Underdim, but most had a coat of whitewash over their ramshackle exteriors, and all of them had a neatly trimmed strip of lawn in front.

Gorm stopped by a street vendor selling ten cent beef rolls near a small park, which is to say, a tree and a bench on the side of Mudfog Lane. The hawker's cart was new and sturdy, but it had been intentionally weathered with sanding paper and a careful paint job to resemble the decrepit crates on wheels Gorm remembered from his childhood. He ordered a beef roll for himself, and then a second for Gleebek after the Goblin gave him a pitiable stare.

"Can ye point me in the direction of Foblerson's forge?" Gorm asked as the vendor fished around in the cart for a couple of buns.

"Half a block Wallward, take a left down Maylie Alley by the rose shop."

"Much obliged." Gorm pulled a shilling from his purse for the beef rolls, and nearly dropped it when the hawker asked for three giltin. "Three sovereigns! The sign says ten cent beef rolls!"

"Because we're a franchise of the Ten Cent Transportable Edibles Company," said the vendor with well-practiced indifference.

"But a giltin 'n' a half each? It's banditry chargin' so much!"

"Can't charge what the market won't bear," said the vendor. "Few things in Andarun are cheap, friend. You want these with onions?"

"They cost extra?"

"No, sir. Condiments are free."

Moments later, Gorm and Gleebek made their way toward Maylie Alley, carefully balancing towering mounds of fried onions, sliced peppers, assorted relishes, and spiced mustard atop their beef rolls.

Gorm surveyed the streets thoughtfully as he chewed. The streets were thick with Humans, a few Dwarves, and every variety of Gnome, most dressed in the red or blue coveralls of factory workers. A Dwarf in old mail and a Goblin in a cat-pelt loincloth stuck out enough to attract more than a few glares.

"Listen," he told the Goblin. "Ye got to learn to keep a low profile, Gleebek."

"Grong, nub Gleebek. Tib'rin — "

"No arguin'. There's a lot of fish in the sea, and if ye make any waves, they'll eat you. Got it?"

"Grot?"

"Good." Gorm shoved the last of his beef roll into his mouth and turned down Maylie Alley.

Foblerson's forge was little more than a crumbling hearth and an anvil in front of a decrepit hut. Before Gorm approached it, he ducked down a side alley and pushed around to the back of the shack. He had to search through a pile of crates and rags, but eventually he found the nondescript black trunk he was looking for. With a wink to the puzzled Goblin, he pulled a long ruby dress from the trunk, tucked it under his cloak, and headed back to Foblerson's forge.

A gnarled, old Dwarf with gray streaks through his braided black beard was trying to beat a piece of iron into submission. The misshaped hunk of metal remained heatedly defiant.

"Afternoon, Mask," said Gorm.

"Name's Foblerson," said the smith, without looking up from his work.

"Is it?" asked Gorm loudly. "Well, Mr. Foblerson, can I ask what ye intend to do with this?" He held the red dress up high.

A hush fell over the alley. All eyes turned to Gorm and the smith.

Most of the common folk know little of Dwarven reproduction, as Dwarves are famously taciturn about matters of sex and procreation. However, it is clear to everyone that something is different about Dwarven courtship. There are no Dwarven couples, no visible Dwarven courtship rituals, and, crucially, no Dwarven women. Every Dwarf in existence is male and, by all appearances, solitary, until he shows up with a tiny, bearded baby strapped to his back and flailing a toy hammer. A plethora of humorous theories and jokes about how such a child might come to be born can be heard in any alehouse on Arth, provided there are no Dwarves present.

Rumors of a Dwarf who owned a dress were certain to draw exactly the sort of attention the Mask loathed.

"Quit your jokin'!" barked the smith. "And come inside," he added, under his breath.

"Thought ye might say as much," said Gorm, following the Mask into the shack.

The front room of the smithy was as one might expect: filled with spare tools, dusty ingots, and a number of weapons and tools in various stages of completion.

"You know what you done?" grumbled the smith as he led Gorm and Gleebek into the dingy back room. "This place was perfect. Foblerson's out of town for a month. And now I gotta find a new spot, 'cause folks will be poking around and asking questions." He stepped behind a musty curtain.

"I've come as I need a favor," said Gorm.

"That's the only reason anyone ever sees you." The smith tossed various articles of clothing out from behind the curtain. A pair of heavy gloves. A leather apron. A jerkin and trousers.

"It's been awhile, hasn't it?" mused Gorm.

"Not half long enough." Behind the curtain, the Dwarven silhouette was warping, stretching into something lithe and tall. The Mask peeked around the curtain, and Gleebek squeaked in fear. Its face was like an ash-gray canvas, featureless, save for a pair of eyes the color of sunset.

"Don't worry," Gorm told the trembling Goblin. "The Mask never stays his true self for long."

Already, the creature's skin was changing to a pale pink, with oily gray hair sprouting from its head. His eyes blinked and became dark irises, and a new nose and lips were twisting into a deep scowl as a thin mustache sprouted above it. "Nobody's got a true self," said the Mask in a new, reedy voice—a bureaucrat's voice. "Everybody is trying to look like someone else, even themselves. We're just more honest about it."

"Ha," said Gorm. "Doppelgangers ain't honest about anything."

"Touché," said the Mask, ducking back behind the curtain. A moment later he emerged in a neat, dark suit and a pair of stylish silver spectacles. "So, how can I get rid of you?"

Gorm nodded to his companion. "This here's Gleebek."

"Is he now?" The Mask cast a sideways glance at the Goblin.

"Gleebek. Da gub Tib'rin."

"He needs his noncombatant papers," said Gorm. "You're going to sponsor him."

"And then you'll stay out of my face?"

"Aye, any and all of 'em. We'll be square."

The Mask nodded. "Fine. And who should I go as?" he asked. His face shifted, the nose becoming thick and hawkish, the skin shifting to a ruddy hue, a deep scar tracing over his right eye, an unkempt, rusty beard suddenly spilling down his chest. "Maybe I could go as ye," he said in Gorm's voice.

Gorm shrugged. "Ye want to walk into the guild lookin' like that, it's your funeral. Just see that Gleebek gets his papers."

The Mask laughed darkly as he shifted back to himself. "Why are you helping a Goblin? Why do you care what happens to him?"

"That's my business."

"I know you, Ingerson. You don't stick your neck out for nothing. There must be a reason."

"There is."

"I'd like to know it."

"That's your problem."

"If this goes badly," the Mask said slowly, "I'll disappear, and you won't find me again. This is all on you."

"Look, first thing in the morning, ye take Gleebek here into the guild—"

"*Dab Tib'rin.*"

"Ye sign his papers as a sponsor, ye leave. He scampers off to, I don't know, be a shoeshine, and I clank boots out of Andarun. We'll be done by lunch. What's to go bad?" said Gorm.

The doppelganger studied Gorm carefully. "Well," he said eventually. "I imagine we'll find out tomorrow."

Marten rubbed his elbows as he hopped down off the cart. A cold summer rain chilled the roots of his bones, and the damp alleyway running off one of Aberreth's back streets offered little by way of shelter. It offered little by way of anything. The alley was nothing more than two granite walls with a couple of yards of cobblestone and a single door between them.

Marten's nerves were raw, and there were butterflies in his stomach, but he was fairly certain he had all his angles covered. Not that fairly certain was good enough; fairly certain could get you killed.

Still, fairly certain was the best he could do. This was his first job without Horold, and the planning had always been Horold's gig. Marten didn't like working alone, but nobody was going to associate with someone who owed Benny Hookhand money. Besides, if this job went according to plan, he could pay off Benny Hookhand and have a tidy sum to spare. And if the job went sour, he doubted it could be any worse than what Benny Hookhand did to poor Horold.

"Best get this over with," he muttered to himself. Taking another second to steel himself, he hurried toward the small red doorway at the end of the alley.

The doorway opened to greet him. "Did you get them, Halfling?"

"Course. Just like I said I would," said Marten, brushing damp curls from his eyes. Conventional wisdom said that Halflings were called Halflings because they were half as tall as men, although some liked to add that they were half as smart or worked half as much. Of course, people who said such things were half as likely to wake up with their coin purses; most Halflings held notoriously flexible views on the nature of property and ownership.

A lantern flared, illuminating a face that made Marten jump back.

One good eye studied the Halfling from a gnarled mess of scars and white stubble. "Let's see 'em," the man grunted, pulling his crimson hood up as he stepped out into the rain.

"Surely, Damrod." Marten had never worked with Damrod the Eye before, but the mercenary was well known in some circles, and not for his patience. The Halfling nodded and hurried around the cart. "You might want to cover your nose. They stink, even with the ice."

"Let's see 'em," Damrod repeated.

Marten pulled the tarp off the back of the cart and tried not to retch at the smell. The man in the crimson cloak didn't even flinch. Damp bodies on thick slabs of ice glistened in the flickering lantern light.

"Five?" asked the mercenary.

"Six," answered Marten. "Got an extra, just in case. Extra value, that."

Damrod's eponymous lone eye squinted suspiciously at the corpses. "They already smell. How long will they keep?"

Marten had foreseen such questions. "Months. They smelled like this by the time I got 'em to the wizard, but he says they won't get any worse as long as they're on the enchanted ice."

The mercenary nodded. "That will do."

"And the gold?" said Marten.

"Inside." Damrod pointed to the dark doorway.

Marten was prepared for that as well. In a heartbeat, he drew a throwing dagger and trained it on the mercenary's good eye. "I'd rather not, if it's all the same to you."

"You don't want to get paid?"

"I certainly do," Marten corrected him. "I'll send an associate to collect next week."

"Why go to the trouble?" said Damrod, without much concern for the knife Marten had aimed at him.

"Because this job's out of my league. A big step up for me. And when you work in, ah … covert acquisitions, if you weren't chosen for your reputation, you were probably chosen for being expendable."

"That so?"

"Oh, certainly," said Marten. "It's plain to see I'm good as dead if I step through that doorway."

"I can see you've thought this through."

"Well, I try to plan for everything."

"You almost did, too," said Damrod the Eye. He snapped his fingers. There was a soft *click* from the shadows, and a wet *thump* from Marten.

The Halfling stared down at the shaft protruding from his chest, dark dampness blooming around it. "Hidden crossbowman," he said. "Should have … should've seen that coming."

"Well, to be fair, this job was out of your league," said the one-eyed man. Marten thought Damrod was smiling for the first time that night, but it was hard to tell because the alleyway was starting to run together like ink on a damp page. The ground fell away from him until he caught up to it, and then he was gone.

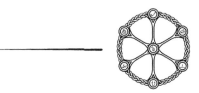

Gorm sat at the fountain in the square of Tamanthan East, on the fourth tier of Andarun, in the shadow of the Wall. The square was set beside two lanes of broad steps divided by two sets of track, running all the way from Base to the uppermost levels of the city. The Broad Steps were the fastest way to ascend or descend Andarun's tiers, despite the crowds streaming over them. People of every race and creed rushed up and down the mountain on the stair, and the tracks were filled with carts of goods and materials being sent up and down the mountain.

Commerce blooms beside streams of people. Street vendors and specialty shops were as thick as weeds around the Broad Steps, enjoying a steady flow of customers trickling in from the stairs. Looking up the mountain, Gorm could see the turquoise dome on the rooftop of the Andarun Stock Exchange. He could hear the shouting of the commodity markets from the lower tiers, and even catch mercifully faint scents of the stockyards drifting in from outside the city walls. The whole Wall thrummed with comings and goings, business and trade.

It was an easy place to go unnoticed, and that made it a good spot to meet with the Mask. This particular fountain was about as high up the mountain, and as close to the Heroes' Guild offices, as Gorm was willing to venture.

When the Mask arrived, he did so as a bow-legged, toothless Human in factory coveralls. Gorm wouldn't have known who it was without Gleebek bouncing after him, happily waving a small green booklet. *"Pauperz!"* the Goblin said excitedly.

"Well, look who got his noncombatant papers," said Gorm, suppressing a small smile.

Noncombatant papers gave creatures that were automatically classified as F.O.E.s a means to become productive members of society. Perhaps more importantly, they enabled them to opt out of being slaughtered and looted by professional heroes. They granted a form of limited citizenship to the bearer, provided he or she was carrying the papers. An adventurer who was found guilty of harming a Noncombatant Paper Carrier risked losing points toward advancement, accruing demerits, and even paying steep fines. The tiny green books were the single most effective defense against professional heroes.

"His conditional papers," corrected the Mask. "He's not an NPC until he gets a job."

"Shouldn't be a problem," said Gorm. "There's plenty of work in Andarun for an enterprising young Goblin, so long as he ain't got standards. All we need to do is …"

Something bright flitted in front of Gorm's face, forcing him to shield his eyes. "Hey! Here he is!"

Gorm looked up at a tiny winged figure glowing with such intense blue light that it seemed to be standing in a sphere. "Blood and ashes," he swore. "A search sprite." He turned to the Mask, but the doppelganger was already elsewhere, and, presumably, else-whom.

The sprite hovered and danced excitedly about a foot above Gorm's head. "Here he is!" it trilled. "It's Gorm Ingerson!"

"Bones!" Gorm swore again, and hurried off toward a Ridgeward side street.

Gleebek scuttled after him. *"Grot gub'ah?"*

"It's a trackin' spell," said Gorm. "It knows where everything and everyone in the area is, and it'll tell ye all about it. Big moneymaker for the wizards. Town guard, tax collectors, anyone who wants to find something or someone, they'll all pay good gold for a search sprite."

Gorm cut through a small alley, crossed a causeway and a small park, crossed Nubble Street, and generally tried any maneuver possible to obfuscate their trail as they made their way toward the stairs down. Gorm considered trying to blend with the crowd, but blending is difficult to do when there is an orb of light hovering above your head and screeching trivia.

"He's walking down the street! Here he is! Look! Now he's turning left! See that! There's a baker shop! You can get bread there! Now he's turning right! It's a weapon shop! Swords are sharp! Hey! He's still walking! Now he's talking to the Goblin!"

"All they are is a bit of knowledge with a mouth," Gorm told Gleebek as they walked. "They only exist to tell ye obvious things, so they don't shut up till they wear off. Could be days."

"Hey! Listen!" shrieked the sprite. "He's ducking down this alley! He's stopping by a rain barrel! Rain barrels collect rain! He's taken the lid off—aaaugh!"

"Ye gotta be quick to catch 'em," Gorm told Gleebek over the tiny, muffled protests. His arm shook violently and pale light flickered between his fingers as the sprite struggled to escape. "And they're stronger than they look!" With a grunt of exertion, he thrust the sprite into the rain barrel. The barrel rocked and splashed and flared with azure incandescence.

Gleebek put his hand over his mouth. *"Nixtit?"*

"Don't pay it no mind," Gorm grunted. "The thing ain't even alive, really. Just a spell." Gorm gripped the side of the barrel and kept his fist submerged until the water was still.

"I think," he added. When he withdrew his hand, it was empty.

"Anyways, it was me or the sprite," he told Gleebek as they made their way down the alley. "Can't have it followin' me if'n I'm gonna dodge the guild."

"Happily, that is no longer a concern," said a Tinderkin, stepping from the shadows.

To Gorm, Tinderkin, as the Gnomes of Clan Kendrin were most commonly known, always looked as if someone had shrunk some Elves until they stood just a little shorter than the Dwarves. The Tinderkin approaching Gorm had sharp features and a lithe frame. His leather armor was as black as the hair he had pulled into a neatly cropped topknot. He wore a slender blade at his hip, a neatly trimmed goatee on his chin, and a smirk on his face that reminded Gorm of a predatory reptile of one sort or another.

"Gorm Ingerson, I presume," he said.

"I'm afraid yer mistaken," said Gorm.

"I should be more afraid that I'm correct, if I were you. My name is Mr. Flinn. I command the Company of Silver Talons acting on behalf of the Temple of Al'Matra." He gestured to a small silver medallion set in his gauntlet, emblazoned with an eagle's outstretched claw.

"So ye ain't with the Heroes' Guild, then?"

"Oh no, not at all," said Mr. Flinn.

It took effort for Gorm to conceal his immense relief. "Well, then—"

"Mr. Brunt here represents the Guild of Heroes," said Flinn, pointing up and behind Gorm.

31

Gorm looked. An Ogre eclipsed the alleyway behind him. Mr. Brunt had a pair of arms like tree trunks, and tattoos of weapons, flames, and half-nude Ogresses covered them like moss. His sloping brow overhung two beady eyes and rushed to connect with his gnarled nose. He wore a vacant, angry expression, as though he was furious at everything and ready to take it out on anything.

"Mr. Brunt and I have some business with you," Flinn continued. "And your … associate as well."

Gleebek held his noncombatant papers out like a shield. *"Pauperz!"* he squeaked.

"Indeed," said Mr. Flinn. "Keep those close, my friend. Who knows what could happen without them? But I digress. We were hoping you'd join us for a drink at Fula's Pot to discuss a promising opportunity."

"Ah," said Gorm. "And we have a choice?"

"Oh, there's always a choice. Choice is a constant." Flinn grinned, a cold glint in his eye. "It's consequences that vary."

High above, Brunt rumbled something unintelligible and yet quite clear.

"Well, well," Gorm said, "I was just thinking how thirsty I was."

Chapter 3

"Nothing like a beer in a private space, eh?" Flinn said.

Fula's Pot only had a handful of customers this early, and when Brunt arrived, every one of them suddenly remembered pressing errands. Now, their party sat at a small grubby table in the back of the tavern's empty common room, watching dust tumble through the thin sunbeams that trickled through the windows.

"Aye," Gorm nodded.

A nervous barmaid delivered pints for Flinn and Gorm, and a cup for Gleebek. The barkeep rolled out a couple of kegs for Brunt.

"Mr. Brunt and I expected to travel all the way to Whitegeld or Monchester to find you," said Mr. Flinn. "How happy to find the famous Gorm Ingerson one tier up from us."

"I suppose that's one way to look at it," said Gorm.

"And traveling alongside a Goblin, no less. I find myself curious as to why."

"I'm wonderin' the same thing, at this point."

"May I?" The Tinderkin reached across the table and plucked Gleebek's papers from the Goblin's paws. "Ah, it seems that your friend here has provisional papers. Where is he employed?"

"He's with me," said Gorm.

"Ah, but being with you isn't the same thing as being employed by you, you see." Mr. Flinn tossed the papers back to the Goblin.

Gorm met Mr. Flinn's cruel smirk with a hard stare. Without breaking eye contact, he pulled a single giltin from his money pouch, placed it on the table, and slid it to the Goblin. "He's my squire," he growled.

"*Skwar?*" said Gleebek.

"Ah, but I'm not sure associating with you would be any better for our friend here." Flinn's smile was both mirth and malevolence as he pulled a slip of parchment from his pocket. "The Heroes' Guild finds several serious offenses and a whole host of minor infractions in your file. Years of heroics with an expired license, failure to procure the necessary insurance, interference with heroics in progress, petty theft, unsanctioned looting ... my, my, such a long list."

"Least I could do for 'em, after what they did to me."

"It seems to me they were lenient. If I recall the ballads, you fled from a quest," said Mr. Flinn.

It would be hard to recall the ballads incorrectly. Songs of Johan the Mighty were sung in every tavern and square from the Freedlands to Ruskan, and even into the southern Empire. All of them told the story of before Johan the Mighty was the Mighty, before he slew Detarr Ur'Mayan or the Bloodworm of Knifevale or the Lion of Chrate, when he was just Johan of Embleden, traveling into the dungeon of Az'Anon the Spider King. All of his companions died or fled, the bards sang. Even a Dwarven berserker ran away, they sang. But not Johan.

Before that quest, Gorm had his own ballads. They called him the Northern Flame, the Pyrebeard. The berserkers called him their finest, and he was the toast of the Khazad'im Clan. He'd needed a caravan to haul loot back from some of his jobs, and when he had arrived in town, throngs filled the streets to scream his name. Then he took a mid-level job with some heroes to bring down a rogue noctomancer, and everything went to the scavengers.

He still wasn't exactly certain what had happened in the dungeon of the Spider King. He didn't remember much of the fight with Az'Anon, though it was true that berserkers seldom remember much of any fight. Still, he had flashes of memory that haunted his dreams to this day. Iheen the Red falling and bleeding, Ataya Trueheart immolated in violet flames, hideous limbs reaching for him ...

And the running. Gorm remembered fleeing blindly, frantically — not just from the dungeon, but for days, running from inn to inn in the grip of a terror stronger than any battle fury he'd ever known. When he'd finally calmed down enough to stop, word was already spreading about Johan, the young hero who'd slain the Spider King alone, abandoned by Gorm, with his other companions dead around him.

"The Heroes' Guild could have had you killed for a deserter," Flinn continued.

The guild made a very clear distinction between common mercenaries and professional heroes. While a mercenary's loyalties were based on current market prices, a licensed hero on a quest was guaranteed to either complete the task or die trying. Whether the hero was trying to finish the quest or trying to evade guild enforcers when he or she died was totally irrelevant.

"All they've given you was an act of mercy."

"Mercy!" snorted Gorm. "Stripped me of my rank and made me a pariah, you mean." Dead, Gorm could have been buried with his father in a quiet ceremony. But alive, as the first berserker ever recorded to have fled from battle, Gorm was a source of shame that no clan could bear. He was cast out of the Brotherhood of Flame and the Khazad'im Clan disowned him, leaving him cold, clanless, and hungry in the streets.

He'd tried finding work, but nobody wanted someone with his reputation on a quest, or even behind a lunch counter. He didn't eat for a week, and only then because some snot-nosed rank-two whelp thought he could take Gorm in a fight. Gorm had lived on his assailant's provisions for a few days, and then beat up another overbold hero for more food and money. Soon, that was more the pattern than the exception, and twenty years later, here he was: a wanted vagrant traveling with a Goblin.

Mr. Flinn shrugged. "We could debate the merits of guild law for some time, but it's probably best if Mr. Brunt doesn't partake too much of the local brew. He's a bit of a violent drunk, you see."

Brunt finished his first keg with a noisy smack of his lips, and then eagerly twisted the tap off a waiting second.

"Ah," said Gorm.

"You've earned more than enough demerits and penalties for the Heroes' Guild to name you a force of evil. And while I'm sure you'd be sad to hear that your indiscretions had invalidated your green friend's papers by association, if you were declared a FOE, you'd doubtlessly be attending to more pressing problems—namely, that Guild regulations should require Mr. Brunt here to show you off for a quick, clean hanging."

"I'm aware."

"Of course, Mr. Brunt has never been one to do things 'by the book,' so to speak. He's developed quite a reputation as a renegade, a lone wolf who takes justice into his own hands."

"Loose … can-non," rumbled Brunt.

"That you are, Mr. Brunt!" said Flinn happily. "So you see, Mr. Ingerson, if Mr. Brunt carries out guild justice for these offenses, it will likely be a bit less quick and much less clean than a hanging."

The air rang with the *crack* of splintering wood as Brunt crushed his second keg against his forehead.

"I see," Gorm said, watching the Ogre laugh. "But since I'm havin' a beer with ye, I suppose yer here to offer me an alternative."

"How very astute of you!" Flinn played with the point of his small dark beard. "You may recall that I represent the Temple of Al'Matra, which has a mission it considers to be of the utmost importance. Have you heard of the Prophecy of the Seventh Hero?"

"I don't know much about their religion," said Gorm. "Is that the one who's supposed to rise up and save the world from something and prove that the Al'Matrans were right about everything after all?"

"More or less," said Flinn. "I believe the Al'Matran prophecies are somewhat more specific."

"Yeah, but every time one shows up, he just ends up getting himself killed. Whole party wiped on some barmy quest that's way out of their league. Last time they went to kill the Dragon of Wynspar, if I remember."

"Ah, well, they do say that madness finds whatever the All Mother touches. The Temple of Al'Matra has had some problems in the past with misidentifying the Seventh Hero. It's rather tragic that hindsight has shown them all to be … less than genuine. Still, perhaps this time will be different."

Gorm choked into his mug, covering himself in a spray of foam and ale.

"I see you've realized the nature of our offer." Flinn smirked. "The Al'Matran Temple is willing to intercede on your behalf with the Heroes' Guild, in exchange for your service, of course. It seems a good deal to me."

"A good deal? The Al'Matrans are all touched by the mad queen! Nobody ever takes quests for the Al'Matrans. It's certain death!"

"Oh, no, Mr. Ingerson. No, no, no." Mr. Flinn leaned in close. "It is almost-certain death. It's probable death. But there is that faint sliver of hope that you won't be asked to do anything too crazy, and that you'll make it home a tad richer and wiser. After all, Rulf the Weary was the forty-second Seventh Hero, and he and his party died from old age waiting for a sign from the All Mother."

The Tinderkin pointed upward, to the vacantly angry figure of Brunt. "Now, Mr. Brunt, on the other hand … Mr. Brunt represents certain death. Contractually obligated death. Death backed by the laws of every government of every city of every nation on Arth."

"Justice … Brunt-style!" Brunt's voice was like thunder in the distance.

"Right you are, Mr. Brunt!" said Flinn. "That, Mr. Ingerson, is certain death. And if that alone doesn't sway you, consider that the deal isn't totally one-sided. The guild will consider you a member in good standing once again: your record erased, your back dues waived, and so on and so forth. You may even advance a rank or two. It could work out rather well for you."

"Then find someone else if it's such a good deal."

"I'm sure you can see the difficulties of finding willing candidates for such a quest," said Mr. Flinn. "And yet the Prophecy of the Seventh Hero has an inherent recruitment quota. My associates and I must look for qualified and semi-qualified heroes with limited options. Such as yourself."

"I have options?" said Gorm.

"Of course. Two options, specifically: take the quest or face guild justice via Mr. Brunt." Flinn drained the last of his ale. "Choice is, as I said, a constant. But I should make it soon if I were you. Mr. Brunt is not a patient Ogre."

"Take matters … own hands!" rumbled Brunt.

"Ha ha! Let's hope not, Mr. Brunt! For Mr. Ingerson's sake, eh?" He placed his mug upside-down on the table. "Well? What shall it be?"

Gorm weighed his options. The Al'Matrans offered a chance to get his life back on track, but chances were far better that they'd lead him to a demise far worse than Mr. Brunt could dream up.

His eyes caught Gleebek's, and in the ignorant yellow orbs he saw a spark of fear. If Gorm was executed for a criminal, Gleebek would be guilty by association. They'd swing from the same tree, which put them in the same boat. Unfortunately, that meant they were up the same creek without the same paddles, as well.

"Fine," Gorm said. "Let's meet this Seventh Hero of yours."

Duine Poldo set the sheet of paper back down on top of the others. He looked down at the man who stood in front of his desk, which was no small feat, as Mr. Snithe was a Human and Mr. Poldo was a Scribkin, or a High Gnome. Standing, Poldo would have barely come up to Mr. Snithe's waist, but Poldo had compensated for his lack of height by designing a mahogany desk and chair ensemble that set him head and shoulders above anyone who entered his office. Scribkin are known for their ingenuity, not their practicality.

"The numbers are not good, Mr. Snithe."

"Yes, sir."

"In fact, they're terrible."

"Yes, sir."

"And here at Goldson Baggs, the numbers are everything."

"Yes, sir."

"So, it is only logical to say that everything is terrible, Mr. Snithe."

"I'm sorry, sir."

Poldo stroked his luxuriant mustache and thought furiously. The numbers hadn't been good before Mr. Snithe had come into his office with a stack of receipts from the Heroes' Guild. Now the numbers were downright awful. He looked at the top slip of parchment. Fine calligraphy on a typeset template read:

7.373 12th OF SUMMERGLOW (OPPO)

Receipt for the Equitable Distribution of Assets
from the Hoarde of

I VENOMOUS CHIMERA OF THE EASTERN MOORS
The Heroes' Guild hereby Holds that
GOLDSON BAGGS SWAMPLAND ADVENTURE FUND
Owning 6 PERCENT of the Hoarde, is entitled to the following:
1 NOTEBOOK (PARTIALLY USED)
6 SHILLINGS, I PENCE

Mr. Poldo let loose a long sigh. The other receipts were essentially the same, save that the names of the plunder funds changed, and none of the other funds got a notebook. "This hoard was projected to be valued at fifty thousand giltin, Mr. Snithe."

Snithe had clearly been expecting this line of questioning. "We had it assessed, Mr. Poldo. Sent a hoard adjuster out and everything."

"And?"

"He never came back."

"And you didn't see that as a problem?"

"It's usually a good sign, sir. The most deadly monsters have usually done the most pillaging, you see. So when a beast takes down a well-trained hoard adjustor, it's generally expected to have more valuable loot."

"That's not always the case, apparently."

"Well, risk is inherent in the system, sir."

"This creature had no money."

"True, sir. The giltin is from selling its meat down at the Base."

"And the notebook?"

"It belonged to the hoard adjuster." Mr. Snithe handed up a small black booklet with an Adventure Capital seal embossed on its cover. "Very good condition, all things considered."

Poldo flipped the notebook open. The first page was the only one with any writing. It read:

> Venomous Chymera of the E. Moores:
> The beaste hath nothing.

"Ah. This would have been useful three weeks ago."

"Three weeks ago, sir?"

"Yes. When our plunder funds invested some sixteen thousand giltin in the bloody monster's thrice-cursed hoard!" Mr. Poldo shouted, slamming the notebook down on his desk.

"Right, sir."

Poldo dismissed Mr. Snithe and polished his spectacles. He picked up a quill and adjusted his calculations. He ran the numbers again, just to be sure. They were still bad.

Sighing, Poldo pulled his stepladder and climbed down from his desk. He adjusted his impeccable black suit, picked up his notes, and stepped out of his office.

He quickly made his way through the familiar maze of ebony marble corridors, ignoring the clerks and agents that scrambled to get out of his way. As he rounded a corner, he extended a hand, and a leather folio was placed in his grasp before he had taken three strides. He lifted his chin, and an attendant ran up beside him, stooping to wax his mustache. He plucked a tumbler of mineral water from a waiting attendant's hand, drank a sip, and gargled the rest, and then handed the empty glass to a different attendant as he rounded the corner. The lift was waiting for him.

"Afternoon, Mr. Poldo," said the Gnoll who ran the lift, with a tip of his crimson cap.

"Good afternoon, Hrurk," said Poldo, stepping into the tiny onyx room.

"Good news today?" Hrurk asked politely.

Poldo shook his head.

"Well, next time," said the Gnoll. The lift's smooth black doors crackled faintly with traces of noctomancy as they slid closed. Hrurk tapped a combination on a dial of runes by the door, and they rode up to the top floor in a respectful silence.

Poldo stepped off the lift into a small waiting area. Across the room, massive gold and ebony doors were already swinging inward with an ominous creaking that rivaled the gates of any dark fortress. With a deep breath, Poldo brusquely walked into the top office of the Goldson Baggs Group, Inc.

The office had onyx walls and panoramic windows, and was empty save for two massive ebony desks; behind them, sat the two men often remarked to be the shortest titans on Arth: Fenrir Goldson and Bolbi Baggs. A Dwarf and a Halfling respectively, Goldson and Baggs had dominated business in Andarun and beyond for more than two centuries. They continued poring over a couple of outsized ledgers until Poldo gently cleared his throat.

"Yes?" said Mr. Goldson, not bothering to look up. He was ancient, even for a Dwarf, and age had reduced his once stout figure to a wizened frame with pallid, spotted skin stretched over it. His long white beard, adorned with gold and copper rings and pendants, was his only remaining hair. He wore a dark suit that looked much like Poldo's yet cost more than a good-sized farm in the Haerthwards.

"I have the report for tonight's meeting with the investors, sir," said Poldo.

"Excellent," said Baggs, setting down his quill. Mr. Baggs's curly silver locks settled in over a face touched by the beginnings of a grandfatherly wrinkle, and he wore a jolly smile that looked comfortably appropriate on someone of his considerable girth. He looked like a kindly old man finally enjoying all the amenities wealth had brought him, such as a suit that made Mr. Goldson's seem cheap.

"There are some serious concerns," Poldo said.

Mr. Goldson put down his pen and set his harsh gaze on the Scribkin.

Poldo swallowed hard and continued. "Adventure Capital isn't performing up to the standard that it once did."

Mr. Baggs frowned. "Our revenues are up six percent this year!"

"Yes, but revenue from loot is down by thirty-seven percent, sir," said Poldo, consulting his notes. "Most of Adventure Capital's profits are from selling plunder funds and their derivatives."

In Poldo's mind, plunder funds were growing a bit too popular. Everybody seemed to love buying up and bundling together the rights to shares of different hoards, creating a new financial product to invest in. The Heroes' Guild encouraged upfront investment, as it could be used to pay off professional heroes, regardless of the loot a foe had. Investors were keen on spreading the risk over multiple foes' hoards. Goldson Baggs and its competitors could make a profit selling shares of monstrous hoards before the monsters were slain, and eliminate the risk altogether.

Poldo saw the benefits of plunder funds. However, all of those reasons were built on one vulnerable assumption: that shares of the hoards were worth more than what a plunder-fund paid for them.

"The average hoard seems to be shrinking in value," Poldo said.

"Treasure hoards don't shrink!" Mr. Goldson snorted. "Drakes and scargs and Chitinous Scythers don't give gold away, do they? No, they attack people to take gold, and the hoards grow!"

Poldo flipped through the other reports in his folio. "Monster attacks are down by five and a half percent this quarter, sir. A twenty-three percent decline since last year. The average quest time from offer to completion is down sixty-three percent from last year. There's been a dramatic rise in the number of Shadowkin and creatures of monstrous descent seeking to become NPCs.

"Foes attack less often, live less long when they do, and increasingly are joining the economy as labor rather than common-pool resources. Hoards are rarer and have significantly less loot, and if trends continue I ..."

"Yes?" Mr. Baggs prompted.

"I don't think growth in the heroics industry is sustainable," Poldo squeaked.

Mr. Goldson and Mr. Baggs shared a knowing look.

"Mr. Poldo," said Mr. Baggs, with his kindly smile. "Do you think we didn't see this coming?"

"Oh, no, sir!" said Poldo automatically.

"Our firm represents the best and the brightest minds in all the kingdom," said Mr. Goldson. "Naturally, we're aware of the current ... irregularities in professional heroics. But we're confident the market will correct itself."

"We're already taking measures to help that correction along," said Mr. Baggs. "But in the meantime ..."

"It's your responsibility to let the investors know that this difficult situation is temporary," Goldson continued.

"And that we're on top of it. Reassure them," Mr. Baggs finished.

"It's a somewhat difficult point to make when our share prices are down three percent on the Wall, sir."

"Our share prices will rise when the investors have been suitably reassured, Mr. Poldo," Baggs said meaningfully.

"Yes, sirs," Poldo relented. He bowed as Mr. Goldson and Mr. Baggs returned to their ledgers.

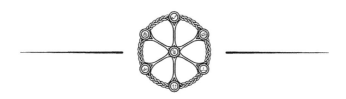

The Temple of Al'Matra was in the middle tiers of Andarun, wedged uncomfortably close to the Ridge. Its grounds were overgrown with thick vines and choking weeds, and its limestone walls were pitted and covered in teal and golden lichen. A couple of green-and-silver banners, each bearing the All Mother's falcon, hung from two old windows, but they had been left in the weather too long and were starting to fade and fray. It was, Gorm thought, as he was led up the wide steps to the temple, a sad state for the house of the Queen of the Gods.

In the Age of Darkness, when the truth was concealed by Mannon and many competing belief systems spread over Arth, most people thought that religious conflict would end if the world could be converted to one faith. Then Arth's gods and goddesses revealed themselves once more and united the world in the worship of one consistent pantheon. Religious conflicts resumed the next day.

Arth's pantheon was essentially a celestial administration that the Creator had left in charge once He decided that His work was good, or at least good enough. Like middle management everywhere, the gods seemed to be mostly concerned with petty conflicts and power struggles. They fought endlessly over believers, and money, and status, and the best temples, and anything else that gods typically want.

By all accounts and any measure, Al'Matra, the All Mother, was not faring well.

No worshippers walked the halls Gorm and Gleebek were ushered through. The mosaics on the floor were missing chips. The murals on the wall were peeling. Some chipmunks had made a nest in the dried-up bowl of the holy font. When they reached the sanctuary, illuminated by shafts of sunlight streaming in through stained-glass windows and holes in the ceiling, a single attendant gave them a halfhearted greeting and trundled off to fetch his superiors.

While they waited, Gorm examined the windows and frescos throughout the room, Gleebek keeping close by his side. The first window depicted a beautiful Elven lady in flowing white seated on a throne next to a great, gray-skinned man with a flowing beard: Al'Matra and Al'Thadan, the All Mother and the All Father. Subsequent paintings showed them reigning as king and queen of the other gods, giving magic to men, and casting Mannon from the heavens.

Another window showed Al'Thadan's betrayal, as he and the treacherous Sten were revealed to be agents of Mannon. The fallen king was depicted as laughing as great Trolls slew Elves and Gnomes and Dwarves below him, while Al'Matra tried in vain to stay his hand. Gorm walked along a wall, watching the rise of Tandos play out in fresco along it. Tandos, the greatest son of Al'Matra and Al'Thadan, rallying mankind to defend against the forces of Mannon in the War of Betrayal. Tandos protecting the warriors of light as they crusaded against the vile Sten. Tandos, striking down Al'Thadan as Al'Matra turned away.

Gorm and Gleebek were at the altar. On top of it was a great statue of two golden thrones: one empty and one with a marble lady slumped upon it. The sculpture of Al'Matra showed a woman wracked by grief, her hair matted, and her eyes staring forlornly into the distance. A queen who held her crown in limp hands. A mother who had been betrayed by her husband, and then watched as her eldest son cut her love down and slaughtered all of his subjects.

It was the kind of ugly end to a relationship that can really mess someone up.

The All Mother's descent from nobility to madness was not so much chronicled as demonstrated in subsequent murals. The scene of Tandos's ascension to divine regent showed him accepting a crown from a cat on its hind legs. The images of the first conflicts between the Al'Matran and Tandosian temples showed Tandos trapped in a spider's web yet still striking at the All Mother with a large mackerel. Al'Matra's fall into poverty showed her walking down a path that bore no connection to any reality Gorm had ever seen, with brightly colored flying shrimp and mocking cherubs following her through a forest of waving tentacles. The last few paintings were nonsense: a diagram of a dissected squid that had ingested a lance. An Elf painted with the angles all wrong, so that both eyes were on the same side of its face. A naturalist's rendition of thirty-seven varieties of olives, only fourteen of which actually existed according to the footnote.

"Bloody insane," Gorm muttered, staring at the olives.

"Some would say," conceded a soft voice behind him.

Gorm turned to see a slight Human clad in Al'Matran robes, all white with green and silver trimmings. He had curly ginger hair and a face that was somehow innocent and weary in equal measure. There was also an oddness about the man's face that Gorm couldn't place. "Hello," he said to Gorm. "I am Niln il'Devin of Al'Matra, a high scribe of Her Ladyship."

"Oh, er, Gorm Ingerson. This is my, ahem, squire, Gleebek."

"Gleebek!"

Niln nodded. "It's good to meet you, Gorm, and you as well, Gleebek." Gorm couldn't see what made the man's face seem so strange. There was nothing wrong with his nose, which was small and round, nor his jaw, aside from needing a good beard.

"Zuggog, da bibbot Tib'rin."

"Er, I meant no offense callin' yer painting insane—"

"It's no matter. We know that the All Mother has certain challenges that she struggles to overcome. As do we all. I-it's my eyes, by the way."

"Ah. Right. That's it," Gorm said. He supposed that he should have been more embarrassed, but he was too relieved to finally identify the quirk in Niln's face. The man's eyes were different colors: one sky blue, the other sea green. "Sorry again."

"No, no. I get that a lot," said Niln. "It's pretty common for those of us who are of the first generation."

Humans were the most common of the races of Man, by virtue of being the genetic default. In ages past, the Gnomes and Elves, and even the Sten, occasionally fell in love with members of a different race, and the result was almost always Human. Of course, when two Humans bred—and it often seemed to the Elder races that they did little else— they naturally made more Humans. Very few Humans could recall their original ancestry.

For a handful of Humans, however, their heritage was much more recent. There were still times when an Elf and a Gnome of some sort would feel Vala's touch and start a family. The children such couples had were something close to what most Humans were, but somehow seemed more ancient.

"So, you're the Seventh Hero, then."

"Uh, yes," said Niln. "Well, so it is written."

"Written by whom?" said Gorm.

"Um, written by me," said Niln, shifting uncomfortably. "Or rather, by the Goddess through me."

"You're the one sayin' that you're this hero of legend? Sounds a bit convenient."

"I'm the high scribe of Al'Matra," said Niln. "The high priestess intercedes on our behalf, and it is I who receive her answers and accounts of history. Most likely."

"Most likely?" asked Gorm.

"There are two high scribes in the temple currently," Niln said with some reluctance. "It's really an unusual situation, especially as there is some … disagreement between my scriptures and Scribe Pathalan's."

"So what's that mean? Is the goddess supposed to be arguing with herself?"

All eyes turned to the diagram of the olives.

"That is a distinct possibility," Niln said carefully. "But it's also possible that Scribe Pathalan, with all due respect, is mistaken."

"Or that ye are."

"Um, yes."

"And a pretty good one, given that you're predicting that you're a legendary hero," said Gorm. "I mean, ye look like ye could barely lift a mace, let alone swing it when an Orcish warrior or Venomous Scarg is bearing down on ye. That counts for more than some inklings that may or may not be the ranting of the Mad Goddess. You're risking your life, to say nothing of my life or Gleebek's, for a pile of silly Al'Matran drivel. No offense."

"You know, saying 'no offense' doesn't count for much after saying something really offensive."

"Fair enough. I'll stop. But face facts. Ye've got no strength, no experience, and ye clearly have no clue what we're doing here. I mean, do ye even have a quest?"

"W-well, not as such," stammered the high scribe. "But the prophecy says—"

"Burn the prophecy. This is supposed to be professional heroics," snapped Gorm. "First ye need someone to find a monster with loot, and they stake a claim on its lair. Then they issue a quest to kill the monster. Then they sell off shares of their claim to investors and use the money to hire heroes to come and kill the beast. And then they split up the loot based on who owns what stake in the hoard. That's the job. That's all it is.

"Ye've got no monster, no loot, no quest, no investors, nothing. This isn't professional heroics. It ain't even amateur heroics. You've just got some fanciful dreams of glory and the writings of a barmy goddess."

"This is actually still pretty offensive," ventured Niln.

"I didn't say 'no offense.'"

Niln's mouth tightened into a tiny, lipless line. "Be that as it may, I … I have to go on."

"So how do ye know what to do? Or when the quest is done?"

"When we have saved the world."

"Ha!" snorted Gorm. "As though that'll hold up in court."

"I think it will." Niln's brow furrowed slightly. "Follow me."

The Inner Sanctum was a small white room with little decoration aside from a painting of the All Mother and a silver sculpture of a strange icon: six silver lines radiating from a rune at the symbol's center, each terminating in a different glyph. Three cords wove around the six outer runes, connecting them to each other so that the sigil looked like an intricate wagon wheel. A thick green folder inlaid with the same icon sat on a small table in the center of the room.

Niln stepped up to the table and flipped open the folder to reveal a heavy document bound with black ribbons and crimson seals that depicted a dripping quill over a well-detailed skull. It was a regrettably recognizable crest.

"Ye hired the Lawyer-monks of Adchul?"

"They're said to be experts on guild law of some renown," said Niln.

"There's an understatement."

The brothers of the Order of Adchul once famously saved a town from flooding by drafting a cease-and-desist letter to the river. Everyone in professional heroics knew that the only way out of a contract with the Lawyer-monks was death, and even that wasn't guaranteed; rumors held they had once successfully filed a motion with the gods themselves to claim a large portion of a Tandosian priest's eternal reward.

"The Lawyer-monks have drafted an agreement using a campaign structure with a set of open objectives," said Niln, carefully reading from the contract. "If that isn't specific enough, just know that you'll be bound to any quests, side quests, bounties, and such that the party engages in, until you are released from service by decree from the Temple of Al'Matra or the Temple of Tandos, or the event of your death."

"The Temple of Tandos?"

"They funded our quest as a gesture of goodwill. Our temples are seeking to end ages of religious conflict."

"That's generous."

"Well, they do have a lot of money."

"I meant calling it a conflict."

Long ago, the wars between the Al'Matrans and the Tandosians had been protracted, bloody affairs, but in recent centuries, the wars had grown progressively more petty, more lopsided, and much more succinct. The last Al'Matran crusade started just over four hundred years ago, when the Tandosian High Priest insulted the All Mother by falling asleep during a holy ritual. The Tandosians crushed the uprising without waking him.

"Hilarious," sighed Niln. "Will you sign the contract and join us?"

"Do I really have a choice?"

"Mr. Flinn would say you do, but since your only other option leads to your execution, I'd imagine that you would say you don't."

"And what do ye say?'

"I'd say you have a destiny, and choices are the steps you take to reach it." Niln offered him a quill.

Gorm took the quill and pulled the contract toward him. "Ye wait till ye've seen a bit of the world," he grumbled, initialing the first page of the contract. "Ye'll stop with such nonsense."

"And what makes you think that I haven't seen enough of the world?"

Gorm looked up from the contract straight into the priest's mismatched eyes. "Yer still tryin' to save it."

Chapter 4

The upper levels of the Temple of Al'Matra were small towers occupied by bunk rooms and private chambers. Niln showed Gorm and Gleebek to the southwest tower on the third floor, to a tiny chamber illuminated by a thin slit of a window on the south wall. It was furnished with two decrepit bunks, two small chests, and an old wash bin.

"You may have your things sent here," said Niln, inviting them in.

Gorm dropped his rucksack on the bottom bunk. Gleebek set down his single giltin and a dead rat he'd somehow acquired. "Done," said Gorm.

"I see. Well, we shall have to pay a visit to the General Store. Come. I'll take you to meet the others."

"So I ain't the first hero you've recruited, then?"

"Oh no, Mr. Ingerson. You are the fifth hero of destiny, and once we have the sixth, I shall become the seventh. We are remarkably close to beginning our quest."

"I'll try to contain my excitement."

They exited the tower to a large rooftop terrace. Topiary bushes and small tea trees grew from decorative pots, while weeds and small shrubs crept through cracks in the cobblestones and shingles. The air smelled of old wood and new leaves.

There were also a lot of statues. Many were the sculptures one would expect: depictions of the All Mother and her saints and her sacred falcons, but they were scattered around pieces that didn't belong in a temple—or anywhere, as Gorm would have it. He glowered at a giant teacup carved from marble, filled with mahogany brew; scoffed at a large sandstone eyeball clasped delicately in a great onyx hand; and was disgusted to see an extensive collection of granite sea creatures scattered though the bushes.

A man was draped over the bench closest to them, plucking a cedar and mahogany lute. He wore a bright gold and vermilion tunic beneath a leather jerkin, and matching tights. He was thin, as was his neat black mustache. His hat was wide, as was his grin. "Hello, Master Niln," he said. "Another successful day?"

"Indeed. Gorm Ingerson, meet Heraldin Strummons, our party's bard," said Niln.

"A pleasure," Heraldin said. "Why does your name sound familiar?"

"Couldn't say," said Gorm.

"Mr. Ingerson is our new warrior," said the high scribe.

"My condolences. What are you in for?" asked Heraldin.

"I'll thank you for not making such jokes, Mr. Strummons," said Niln, frowning.

"I'd wait until I stop first, were I you. What's with the gobbo? Target practice?" The bard produced a throwing knife and casually sighted it on Gleebek, who yelped and ducked behind Gorm.

Gorm decided that Heraldin wasn't quite so tolerable after all.

"Gleebek is Mr. Ingerson's squire," Niln interjected.

"You can't be serious." Heraldin sneered. "Why would we possibly bring a Goblin along? It's unhygienic. And what use would it be?"

"I was thinkin' the same thing about a bard," Gorm shot back. According to the Heroes' Guild's *Official Guide to Professional Heroics*, bards were a class of hero possessing varied talents; uplifting songs could inspire a party to even greater acts of valor and daring. In Gorm's experience, they weren't good for much beyond absorbing incoming arrows.

"Mr. Strummons is more than just a bard," Niln said. "He's actually a rather accomplished, ah, improvisational locksmith? Or perhaps an acquisition specialist?"

"Why don't ye just say he's a thie—"

"Don't say it!" The bard hushed him, leaping to his feet. After a conspiratorial look around, he continued in a hurried whisper. "We don't use certain words to describe certain professional services that I used to provide, because if certain parties were to think that I was engaging in certain professions, a certain Benny Hookhand would certainly take me out to paint the town red. And I'd be the paint, if you catch my meaning."

"We're on top of a building," said Gorm. "Who's going to hear?"

"Don't underestimate Benny Hookhand. Besides, I prefer to be a bard."

"What, really?"

"Oh yes," Heraldin added, strumming a chord and waggling his eyebrows. "You'd be surprised what women will do for a man with a lute."

"Now that's unhygienic."

"Perhaps we should continue on," said Niln hurriedly.

They walked across the terrace to where Gorm could see two figures facing away from each other on opposite ends of a stone bench, near the balcony that overlooked the city. One was a man in royal purple robes, reading a book. His head was shaven, although he had a neat black goatee. The other was a young woman in vibrant orange. Her long dark hair was loose, save for a single thin braid. She was not reading anything but was instead very actively engaged in not looking at the man. Both wore deep scowls.

"Oh gods," said Gorm. "Ye hired a solamancer and a noctomancer?"

In the threads of magic that weave the world of Arth, there are two directions: the warp and the weft. A mage is a person who, through birthright and scholarship, can see and harness these threads for power or profit, or, as is so often the case, both. The great orders of wizardry are most notably distinguished by the threads of magic their members can see and touch. Solamancers, of the Sun, grasp the weft — the powers of fire and water, light and life. Noctomancers, of the Moon, wield the warp of magic — the forces of air and earth, shadow and death. There are many other differences between solamancers and noctomancers, of varying degree and nature: ceremonial, cultural, philosophical, and, all too often, violent.

"Oh, it gets better than that," said Heraldin.

"Master Jynn, Lady Laruna," said Niln. "This is Gorm Ingerson, our new warrior, and his squire, Gleebek."

"*Gleebek!*"

The wizard looked up with a face too gaunt to be friendly. Narrow Ruskan eyes peered from within pools of shadow above a hawkish nose and a thin mouth. "I see," he said, scratching his beard. His vowels spun out slightly longer; traces of a Ruskan accent. "I am Jynn Ur'Gored of the Order of the Moon, High Councilor of the Circle of the Red Hawk."

"I'm Laruna Trullon, Order of the Sun," said the solamancer, talking over Jynn. "Eighth-rank mage with the Heroes' Guild." Her face, like the rest of her, was sharp and thin, and not unhandsome.

Gorm introduced himself and Gleebek. "I find it hard to believe ye two don't mind workin' together," he added.

"Actually, I'd prefer if we don't talk about it," Jynn said.

"It's best if you address us one at a time," said Laruna, staring at Gorm pointedly. "And pretend the other isn't there."

Gorm turned to Niln. "Is this how it's to be? They spend the whole quest not acknowledgin' one another?"

"Gods, let's hope so," said Heraldin. "It's so much better this way."

"I think Mr. Ingerson was hoping to see that you can act as a team," Niln told the mages, nodding in earnest encouragement.

"Oh, I've worked with many apprentices before," said Jynn. "She won't get in our way."

Laruna spoke over him. "The newblood? Rank-one heroes go on quests all the time. He'll catch up."

The mages shot each other loathing glares.

"I don't trust the Heroes' Guild on matters of magic," said Jynn to Gorm loudly. "They're clearly working with forces they don't understand."

"I'd say the guild knows a lot about effectiveness," Laruna remarked to no one in particular. "They're far more able to get things done than stodgy old councilors from the academy."

"Old?" Jynn demanded. "I'm not yet thirty. I'm the youngest man ever to sit on the Academic Council of Mages."

"And it's gone straight to his head," Laruna told Gorm. "Besides, it's all books and theory at the academy. I've actually been on quests. I'm eighth-rank."

"Perhaps you'd value academic achievement more if you had any, apprentice," snapped Jynn.

Laruna ignored the wizard. "I only need one more councilor's vote and I'll advance instantly," she told Gorm. "Guess who's holding me back?"

"You'll have my vote when you're ready," said Jynn.

"I am ready," said Laruna. "You're just too stuck up and self-important to see it."

"It only seems that way to the ignorant."

"Watch your mouth, candle-wand!"

"Enough!" said Gorm. "Honestly, if ye two find each other so awful, I don't see why you've chosen to sit at the same bench."

The mages seemed somewhat perplexed by the sentiment.

"This is the best view in the temple," said Jynn.

"Why should he have it?" said Laruna.

"Just ... please don't burn anything down," sighed Niln.

They left the mages to their silent feud and worked their way to the side of the terrace, opposite Gorm and Gleebek's bunk.

"Well, there's an interestin' party dynamic," Gorm remarked. "Solamancers and noctomancers don't always get along so great, but that was somethin' else."

"They share an unfortunate history," Niln conceded. "After Jynn objected and blocked Laruna's ascension to full magehood, they had a rather nasty duel."

"So? Mages blast each other all the time."

The Academy of Mages recognized sorcerous duels as a valid method of establishing social standing, or settling personal disagreements, or figuring out whose turn it was to do the dishes.

"Yes, but said duels are supposed to be sanctioned," said Niln. "Unsanctioned duels must be reviewed in a committee hearing to determine how said duel started. That's the problem."

"Why? How'd the duel start?"

Niln stopped short. "Please don't ask that question," he said, pointing at Gorm. "Ever."

Heraldin stepped in. "They'll each swear the other started it, and then they'll just swear at each other, and then the fireworks will begin."

"They've burned down three courthouses so far," said Niln, shaking his head.

"They're that bad?" said Gorm.

"Bad enough to land them here," said Heraldin with a grin.

Niln rebuked the bard again, but Gorm wasn't listening; he was watching a tall figure who leaned against the far wall, a very large man wearing dark leather armor and a black hood. Most of his ebony face was concealed behind a crimson scarf, but even at this distance, Gorm could recognize him. The man's face had haunted Gorm for twenty years.

"Iheen," Gorm whispered.

"Who?" asked Heraldin. "No, that's Gaist."

Gorm shook his head. "It's Iheen the Red."

"Iheen the Red?" Realization lit up the bard's face. "That's where I know your name! You're the berserker who ran and abandoned Johan!"

Gorm had already stopped paying attention to the bard again. A flicker of surprised recognition crossed Iheen's face, but he quickly resumed staring stoically into the distance.

"Iheen," Gorm said, extending a hand. "Iheen, it's me—Gorm Ingerson."

Iheen, or perhaps Gaist, said nothing.

"Iheen? Or Gaist? Whatever ye call yerself, I can see ye know me."

The man didn't move a muscle.

"Don't take this the wrong way," said Niln. "Gaist does not speak."

"Not at all?"

"Not for over twenty years, according to guild records. Not since the Dungeon of … ah." Niln trailed off awkwardly. "I suppose you know."

It had been twenty-one years since the dark magics of Az'Anon the Spider King had bestowed a renewed vigor and a misanthropic worldview upon every corpse within a hundred miles of his black lair. It had taken Gorm and his party over a full day to carve a path through the dead army to Az'Anon's front gate, and then the real horrors had begun.

"I ain't been the same since," said Gorm. "I don't know why I thought he would."

"Indeed," said Niln. "However, I believe him to be a valuable member of our team. He was our first volunteer, after all."

"Yeah, no surprise there," said Heraldin.

"Oh?"

Niln tried to interject. "I don't think—"

"Go look up the statue's file at the Heroes' Guild," said Heraldin, gesturing at Gaist. "His license has more points than a Dire Porcupine's backside, because for the past twenty years he's been throwing himself at the biggest, nastiest monsters he can find—usually alone. All since he was horribly shamed. Any guesses as to what's going on?"

Gorm knew. "He wants to die."

"There's a clever Dwarf," said the bard. "And remember, he's the only one who volunteered for this gig."

"Yes, well … thank you, Heraldin," said Niln, without gratitude.

"How do ye know any of this if he doesn't talk?" Gorm asked.

"Oh, he can communicate," said Niln. "He has official papers, and he fills out enough paperwork to follow guild procedures. And it's amazing what you can say with body language."

"Especially when you're using someone else's body," added Heraldin.

Gaist was as still and silent as the stone walrus he was standing beside, yet there was something in his posture, in the manner with which he set his jaw, or in the way his eyes managed to always be staring somewhere else, that said, very clearly, *go away.*

"Perhaps it would be better to continue this discussion elsewhere," said Niln. "Come. I'll see you back to your room."

Heraldin waved to Gaist. "So long. Watch out for those pigeons."

"Don't worry," Niln said as they made their way back across the terrace. "Gaist may not do much here, but he's actually quite good with a blade. A rank-six weaponsmaster, in fact."

"All the more reason to worry," said Gorm.

"Excuse me?" said Niln.

"Do ye know the number one cause of death among professional heroes?"

"I'm fairly certain it's getting eaten by something or other."

"Maybe a long time ago, but not anymore."

"Oh! Is it falling in pits?" Niln guessed. "I heard a lot of heroes die because they don't have a rope."

"Ain't pits."

"We've bought several ropes," Niln offered feebly.

"It's inter-party conflict." Gorm spoke with a weariness born from experience.

He had lost many friends to fights within their party. Sometimes a hero had something to prove. Sometimes they had a different agenda. Sometimes there were spectacular battles, and sometimes there wasn't even a fight at all; a "forgotten" healing potion or a lever pulled at the wrong moment was all it took to be rid of an inconvenient companion. Whatever the cause or method, the leading killer of professional heroes was other professional heroes.

"You've got an unstable, suicidal man with a small arsenal in our camp," said Gorm. "And then you brought in a pair of mages with a history of burning down buildings. And a bard who keeps talkin' like he wants a punch in the face. No offense."

"None taken," said Heraldin. "You'd be surprised how often I hear that."

"I don't think I would," said Gorm. "The point is, you've assembled a better powder keg than a party. Ye think these people are going to fight together? Could ye stand and face a tentacled horror from beyond time and space and know, absolutely know, that they'll have your back?"

Niln seemed at a loss for words. He looked to Heraldin, but the bard gave the scribe nothing more than a shrug before walking away.

"It's like I said before. Ye don't know what you're doin'," Gorm pressed. "Ye can only play at being a hero for so long before the truth catches up to ye and kills ye in some horrible way. Professional heroics is all a laugh, until it isn't anymore."

"I'm not playing!"

"Well, ye sure as fire ain't a professional. And amateurs don't last long in a dungeon. Ye want to die for the mad queen, it's your business. But you're taking me and Gleebek and the others along as well. Why drag all of us into it?"

"I …" Niln began, and then thought better of it and started over. "People always say that we must stand up for what we believe in."

"They're not talkin' to you!" barked Gorm. "They're talkin' to people who don't believe in stupid things! They're talkin' to people who think the same way everyone else does, or something close enough!"

Niln's mouth opened and closed like a fish on the shore.

"Come on, Gleebek," Gorm said.

"*Spooty, Gleebek zuggog nub da bibbot.*"

Gorm made it to his chamber before Niln caught him.

"I can learn!" the high scribe called, running down the hall. "Maybe I don't know what I'm doing. But you do. You did it for years. I read about it: the time they called you the Pyrebeard. I'm willing to learn."

Gorm could see the earnestness in the man's eyes, next to the inexperience and the folly. "But I ain't willing to teach," he said, and closed the door.

Gorm was half undressed for bed when he heard a knock on his door. Technically, Gleebek was too, but the Goblin was always half-undressed. Gorm took a moment to throw on his chain mail and cloak before answering the knock.

A relatively small member of the Silver Talons, wearing ill-fitting armor, informed them that Mr. Flinn expected Gorm to come and assist him with some recruitment.

"Why me?" asked Gorm. "Ain't he got a whole troupe of ye Talons?"

"Oh yes, sir," said the mercenary, pulling Gorm aside. "But if we were to, aha, convince a hero to join us against his or her will, that's very much akin to capturing them, and attempting to capture or restrain heroes is very clearly thuggery. But the bulk of the Silver Talons' certified thugs are stationed in Aberreth, and here in Andarun we're mostly just goons."

"That makes sense," conceded Gorm.

The Thugs' Union and the League of Goons existed to provide discreet protection and rule enforcement to private entities, but thugs also specialized in the control and suppression of licensed heroes. Plenty of taverns, shops, and politicians had a vested interest in keeping nearby heroes in line, and even the Heroes' Guild employed thugs to retrieve or discipline wayward members. The Thugs' Union maintained that heroes belonged deep in dungeons, not in intrigues, and it worked to protect the image of thuggery as a respected and valued part of society.

"Attempting to coerce guild members is very dangerous work," said the pimply little Silver Talon, which was true. Good thugs were nearly as fearsome as professional heroes. Mediocre thugs were famously short lived. "Do you know what health insurance costs if you're dealing with professional heroes without thug certifications?"

"The premiums must be mad."

"Totally insane, sir. Technically, my policies could get voided just for talking to a hero for too long. So, uh, if you could …"

Gorm thanked the young mercenary and sent him on his way. Once he was properly dressed, he made his way down to the sanctuary.

Mr. Flinn greeted Gorm with a mocking bow. "Ah, Mr. Ingerson. An honor. It's not every day that I stand in the presence of a hero of destiny."

"I was hopin' it wouldn't be today either. We've no business, mercenary."

"I'm afraid I must correct you there."

"I signed the contract. I'm already recruited."

"Yes, and now you and I share an employer," said Mr. Flinn. "Master Niln sends a request that you join Mr. Brunt and myself in recruiting the sixth and final hero."

"Don't see why ye'd need my help."

"Our candidate is currently in one of the most disreputable establishments in one of the most unsavory districts of Andarun. More arms are always welcome."

"Brunt seems like a capable lad," said Gorm. "I'm sure ye can manage."

"Perhaps you have forgotten the nature of the employer–employee relationship, Mr. Ingerson. When Master Niln sends an order, your opinion on the matter is optional. Your compliance is not." Mr. Flinn produced a small slip of paper with an address scrawled on it. "You will meet us at this address in one hour. Wait outside for us, preferably with a professional smile."

Gorm gave a professional smile, which was very much like baring his teeth at the Gnome. "See ye in an hour," he growled, and left the Gnome to his own devices.

The address was outside of Andarun's walls in the Riverdowns, a network of rickety docks and ancient warehouses that looked to be slowly sinking into, or perhaps pulling themselves from, the Tarapin River. Gorm and Gleebek made their way along a rotting boardwalk, past decrepit hovels and timber skeletons of boathouses, until they came to the tavern Flinn had directed them to.

The Randy Goat leaned over the river's main channel, leering at the trade barges and river skiffs that bobbed on the water. Its broken windows glowed with golden light in the sapphire evening; through them rang laughter, swearing, and raucous commotion. Battered men, broken stools, and other wreckage from a bar brawl were heaped along the boardwalk outside.

Gorm stamped up to the tavern, eyeing a sign that depicted a young barmaid trying to preserve her modesty while a mischievous goat consumed her skirt.

"He calls this disreputable?" he said to Gleebek. "Me Da took me to worse places when I was knee high."

An unfortunate patron burst through a third-story window and plunged screaming into the swirling river. Gleebek edged closer to Gorm.

"Fair 'nough," Gorm said, scowling at the window. "I still seen worse."

Gorm leaned against a dock post while he waited, and Gleebek sat down uneasily on a large coil of barge rope. Whenever the Goat's patrons quieted to a dull commotion, they could hear the Tarapin burbling beneath them and the creaks and bumps of the barges tied at the docks down the way.

It was well past the hour they had agreed upon when Mr. Flinn finally arrived, Brunt thundering along behind him. The Tinderkin greeted Gorm and Gleebek cordially and thanked them for waiting.

"Just tell us what ye want us to do." Gorm snorted.

"Wait here," said Flinn.

Gorm felt the veins in his forehead throbbing. "But ye—"

"Not all of the heroes we recruit are as cooperative as yourself, Mr. Ingerson," said Mr. Flinn with a small laugh. "We need the exit covered should our newest recruit decide to flee."

"So we're just to stop anyone who comes runnin' from the tavern."

"Indeed," said Mr. Flinn. He watched a figure lurch out the bar door and shamble down the causeway. "But with any luck, it won't come to that. People usually can't walk straight after a stint at the Goat, let alone make a successful run. Come, Mr. Brunt."

Gorm glowered after the Gnome and the Ogre as they pushed their way into the bar.

"Grot ga gi'zub?"

"Nothin' to be done," snorted Gorm. He leaned back against the wall and startled something some way down a half-submerged alleyway.

"Hey!" called a pile of rags, dragging itself from the shadows. It was a man, draped in old cloths and rusting chain mail. He stared at Gorm with dark eyes set in sallow skin, and clutched his freely bleeding forearm. "Hey, you gotta help me!"

"Get lost," Gorm told him.

"I've been wounded," he gasped, crawling over to Gorm. His words came in bursts of gravelly slurring. "I need salve. Bad. Got any … got any salve?"

"Gub ga'dubba sa?" said Gleebek, glancing worriedly at the man.

"What? No, don't worry about him. He's a salve-head." Gorm pantomimed a swig from an imaginary bottle. "He's addicted to healing potions."

The miraculous elixirs known collectively as healing potions saved countless lives, but easy access to draughts that could bring a man from the brink of death to perfect health in seconds had some less-pleasant consequences. It wasn't unusual for a hero to sustain multiple life-threatening wounds on any given quest, and a hero in demand might end up consuming his or her weight in salve during a busy month.

After that much exposure to sorcerous healing, a person could begin to like the sensation of the elixirs, or even to need it. The streets of Arth's cities were littered with ex-heroes who had become too dependent on salve to adventure, or to find another job, or to do anything beyond acquire more healing potions.

They sat in gutters and alleyways, hacking at themselves and bleeding on passersby until they found someone either kind or disgusted enough to toss them the potion they craved. Some of the greatest heroes in history wound up bleeding to death on a busy sidewalk, waiting for someone to pass them a taste of elixir.

Gleebek tugged at Gorm's cloak. *"Sa'kubbat,"* the Goblin insisted, pointing at the wounded man.

"No, look, you're being ..." Gorm shook his hands in consternation, and then tried to pantomime a man slitting his own wrists. "He ... cut, see? Cut ... himself. He did it to get free potions."

The addict shook his grisly appendage at the Dwarf. "No, no, I didn't ... Look ... Help! I got cut on ... on a something! It was sharp."

"Sod off. I ain't got any healing potions, anyway."

"How ... how about some gold, then? I can buy some at the Goat."

"That's the last thing ye need," Gorm grumbled, eyeing a couple of bleeding figures slumped outside the Goat's door. "Go see the Temple of Fulgen instead. They'll help ye."

"Hey ... Hey, I'm a hero," tried the addict, pulling himself to his feet and staggering after them. "I ... I can kill that Goblin for you. For some gold. Or salve."

Gleebek squeaked and ducked behind Gorm. "Easy on the threats, lad," Gorm said. "He's an NPC."

The addict squinted in confusion. "You ... you don't want me to kill the Goblin?"

"Course not."

"Okay, fine." The hero took an unstable step forward as he drew a bloody knife. "Give me some gold or I kill the Goblin."

"*Pauperz!*" Gleebek chirped, presenting his documents.

"I ain't got time for this," grumbled Gorm, standing. He stamped up to the bleeding addict, grabbed him by the collar, pulled him closer, and delivered a punch like a hammer blow to the man's forehead. The man's eyes rolled back, and he collapsed with a feeble groan.

"Thrice-cursed salve heads," Gorm muttered, shaking the grime off his hand. He started away, but then thought for a moment and returned to bind the man's wound with one of the fellow's cleaner rags. When the wound was stable, he relieved the unconscious hero of the dagger.

"*Grot zub?*"

"Payment for medical services," he explained to Gleebek, cleaning the blade on his cloak as he leaned back against the side of the Goat. He offered the knife to Gleebek. "Here," he said.

The Goblin seemed unsure what to do, as if this was the first time someone had ever pointed the dull end of a blade at him. He pointed to the weapon. "*Ra gub'pogti Tib'rin ixit nork?*"

"Aye, whatever ye said. Take it."

Gleebek lifted the weapon with reverent claws and stood up straighter to carefully slide it into his fur belt. *"Ra da'pogtiz,"* he said fiercely. *"Da'klibbo."*

"Aye. Look, it's just a knife," said Gorm, trying to suppress a grin.

Flinn's voice rose above the Goat's din. "No, Mr. Brunt, this way! Yes, and mind that table. Oh, please excuse me."

"Sounds like Mr. Flinn'll be needin' us soon," Gorm told Gleebek.

"Grot?"

Someone else was shouting something, but Flinn cut him off. "Mr. Brunt! Would you assist this fellow in excusing us?"

Gorm took a step back, directing Gleebek to do the same. A moment later, the door was blasted from its hinges by an airborne bouncer, who skidded across the boardwalk and barely managed to avoid falling into the river by catching the edge of a plank.

Brunt rumbled through the newly widened portal. "Beg … pardon!" he roared, and then, noticing the bouncer dangling from the plank, he stomped heavily on the boardwalk. Boards shook and cracked under the force, neatly depositing the hapless bouncer in the river. The Ogre gave a semi-satisfied snort.

"Woo! Look out!" called an Elf, stumbling through the doorway.

She was tall, with slender features and long pointed ears, as is the nature of Elves, but she was shouting and gesturing in a way that wasn't Elven at all. Her fern-green leather armor and matching jade and drake-hide bracers were stained with what Gorm could only hope was a spilled drink. She was the very image of grace and beauty, leaning on Flinn's shoulder to avoid falling on her face.

"Ah, Mr. Ingerson," said Flinn through gritted teeth. "Perhaps you and your squire would be so kind?"

"I suppose." Gorm threw the Elf's other arm over his shoulder. She reeked of spiced wine and grog.

Flinn handed Gleebek a rucksack and a fine bow. "Ah, excellent. It has been, shall we say, an eventful outing."

"I'm a hero of destiny!" hollered the Elf.

"Apologies. I forget my manners," said Flinn, grimacing. "May I introduce—"

"Ay! Someone's gonna pay for that door!" someone shouted from behind them.

"Settle the bill, Mr. Brunt!" snapped Flinn.

A scream and a splash indicated Brunt had done so.

"Now then," said Flinn as they continued down the boardwalk. "May I introduce—"

"Shhh," hushed the Elf, slapping her hand over the Gnome's mouth. Her head inclined back, and she rolled her eyes at Gorm. "Are you a hero of destiny?" she whispered.

"So they say," Gorm ventured.

"Me too!" gushed the Elf.

Flinn finished prying her fingers away from his lips. "This is Kaitha!" he snarled.

Kaitha vomited, prompting a momentary halt in the procession.

"Charmed," said Gorm.

When he awoke, it took Gorm a moment to take stock of the situation. He was still in the Temple of Al'Matra, which was bad. He had been out late at a tavern, which was usually good, but he hadn't had a drop to drink there, which was unusual and bad. He wasn't hungover, which was unfamiliar but not necessarily unpleasant. Now he could see the sun rising through his window, which was also unfamiliar and certainly unpleasant, and someone was quietly knocking at his door.

All in all, Gorm was in a pretty foul mood when he answered it.

"Hello. Sorry," said Kaitha. She had cleaned up and pulled her long hair into a ponytail. Her lips were set in a playful, helpless pout that would make most men subconsciously shift from groggy annoyance to alert and helpful. Dwarves, however, are closer to eunuchs than they are to most men.

"What are ye doing here?" Gorm growled.

"That's just the thing I'd like to know," said the Elf, stepping into his room. "Well, one of the things. Also of interest are: where am I, who are you, and why is there a Goblin with a dead rat in your bedchambers?"

"Ye don't remember a thing?"

"I remember several things. Just not how they fit together. Or what goes in the middle."

"I'm Gorm Ingerson. The Goblin's me squire."

"Gleebek!"

"Unusual. The dead rat?"

"I don't know where he gets them, but I'm pretty sure it's breakfast."

"I see." Kaitha thought for a moment. "You can call me Kaitha."

"We met last night."

"About that," said Kaitha. "Any idea what happened?"

"Do ye remember the Al'Matran Prophecy?" Gorm asked.

"Is that a new name for a Tarapin Topspin? I think I had one of those."

"A what?"

"It's moon wine, grog, and a twist of grundant juice on salted ice."

"What?"

"It's good. You can't even taste the grog."

"I ain't talkin' about a drink."

"Then I don't know what you are talking about."

"I'm talking about how ye signed on with the Al'Matran temple to be one of the seven heroes of thrice-cursed destiny."

Kaitha shook her head. "No. I'm pretty sure I'd remember if I did."

"And I'd remember vomiting on someone's boots, but ye still ain't apologized for that."

"Oh, sorry," said the Elf, rubbing her temples. "Gods, I probably did sign up with … who? The Al'Matrans? Bones!" she swore.

"Aye. That must have been one titan of a drink."

"Or four," said Kaitha. "Okay … Okay. I can handle this. We'll go get breakfast. I'll get Leiry. He can get me out of this."

"If ye say so," said Gorm. "I'm going back to bed."

"Sure you won't come? I'm buying."

Gorm was already brushing past her down the hall. "Let's go, Gleebek! Leave the rat."

Mr. Flinn and Mr. Brunt were seated near the front door. A board with a set of thrones pieces was set between them, but Gorm noticed that only Flinn was making moves.

"Ah, Lady Kaitha and Mr. Ingerson, might I ask where you're off to?"

"Breakfast," said Kaitha. "We'll be back once I've sorted this contract out."

"That's fine," said Mr. Flinn. "Provided you have it sorted out by lunch. The Heroes of Destiny are expected at a meeting of the utmost importance."

"Oh, I hope to be back well before then."

"See that you are. Mr. Brunt didn't get enough sleep last night, and now he's in a foul mood."

Gorm looked up at the Ogre's vacant, angry stare. "With Brunt, how can ye tell?"

Mr. Flinn's lips curled into a dark smile. "I'd encourage you not to find out, Mr. Ingerson."

An hour later, they were seated around a tiny wrought-iron table on Pinnacle Plaza, the great terrace on the topmost tier of the city. Boutique shops, coffee stands, teahouses, and popular eateries formed a neat semicircle around the plaza, sending small tables and chairs creeping toward the statue at the plaza's center. Behind the statue sat the Temple of Tandos, and beyond that, built into the highest slopes of Mount Wynspar, was the Palace of Andarun.

"You haven't touched your breakfast," Kaitha said.

"I'm scared it'll blow away if I disturb it," said Gorm, looking in disgust at his plate. He was a firm believer that the best meals were made by holding dead things over a fire until they smelled good. As far as he was concerned, the tiny pile of twisted fruits and exotic extracts set before him was a blasphemy.

It was Elven cuisine, but then most things up at the Pinnacle were Elven. Many Elves had old money; some of them were already rich when the Freedlands were still forming.

"It's good. Try it."

"This stuff cost more than me boots," Gorm grumbled. He scooped up a forkful of mashed plant matter and chewed thoughtfully. "And I'm pretty sure it don't taste as good," he added, sliding his plate to Gleebek.

"Kaitha!" The heaviest Elf Gorm had ever seen charged toward them, holding his thick black spectacles to his head as he ran. He wore his silver hair pulled back behind his pointed ears, and a thin beard traced the generous circumference of his uppermost chin. "Kaitha te'Althuanasa Malaheasi Leelana Ter'ethe…"

"I always know I'm in trouble when Leiry uses my full name," Kaitha said to Gorm.

"Who is this guy?"

"Leiry? He's my agent."

"…Liliea Musanatila Bae Iluvia…"

"You've got an agent?"

"Oh yeah. I'm in high demand. I mean, not as much as I used to be, but still."

Gorm suddenly recalled hearing tales of a woman with jade and drake-hide bracers, a shadow in an emerald cloak who slew terrible monsters before the beasts ever saw her. "You're the Jade Wind!"

"Yeah, that's right," Kaitha said with a small smile.

Leiry was growing scarlet in the face. "…Yi'Nailn Loela Toranga Migracie …"

"Me Da used to tell me about you! You saved his Da from the Hydra of Gauntcragge when he was a wee lad!"

"Oh?" Kaitha's smile was losing steam. "That's great."

"… Asanti Tilalala nil Tyrieth!" Leiry finished. "What am I to do with you? Signing on with the Al'Matrans!"

Kaitha ignored him. "Gorm, this is Leiry. Leiry, Gorm Ingerson, and his squire, Gleebek."

"Pleasure," said Leiry. "The Pyrebeard, right? Tough luck on the Az'Anon business, kid. Pay us a visit. Maybe we can make it work." He flipped Gorm a small white card, which said in embossed, cardinal red letters:

LEIRY, Hs. Alintal
AGENT OF HEROES
34 Greenwyne Avenue
42nd Tier, Andarun

Gorm read the card. "Not many agents are interested in working with me these days."

"You'd be surprised. I work with a lot of problem cases," Leiry said. "Look at this one here. Am I right? I mean, Kaitha, sweetheart, how many gutters have I dragged you out of? How many times have I had to convince the mayor of some backwater that you weren't too wasted to kill a Bugbear or an owlbear or an owlverine? And now this? This is how you repay me? The Al'Matrans?"

"I know, Leiry. I know." Kaitha sighed. "That's why I sent for you. You've got to fix this."

"Fix this? Fix it! What is there to fix? I—" A thought struck Leiry. "Gorm, and, uh, Glubduck. Whatever. Listen. I need a moment with my client."

"Right you are," said Gorm. He grabbed his coffee, motioned for Gleebek to follow him, and walked closer to the edge of the plaza. All of Andarun spread out before him, gray granite and white marble and cobalt and teal slate roofs, and beyond it, the Plains of Bahn. The view was all the more breathtaking for the cloudless azure sky.

Behind him, things sounded like they were considerably stormier.

Much of the fight was too low to be heard—whispered, or hissed, or choked in fits of sobbing. Gorm could only make out small, unpleasant snippets of conversation. The Lawyer-monks of Adchul were brought up more than once, as was the Randy Goat, and alcohol, and Kaitha hanging out with losers.

At the mention of losers, Gorm mentally added Leiry to his list. It wasn't a good list to be on; it was said that the only thing that could outlast Dwarven craftsmanship was a Dwarven grudge.

"You're a carriage wreck," Leiry thundered. "You were a spectacle, and now even that's getting old!"

"You can't say that!" said Kaitha. "You can't …" She trailed off, weeping.

Gorm noticed a noblewoman sneering at Gleebek and shot her his most vicious professional smile. She scowled and hurried away. Satisfied, he turned back to the view of the city. Gleebek sat next to him, eating a dead rat. "Where do ye find those bloody things?" he asked the Goblin.

"Grot?"

The fight blew over eventually. Leiry thundered and blustered himself out, and then moved on. Gorm turned to survey the wreckage.

Kaitha was slumped over the table, looking smaller and sadder than an Elven breakfast. Her red-rimmed eyes watched her fingers trace a small pattern on the table. She didn't look up when Gorm and Gleebek took their seats again. "I haven't finished a quest in more than forty years," she said. "I can get them started. I try, I really do. And then … I just feel like I need … you know? Something to take the edge off … and it gets all messed up."

Gorm nodded. It wasn't exactly his song, but it was in the same key.

"And, of course, everyone's heard of the Jade Wind," she said, her voice a hollow husk. "And they all know what I used to be. And they keep on telling me the stories, the thrice-cursed stories, of what the Jade Wind did, and who she saved, and how she did it. And I hear them whispering about what a shame it is that such an amazing ranger could come to this. And I'm sick of hearing about that Jade Wind, because I don't know her any better than you do."

The oldest Elves were older than Andarun, some even older than the race of Dwarves. However, it was almost impossible to identify the eldest among them with any certainty, because how Elves look does not change over time while, crucially, who they are changes quite a lot.

An indefinite lifespan is not the same thing as an infinite memory. Time erodes events into stories, stories into recollections, recollections into impressions, impressions into vague sensations that eventually dim altogether. An Elf's old life was always trickling away, being replaced by new memories, new ideas, and eventually, for all intents and purposes, a new Elf.

"I haven't been the Jade Wind for a long time," Kaitha said. "I've been the person trying to be the Jade Wind again. Leiry said he could make it happen, but now he's gone. And he was the last agent who'd take me, so I guess my career is too."

Gorm watched a falcon circling overhead. "They used to call me Pyrebeard," he said. "I used to run the biggest quests, slay the nastiest beasts. I was gonna be as big as … well, as big as ye were. And then I messed up once. Just once. And now I'm here."

The moment of camaraderie brought a small smile from Kaitha. "And now we're a part of this … this Al'Matran madness." She laughed and gave a long sigh. "How are we going to get out of this?"

"I don't think we are," said Gorm. "Not anytime soon. Might as well get used to it."

Kaitha looked out over the edge of the plaza, across the city. "Did you ever hear of the *aithanalasi?*"

"My Elven's a little rusty. On account of me never learning it."

"The Imperial tongue calls it the Wide-gulleted Bobbinjay." Her mouth twisted at the taste of the translation.

Most Elves consider the Imperial language to be crude, graceless, and discordant—largely because it is. It's also precise, broad, and nearly universal, making it a necessary evil.

"It's a beautiful little bird with a sacred voice. The Lords and Ladies of my people will gladly spend thousands of giltin to entice them to their balconies, just in the hope of hearing a song."

"Thousands?"

"Easily thousands. Tens of thousands. *Aithanalasi* need the right trees. The right flowers. It can't be too cold or too warm. The balcony has to be at the height they like. And if you do it just right, an *aithanalasi* may decide to perch on your rail and sing for hours."

"I can buy a bird cage for twelve giltin," said Gorm.

"That's the point. If you want the song, you can never cage one. Once it's behind the bars, it goes silent. It might even beat itself to death against the cage. Do you see what I'm saying?"

"Birds are daft?" Gorm grabbed a roll off a passing waitress's platter.

"No. The bird won't be caged!"

"I'd take it over being beaten to death against iron bars," said Gorm. He broke off a piece of the roll and offered it to Kaitha.

"That is the song of the *aithanalasi*," she said, waving the bread away. "That is why its voice is sacred. Wherever you go, go because you decided to. Never let anyone cage you. Find your freedom."

"All right, I got one for ye," said Gorm, handing half of the roll to Gleebek. "Ever hear of the Warbling Slateclaw?"

"No, I don't think so."

"Big, ugly badger with claws like stone. Digs tunnels up in the Ironbreaker Mountains and the Black Cliffs. Only singin' mustelid in the world. Dwarves everywhere used to want 'em as pets, till they found out what miserable beasts the slateclaws are. Take one in, and it'll claim your favorite chair and sing songs that'll run your spine inside out unless ye give the furry bastard its favorite treats." He mimicked a horrible yodeling, and then silenced himself with a bite of bread.

Kaitha smiled. "I'm wondering where this is going."

"That's the song of the Warbling Slateclaw. Wherever ye go, there ye are. Try to find the comfy chair." Gorm leaned back in his seat and shook the half-eaten roll at the laughing Elf. "And see if ye can grab a free meal."

Chapter 5

The Temple of Al'Matra was bustling with activity by the time Gorm and Kaitha returned. Attendants rushed about the gardens and lobby. Silver Talon mercenaries marched through the halls at rigid attention, clad in the same black leathers that Mr. Flinn wore.

They found Niln in the sanctuary, and the high scribe excitedly informed them that they were summoned to an audience with the king.

"What's the occasion?" Gorm asked.

"We are to be recognized as the Seven Heroes by His Highness. He has also indicated that he will give us our first quest."

"Well, that was fast."

"Destiny," said Niln, wearing a broad smile.

"We'll see," said Gorm.

"The king expects us soon," babbled the high scribe. "We've only got an hour to get ready."

Wisps of steam drifted from the copper basin in Gorm's room when he took his bath. The water had cooled to lukewarm by the time he convinced Gleebek to get in. The Al'Matrans had provided him with a coat of shining mail, a deep indigo cloak, sturdy boots, and soft leather gloves. His outfit was complemented by a new round shield, painted sapphire blue, with shining steel braces and a drake-hide rim; a couple of gold and brass rings for his beard; and a new steel helmet encircled with runes. They had also provided a replacement war axe, covered in gold etchings and runes of power, but he forgave them for it as he tucked his trusted old weapon into his belt loop.

When he looked at the Dwarf in the looking glass, he could see Pyrebeard staring back at him, eyes hard, jaw set. He could almost hear the roar of the crowds, almost see the banners with his emblem hanging from every turret in the town. He remembered the smell of summer nights in Scoria, when everyone knew him for slaying the Hydra of Hangman's Grotto, when friendly shouts greeted him as he rounded every corner, when he never bought his own drinks at the bar.

Gleebek stumbled into view behind the Dwarf, struggling to hike up a pair of breeches beneath his new squire's tunic, effectively shattering the illusion. Pyrebeard was gone. In his place was a clanless drunkard with a Goblin for a squire.

"Come on," Gorm said. He stalked past Gleebek into the hallway. "Let's get this mummer's farce over with."

The procession was taking shape when he stepped out onto the palace grounds. Niln sat mounted on a great white stallion at the head of the line, arguing with a pair of Al'Matrans in even more decorated robes. Gorm surmised they were the high priestess and the alternate high scribe of Al'Matra. Behind them, Jynn and Laruna rode side-by-side on a pair of chestnut mares. Gaist sat behind them, so stiff and motionless on his black stallion that even the beast seemed uncomfortable. Al'Matrans and Silver Talons hurried around the heroes, preparing for the procession to depart.

Kaitha found Gorm as an attendant was helping him mount his own horse, a ruddy stallion with a foul temper. "There you are," the Elf said. "Finally. Have you met these people? You're the only one I can talk to."

"Tried talkin' to Ihee—er—Gaist, eh?"

"It's like having a conversation with a mural. I wouldn't even know his name, except someone hung a sign on his horse. And that's still preferable to the mages. Anything you say is just an excuse for them to indirectly insult each other."

"I don't know why they're ridin' next to each other," Gorm said.

"Simple. Neither one will ride behind the other. Is your, er, squire all right?"

Gorm looked behind him. An Al'Matran attendant was attempting to coax Gleebek onto a trained mule, without much success.

"Gleebek. Get on your mount."

"Da nub'hig a'skubber!"

"None of that. We're mounting up. On the mule with ye, Gleebek."

"Prog da'root spooty! Tib'rin! Da'gub Tib'rin!"

"No more arguing! Up ye go, on your donkey."

Gleebek crossed his arms and muttered something unintelligible, but he allowed an attendant to hoist him atop the mule.

"You speak Shadowtongue?" Kaitha asked.

"Not a word," said Gorm.

"Then how do you know what he's saying?"

"Haven't the foggiest."

"Then how do—uh, hello." Kaitha was taken off guard by the sudden onset of a bard, clinging to her right hand.

"My darling, my flower, you are a vision," said Heraldin. "A sonnet striding among mortals."

"Hand," said Kaitha.

The bard walked his fingers up Kaitha's arm. "Your eyes, like pools of jade. Your hair, a cascade of auburn, a fount of autumn hues. Your skin, like almond milk."

"Hand," Kaitha reiterated.

"Yes, your hands are like doves, gentle and elegant. They said you were a diamond in the rough, a rose among weeds, but their words fell short," Heraldin said, impervious.

"Hand."

"Nothing could prepare me for this moment—awk!"

Kaitha moved in a quick succession of maneuvers, a fast and forceful choreography carried out with a precise grace. The bones in Heraldin's hands crunched, and he sank to his knees, making a sound like a teakettle about to boil over.

"I guess you weren't prepared after all," Kaitha said, giving the bard's wrist another half-turn. "Gorm, do you know who this is?"

"It's our bard. Heraldin Strummons is his name, I think."

Heraldin kept making the teakettle noise, which sounded like "eep."

"Well then, bard, as we're contractually obligated to work together, let me give you a few pointers for the next time our jobs force us to speak." Kaitha twisted his hand further. "I am direct. If I were interested, you'd know it. As I'm not interested, you should know it. And if you annoy me again, you'll regret it in ways that you are only now beginning to imagine. Are we reading from the same scroll here?"

"Eep," said Heraldin, but this time it sounded like an affirmative "eep."

"Good." Kaitha released the bard's hands and let him collapse into a ball. "Well, it seems the procession will be moving shortly. We'll talk later, Gorm."

"Aye, good riding," said Gorm.

"Eee-aawww — by the bones!" swore Heraldin, shaking his hand. "Did you see what she did to me? I'm going to need a healing potion."

"It was impressive," Gorm admitted.

"She has all the warmth and friendliness of an Ice Drake," Heraldin said. "And here I thought there might be a little fun to be had on this trip."

Gorm scowled. The bard's callous lechery seemed shameful, but in Gorm's experience, the other races of men did and said things that would make a decent Dwarf blush without a second thought: they talked of love in public; they wore their emotions like clothes, and they wore clothes that hid nothing; and they held huge harvest festivals with flowers everywhere. Living among such wanton debauchery had been a culture shock, as it was for any young Dwarf leaving the mines, but Gorm liked to think he had grown fairly well accustomed to living among non-Dwarves. "Well, I'm sure ye'll find someone on this trip to keep ye company," he said diplomatically.

"A wishful thought. The only other woman in our party is the mage. And it's no use trying my luck with the pyromancer. I've been burned before."

"Ha!"

"It wasn't a joke," said the bard, clutching his hand. "It took the temple healer over an hour to regrow my eyebrows."

"All the funnier," said Gorm, spurring his horse on its way.

The procession of the heroes of destiny left the temple and made its way toward the Wall, where it took the Broad Steps up to the Pinnacle Plaza. Niln led the heroes, while a contingent of Silver Talons marched on either side, with Mr. Flinn and Mr. Brunt following behind them. Mr. Flinn walked with a relaxed purpose, the kind of gait that says *move along*. Mr. Brunt stamped along beside him in a manner that added *or else*.

Onlookers stopped to watch them proceed. The heroes were heckled by a couple of people who had failed, against all odds, to notice Mr. Brunt. Gorm was grateful for the shield the Al'Matrans had provided. It gave him a way to hide his face.

Heraldin nodded as they rode down the center of Pinnacle Plaza. "Conveniently, our path to the king runs just beside our ultimate foe."

"What?" said Gorm. "Where?"

"Has no one told you?" Jynn asked. "The statue is our nemesis."

Gorm looked back at the old statue in the center of the plaza. The sculpture was a tall man, roughly hewn from black granite, beard streaming in a silent wind, sword held at the ready. His stone face was twisted into an expression that could have been horror, or perhaps rage, his gaze fixated on something unseen at his feet.

Gorm had seen the statue a thousand times before, but had never looked close enough to notice the details of the man. The broad shoulders on such a tall figure, the wide nose, and the flat features of the warrior's face were unmistakable, despite the fact that nobody living on Arth for over three ages had ever possessed them.

"It's a Sten," said Gorm.

"That he is," said Heraldin.

"How are we to find a Sten? They're all long dead."

"Oh, it shouldn't be too hard once he comes back to life," said Jynn.

"Right." Gorm sighed.

"Or perhaps we're to kill the sculpture if it animates itself," said Laruna.

"The Sten were masters of the old magics, Mr. Ingerson," Niln called back to them. "The magic of stone and bone and blood."

Gorm jabbed a thumb toward the grimacing sculpture. "So ye think this fellow is going to come to life?"

"Back to life," corrected Niln. "Or return in some other fashion. Yes. The prophet Klinesh says that 'the thrice-cursed is thrice born, the third time to unmake what was made.' He is the Dark Prince, the last king of the Sten."

"He's a hunk of granite."

Niln didn't seem to be listening. He stared defiantly up at the Dark Prince's cryptic visage, and recited another prophecy:

> *Blood and tears rain on stones,*
> *The weeping of light's children fades*
> *As the Maiden of Tears sings her dirge.*
> *This is the music of the Stens' rebirth.*
> *The song of Al'Thadan's rise.*

"So wrote the prophet Asepth," Niln finished ominously.

"'He shall lament the lack of hot beverages,'" recited Jynn. "I'm fairly certain Asepth wrote that one too."

Gorm shared a smirk with Kaitha, and a couple of the Silver Talons walking with the company stifled laughs.

"Yes, well …" Niln shifted in his saddle. "Some of the scriptures are more difficult to interpret than others."

"They're all equally fatuous," said Jynn.

Niln straightened in his saddle and spurred his horse forward.

"Careful, Master Jynn," Mr. Flinn said from the rear of the heroic procession.

"Apologies, Mr. Flinn. I had no idea you were such a believer in the idea of an immutable destiny."

"Immutable? Oh no, sir."

"Master … own … destiny!"

"Right you are, Mr. Brunt. The choices we make shape our lives. For example, poor judgment can make a life remarkably shorter."

"I see," said Jynn. Not another word was spoken until they were well inside the High Palace of Andarun.

The High Palace was set into the side of Mount Wynspar, at the very back of Andarun's topmost tier. Marble towers and columns seemed to flow from the white stone of the mountain, spilling around and under domes tiled with navy and burgundy. Crimson and blue banners of Andarun hung from the highest ramparts, but below them were a rainbow of banners from all the city-states in the Freedlands, and beneath hung pennants beyond counting: the sigils of all of the various companies of bannermen.

The Silver Talons stopped at the courtyard, marching into waiting formations as Gorm and companions dismounted. "Ye leaving us?" Gorm asked Mr. Flinn.

"It would be above my stature to associate with the heroes of destiny in such a manner," said Mr. Flinn, though his wry smile indicated that just the opposite was true. "But worry not. Mr. Brunt and I will be in the audience."

"There's to be an audience?" said Kaitha.

Mr. Flinn only smiled and waved.

A contingent of palace guards, decked in shining steel armor and blue and red livery, took the Silver Talon's place, as the heroes were marched through the palace to the throne room.

The throne room was a long hall, with high, arched ceilings and marble floors that were packed with nobles and servants of every race. There were Elven Lords and Ladies, Dwarven Fathers attending a prominent Ancestor, the Dukes and Duchesses of the Human nobility, Halfling emissaries, Tinderkin ambassadors, and representatives from the other clans of Gnomes. Gorm could feel all of their eyes fall on him at once when the crier announced that the Heroes of Destiny had arrived.

"I guess this would be the audience," said Gorm.

"It's more like a funeral for our careers," said Kaitha, trying to cover her face.

Gorm recognized the polite smirks on the faces of the lightly applauding nobility. It was an expression common to the successful playing host to failures: trying to keep up the appearance of manners while simultaneously hoping for an amusing disaster. Above the cruel crowds, a vision of shining armor and gleaming teeth stood before the thrones, clapping loudest of all. Johan. The greatest hero of the age, the slayer of Az'Anon and Detarr Ur'Mayan, the savior of Hap's Bend, the Champion of Tandos.

"Didn't know they'd bring in Johan for this," said Gorm.

"Nor did I," said Jynn, hiding his eyes.

"They had to bring in the guild's top hero?" said Laruna. "It wasn't enough to embarrass us in front of the king and queen?"

The king and the queen had been prince and princess the last time Gorm had seen them. The years had weathered King Handor from the plump and pleasant prince to a leathery scarecrow in fine robes. Time had the opposite effect on Queen Marja; she could barely fit on her throne. The crowd fell silent as Handor stood.

"All rise!" called Johan. "The Crown now calls the Champion of Al'Matra—the Seventh Hero of prophecy—and his valiant companions to come before the court!"

"Here we go," said Gorm. The ceremony began.

As far as Gorm was concerned, a ceremony was the most efficient way to expunge the joy and excitement from any event, refining it into the purest tedium. It was like watching a play that he already knew the ending to, only with more dialogue and usually less swordplay. He wasn't sure what quality of a ceremony invited people to speak at extreme lengths on subjects that everyone was already familiar with, but it was probably the same force that invariably compelled some participant to wave a stick or a sword over a small fountain, or a cup of wine, or something extra symbolic.

The ceremony kept going.

Gorm had stopped paying attention around the point when the king had admonished the crowd about the importance of believing in your own heart or some other such nonsense. The audience's attention was drifting as well; their interest had waned once it became clear that the heroes weren't going to do anything spectacularly embarrassing, or at least nothing beyond showing up in the Al'Matran party. By the time Johan waved his sword over a horn of ale, the air rustled with the sounds of an anxious crowd.

Gorm glanced at Niln. The boy drank in Johan and Handor's grandiose words; his chest seemed to swell with every mention of honor or destiny. There may have even been a tear glistening in Niln's eye.

The ceremony's end was long and laborious, like a dying beast that refused to be put down. Johan finally ended it with a sharp, decisive declaration that the Seven Heroes of Destiny were officially commissioned, prompting a smattering of applause and a stampede for the door.

To Gorm's surprise and dismay, the heroes weren't allowed to leave with the rest of the crowd. Instead, they were ushered through a small door behind the thrones, to a small stone room with a round oak table. Gorm and his companions sat around the table, and then rose as Johan entered. They immediately dropped to their knees when King Handor strode in behind Johan, flanked by several attendants.

"Oh, none of that, none of that," said Handor. He looked far more relaxed than he had on the throne. "Look, the big one has the right of it," said the king with a nod to Gaist, who hadn't sat, or kneeled, or acknowledged the king addressing him. "On your feet, or in your chairs. It matters not. The ceremony is over, and we have business to attend to. Johan?"

"Your Majesty!" said Johan. He pulled a velvet pouch from his belt. It contained a single object: a large, milky-white stone. He placed it on the middle of the table, where it stared at Gorm with the weathered remnants of tiny eyes and menaced him with a tusked grimace.

"This," said King Handor, "is one of the Elven Marbles."

"It's an Orc," said Laruna.

"Indeed it is," said the King. "It was likely carved by ancient Orcs in the Fourth Age."

"So why do they call them the Elven—"

"The marbles were ripped from the inner chambers of an Orcish temple by the Elves of House Tyrieth during the sack of Chief Ug'Ruck Big Tooth's fortress," said King Handor. "This was at the end of the last age, in the days before Orcs could obtain noncombatant papers, you see. You're familiar with this sort of problem, I'm sure."

Gorm nodded. Tens of thousands of Orcs, Goblins, Gremlins, and other Shadowkin had decided that it was better to join the margins of society as NPCs than to become a footnote of history. With a growing multitude of reformed monsters walking the streets of the Freedlands, increasingly often a Shadowkin would notice a sacred relic or holy weapon long lost to their people displayed in a shop window or hanging from some nobleman's wall. The town criers were particularly enamored with a story about the urn of a revered Kobold ancestor that had been repurposed by the High Clerk of the Scorian Heroes' Guild as an ashtray.

"The Orcs and the Elves nearly went to war over it years back, in the reign of my father," said the king. "The Orcs took the Elves to court over it, and most scholars agreed they had a chance of winning. But three days before a verdict, the marbles disappeared, and each side accused the other of the theft. The Orcs went mad—totally mad. You had NPCs defecting and riling up the Orcish tribes over the marbles. We had to put whole armies of them down, all for some rocks that went missing."

Gorm remembered it well. In prouder days, he'd led the party that had dispersed a portion of the Iron Bone Tribe. He'd even struck the killing blow against their chieftain.

"Those statues brought my father nothing but trouble. So I'm sure you can imagine how unhappy I was when the marbles turned up in a wyverns' hoard a few weeks ago," said the king. "And how much more so when most of them went missing en route to Andarun."

"Ah," said Niln. "Yes, Your Majesty."

"The Freedlands exists because of one thing," King Handor said, leaning forward. "Stability. The people in the streets claim their freedom or their virtue binds our kingdom together, but in a famine you're only free to starve, and in a drought there is no virtue but survival. No, liberty and piety are well and good, but a kingdom needs stability to survive; a healthy stalemate wherein every people, every faction, every city finds the status quo preferable to the price of change."

"Yes, Your Majesty."

"I will do anything to preserve that balance. Anything. This theft, this intrigue ..." Handor shook his head as words failed him. "There are tens of thousands more Orcs in Andarun than there were twenty years ago, and already their leaders are wondering aloud who has taken the stones. The Elves of House Tyrieth have skipped questions altogether and are making bald accusations against the Orcs. It is imbalance. It is strife. It is the first crack in my kingdom's foundations. I will not have it."

The king stood. "This, then, is your quest. I charge you to find the marbles and return them to their rightful owners. I care not who those rightful owners are; give the stones to the Elves, or the Orcs, or to the wyvern's corpse, so long as this matter is done and settled and my kingdom is stable once more."

"We won't disappoint, Your Majesty," said Niln.

The king smiled. "I know," he said. He nodded to Johan, and took his leave.

Johan put the lone Elven Marble back in the velvet pouch, took a small maroon binder from a waiting attendant, and handed both to Niln. "This is the first of the Elven Marbles, and the file with all of our information on the missing four. You will reunite the set and put them in their proper place. Wherever that is."

"I accept this quest," said Niln breathlessly, his face rapt and reverent as he accepted the marble and the documents.

"Ha ha! I like your spirit. I wish I could stay and chat, but you know how it is," Johan said. "It'd be good to catch up with a few of you. Gorm and Iheen, I'm looking at you two. It's been too long, guys, really. Let's have lunch after all of this. And you. What was your name again? Is it Keetha?"

"It's Kaitha."

Johan shot her a wink and a winning smile. "You and I should definitely get better acquainted. Sometime soon. Great ceremony. Great team. It's gonna be great. I know it. Tandos bless you. Ha ha!" With a swirl of his crimson cape, Johan was out the door.

The seven heroes, plus one Goblin, sat in a perplexed silence. Even Niln looked puzzled, the awe and wonder draining from his face as they sat quietly. "Is that it?" he asked.

An attendant placed a scroll bound with a scarlet ribbon on the table. "You'll find these documents lay out the key objectives of your quest," she said. "We've taken the liberty of scheduling a meeting with the ambassador from House Tyrieth for the day after tomorrow. I'm told a Mr. Flinn will have the details."

"I just expected something a little more ..." said Niln, clutching the pouch and the maroon binder. "It's just not what I was ... I mean, we're the Heroes of Destiny." It was almost a question to the royal attendant.

"Yes, well, right now, we need this conference room," said the attendant, making an apologetic face. "I'm afraid I have to ask you to continue your meeting elsewhere."

The heroes were ushered out of the room and directed down the hall. Rather than follow the others, Gorm excused himself and set off down the stone hallway in the opposite direction. Gleebek came skittering after him.

Something didn't settle well in his stomach. It was good that the job was a simple fetch quest, and it sounded more dull than dangerous. Years of adventuring had taught Gorm to appreciate an uninteresting adventure; fewer heroes came back from the exciting ones. But as good as the quest for the Elven Marbles sounded, it didn't make any sense, and only one man had answers.

He caught up to the man in a small atrium at the top of a short staircase. "Johan," Gorm called up to him.

"Oh. Gorm. Look, I really do want to catch up, but no time to talk. You can thank me for getting you the gig later."

"Ye can spare a few minutes for a hero of destiny," said Gorm. "Wait. Ye recruited me for this … this Al'Matran nonsense?"

"Well, we had the Silver Talons recruit you. Ha ha! But I was the one who suggested it. Like I said, thank me later."

"I ain't thanking ye. I'm blaming ye."

Johan's perpetual grin finally broke. "You … I thought you'd be ecstatic."

"Oh, aye, I'm sure ye hired mercenaries to haul me along because ye thought I'd be ecstatic for bein' wrapped up in the Mad Queen's schemes."

"Hey, listen, I knew I'd need some muscle to keep some of the heroes in line," said Johan. "People worry about career and image and things like that. A couple of union thugs helps them get their priorities straight. But you, and I say this as nicely as possible, you don't really have that problem, right? What career or image do you have left to damage? I mean, you're traveling with a Goblin, Gorm. No offense, little guy. Ha ha!"

"*Gleebek!*"

"I thought you'd jump at the chance to clear your record," said Johan. "It's the chance to be a hero again, the chance the guild never gave you. You could get a few points, make it back in the game."

"Aye, back in the game for long enough to get cut down in some sort of lunacy. Ye know what happens to Al'Matrans on quests. It usually involves cleaning 'em up with a mop."

"Yes, but this is sponsored by the Temple of Tandos. We're not going to let that happen."

"And there's another thing that don't smell right. Why are you Tandosians helping the Al'Matrans? Why's the king involved? Why send the prophet of an insane goddess on an important diplomatic mission? Ye ain't playing straight with me."

"All right, all right!" said Johan, holding his hands up. He dismissed his attendants with a nod, and turned back to Gorm once they were out of earshot.

"Look, the Al'Matrans have a problem." Johan leaned in, speaking low and close and fast. "A second high scribe pops up and starts stirring things up with more Seventh Hero prophecies. The Al'Matrans don't want another batch of dead heroes on their record any more than you do. Plus, most of the last wars between the Al'Matrans and Tandosians were started by so-called Seventh Heroes, and nobody thinks the Al'Matrans can survive another war. And then King Handor has a problem, because this business of the Elven Marbles is blowing up. The markets are down, Gorm, and the king's coffers are emptying. The last thing he needs is some strife between the Elves and the Shadowkin.

"So I had an idea. The Temple of Tandos sponsored this Seventh Hero, and now we get a say on where he goes and what he does. The Al'Matrans can save face, because if he doesn't like his quests or his treatment, they can blame the Tandosians for holding him back. Do you follow?'

"Aye," said Gorm, still reluctant. "So why put him on an important quest?"

"Because at the end of all this trouble someone is going to be angry that they didn't get all of the Elven Marbles, be it the Orcs or the Elves. By appointing the Seventh Hero to sort out the business and choose who gets the stones, we make sure they'll be angry at you, or the Al'Matrans, or maybe even the Tandosians. Ha! But they won't blame the crown, or at least not as much as they would have, and that's the key. Stability."

"True," said Gorm.

"Everybody wins," said Johan. "The Al'Matrans are spared embarrassment or even a war over this Seventh Hero business. The Temple of Tandos avoids an unsightly conflict with the Al'Matrans and gains influence with the king. The king gets to hand this headache with the marbles to somebody else. And you and your friends traveling with Niln get your careers back on track after one simple fetch quest."

"Aye, but only until Niln dreams up some sort of suicide mission," said Gorm.

"Gorm, if he does that, how do we benefit? People knew the last Seventh Hero was mad once he took on the dragon, and it was a public relations nightmare for the Al'Matrans. Why would I want that for my own temple?"

"I suppose ye wouldn't," Gorm conceded.

"I definitely wouldn't," said Johan. "I just need you to be on board with this one job. You settle the matter of the marbles, we declare your quest a success, and then we say the Seventh Hero is awaiting his destiny or something. You can even take on other gigs while you wait. You'll have a career again."

"Just one quest," said Gorm. All that stood between him and his old life, the good life, was finding a set of rocks and handing them to the Elves.

"That's all I'm asking," said Johan. "Unless that statue comes to life. Then we might have to call you up again. Ha ha!"

"Ha." Possibilities danced before Gorm's eyes. The Khazad'im Clan might take him back in. He could see his brothers, visit Da's urn at the ancestral shrine. He might even make it to this year's Feast of Orchids. If they could finish the quest in time.

"I'll do it," he said.

"Ha ha! I knew it!" said Johan. "That's why I chose you for this mission. I know that in the end, you'll always do the right thing."

"Aye." Gorm nodded, barely listening. They'd need more training, of course. It was just a matter of managing personalities and getting the combat dynamics down. They could start preparations tomorrow. Tonight, even. With any luck, he'd be catching an orchid in the autumn festival.

"Look, I can see you're already excited about the job," said Johan. "I'm excited. This is exciting. But I really need to be going. Are we good?"

"Aye," said Gorm, momentarily surfacing from his plans. "Aye, we are."

"Great. And let's keep this conversation to ourselves, shall we? The whole plan will kind of go south if Niln gets wind of it, I'm sure you can imagine."

"Aye. Aye, I'll not speak of it. I … thank ye, Johan."

Johan's teeth gleamed an uncanny white, "Don't mention it, Gorm," he said. "I'm counting on you."

Chapter 6

Something had excited the market.

Whenever something riled up the traders around the Wall, the Broad Steps would fill with merchants and businessmen waving certificates and bank notes. They whirled around the banks and markets in a raucous squall, buying and selling shares in a flurry of trades. Dungeon hoards, plunder funds, companies, and commodities changed hands rapidly, driving impossibly complex trends that every broker was desperately trying to predict.

Gorm didn't care whether the prices were rising or falling, but he had a lot to say about the market activity—especially the parts of it that were blocking the Broad Steps.

"Bloody thrice-cursed ashen bones," he shouted as another trader bumped into him. "Get out of my way!"

The merchant ignored him, and rushed off shouting for someone selling Dragon of Wynspar.

"We've got to make it back to the temple before dark," Gorm told Gleebek. "We start training tonight."

"Grot?"

"Burn this mob. This way!" Gorm ducked off the Broad Steps, turned down a side street, and headed Ridgeward. He moved like a Scribkin steam engine, pounding down the street so fast that Gleebek had to run to keep up. As fast as he moved, he couldn't catch up to his mind. A professional hero again! A reinstated license, a clean record, and all the riches and fame that professional heroics could bring were within reach once more. Success wasn't a certainty, but it was a possibility, and that was better than he'd had a couple of nights ago.

"Suggich! Ra gi'deek nub zib!"

"Of course I'm going for it!" Gorm barked. "I got a chance to get back everything I lost, everything I dreamed of for the past twenty years. And me only other options are facin' guild justice or sulking until the so-called Seventh Hero gets us all killed. I'd be mad not to try to make it work."

"*Grot?*"

"The high scribe is totally green, if ye'll pardon the expression. He wouldn't last two minutes against a Goblin, no offense. Eh …" It dawned on Gorm that a surprisingly large portion of heroic jargon centered on demeaning, if not killing, Shadowkin, and for once he was glad that Gleebek probably had no idea what he was saying. "Look, point is, he ain't really a professional hero. We've got to get him enough skills to stay alive."

"*Spooty, da zuggog na'guggin ra'root.*"

"Aye, and ye too. I'll teach ye knife work with Niln. Just enough to keep ye on your feet while we're on the quest. Then we can get ye a real job …" Gorm trailed off. Of course, once the quest was over, Gleebek would need a new line of work as a servant in a tavern, or a stable hand, or a farm worker. Almost any job would be better than roaming about with Gorm; Goblins, as a general rule, don't last in close proximity to professional heroes.

Gorm shook his head and charged on.

"I don't know how good the bard is. If he used to be a thief, he should know how to handle a dagger or a short sword. And we'll have to find a way to get the mages fightin' like a team if they're to be any use. But they've got the foundations of heroics, something to build on. This could work."

They took a shortcut through a small park, to stairs that led down another three tiers.

"And we've got a top-notch ranger. Well, at least she's been on big campaigns before. I know it's been awhile, and I've heard about the bad spells, but let me tell ye, Gleebek, Kaitha used to be something."

"*Tib'rin!*"

"All the bards were singing about her back when I was on me Da's knee. There's greatness just beneath the surface. We just got to bring it out. Keep her head in the game and out of the bottle. I can make it work."

"*Gi'nub zib been.*"

"Well, of course I can always count on Iheen. Or Gaist. Whatever he's callin' himself. Might be a bit unstable now, but it sounds like he can still handle a sword."

They were almost to the Temple of Al'Matra. Gorm was nearly running.

"Take me, and that's three veterans. Then we've got three unknowns, the high scribe, and a Goblin squire." Gorm rushed through the temple gate. "We won't be slayin' any dragons anytime soon. Ha! I doubt we could take on a young wyvern." He bounded up the temple stairs. "But for a fetch quest? We'll be fighting bandits and giant rats. Maybe a few Orcs, if things go badly. We can handle that."

Heraldin was waiting at the top of the steps. "There you are," he said. "I was asked to—"

"We can do this," Gorm shouted, grabbing the bard by the arms and shaking vigorously. "It's going to work!"

"What's going to work?"

"This quest. This plan. We're goin' to make it, lad! We just need to work together. It's going to—"

The temple wall erupted, a wall of scarlet fire blasting from it like a sideways volcano, spouting over the edge of the stairs just a few feet from where Gorm stood. Marble pillars around the obliterated wall began to glow red with the heat. Ceremonial shrubs ignited. Gorm could feel his whiskers singing.

Heraldin shot him a knowing grin. "Good luck with that," he said.

Gleebek stared at the flames, his arms limp by his sides. *"Spug ..."*

A figure became visible within the torrent of fire, steadily skidding backwards as the force of the assault drove him toward the edge of the stairs. Jynn's sorcerous shield winked out as the flames subsided. The cobbles on either side of him were charred and bubbling, but the wizard and the stones behind him were unharmed.

"Do you see?" Jynn snarled at Gorm. He waved a hand at the smoldering hole in the temple. "Do you see what I have to deal with here? This is the kind of rank amateurism that marks an apprentice! I … uh!"

The noctomancer barely had time to re-weave his shielding spell before another blast of fire slammed into him. Gorm could hear Laruna shrieking something unintelligible over the roar of the fire.

"Oh, very mature!" Jynn hollered. He strode back into the smoldering temple as his shield blinked away again. "As if that's a rational argument!"

Heraldin turned to Gorm. "Well, it was a nice thought," he said. "But I still don't think our chances are good."

"I didn't say anything about chances," Gorm growled. "I said it's going to work. Come on."

Inside, the temple was chaos. Acolytes rushed around with buckets and urns of water, while several priestesses tried to spare some ancient scrolls and statues from the growing flames. The other heroes were rushing toward the fight as well. Gorm spotted Niln shouting and waving his arms at Jynn. The wizard, however, was engaged in a shouting match with a pillar of fire that was rising from the floor. And at the center of the pillar was Laruna.

Blazing energy spiraled around the solamancer in a sorcerous cyclone. The young woman's face was a mask of rage, and something behind it burned with a fury bright enough to send a fiery orange glow streaming from her eyes and mouth.

"Blood and ashes, that's a lot of fire," said Gorm.

Heraldin nodded in agreement and subconsciously checked his eyebrows.

"Still, only one thing to be done for it," said Gorm. He leaped over a fallen pew and started at a full sprint.

Gorm had fought his fair share of wizards and mages in his day. They tended to turn villainous more than any other class of hero. When one made a habit of unraveling the fabric of the universe and twisting the strands back together to suit one's whims, things like guild rules and the law and basic decency seemed less and less immutable. And since there were so many magic-using foes out in the field, warrior heroes came in only two varieties: those who knew how to fight mages, and extra crispy.

Gorm ran around the sanctuary until he was directly behind Laruna, and then he switched suddenly to a full sprint directly toward her. The Solamancer was so engrossed in her conflict with Jynn that she didn't even turn until Gorm was launching himself into the air. The pillar of fire around her dissipated as Gorm's shoulder slammed into her, sending her flying into the wall. She slid to the ground with a faint cry.

Jynn approached as Gorm was struggling to his feet. "I must say, that was surprisingly effective," said the wizard.

"Aye. On account of the first principle of fightin' wizards."

"What's that?"

Gorm dropped him with a hammer punch to the jaw. "Surprise," he said.

It took a bucket of water to rouse the mages. By the time they were standing, the other heroes had gathered around.

"Listen up," said Gorm. "I know better than to say there ain't going to be any more fights in the party. Nobody ever stopped inter-party violence just by askin'. But I will say that if there are any more fights in the party, I'm gonna join them. And I'm gonna win. And whoever loses is going to very much regret it. Understood?"

He stared at each of them in turn. The mages nodded sullenly. Kaitha and Heraldin seemed more surprised. Niln looked decidedly suspicious. "Why do you care all of a sudden?" the high scribe asked.

"Because we're going into the field soon, and this kind of nonsense gets heroes killed every day. So tomorrow, first thing, we start training. And we're going to work together, like a bloody team of thrice-cursed professionals who know that our lives depend on each other. And then we're going find those thrice-cursed marbles, and finish this bloody quest, and we're going to do it fast! Because this is going to work, burn it!"

Niln sat at his desk. A honeycomb of cubbies and drawers ran around the walls of his study, all crammed with scrolls and parchments. Pale moonlight shone through his solitary window; candlelight illuminated the blank page in front of him. He held a quill at the ready, waiting.

The scripture began.

And Lo, the six were gathered by the High Scribe and blessed by the King, as was foretold by the prophet Asepth.

89

Niln's quill glided across the page quickly, effortlessly, and without thought. Holy text was left in its wake.

> *And I saw two vines: one growing from the sea, and one from the forest.*

A vision of two titanic vines, spread from the ocean to the Green Span, appeared behind the goddess's words.

> *The vine from the sea grew up a great mountain, and entwyned the top, and set out roots. And the vine from the forest grew up the same path, and bloomed in Death, and smote the vine from the sea. And the sea vine burned, and the blossoms of the forest vine rose up, and the vine of the forest Lived once more, and entwyned the mountain.*

The vision departed as suddenly as it had come. Niln dutifully finished transcribing it, though he had no idea what it meant. Incoherent, rambling scriptures were a hallmark of the All Mother; indeed, those who believed Scribe Pathalan was the true high scribe, instead of Niln, were quick to point out that most of Niln's writings made much more sense than any words of Al'Matra for more than three hundred years. His predecessor's life work had been a treatise on the similarities of toenails to prawns. Scribe Pathalan's latest work was an inventory of all the items built into mouse nests within the temple, including personal names for all of the buttons.

The Book of Niln, by contrast, was filled with relevant stories, verifiable history, and direct commandments. Naturally, the other Al'Matrans held it as suspect.

> *And the Wizard Jynn did provoke the Mage Laruna, who did throwe a Mighty Spelle at him, and he did return another spelle, and so forth. And their battle did smite the Temple Mightily.*

Niln sighed. He had hoped that this particular incident wouldn't have made it into the scriptures, but he didn't have any say. The words of the holy texts burned across his mind, and his only recourse was to write them down. What the goddess willed, he wrote.

So Gorm, Son of Inger, Son of Hruxo, did smite both of yon mages, and tell them to shape up, for he held a Great Fire in his heart for the Quest.

Gorm's newfound enthusiasm was an interesting development. Sometime between the king's ceremony and arriving at the temple, the Dwarf had transformed into a veritable zealot. He had ordered training gear, scheduled a time for practice in the morning, and delivered a rousing speech, all before dinner. Niln couldn't see any reason why Gorm would become so passionate so quickly. Still, Niln had little choice but to accept the Dwarf's sudden support, whatever the cause. The All Mother knew he needed it.

That night, Heraldin Strummons, the Bard, went to the room of Kaitha of House Tyrieth, for he held a Great Fire in his pants. And he did profess his desire for her.

Niln shook his head and sat back to listen. A yelp of pain rang out from across the temple. Niln resumed writing.

But yon Elf made it clear that she was Not Interested. And in so doing, they awoke Gorm, Son of Inger.

Bootsteps echoed in a distant staircase, loud and fast.

And Gorm did correct Heraldin Strummons, and tell him to Behave Professionally.

Gruff shouting echoed in the staircase.

With much emphasis.

Niln winced at a low thud and a cry of agony.

And this was a distraction to the High Scribe Niln, but his work was not yet completed. For his Fate was to assemble the foretold

Heroes, and to lead them to their Destiny, as was foretold in the First Book of Niln.

The conflict was a distraction, Niln thought, as the goddess's words faded from his inner sight. But he was undeterred. The scriptures made it clear that he was the Seventh Hero. Although …

Niln set the quill down. A thought tugged at the back of his mind, a seed of hesitation that had plagued him since the verses of prophecy first bloomed in his mind. The verses he wrote never directly named him as the Seventh Hero, or even one of the heroes. He would assemble them, and lead them, and quest with them, and guide them … but he was never said to be one of them.

Still, what else could the scriptures mean? He was called by name to lead the Heroes of Destiny. He was chosen to assemble the six. He was explicitly told by the goddess that his works would save the world.

Niln shook off the lingering doubts and left his study. There was much to be done before bed. Most pressingly, the bard would likely need a healing potion.

Gorm ascended the tower steps, carrying a hunk of bread and several slabs of cheese from the larder. Gleebek followed him, laboring under a load of loaves, cheeses, fruits, and pastries.

"I admire a good appetite, lad," Gorm told the Goblin. "But I think ye may be overdoing your breakfast."

"*Da grong.*"

"Ye keep eatin' like ye'll never see food again. Oh." It didn't occur to Gorm until it was too late that, up until recently, every meal that Gleebek had eaten had likely been served with a side order of uncertainty. Aside from heroes, starvation was the greatest threat wild Goblins faced.

They could hear the voices of the other heroes on the terrace as they neared the top of the stairs. Gorm slowed when he realized that he was the subject of discussion.

"He's out of his right mind," Jynn was saying. "He seemed like the normal sort at first, but yesterday he came in practically frothing at the mouth to tell us to get ready for this quest."

"That was after he assaulted us," Laruna added.

"Absolutely bonkers," Heraldin said.

"I think we should give him the benefit of the doubt," said Kaitha. "I was excited about the job at first too."

"You were inebriated to the point of oblivion," said Jynn.

"Exactly. He was probably drunk last night. It seems more likely than him suddenly going insane."

"It makes sense that he would join the Al'Matran's madness," Heraldin said. "He's a berserker, you know."

"Aren't those the Dwarves who get so angry they go crazy in battle?" asked Laruna.

"Berserkers are members of the Brotherhood of Flame, the most elite of the Dwarven fighters," said Jynn. "The highest honored among their armies."

"And?" prompted Heraldin.

"And yes, they get very angry and go absolutely crazy in battle," Jynn said.

"It ain't anger," said Gorm, stepping out from the stairway.

The other heroes had been breakfasting around an old oak table, and upon Gorm's appearance they attempted to arrange themselves around it to affect maximum nonchalance.

"Oh, good morning, Gorm," Heraldin attempted.

"I mean, of course there's some anger. You're fightin' after all. But anger ain't what makes ye berserk." Gorm stood next to the table and looked out across the terrace, to the city.

"It's purpose. Ye find something in the battle to fight for, something ye'd die for. Your brothers back in the clanhome, the honor of your Da's name, the lives of innocents. A reason to fight, if nothing else, like a tiny fire, and ye reach out and grab it. And ye hold it no matter how it burns. And soon ye can't separate yourself from your purpose, any more than ye could take the light from a candle flame. Ye live to win. Ye can't lose; ye can only die."

"Whoa," said Laruna.

"And later, they'll say ye looked crazed, or ye howled like a beast, or ye seemed possessed, but their words are nothing but a vapor in a breeze. 'Cause ye can still feel a flicker of the fire ye held inside, and ye know now what ye knew then, and ye'll never be the same. That's what it is to be a berserker, and I'd never trade it for anything. Or I wouldn't have, until I ran. A berserker doesn't run."

He caught Gaist's eyes and saw his own painful memories reflected in them. Memories of death, and fear, and flight.

Gorm sighed. "I lost me flame at the dungeon of Az'Anon. Call me what ye will, and say I'm crazy if ye like, but don't call me a berserker. I ain't one anymore."

"So this is just your normal, run-of-the-mill insanity?" said Heraldin.

Gorm shot him a sidelong glance. "I don't believe this campaign will be as bad as ye think. This quest ain't half the danger we thought'd it be, and who knows, maybe they'll be done after that?"

"Or maybe they'll send us after the Dragon of Wynspar. Or Troll hunting," Heraldin said. "The Al'Matrans are half as mad as their goddess."

"The Tandosians ain't, and they're behind the quest."

"You're a bigger fool than I thought if you trust the Tandosians," said Jynn.

"Ain't got much of a choice, do we?" said Gorm. "We're on the quest either way. As far as I can see, we can either do what we can to make the job better, or we can sit back and make snarky comments."

"I'm happy to say that Mr. Ingerson has the right of it." Mr. Flinn materialized from the shadows behind them.

"Don't do me any favors, mercenary," said Gorm. "What are ye here for?"

"Why, only to deliver a couple of messages."

"So deliver them."

"Naturally. The first is that you are to meet the esteemed ambassador from House Tyrieth for lunch tomorrow. You will join Her Ladyship at the Elven Embassy at noon. And as for the second, it almost seems unnecessary, but I do want to make sure you realize that Master Niln's safety on this adventure is paramount."

"He'll be fine. We're gearing up and training today," said Gorm.

"Ah yes, but I'm sure you're aware that some of the greatest threats to professional heroes come from within the party, do they not?" said Mr. Flinn. "And given your reluctance, I'm guessing at least one of you wouldn't be above slipping a dagger between a scribe's ribs to be free of this quest."

"Hold on. Are you suggesting we'd kill Niln and make a break for it?" said Laruna.

"Not all of you, certainly. Maybe not even most of you. But there might be one or two among you who have thought that the open road would provide an opportunity for freedom. Most likely the bard," he added, pointing.

"Fair enough," said Heraldin.

"Sounds more like something ye'd do, Flinn," said Gorm. "I know your type. Ye'd kill your own mother for tuppence."

"Ah, you see, that's where you're wrong," said Flinn. "I know the value of a life, usually within a few cents. When I killed my mother, it was for well over five thousand giltin."

"That's disgusting," said Kaitha.

"That's economics. Everyone is worth something, and some people are worth a lot more posthumously, which is rather the point, you see. Think what you will of him, but Master Niln's identity as the Seventh Hero means that he is worth more than any of you. And what's more, essentially all of your worth comes from the fact that you're on Master Niln's quest. If he were to meet an untimely end, there'd be no quest for you to be on, and subsequently no value in you being alive. The price on your heads, on the other hand, would be more than enough to compensate for the trouble of finding and collecting them."

"Ye through?" said Gorm.

"Merely a friendly warning."

"Ye make a lot of friendly warnings," said Gorm. "They're all starting to run together. Sounding like a bunch of noise."

"I assure you that I'm more than capable of backing up my good word, Mr. Ingerson."

"Perhaps, but then who'd be on the wrong side of the law? We're heroes on a job now," said Gorm. "I've enough of your crowing. Be off."

Mr. Flinn's smile was like an autumn frost. "It seems you won't be so easily manipulated."

"Seems as much." Gorm grinned back at him.

The standoff was interrupted by a distant rumbling. "COO! COO!"

"Yes, thank you, Mr. Brunt!" shouted Mr. Flinn. "We must work on those birdcalls!" He tuned back to the heroes. "That signal means Master Niln is on his way. I must bid you good day. I must also insist that this conversation never happened."

"It seems more like it never ends," said Jynn.

"You stand corrected, sir," said Mr. Flinn, and took his leave.

"What a little Goblin snot," said Laruna, watching the Gnome walk away. "No offense."

"*Nub Hupsit.*"

Gorm spotted Niln walking across the terrace and carrying a small bowl of oats and a cup of tea for breakfast. "I think there's something wrong with that Ogre," said the high scribe. "Well, regardless, I believe you said we were to start training this morning, Mr. Ingerson."

Gorm grinned.

They started with assessments. "We'll run several drills to assess where ye are in your fighting skills, and where ye need work," Gorm explained. "When we're done, we'll see where we need work, and the top performers will train those who lag behind."

They ran sprints and did an obstacle course. They shot targets and sparred with a training golem. They held a mixed skirmish fought with wooden swords. By mid-morning, Gorm had a good idea of where they were.

"We're dead," Gorm said.

"It's not all bad," said Kaitha.

"He needed a healing potion after fighting a training golem. A bloody training golem," Gorm said.

"Well, it is a sorcerous automaton built for combat."

"It has pillows for arms! I can't see how he even got nicked fighting one, let alone needed a potion." Gorm rummaged through the medicinal rucksack. "How many did he drink, anyway? I thought we had more elixir."

"So Niln needs work," said Kaitha. "Look on the bright side. The wizard was better than expected."

"Well, set the bar low enough …" grumbled Gorm.

"And the bard can fight better than you thought," Kaitha said.

"He's got no sense of the battlefield. Too used to questing solo. Doesn't look past his own nose in a fight."

"Well, we're here to work on that," said the Elf.

"Aye. I suppose we are."

He set Kaitha up training both Niln and Gleebek, starting with stave drills. "We'll try to move ye up to daggers this afternoon," Gorm told them. "Assuming ye've made enough progress."

"I must confess, I'm a little surprised that you've put me with the Goblin," said Niln.

"Don't worry," said Gorm. "You'll catch up."

"Lob'dod!" Gleebek brandished his staff.

For Heraldin's training, Gorm had a couple of attendants bring in an hourglass and a small wooden box. It contained a fine board inset with a grid of mahogany and pine spaces, and two sets of ornately carved ivory and ebony pieces.

"I'm to play a board game?" Heraldin said incredulously.

"You're good with a blade," said Gorm. "Good enough that a day's drills ain't going to do much for ye, at least. But ye lack strategy. A plan. A mind for staying ahead of your foe." He set the final piece, an ebony king, on the board with a faint click. "Thrones teaches all that."

"So we're just going to play thrones all day?"

"Not me," said Gorm. He nodded to Gaist.

"What? The mute?" demanded the bard. "Why not pit me against one of the topiary shrubs? I've seen them move more today."

Gaist regarded them with the cold, tenuous serenity of thin ice.

"Make a move."

"He didn't even participate in the drills. For all we know, I should be training him."

"Make a move."

"We'll start by teaching him to speak."

"Just make a move."

Heraldin sighed, advanced an ivory bannerman, and flipped the hourglass.

"There," said Gorm. "Now, I can't speak for this Gaist fellow, but Iheen the Red never lost a game of thrones in all the years I knew him. Never turned down a challenge, and never failed to win. But hey, maybe he's changed." He nodded to the sand pouring through the hourglass. "Maybe he doesn't mind losing by forfeit."

Gaist stared out over the horizon.

"Losing to a bard."

The weaponsmaster didn't so much as flinch. The sand had almost totally drained from the top of the hourglass.

"All right. Well, I'm surprised," said Gorm. "Seems he's willing to let his thrones record go without a fight. Never thought it'd be broken by a common bard working for the Al'Matrans."

"This is starting to get insulting," said Heraldin. "Anyways, time is u—"

Gaist moved like silk in the wind, gliding up to the table and advancing an ebony bannerman in one swift motion. He quickly flipped the hourglass, seated himself across the table from Heraldin, and resumed staring silently into the air.

"Oh-ho, that's your move?" said Heraldin. "Nobody moves the outer bannermen to start. I thought you were supposed to be good at this." He advanced a paladin.

Gorm smiled. "Enjoy your education," he said. He hadn't made it halfway across the terrace when he heard the bard shouting.

"How have you won already? I didn't even get to take five turns! I demand a rematch."

That left the mages. Gorm took them down to the back courtyard of the temple. It was a good-sized expanse of grass and stone pressed against the ridge of Mount Wynspar, with few features but a couple of stone benches and an old plum tree. The fact that the courtyard was so big, and contained so little, was exactly why Gorm had chosen it as the site for Jynn to train Laruna.

Both mages erupted into immediate protests upon hearing Gorm's plan.

"I'm not going to work with that pompous Orc-sired fool."

"I can't work with someone so absolutely ignorant."

"What could I learn from him?"

"What could she learn at all?"

Their arguments washed over Gorm like waves over a stone. When it became clear that their dislike of each other wasn't going to sway the Dwarf, the mages moved their arguments to a unified front.

"I can't even touch solamancy, let alone teach it," said Jynn.

"There's a reason there are two orders," said Laruna. "Mages can only see one side of magic."

"All the mages worth mentioning, anyway," said Jynn. "The point is, I really don't think I can teach her."

"I mean, I don't like the guy, but he's not a filthy omnimancer. He's not going to have any idea about solamancy."

"Well, I have some ideas of the theory."

"The theory seems like what she needs," said Gorm. "She's got plenty of power. No technique."

Laruna shot Jynn a venomous glare. "I don't need technique," she growled. "Look, it's simple. I'm going to be a pyromancer. I burn things. I throw fire at them, or set them alight, or make them explode. This is not complicated."

"Except in that last fight, ye didn't fare so well. Ye couldn't burn the noctomancer, or stop me from takin' ye down. All ye managed to do was cause a lot of damage to the temple, and maybe cost the Al'Matrans their property insurance."

"Well, I ... I—"

"They ain't happy about that, by the way. Point is, this magic business seems to be a little more complicated than ye think."

"Thank you," said Jynn. "That's what I've been saying all along. She may have some raw talent, but it's simply unacceptable that she should advance beyond an apprenticeship while using such crude weaves."

"And your weaves are much better," prompted Gorm.

"Oh, there's no comparison," said Jynn. "I'm the youngest wizard in three centuries to teach classes at the academy. Archmages have personally attended to see my weaves. I'm one of the most highly regarded spellcasters in the Freedlands. Some say I'll make Archmage by thirty-five."

"Good! Training Laruna here won't be a problem, then. I'll expect an update on her progress this afternoon. Don't start any fires. Or else."

Gorm turned and walked away without giving the mages a chance to respond.

"'Oh, there's no comparison,'" he heard Laruna mimic. "'One of the most highly regarded spellcasters in the Freedlands.'"

"Shut up," said Jynn.

"That's excellent advice," said Laruna. "If only we had thought of it before talking the Dwarf's ear off about what a great teacher you are."

"Let's just get started," sighed the wizard.

They spent the day in drills and games, sparring and spell casting. Gorm wandered between each of the three stations, offering encouragement and barking orders in turn. A long-forgotten thrill was creeping back into him, notes of excitement that rang in his voice and hummed in his bones. The open road was before him, with mysterious lands and unknown foes and treasures waiting to be discovered.

Of course, he had spent the last twenty years with the open road before him, and certainly there were plenty of unknown foes along his way. But now he had a task, a reason to roam, rewards to be reaped.

Not all who wander are lost; some are on quests.

Gleebek made it through his stave drills with ease and started the basics of dagger work. He insisted on using the knife Gorm had given him, taken from the threatening salve addict. In the same amount of time, Niln had gotten to the point where he was able to make it through a staff routine without injuring himself.

"We'll call it progress," said Gorm.

After losing forty-two straight games without ever mounting an offense, Heraldin managed to last for more than twenty turns and threaten Gaist's throne in their final match of the day.

"I prefer to quit while I'm ahead," Heraldin explained.

"Ye've a funny definition of 'ahead,'" said Gorm.

"I prefer to define words in ways that suit me," said Heraldin.

The mages accomplished little, if anything. When Gorm arrived looking for a report, they spoke over each other as they attempted to shift blame. Soon, they were yelling, and then they were screaming at each other, and then there likely would have been another magical battle had Gorm not intervened.

"At least they didn't burn anything down," Niln remarked.

"We'll call it progress," sighed Gorm.

"See how much better that is?" said Heraldin.

Kaitha retired to her rooms after the so-called feast. Tonight's dinner had been a cruel mockery of the elaborate celebrations that had preceded her old quests. Before she'd headed out to take on the Ratmen of Warpspyre Peak, they'd served half a barn's worth of livestock to hungry crowds of nobles; that was back when being the Jade Wind was something to be proud of. When she was somebody.

Now, even the Al'Matrans couldn't hide their contempt or amusement at her plight. And why should they? She was training a newblood and a Goblin. It seemed like such a waste for a heroine of her caliber.

Then again, she wasn't what she used to be. Or so she was told.

The whole situation set her on edge. She liked Gorm and could respect his newfound energy, but his enthusiasm was misplaced. They were on a quest with the Al'Matrans, and even if they survived, their hero careers were over.

Her hands were shaking. She needed something to relax her, just for a little, just this once. Then she'd be fine, and she could move onto the next quest. She arrived at the foot of her bed before she knew where she was going, her hands already slipping past a false bottom in her rucksack to find a few glass vials.

She pulled out a small vial filled with warmly incandescent liquid. Kaitha had long forgotten her first healing potion. Somewhere, on some adventure, she'd doubtlessly found herself wounded and bleeding with more foes to fight. A bottle of elixir could mean the difference between life and death.

Once she began spending too much time in the taverns, however, she started taking elixir less cautiously. She'd drink healing potions after any wound, not just the life-threatening ones. She'd keep them on her belt loop, so she could grab them faster when in a fight. She found herself running headlong into danger, not caring if she was wounded — no, even hoping that she would be, so she could drink the sweet fluid and feel the sweet fire run through her veins.

Somewhere along the line, she'd started taking it when she wasn't on a job, sometime back, when she was just starting to mess up on jobs and lose clients. She knew that taking elixir was risky; everyone had seen the addicts wandering around, hacking at themselves and begging for healing potions.

Kaitha wasn't that bad, she told herself, as she sat down next to her bed. She laid a few small rags around her, and then drew her long hunting knife. She just needed it once more, one more time to take the edge away. And then she'd stop. She had to stop.

A tear trickled down her cheek. Of course, every time had been the last time. Just like, some small part of her knew, the next time would be.

Kaitha started near her wrist and cut down the front of her forearm almost to her elbow. She sat back and grimaced, feeling a familiar thrill as she watched her life pour down her arm. She wondered if she'd bother to stop it this time. People would say it was a waste, a horrible shame that one so great should wind up like that. But they said it now, and if she died, she wouldn't have to hear it anymore. Or know it anymore.

Kaitha threw her head back and drank the elixir, tasting its fire and copper flavor, feeling it burn sweetly down her throat. She rested against her bed as the gash in her arm closed itself. Warmth spread from her wrist through the rest of her body as the magic began to replenish the blood she had lost. Her eyes glazed over.

It was the warmth that she craved; it enveloped her, a rapturous glow took her in its arms and loved her unconditionally. It drained away all of the memories, the fear, the shame. Everything painful floated away on velvet wings, and in the warmth, Kaitha could finally be herself. Whoever that was.

Chapter 7

The Elven Embassy was just a couple of tiers down from Andarun's pinnacle. It was a palatial mansion built from granite but in the spiraling, flowing style of the Elves, so that the building seemed to be poured from the heavens rather than built from the ground. House crests were grown from the wall, living emblems made from trees guided into impossible shapes by Elven wyldsingers and decorated with the totems of each Elven House. Oak branches grew through a bear skull for House Galantia, while maple entwined boar tusks for House Lleweryn, and cherry wrapped around a stag's antlers for House Tyrieth, and so on.

"This place clearly has some gold about it," Laruna noted, admiring the architecture. "It's got real gargoyles, not the cheap carvings."

Gorm harrumphed.

"Look! That one's sunning its wings," Laruna said. "How do they even get them to stay on the roof?"

"You have to raise the gargoyle from hatchlings to get them that tame," said Kaitha. "And even then, you should keep small pets indoors."

Gorm harrumphed again. "It's ridiculous extravagance. Ye can't trust someone with too much gold."

"And how much is too much gold?" said Kaitha.

"Ye can jus' tell when someone's got too much," Gorm said. "Trainin' monsters to be ornaments or puttin' cats in chain mail or hirin' Gnomes to dress up and prance about the garden."

"Interesting," said Jynn. "I've always thought Dwarves were particularly enamored with gold."

"I liked it more back when it was actually gold," said Gorm. He produced a giltin and bit it. The coin bent easily, flaking gilt away from its tin center. "Gold today's like a child's trinkets."

Jynn shrugged. "A giltin is just a symbol, a tiny unit of power. Currency is a system of control, and coins and bank notes are how it's measured."

"I've never thought of it that way," said Heraldin.

"Most people don't. Then again, they don't see the warp or the weft of magic either," said Jynn. "It's the way of the world. Power eludes the masses, and so the masses are ruled by the few."

"And then the few go crazy and start carrying Kobolds in their purses," said Gorm.

They were stopped at the front gate by Elven bannermen in jade and gold armor. Niln presented their credentials to a tall Elven captain wearing a striking golden cape. The guard reviewed the quest paperwork, the embassy invitation, and each of the Heroes' Guild certifications. He paused when he looked at Gorm's license.

"Rank one?" he asked with a smile.

"Technically," Gorm said. He mentally added the captain to his List of People Who Had Made the Wrong List.

The Elf grinned, handed the papers back to Niln, and waved them along. "Move through. Not you," he added.

"*Grong, Grot?*" asked Gleebek.

"No Shadowkin in the embassy," said the guard. "He can wait over there. Hear that, Gobbo? You. Wait. There."

"Ain't a Shadowkin. He's me squire," said Gorm.

A few of the guards chortled. "I've never heard of a slimeskin squire, even for a mine-drek at rank one," said the captain, cramming multiple slurs into what was perhaps the most spectacularly ill-advised comment of his life.

Gorm grinned, or perhaps bared his teeth—even he didn't know, truth be told. The only thing that was certain was that whenever he smiled that way, events tended to get interesting. His first punch took a few teeth from the guard's smile, his second cracked the Elf's ribs, and after that he lost track until Kaitha interrupted him.

"Mister Ingerson," the ranger shouted, "is looking forward to having the remainder of his ranks restored, because now he is a proper hero once more and doing things within the bounds of the law."

"Well—" Gorm started to protest.

"Plus, we wouldn't want to upset Master Niln," Kaitha added pointedly. The high scribe stared at the prone guard, pale and slack jawed.

Gorm reluctantly lifted his boot off the captain's face. "Aye, sorry," he said, sheathing his axe. "Been livin' the rough life on the road too long, I guess. Forgotten me manners."

He offered a hand to help the captain up, but the terrified Elf slid himself back on his good arm and gurgled something or other. It was hard to understand a man without a functioning jaw. Several of the other guards shrank away, clutching their weapons in feeble imitations of defense.

"Somebody get the man a healing potion," Jynn said.

"Aye. That'll grow those teeth back," Gorm told the terrified captain.

"We'll continue to our meeting," Kaitha said. "Squire Gleebek will wait for us here."

"But—" Gorm started.

"We've created enough paperwork here already," Laruna said.

"I think discretion is the better part of whatever that was supposed to be," Heraldin added.

Kaitha nodded. "No disrespect, but Gleebek can remain outside."

Gleebek approached Gorm and patted his arm. *"Gi'deek. Ga'gub zug."* The Goblin nodded reassuringly as he went to sit on the bench the Elven captain had directed him to.

Gorm sighed. "Come on. Let's get this over with."

Niln, rubbing his forehead, fell into step beside Gorm once they were through the gate. "Mr. Ingerson, we can't ... what do you think the guild will have to say about us assaulting embassy guards?"

"Oh, I'd say thirty or forty."

"Years? In prison?"

"What? No. We'll be fined thirty or forty giltin."

"That's all? You assaulted bannermen!"

"Aye, but we're heroes in the line of duty. Happens all the time. The rules are different for us, lad."

"A man on the street could lose his head for throwing a stone at a bannerman, and you're saying we'll pay a small fine for ... for ... I'm not even sure what exactly you did to him back there."

"Broken jaw, fractured ribs, fairly certain he lost several teeth—"

"That wasn't a request for more detail."

"Fair enough." Gorm shrugged. "Point is, we might have more leeway with city guards than a man on the street, but that man wouldn't hang for breaking a contract, would he? Now me, if I left your temple tonight I'd be swinging from a rope in the morning. We're under guild law now. Some rules matter less, and some matter a lot more."

Niln scowled. "Still, Mr. Ingerson, I think we should abide by all of the law, not just the parts that you think matter."

"Aye. Sorry. Old habits die hard."

"Diplomatic relations die easy."

"Then they shouldn't have barred me squire from entering."

"I'm sure no harm will be done to him."

"Harm's already been done," snapped Gorm.

The chambers of House Tyrieth were on the top floor of the embassy. The house's sigil grew in the sun provided by a large oculus in one of the building's twisting domes. It was a cherry tree, grown into a perfect circle that spiraled around a great pair of antlers, yellow and white banners streaming beneath. Trained songbirds flitted among the leaves.

"You should see it in the spring, in bloom," Kaitha said.

A waiting attendant guided them through the house chambers. The floors were stained oak and the granite walls were decorated with mosses and rare blooms. The furniture was made from dark cherrywood carved into sleek, fluid shapes and decorated with carvings of leaves and cherry blossoms.

The heroes were led to a medium-sized room with an oblong table and broad picture windows overlooking the embassy gardens. Gorm walked to the window and gazed out over the exquisitely manicured trees and flowers while he waited. One by one, most of the other heroes joined him.

"It's beautiful," said Laruna,

"It has to be," said Kaitha.

"Kaitha?" said a voice from the door.

Gorm turned to see an Elven woman in the doorway. Her amber hair was pulled into a tight bun, and she wore a smart suit jacket and short skirt, both in shades of cherry-blossom pink. She also carried a large leather purse.

"Jalana?" said Kaitha.

The two women emitted a high-pitched squeal of the kind Gorm had heard when horrible monsters attacked villages, and then they ran across the room and clasped each other in a lukewarm embrace.

"How long has it been?" Jalana asked.

"I don't know. Forty years?" said Kaitha.

"And so much has changed!" said Jalana. "I'm the ambassador to Andarun now. And you're with the Al'Matrans. Oh, Mother always said you were touched by Al'Matra."

"And somehow, everything seems to stay the same." Kaitha's smile suddenly seemed more brittle. "Speaking of which, how is Mother now?"

"Oh, you know. The same."

"Ye two are sisters?" Gorm said. Now that they said it, he could see a distinct resemblance.

The Elves shared a knowing look. "Sort of," said Jalana.

"Queen Gwelineth always has three daughters," Kaitha said.

"You're princesses?" exclaimed Laruna.

"We used to be," Jalana said. "Mother follows the old ways."

Gorm had met a few Elves who stuck to the "old ways." Some couldn't stand the idea of losing their identity as their memories faded, of literally losing themselves every few centuries and having to find someone new again. When you couldn't trust your own mind to tell you who you were—and thus who you are now—the only way to know for sure that you hadn't changed was to never change at all.

Followers of the old ways stayed within the same cycles, endlessly repeating the same events and reinforcing the identity they clung to. Some did so at great expense and effort. Gorm recalled hearing about the sad case of an Elven couple that forever lived on the edge of poverty so they could save enough to marry each other in a lavish ceremony every decade or so.

"The queen always has three daughters," said Kaitha. "The babe, the girl, and the maid."

"When the time comes for a new daughter, the babe becomes the girl, and the girl the maid, and the maid moves on," said Jalana.

"So what does she do if she has a son?" Heraldin asked.

"There's a reason we couldn't socialize with the stable boys," said Kaitha.

"It works well. We're offered prominent positions: ambassadors, advisors, treasurers, and the like," said Jalana. "Of course, some of her daughters wander away, much to Mother's disappointment."

"Mother never liked my career choices," Kaitha explained.

"Oh, I wouldn't say that. She didn't mind them when you were successful."

An icy silence descended. Jynn cleared his throat.

"Well, shall we get to the business at hand?" Niln said, beckoning them to sit at the table.

Jalana's handbag shook and wriggled when she set it down. "Looks like someone's waking up!" she said. A gnarled canine face peeked over the top of the bag. It had bulging eyes and mismatched teeth and wild tufts of white hair sprouting from its eyebrows and chin. A Kobold.

Gorm shot Jynn a pointed look. The wizard shrugged and held up his hands.

The Kobold yawned, stretching his arms as he stepped out of the bag. His tiny blue and white suit had a small hole in the seat for his tail. "Isn't he the cutest? Oh, he's the cutest! Yes he is."

"I thought ye didn't allow Shadowkin in here," said Gorm.

"Well, we make exception for the cutest widdle Kobold ever, don't we?" Jalana set the Kobold on her lap. "Boots is the Honorable Ambassador of Adorable, isn't he? Yes he is. Yes he is."

The Kobold nuzzled into the Elf's lap and gave Gorm a smug smile.

"If we could focus on the business at hand," said Niln. He removed the velvet pouch from his robes, and from it he produced the lone Elven Marble.

Jalana's face lit up when he placed the stone on the table. "You found it already? Oh, thank Tandos. That didn't take nearly as long as I expected."

"There are said to be four more of the marbles, my lady," said Niln. "This one was entrusted to me by the king."

"Oh," Jalana seemed annoyed. "Well, look, House Tyrieth is very upset about this whole business with the artwork. It's a cultural treasure or something."

"From what I hear, that's what the Orcs are saying too," said Gorm.

"What? Really? Well, who cares?" Jalana gave the Kobold another treat. "Besides, the Orcs can't take proper care of the sculptures or protect them, right? I mean, the sculptures were broken and looted, right?"

"By your house," said Gorm.

"Thank you, Mr. Ingerson," said Niln.

"Look, it's simple. House Tyrieth demands that the marbles be returned." Jalana's grimace faded as she turned her attention to her Kobold. "Is that a good nom-nom, Boots? Yes it is. Yes it is."

"Can you tell us who might have wanted to steal the marbles?" Niln asked.

"Well, the Orcs, like your Dwarf said. And House Galantia has always envied our artworks. They're collectors too, you know. Last week at the Embassy Ball, Kalithan of Galantia had the nerve to call our gallery 'banal.' Can you believe it? Well, I wouldn't stand for it."

The meeting degenerated into an update on the latest gossip as lunch was served. Gorm was starving, but the food was Elven. He halfheartedly poked his spoon at what seemed to be a piece of jellied spinach before turning his attention to the marble in the center of the table. He picked it up, stared into the angry eyes, and felt the tusks from the vicious underbite. Something caught his eye when he flipped the statue over.

A small sigil was stamped in faded indigo ink onto the bottom of the statue, at the base of the neck, where the head had been sawn from the original sculpture. It was a fish pointing downward, but its mouth opened in a fearsome, sharp-toothed star ringed by a pattern of tentacles. Two appendages were longer than the rest, wrapping around the fish to create a perfect circle.

"What's this symbol here?" he interrupted the story of some house's slight against some other house.

The marble was passed around the table, but nobody seemed to have seen it before.

"I don't know," said Jalana, examining the stamp. "Maybe the museum curator put it there for some reason? No, Boots! Down! Down! There's a good boy."

A knock sounded, and an Elf dressed in a smart suit entered. His face looked remarkably like that of the captain of the guard at the front gate — or, at least, before Gorm was through with him.

"A message for you, Madam Ambassador," the Elf said.

He handed Jalana a dossier.

"Oh, this is wonderful news," she said, reading the files. "We think we know where the other marbles are."

"We have word that suggests the marbles were taken by bandits," explained the messenger. "They've made camp in the outskirts of the Myrewood, not half a day's ride from Ebenmyre."

An uncomfortable silence settled around the table. "That's … excellent," said Heraldin. "Heroes of Destiny, quick huddle?"

The heroes pulled into a tight ring at one end of the table and leaned their heads in close.

"How is that wonderful news?" Heraldin hissed. "The marbles are in the bloody Myrewood!"

"Ugh," said Laruna. "I don't want to go wading through some festering swamp brimming with foul monsters."

"Isn't that professional heroics?" said Niln.

"Professional implies there's money involved," whispered Kaitha. "The Myrewood got looted clean thirty years ago. Everything that's crept back in is poorer than dirt."

"And also homicidally insane," said Heraldin.

"You can make a name for yourself killing horrible monsters, but it's loot that pays the bills," said Laruna.

"The Myrewood is a lot of risk for little reward," said Jynn.

"Not if the Elven Marbles are in there," said Niln. "They're the object of our quest."

"Yes," said Heraldin. "The quest that was supposed to be easy, right, Dwarf? A simple walk to pick up some sculptures and be on our way, wasn't that what you said? And now we'll probably be eaten alive by giant blood leeches."

Gorm had been through the Myrewood before. He'd helped clear the thrice-cursed swamp of monsters in one of his early campaigns. But he'd been with a well-organized party then, every hero a hardened veteran with years of monster-hunting experience. And they'd still lost a few. You couldn't bring newbloods like Niln or Jynn into the Myrewood. They'd just be dead weight—in more ways than one.

Still, that had been on a journey to the swamp's center. "That fellow said the marbles are on the outskirts of the swamp," Gorm said.

"So what?" said Laruna.

"The edges of the Myrewood ain't so bad," Gorm explained. "That's why bandits camp there. Everyone's scared of the swamp, but the nastiest things of the mire stay nearer to the middle. We should be fine, provided we stay near the outskirts."

"Assuming he's right," said Heraldin.

All eyes turned back to the Elves of House Tyrieth. The messenger smiled at them and handed Niln the dossier of intelligence. Jalana treated Boots to a vigorous tummy rub.

"How sure are you that the marbles are on the outskirts of the swamp?" said Niln, studying the documents.

"And not in the parts with the giant blood leeches?" added Heraldin.

"We have good information indicating as much," said the messenger.

"What kind of information?" asked Gorm.

"Good," reiterated the Elf in a manner that clearly indicated he wasn't revealing his sources.

The heroes resumed their huddle.

"Do we trust him?" said Jynn.

"Do we have any better leads?" said Niln.

"Do we even have a choice?" said Heraldin,

"No, no, and no," said Gorm. "Unless we get a better lead, we're going to the Myrewood."

Duine Poldo entered the black marble and glass office of Goldson and Baggs with a growing sense of trepidation. The binder in his hand overflowed with reports and charts and tables of numbers; none of them were encouraging.

"Welcome, Mr. Poldo," said Mr. Goldson, without glancing up from his ledger.

"We trust you have news," added Baggs, scrawling on a parchment with his heavy quill.

"Yes, sirs," said Poldo, stepping forward with a nervous cough. He opened his file and read from his notes. "Sethiroph the Serpent Priest is dead, and the cult of Sitha has been cleared from the Black Temple."

"Ah, excellent," said Baggs. "I'm sure the citizens of Berleycrest and Fenrose Heath are resting easier tonight."

"How was the loot, then?" asked Goldson.

In Poldo's experience, Mr. Goldson was always more to the point than Mr. Baggs. The point was always money.

"The hoard was approximately forty percent of projections," said Poldo. "All of the plunder funds have taken a massive loss. Three smaller firms folded when the haul came in."

"I'm sure our funds were suitably insured," said Baggs.

"Yes, sir," said Poldo uncertainly.

Goldson finally looked up from his ledger. "And yet you don't seem reassured."

"All of our funds were insured by Lamia Sisters through one of their subsidiaries, sirs," said Poldo. "And as we've insured all of their funds through one of our own subsidiaries, we've ended up owing each other about five million giltin, with the balance sheets no better off for it."

Mr. Baggs was about to respond when a small chime rang out. They turned to the back wall of the room, where numerous crystals were arrayed in a neat grid, each with a small bronze plaque beneath it. One of the crystals glowed with a faint emerald light and still hummed with residual sorcery.

"Mr. Poldo, would you be so kind?" said Mr. Goldson.

"Yes, sir," said Poldo. He hurried across the room, adjusted his spectacles, and read the small, polished placard beneath the crystal. "It's a green light from one Relic Investment Group, sirs."

"Ah," said Mr. Baggs. "It seems things are shaping up nicely."

"Perhaps. Mr. Poldo, join us for a drink," said Mr. Goldson.

Poldo wasn't in much of a mood for celebration, but he hurried to retrieve the drinks from an ebony cabinet regardless. He set three glasses and an ice bucket on an ornate mahogany tray, selected a bottle of fine Dwerrow spirits, and poured three drinks. Mr. Goldson took his liquor with two ice cubes. Mr. Baggs preferred his neat. Poldo made his a double; it was that kind of day.

"I'm not so sure things will turn out as well as you think they will," said Mr. Goldson as Poldo set his drink on the table.

"I'm completely sure they won't," said Mr. Baggs. "That's why we have contingencies."

"One contingency."

"I'm told it's a good one." Mr. Baggs raised his glass. "To plans well laid and profits well earned."

"To new beginnings," said Mr. Goldson, joining the toast. "And the good old days."

Mr. Goldson and Mr. Baggs turned to Poldo, both wearing small, expectant smiles.

Poldo raised his own glass. "Cheers," he said.

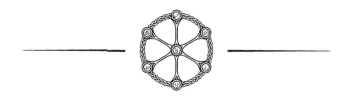

Gorm and the heroes were leaving the courtyard of the Elven Embassy when an aide in green and indigo robes rushed to catch them. The messenger breathlessly greeted them all and paid respects to Niln before he addressed Gorm directly. "Mr. Ingerson, if we may detain you a little longer, your presence is required in the lower chambers."

"What about?" said Gorm.

"I'm not at liberty to say, sir."

"It might have something to do with the spontaneous dental work you gave the captain of the guard," said Heraldin.

"Thank you, Heraldin," said Niln.

"It's probably bloody paperwork," grumbled Gorm. "Insurance forms and all that."

The aide assured Gorm that it wasn't paperwork and wouldn't take long. Niln assented to the diversion, and so Gorm agreed to meet them back at the temple. "Take Gleebek back with ye," he told them.

He followed the aide back to the embassy, but instead of entering through the front door, they walked around the side of the building. They took servants' paths past the sprawling gardens, hidden by carefully placed hedges and strategically grown trees. A cleverly concealed staircase led them down to a small grotto where the Elves kept their servants' entrance. The aide took his leave.

For a while, Gorm leaned against the grotto's mouth and listened to the songbirds above him. The air smelled of moss and summertea blossoms. He heard the oaken service door open and close behind him, but he didn't see anyone standing there when he turned.

"Down here," said a raspy voice.

Gorm adjusted his gaze earthward. "Boots?"

"Ha! That's my stage name," said the Kobold. He leaned against the wall opposite Gorm, struck a match on his teeth, and lit a small cob pipe. "You can call me Burt."

"They brought me back here to talk to a purse Kobold?"

"Whoa, hey, look at Mr. High and Mighty denigrating my career!" said Burt. "And here I thought I was trying to help, but what could a lowly handbag performer offer a professional hero?"

"I was just surprised—" Gorm backpedaled.

"Shocking that a purse Kobold would dare talk to a hero, huh? Maybe I should have looked at all of the other great career options available to a young Kobold, right? I could've been a sewer worker like my cousin Tibbo. Course, he got eaten by something down there, but this is Andarun, right?"

"All right, all right, settle down."

The Kobold champed on his pipe and waved his hands animatedly. "And hey, I could have been a gutter runner, right? I mean, I've known a friend or two who got blown off the rooftops. But if they pooled their wages, they could almost afford food and rent."

"Ok, look—"

"I get food, I get good pay, and I ain't at much risk of dying. It's a good gig. More Kobolds should be so lucky." Burt scratched a tuft of hair above his bulging eyes. "Course, most ain't got the face for it."

"I didn't mean nothin', all right?"

Burt chewed his pipe furiously and glared up at Gorm, his paws firmly on his hips. "Yeah, I guess not," he said. He took a deep breath. "Is it true what they said? You took down old Captain Nethallar in a fight?"

"Bones," swore Gorm. "Word travels fast."

"You hear things, when you're in a purse. People forget you're there. Or that you can talk." Burt puffed furiously on the pipe, conjuring clouds of glaucous smoke. "So it's true, then."

"Aye. It's true."

"And you did it for a Goblin? Just because the guards wouldn't let him in?"

"I suppose I did."

"Not many Dwarves would stick their neck out for a Shadowkin," said Burt. "Then again, not many Dwarves would have mentioned the Orcs' claim on those statues to the Elven Ambassador."

"I'd like to think that quite a few would," said Gorm.

"I'd like to as well. But you and I both know they wouldn't."

Gorm shrugged. The Kobold was right, but acknowledging as much was difficult. It was always hard to talk about Shadowkin with Shadowkin.

"Takes a strange kind of Dwarf to stick his neck out for a Goblin and some Orcs," said Burt. The Kobold scrutinized Gorm with bulbous, mismatched eyes, looking for some hint of reaction. When Gorm gave him none, he pressed further. "Maybe the same kind of Dwarf who'd give the statues to the Orcs, if he found them?"

"Whoa, slow down," said Gorm. "I ain't agreeing to that."

"No, no, course you ain't," said Burt. "But you may be the type who might do it, if he had good reason."

"It ain't my decision to make."

"You got influence. I saw the way the high scribe looks to you for advice. The rest of them listen to you. You could put in a good word."

"Why does a Kobold care whether the Orcs get the marbles anyway?"

Burt shook his head and took a slow drag from his pipe. "Because if they get them, that would mean somebody recognized them. That the king, or his chosen champion or whoever, picked the Shadowkin over the Lightlings. It'd make them somebody. And then we Kobolds, all the Gnolls really, and the Goblins and the Gremlins, we'd all be a little more somebody too, you know?"

"Don't talk nonsense. Everybody is somebody," said Gorm.

"I'm somebody as long as I got these thrice-cursed papers," said the Kobold, pulling a tiny green booklet from his coat. "I'm somebody as long as a washed-up princess wants me in her purse! We ain't like you

Lightlings, waking up every morning and wondering what you want to do, where you think you should go. I wake up every morning and wonder what they'll let me do, what I can get away with. 'Cause any day I cross them, they'll take away my papers and then I'm nothing again. Fodder for some hero's license, a dead dog walking.

"Think about the Orcs and Ogres, the Kobolds and Gnolls, the Slaugh and the Naga, the Goblins and Gremlins. Know any rich ones? Know any nobles? Thinking of any connections you're glad you have, or would like to make? No? Because we're nobody. Or, at least, we're less somebody than you. Shadowkin never win, Lightling. We can't win."

"Er … sorry," said Gorm.

Burt waved off the empty apology. "I know you can't promise me anything. I know you don't get to make the call, and even if you did, you might not be able to make it our way. I get it. Just make me this deal. I give you a tip about those rocks, and you think about giving them to the Orcs if you find them. Just a thought. That's all I'm asking."

"Aye," conceded Gorm, shaking his head. "I can't say it will do ye any good, but I'll think it over."

"Good." Burt leaned back against the wall and looked around conspiratorially. "I recognized the stamp," he said.

"The what?"

"The stamp. Blue ink on the bottom of the statue? Looked like a fish-squid?" Burt leaned toward Gorm, stood on tiptoe, and whispered, "That's the seal of the Leviathan Project."

"What's the Leviathan Project?"

"Shush! Shh!" hushed the Kobold. "Look, I don't know what it was. But I know a guy who knew a guy who was on it, and it was bad. We're talking about some heavy stuff here, Dwarf. Dark magic and dark secrets, right? I don't know why the stamp's on the statue, but it isn't good news for you or for anybody. You want to know more, you go talk to One-of-Each Magrash."

"How many Magrashes are there?"

"Oh, there's only one of him. One-of-Each is his name. You'll see. Orc working the sewers down near the Base. Look in Sculpin Down."

Gorm nodded. "That all?"

"That's a lot."

"Aye," said Gorm. "Aye, it was. Thank ye."

"For what?" said Burt. "This conversation never happened. I was never even down here. I was up getting ready to head to the groomers, see."

"Course ye were," said Gorm. "Goodbye, Burt."

"So long, Lightling." Burt stopped at the door and shot Gorm a pointed look. "What's a guy gotta do to get let in?"

"Oh, sorry." Gorm opened the old oak door.

Burt stopped halfway indoors. "You'll think about them Orcs, won't you?"

"Aye," lied Gorm. "I will."

The Kobold nodded and left Gorm to his thoughts.

He had a lot of them.

Jynn shook his head. "Wrong. Again."

Laruna knew he would say that. The phrase was the beat behind the endless drone of these thrice-cursed training sessions. She had spent every spare moment of her day standing in the same bleak, empty, and recently charred courtyard behind the temple, hurling fire at a wall of scorched stone while listening to Jynn's ceaseless litany of correction.

She'd sent more flame blasts and fireballs at the far wall than even she thought possible, leaving her drained. Exhausted. She felt like a husk of herself. "I need to rest."

"Again," said Jynn.

A sudden flash of annoyance flared up within her. Laruna stoked her irritation by thinking of Jynn and his inept lessons, of the Dwarf who had suggested this ridiculous arrangement, and of Niln, who had allowed it. The spark grew into anger, and then into a rage that seared down her arms and leaped from her hands as a pair of fireballs, which she flung at the stone ridge.

The spells hadn't hit the ridge before Jynn spoke. "Wrong. Again."

"How many times do I have to do this?" breathed Laruna. "I don't even know what you want."

"I want you to channel two threads. Try again."

"I can't." She was beyond anger. Beyond caring.

"Again!"

"Don't talk to me like I'm an apprentice," she said.

"An apprentice? This is how I train neophytes. This is the first lesson on the first day."

Tears welled in Laruna's eyes. She was too tired to care. "I can't."

"You can. You have enviable power, Laruna, but you don't wield it like a mage. You must learn to weave magic instead of just throwing it. Now, again."

"This is how I cast spells!"

"We are here to unlearn your bad habits. Again."

Laruna raised her hands and reached out, straining to find magic that wasn't tied to her emotions. To her surprise, she felt something, a faint heat, a whisper of fire building around her fingertips. She gasped as two thin tendrils of golden light spouted from her palm and wavered upward. The magic wasn't flame, yet it was the essence of flame, dancing uncertainly in her hand.

"I did it," she whispered. "I'm weaving."

Jynn nodded. "Now split the thread."

"No, I'm actually weaving! I've never done this before."

"You still haven't, technically. Split the thread, and then we'll weave them."

"I mean, this is new. This is progress. You could say as much," growled Laruna, shaking her hands at the wizard in frustration. The gesture disrupted her concentration, and the feeble threads of magic dissipated.

"Wrong," said Jynn. "Again."

Laruna looked at her empty hands, and then back to the wizard.

Jynn stared back at her impassively. "Again," he repeated.

The apathy and exhaustion burned away in a blaze of white-hot fury, searing from her very core outward as she loosed an enraged scream. A pillar of flame erupted from the ground beneath her feet, soaring higher than the temple walls for a moment before she loosed the spell. The whole courtyard was lost in a maelstrom of fire and heat, with Laruna screaming her hatred and anger in the middle of it.

By the time the flames left her, Laruna didn't even have the strength to stand. She dropped to the ground next to Jynn just as his magical shield winked out of existence. It seemed like an eternity before she felt her arms again, and even longer before her breathing calmed.

"Are you all right?"

"Shut up," Laruna rasped, pushing herself to her knees.

"Good," he said. "That was wrong. Again."

Chapter 8

"A titanium rune-forged blade with pyromantic sharpening and recursive honing enchantments," said Gorm, reverently holding the battle-axe. He could feel the sorcery hum within the weapon as he tested the weight of it. "Magically calibrated haft balancing with a strength-enhancing shoulder, trademarked thunder-strike axehead, and a drake-skin comfort-fit grip."

"I can see I'm dealing with a Dwarf of discriminating taste," said the man behind the counter of The Weapon Store, a wholly owned subsidiary of The General Store Incorporated.

Gorm smiled and set the enchanted blade on the counter. "I pick up a little here and there," he said with false modesty.

Niln stood next to him, clearly attempting to conceal his ignorance with the most thoughtful and focused expression he could muster. It wasn't working; Gorm thought the high scribe looked like he was sick in the bowels, and it was still plain as day that he didn't have a clue what he was looking at.

"How much does it cost?" Niln asked. He tried to heft the axe, failed, and settled for testing its edge instead.

"A thousand giltin," said the clerk.

"A thousand — ow!"

"Do be careful, sir," said the clerk, wiping the blade clean with a little cloth. "It's very sharp."

Niln sucked the tip of his bleeding thumb and glared at them both.

"Will you be purchasing the axe, then, sir?" the clerk asked Gorm. "Or perhaps some time with the training golems would help you make your decision?"

"Nay," said Gorm. "I'd wager ye'd have to be rank four before the Heroes' Guild would let ye use that axe."

"Five," said the clerk.

"Well, either way ye slice it, I ain't got the ranks. Not anymore."

"A pity, sir. You held it well."

"A pity for sure, but the guild does as it must. If ye let just anyone off the street wield enchanted weapons, well, ye know what would happen."

Gorm and the clerk both looked at Niln, who was still attempting to staunch his bleeding thumb.

"Indeed, sir," said the clerk. He offered Gorm a short sword. "Perhaps you would consider a sword of truth?"

Gorm took the blade and gave it a thorough examination. "What's it do?"

"It glows white-hot whenever you have an epiphany," explained the clerk.

"Ain't sure how often that happens in the heat of battle," said Gorm. "How much ye asking?"

"Eight hundred giltin."

"Eight hundred?" snorted Gorm. "This thing's overpriced."

The sword flared with white light as Gorm set it back on the counter. "No, I think a couple of vials of blade-flame for old reliable will do it for me weapon," said Gorm, patting his old axe.

"Certainly, sir." The clerk made a small note on the heroes' tallysheet, which was growing rather long. "Anything else?"

"What have ye got for armor?"

"I think you'll be quite pleased with the newest full plate, sir," offered the clerk. "Made with Tru-lite Steel and forged with crystals harvested from snow elemental hearts. Doesn't smother you like the old full plate models. Guaranteed to stay cool and breathable in battle."

"Party's not running any heavy duty," said Gorm. "More of a skirmishing outfit."

"With two mages? Who takes the punishment?"

"Well, hopefully the other guy," joked Gorm. He and the clerk shared a good laugh.

"Well said, sir. We do have a chain-mail model from the same line. Very resilient. And a padded-leather interior."

"Ye've got me attention," said Gorm. The clerk nodded and headed out back.

Niln and Gorm watched the other heroes moving through the store, browsing racks that bristled with every sort of weapon imaginable. Laruna and Jynn hovered around a collection of staves. Heraldin was experimenting with glass globes that burst into brightly colored clouds when thrown to the ground. Gaist stood, arms crossed, in front of a huge rack of knives and swords, while Kaitha browsed through a collection of bows. Gleebek roamed aimlessly throughout the store, followed by an uproar of sound and light as weapons sang, leaped, lit aflame, and glowed various colors whenever the Goblin walked too close.

"What was it you and the clerk were discussing?" said Niln. "About running heavily or being punished?"

"Oh, that? We don't have anyone in heavy armor to get in close and keep a monster busy while the mages kill it," said Gorm. "Instead, we have a ranger and thief—"

"Bard!" yelled Heraldin from across the store.

"Which basically fills the same job twice," Gorm continued. "It's your standard hammer and anvil arrangement, except we're all hammer."

"It's not just about filling jobs," said Niln. "We were chosen by the All Mother. We are all here for a reason."

"Well, unless that reason is to die as a spectacular example of how not to pursue a career in professional heroics, I suggest we gear up. And seein' as we're likely headed for the Myrewood, we'll want armor that's venom- and water-resistant, maybe some flamin' weapons. That sort of thing."

"I've heard it said that gear does not make the hero."

"Aye, but gear does make the hero live longer," said Gorm.

"If you say so," said Niln's voice. His face very clearly said, *but it's not supposed to be this way.*

Gorm remembered seeing the world through similar lenses. There was a time when he once thought heroes could set out from home with little more than a walking stick and a plucky attitude and return a few short years later stronger, wiser, and rich enough to bleed silver. Back then, he thought character and perseverance brought a hero through a quest, rather than flaming weapons or enchanted armor. But those dreams died quickly in the world of professional heroics, as did the adventurers who held on to such ideals too tightly.

He put a hand on Niln's shoulder. "You're still thinking like it's a story, lad," he said. "This ain't a legend. It's a job. A career. Ye need to set aside your ideas about what should be and start thinking about it like a professional. Quests succeed and fail now, lad. Right now, before the heroes are on the road. Because a party of heroes is like a Gnomish flame cannon: give it the right chemistry, point it in the right direction, and it'll do wonders. Do any one part wrong, and the whole thing blows up in your face."

Gorm waved a hand out at the retail armory. "This here is the chemistry part. This is where ye get the right team filling the right roles and wearing the right gear; it's all got to come together in this strange alchemy that fuses a small mob of sell-swords into a company of heroes."

Niln struggled to take in the advice. "I will try to learn," he managed.

The clerk returned with a fine suit of chain mail. The armor felt light and comfortable when he tried it on, but it was strong enough to shatter the fist of a training golem that punched it. Gorm added it to the pile of purchases the other heroes were heaping upon the counter. The clerk hummed happily as he made an additional note on the heroes' tallysheet.

"And I suppose you're expecting me to ensure that the temple sees to the bill," Niln said to Gorm.

Gorm grinned. "Well, we're all here for a reason."

Laruna tried to act naturally as she made her way through the aisles of The General Store. Kaitha hadn't given her any reason not to be comfortable, after all; Laruna had met many famous heroes, and few had been as down to Arth as the Elf seemed to be.

Still, this was the Jade Wind, the ranger who had helped clear the Temple of Elemental Unpleasantness, the scourge of the Slave Lords of the White Sea, the heroine who brought down the Duchess of Jackals. In her heyday, the Jade Wind had been a legend even among her peers. And now she was standing just down the aisle from Laruna, loading a market basket with vials from a shelf of health potions. How could Laruna not be nervous?

"That's a lot of healing potions," Laruna said, immediately cursing her awkwardness under her breath.

The ranger glanced at her and shrugged. "You have to be prepared in the field. Accidents and ambushes happen."

"Buying anything else?"

Kaitha glanced through her basket. "Just a Poor Man's Quiver," she said, pulling out a plain leather quiver with a single protruding arrow.

"Why do they call it a Poor Man's Quiver?"

"Two reasons," said the Elf. She drew the arrow from the quiver and set it on the shelf, and then nodded back to the quiver.

"Wow," said Laruna.

"It's always got one arrow," said Kaitha, drawing forth the quiver's lone arrow. Another lone arrow sprouted behind it.

"That's some expensive enchantment," whistled Laruna.

"That's the other reason it's called a Poor Man's Quiver. After you've bought one, you're poor." The Elf nodded to Niln, who was up at the weapons counter with Gorm. "Professional tip? Always buy your best gear on a well-financed project."

"Good idea," said Laruna. Emboldened by camaraderie, she added, "I'm sorry if you get sick of hearing this, but can I just say that I'm a great admirer of your work. Any pointers you can give me are much appreciated."

Kaitha seemed to scrutinize her for a moment, though it was common for Elves to do so. As strange as the fair folk often seemed to Humans, Laruna reminded herself that from an Elven perspective, Humans seemed remarkably difficult to keep track of. One of her Elven professors at the academy had frequently mistaken Laruna's classmate for his ancestors.

"Don't let anybody take advantage of you," said Kaitha eventually.

"Excuse me?"

"You're young. You still have that sparkle in your eye, that drive to go out and save the day and let the rest sort itself out. But when you think like that, people can take advantage." The Elf got a distant look in her eye. "Employers want your services. Agents want a cut of your pay. Companies want your image to sell their products. And men want, well, what men always want. If you're not careful, you give yourself away for less than you're worth. You trust people that you shouldn't. You play with fire, and you get burned."

The ranger shook her head and gave Laruna a small smile. "That's my tip. Don't get burned."

"Oh, I usually don't get burned," said Laruna. "In any sense of the word. I was more looking for things like fighting advice and keys to advancement."

"Oh … that. Just survive. Live through enough quests, and you'll rank up. For a strong heroine with your kind of magic, that's the easy part. But if you do that long enough, eventually you learn that your job isn't about being self-sufficient in the wild or defending the weak or the pursuit of justice. Really, we just kill things for money. And when that finally starts to sink in, you face the hard part of professional heroics: the big questions."

"The big questions?"

"Yeah. Is there more to life than just killing and looting? Are we more than just numbers in some Guild Master's ledger, statistics written on our license? And the big one, the one that haunts you every night on the job: Why are we doing this anyway?"

"Why are we doing this anyway?" Heraldin asked.

"We're following a lead," said Gorm. He led the other heroes through the back alleys of Sculpin Down, a craggy slum shrouded in the shadow of the Ridge.

"I thought the lead pointed us to the Myrewood," said Kaitha,

"That would probably be preferable," said Jynn, stepping over a figure slumped in the street.

"Well, the smell wouldn't be so bad," said Heraldin. Sculpin Down had an unenviable position, sitting just above the stream where the stockyard waste met the city sewers. The sorcerous devices employed by the League of Sewer Workers kept most of the district merely unpleasant, but small faults in the system left pockets of stench powerful enough to bring tears to the eyes.

"We follow all our leads," said Gorm, shrugging off their complaints. He'd never worked in a party of heroes that could entirely agree on what to have for breakfast, let alone how to complete a quest. Managing egos was as much a part of the job as slaying monsters, and often far less pleasant. The other heroes could gripe and complain until they were bluer than a Slaugh in summer, so long as they got in line.

They walked along one of Sculpin Down's fouler alleys, which teemed with unsavory characters. The beggars carried daggers here. Glowing eyes watched from every corner. Gorm tried asking for help finding One-of-Each Magrash, but his inquiries earned him little but sneers and snarls from retreating figures.

A coven of three omnimancers walked by, drawing dark looks from Jynn and Laruna. Mages of the Twilight Order had sided with the Sten in ancient ages, and they had been all but wiped out for it. Now the third order of wizardry was nothing but an informal gathering of those mages cursed with the ability to touch both solamancy and noctomancy, but without the decency to suppress it.

The alleyway opened up into a small cobblestone square with a broken fountain at the center. Even for the late hour, the square seemed preternaturally empty. Its only inhabitant was an old man in black robes who sat near an alcove carved into the base of the next tier up, laughing sporadically. A blood-red light flickered behind him, casting ominous shadows in the falling twilight.

"Where are you going?" Niln asked when Gorm started crossing the square.

"To see if he knows where Magrash is," Gorm said.

The man in the distance cackled. "So long!" he screeched to himself. "Off you go! I bet you didn't see that coming!"

"You don't set much of a standard for whom you'll seek out for advice, do you?" said Heraldin.

"Of course I do. Ye just don't meet it." Gorm headed toward the strange man.

The red light turned out to be coming from a statue set within the alcove. It was a granite representation of a skeleton seated on a small chair, its fleshless hands steepled beneath its lipless grin. A shrine of Mordo Ogg, the god of death.

Tiny crimson pinpoints intermittently flared within the skull's eye sockets, prompting hoots of delight and comments from the robed man. It took a special kind of person to serve the Lord of the End — the same variety that made undertakers smile politely and edge toward the door.

"There goes another one," the man told Gorm as the sculpture's eyes flared again.

"Another what?" Gorm asked, against his better judgment.

"You can't really tell. Could be a man, could be a Shadowkin. Don't matter. They're off to meet the Master."

"That's people dying?" Laruna stared at the crimson light.

"Just one," said the man. "Oop. And another. And there's another!"

"But—"

"There goes another," said the man, flashing a grin that displayed as many gaps as teeth. "Name's Ignatius. A humble priest of Mordo Ogg, at your service."

"Gorm Ingerson. Ever hear of an Orc named Magrash?"

"Old One-of-Each? Course I know him. I—oop! We got a fighter."

The lights in the shrine were glowing steadily, becoming more crimson with each passing second.

"Sometimes they don't want to go wherever it is they're off to," said Ignatius with a chuckle. "They try to fight old Mordo Ogg. He don't much care for that, does he? There it goes."

The lights winked out. A moment later, they resumed their irregular flashing.

"I can see why this square is so empty," said Niln.

"Ye were saying?" Gorm prompted Ignatius. "About Magrash?"

In between particularly interesting flashes from the shrine's eyes, Ignatius informed the heroes that One-of-Each Magrash was generally to be found at Moira's, a tavern just outside Sculpin Down's West Gate. Gorm thanked the priest, and the heroes hurried from the square.

Moira's was marked by a simple sign painted with a white tree. Inside, the fire hissed and crackled as it died in the heap of bricks that had once been a fireplace. Several figures were bent over lonely tables, nursing beers and drowning sorrows.

Gorm and the other heroes sat at a big table in the back corner and ordered a round of drinks and an assortment of breads, cheeses, and dried meats. Gorm taught Gleebek the proper way to make a sandwich, which is to ensure that the meat is thicker than the bread. Kaitha and Laruna compared wines, and found them both lacking.

The atmosphere was lackluster and the food worse, but the heroes were enjoying themselves nonetheless, glad to be done with training for the day.

Heraldin, however, found a thrones board and started setting up a game between himself and Gaist. "I think you'll find that I've some new tricks, my friend. Your move first this time."

Gaist glanced at Heraldin, advanced a bannerman, and turned back to staring into the center of the room.

"Haven't you had enough of that game?" asked Laruna.

"I'll be finished once I've tasted victory," said the bard, advancing his own piece. "I think tonight is my night. I've figured out the trick."

"Oh?" asked Niln.

"Yes. In thrones, if you move atop an enemy piece you kill it, but if you leave it only one safe move, it becomes your own. At first, I thought I should just steal all the pieces I could, but that left me with too few moves, and Gaist just took them back. So I killed all the pieces I could, but clearing the board gave him enough maneuverability to steal my pieces. The trick is knowing when to steal a piece, and when to go for the kill."

"Seem like you're learning something after all," said Gorm.

"I'll have you know I pick things up rather quickly, if I do say … if I … I …" Heraldin trailed off as Gaist advanced a knight. "All right, why would you move there? What are you doing now? How does that even make sense?"

Gaist's stoicism had a hint of smugness about it.

It was more than a little amusing to watch the bard learn his place, but Gorm was here on business. He looked around the tavern. A few Orcs stood about the bar, green-skinned and square-jawed, and Gorm quickly saw that one of them was Magrash himself.

It was hard to misidentify One-of-Each Magrash, a wrinkled, gray-haired Orc with an eyepatch that kept slipping because one of his ears was missing. Only one tusk protruded from his lower jaw. His left hand was a metal hook. His right leg ended in a peg.

"I found my source," Gorm told the other heroes. "I'll be back."

"Look who's splitting the party," said Kaitha. "And I thought you were pro."

"Ha! Right," grinned Gorm.

"What are you talking about?" asked Niln. "Is there some sort of problem?"

"No, no," said Gorm. "I ain't splitting the party. She's making a joke, lad."

"So splitting the party is bad, then?" said Niln.

"You never split the party," said Laruna.

"It's right in the *Heroes' Guild Handbook*," said Jynn.

"Someone always wanders off to grab something shiny or test a lever or something, and the next thing you know they're coming back with some horrible monster following them," said Kaitha.

"Usually when you're in the middle of a massive fight with something else," said Gorm.

"If they come back at all," said Heraldin.

"I remember in the Tomb of the Horortep, a rogue snuck off to grab a statue he saw, and wound up sprinting back with three stone golem guardians on his heels while we were trying to get over a pit trap," said Kaitha. "Lucky for us, the pit was deep and golems have poor balance."

"I got a story that will top that one when I get back." Gorm laughed.

He made his way across the bar. The air was thick with smoke from the back kitchen. The Orc's one good eye was filled with mistrust and apprehension as Gorm approached.

"You One-of-Each Magrash?"

"If I wasn't, that'd be a good name for me," said Magrash. "Who wants to know?"

"Nobody in particular," said Gorm. He dropped a coin purse on the table as he sat down. "Just someone looking for information."

Magrash looked back at the table where Kaitha and the others were laughing at some story or another. "I don't want no business with heroes," he said.

"Look, ye can see I got more than enough muscle back there to get my answers," said Gorm, "but doing things that way means paperwork, and guild reviews, and all sorts of other hassles. I'd much rather ye take this here thirty giltin, answer a few questions, and get back to drinking. But it's your choice."

Magrash further scrutinized the party. "You got a Goblin with you."

"That's me squire."

"You the one who sent the Elven guardsman to the healers?"

"I … he didn't go to … How did ye hear about that?"

"It's all over the city. Is it true that you did it because he insulted the Goblin?"

"Look, I don't need that getting around, not anymore than it is."

Magrash's demeanor warmed noticeably. "What do you want to know?"

"I'm looking for info on the Leviathan Project."

Surprise flashed in Magrash's eye, but he recovered quickly. "Let's talk outside," he said, nodding toward the door.

The alley out back of Moira's was illuminated only by the full moon. A light flared in the darkness as Magrash lit a cigarette.

"People hear you talkin' about the Leviathan Project to me, and I'm going to get my noncombatant papers revoked," said Magrash.

"Why?"

"You can't be an NPC if you used to work for a villain," said Magrash. "Run around with a bloodthirsty warband of Shadowfolk all you like, and they'll take you with open arms. But lift some boxes for a Lightling that's gone foe, and twenty-five years later you're still unclean. Oh, hang on."

Magrash hobbled over to Moira's back door and stomped on a thick, meaty tentacle. Something beneath them shrieked in displeasure as the rubbery appendage retreated through a sewer grate.

"Thrice-cursed Krakens," Magrash grumbled as he hobbled back. "Sure, they're cute when they're the size of your hand and they'll sit on the shoulder, but people always dump 'em down the sewer once they start going after cats. And then who do you suppose has to deal with them? The lowly sewer worker, that's who."

"There's more than one of them in the sewers?" Gorm asked.

"There's far more and far worse than those watching from the water," said Magrash. "Heroes clean the sewers out every few years, but new critters come up from the depths or down from the top all the time. Still, monsters are better than taxpayers, right?"

"Sorry?"

"Both will try to squeeze the life out of you, but you can take an axe to the monsters. Ha ha! Sorry. Little civil servant humor there. What were you talking about?"

"I didn't know the Leviathan Project was run by a villain."

"Not just one. All the big wizards from back then: Detarr Ur'Mayan, Teldir of Umbrax, Aya of Blades, Win Cinder, Az'Anon."

"Az'Anon the Spider King?" A chill ran up Gorm's spine at the thought of the dark wizard who had ended his career.

"Well, they called him Az'Anon the Black back then," said Magrash. "It was before his trip to Nagarok, when he was just one of the five on the Leviathan Project, or so I hear."

"Ye didn't work on the project, then?"

"No. Had a brother who was on it, working for Detarr Ur'Mayan. He'd tell me about it and try to recruit me. Back then, I was a warrior with my tribe, and we raided the Lightling towns from the Eboncrags down to Knifevale."

"So can I talk to your brother?" said Gorm.

Magrash shook his head with a sigh. "He got killed. Was on the first floor of the tower when Johan the High-and-Mighty came to chop off Detarr's head. Bloody hero didn't even care about the Leviathan business either. He only wanted that fat queen of yours to marry Handor instead of Detarr's boy.

"I figured it was only a matter of time before the heroes came for my tribe too. Put in for my noncombatant papers the next day. Thought

I'd be safer." Magrash gave a dark, mirthless laugh. "See how well that turned out? I was just One-Eye Magrash before I started working the sewers."

"Know anyone I could talk to who worked on the Leviathan Project?" Gorm asked.

"I can give you a name, but if it gets out he was on the project, both he and I are as good as hung."

Gorm nodded. For NPCs, guilt by association was a capital offense.

"Head to Bloodroot," whispered Magrash.

"Bloodroot?"

"It's a town up by the border with Ruskan. Old beet-farming village. It used to be called the Baetwolds till a tribe of NPC Orcs took it over. Look for Ghabrang. He's your Orc."

"I may do that," said Gorm, hoping he'd never have to. "Any chance ye know anything about how the Elven Marbles got wrapped up in all of this?"

Magrash snorted. "The stolen burial stones? I don't know what they'd have to do with Project Leviathan. The noctomancers collected a lot of random stuff for the project. Why?"

"They were stolen. Er, again. We're on a fetch quest for 'em."

"I did hear they went missing on the road from Scoria. Usually, that's a very safe road."

"Ye know somethin' else?"

Magrash considered Gorm carefully. "Not for sure. But I did hear that a band of Lizardmen drove some omnimancers out of an old tower out by the Sudden River a couple of weeks ago. That's just a few days off the road to Scoria. Sounds like something they could have done."

"Probably coincidence," said Gorm.

"Could be," said Magrash. "But a lead's a lead."

Gorm tossed the giltin to the Orc with a word of thanks.

His mind raced as he headed back into the tavern. He'd never suspected a connection between Detarr and Az'Anon, aside from the hero who slew them, but apparently they had collaborated with the most evil wizards of their time for art theft. And now someone else wanted the stones, though all of the wizards that Magrash had mentioned were long dead. Was someone starting the Leviathan Project again? Would that even matter? For all Gorm knew, the project was an underground museum putting Orcish relics on exhibit.

The other heroes were still comparing tales of past quests when Gorm sat down at the table.

"I'd blasted both of his legs and one of his arms off, and we planned to just leave him, right?" Laruna was saying. "So we started to head out, and the crazy blighter starts true forming!"

"What's true forming?" Niln asked amid the heroes' laughter.

"Oh, you think you've defeated me," mimicked Kaitha, "but now let me show you my true form! Har har har!"

"For some reason, I let you break my Human body and trash half of my lair before I really started fighting! Bwa ha ha!" said Laruna. "Gods, it's annoying."

"So what happened?" asked Niln, interrupting the heroes' mirth.

"What?" asked Laruna, wiping a tear from her eye.

"With the warlord in the volcano? What happened when he true formed?"

Laruna looked uncomfortable. "Oh, er, he turned into a two-story-tall demonic slug, ate our rogue and our priestess, and crippled our fighter before we put him down."

The laughter at the table withered into an awkward silence.

"That's horrible," said Niln eventually.

"That's professional heroics," said Gorm darkly. "Kill and loot until you're killed and looted."

"Yes, well, it's risky, but the work we do is important," said Kaitha.

"We're keeping the world safe," said Heraldin.

"Are we now?" asked Jynn. "It seems to me the Dwarf had the right of it. In the end, this is all about gold."

"It's about keeping citizens safe," said Laruna.

"Then why is the Myrewood infested? Why isn't the Underdim cleared?" asked Jynn. "Why is nobody killing the impoverished monsters? Because it's for the gold."

The horrible silence returned, leaving each hero to think of the implications of the wizard's words.

Gorm shook his head. "Wasn't always this way. I took me first jobs for free. Me master in the Brotherhood was a hero, and he worked for almost nothing. Saved a whole city for supper once. Things should … if they could just go back to the way they was …" He trailed off into silence.

"They can't," said Jynn. "Surely you're familiar with our gross domestic product."

"Of course I am. Why do ye think I'm drinking imported?" said Gorm, shaking his tankard at the noctomancer. "What's that got to do with anything?"

"No, I mean our GDP — the total value of everything that's made or done in the Freelands. It's a big number, but if you break it down, four out of every ten giltin are linked with professional heroics."

"Forty percent of the economy is loot?" said Kaitha.

"Loot, or plunder funds, or weapons and armor manufacturing, or potion brewers, or inns that cater to adventurers, or hoard-appraising, and so on," said the noctomancer. "There's a lot of work done and products sold to support questing heroes. If we stopped, what happens to the workers and the sellers? They'd lose everything. They'd starve in the streets."

"You think it would be that bad?" said Laruna.

"Is there a good way to be bankrupt?" said Jynn.

"Morally," suggested Heraldin.

"Professional heroes defend a portion of the population from poverty at the expense of other parts of it," said Jynn.

"That's not why we're here," said Niln.

"Well, I'm here because your mercenaries strong-armed me into joining the guild. I'd never have been a bloody hero otherwise."

Everyone stared in shock at Jynn's forthrightness. Gaist gently took the wizard's tankard away.

"Sorry," mumbled Jynn. "But you know it's true."

Doubt was creeping into the heroes' faces. Even Niln was faltering.

Gorm could feel them slipping off course. "Well, it don't have to be," Gorm said. "It don't matter how we got here, or what the whole economy is doing with gross products, or anything. What matters is what we do, and why we do it. Maybe we can't save the world, but maybe we'll make the world a tiny bit better."

He could see a spark of hope retuning to the other heroes. He nodded to Niln.

"Oh, er, right!" said Niln. "I know we didn't meet under the best circumstances, but I know we are a part of something bigger than a few gold coins. Bigger than any of us. We can accomplish great things, my friends."

Gorm raised his tankard. "To saving the world."

The other heroes raised their drinks as well and toasted to heroic deeds, and a measure of mirth and happiness returned as they drank.

Gorm drank as well, and smiled and laughed with them. But the joy didn't return for him. All he could think of was why he was really on this quest: for the money, and for the fame, and for the past he so desperately wanted to bring back.

Poldo stood a few feet from the table, clutching a packet of charts and drawings. He absently fidgeted with his spectacles and groomed his mustache. He was always nervous when meeting with Mr. Goldson and Mr. Baggs, but they weren't the only important figures sitting at the table a few feet away. King Handor sat at the table, flanked by Johan the Mighty — the champion of Tandos — and Weaver Ortson, the grandmaster and high councilor of the Heroes' Guild.

The dinner was ostensibly a casual evening wherein the king was hosting some old friends. They sat in comfortable leather chairs before a cozy fire in an old study high in Castle Andarun. While the meal was certainly informal, Poldo noted that conversation turned to business before the end of the soup course.

"We have heard that Your Majesty was considering a tax on loot by professional heroes," Baggs said with a disarming smile.

"If by considering it, you mean I'm days from enacting it, then yes," said Handor.

"But, sire," Goldson said. "Surely that will jeopardize much of the prosperity we've all worked so hard for. Poldo, the charts, if you will."

Poldo stepped forward.

"Save your charts," said the king. "I've seen plenty of charts."

Poldo stepped back.

"Tax revenues from professional heroics are down by a tenth," Handor said frankly. "And the rebuilding costs for collateral damage caused by monsters and questing heroes are up by a quarter. The kingdom's coffers can't take it."

Baggs intervened. "Majesty, nobody benefits from the current situation—"

"You seem to be handling it quite well," Johan said. "Ha! I hear your revenues are up seven percent."

"Six, Your Honor," corrected Goldson.

"I imagine that was helped by the Griffin of Whitegeld," said Handor.

"I'm sorry, Your Majesty, I'm unfamiliar with that particular quest," said Baggs.

"Oh? Well I'm sure your Gnome has a chart for that. Right, Scribkin? Do you have anything on the Griffin of Whitegeld?"

Poldo stepped forward.

"That won't be necessary, Poldo," snapped Goldson. "I do recall something of the case, Your Majesty."

Poldo stepped back.

"Let me refresh your memory," said the king. "Adventure Capital estimated the griffin's hoard to be worth more than a hundred thousand giltin, and investors spent over eighty thousand for the rights to its loot. And when your heroes put the beast down last week, it had nothing but a broken shield and some beads. The whole quest brought in eighty-seven giltin, and that only after the carcass was sold to a tannery."

"Sire—" Goldson attempted, but Handor could not be stopped mid-charge.

"The city-state of Whitegeld pocketed sixty thousand giltin, Adventure Capital walked off with twenty thousand more in fees, and investors got back eighty-seven giltin. The Royal Guards' pension had invested huge sums of gold in the project and walked away with half a week's wages. Now old Guine has to work for another two years!" The king pointed to a leathery bannerman in rusted armor that rattled with each geriatric shake.

Goldson and Baggs wrestled their faces into a reasonable facsimile of empathy and nodded at the old soldier. "Your Majesty, we're aware of current hardships, and we're sorry for the losses," said Baggs. "But everyone involved understands that risk is inherent in the system. We all would have shared in the gains, and sadly we all must share in the loss."

"Recall that our business had to hire six heroes," continued Goldson, "equip them with expensive magical gear, and pay a portion of the death benefit for the two who gave their lives slaying the griffin. It's a considerable expense."

"Ah yes, that," said the king. "Mr. Ortson, can you tell me how much Adventure Capital paid in expenses for the quest to slay the Griffin of Whitegeld?"

Weaver Ortson was caught with a mouthful of bread and soup dribbling through his straggly beard. "Ahem, yes," he said, swallowing and using a napkin. "Er, I believe it was fifteen thousand, one hundred and two giltin, Your Majesty."

"Thank you, Mr. Ortson," said Handor.

"And worth every copper, Your Majesty," said Ortson. "Our heroes are putting their lives on the line every day for the sake of the kingdom and its citizens."

"Yes, thank you, Weaver. We're all familiar with the Heroes' Guild," said the king. "Now then, Mr. Goldson, twenty thousand in fees, minus expenses, sounds like almost five thousand giltin in profit to me, which is quite above what one would expect for a quest that cost investors tens of thousands."

"Sire, please!" Baggs protested. "Remember that we were projecting a much larger hoard, which would have allowed us a share of the net loot."

"Meaning that our profits were about a fifth of what we expected, Your Grace," pressed Goldson hurriedly. "That drives our stock price down, making our company as a whole worth less."

"Which is just as bad as a loss," said Baggs.

"Perhaps even worse," finished Goldson.

"Nearly," said the king, with pointed doubt. "Regardless, in recent years you've profited from the public's gold. The only hoards that have met your projections have belonged to monsters that ransacked city-states and towns, and those are the very beasts that burden kingdom coffers with heavy repair bills."

"If that is the case, sire, taxing loot will hardly fix the problem," said Goldson.

"You could have covered the expenses for damage that way years ago, but not in today's adventuring climate," agreed Baggs. "Poldo, if you'd bring the charts ..."

Poldo stepped forward.

"There's no need for that. I think we all know that loot isn't what it used to be," said Handor.

Poldo stepped back.

"And that's precisely why I also plan to tax profits from the sale of looting rights."

The little color that remained in Goldson's face drained away. "Sire, that ... that would be ... disastrous."

"Would it?" Handor asked with a wry smile. "For whom?"

"Your Majesty, think of the consequences," wheezed Baggs. "The kingdom's coffers may swell, but the losses sustained by city-states and businesses would be phenomenal. Everyone from sewer-urchins to Poldo here would find their jobs in jeopardy!"

Poldo nearly dropped his charts.

"The problem, sire, isn't tax policy," said Goldson. "Professional heroics have never generated revenue for the kingdom directly. Rather, heroics promote economic growth and reduce city-states' dependence on kingdom funding. The recent loot situation has just made that more difficult."

"Much more difficult," added Mr. Ortson.

"That's why our side project is so important," said Baggs. "If successful, we could return professional heroics to where it was twenty years ago. We could experience that kind of growth and mutual prosperity again."

"Perhaps we should hold off instituting taxes until after we see the results of the project," suggested Goldson.

Handor pursed his lips. "The plan may fail."

"We have a contingency," said Ortson.

"The one you told me about, Johan?"

"Indeed, sire," said Johan.

The king nodded and fell back into thought.

"Speaking of which," Johan said. "I had to deal with an incident at the Elven Embassy today. One of the Al'Matrans' Seven Heroes beat the captain of the Elven guard senseless for insulting a Goblin."

Poldo wasn't sure why, but the champion's anecdote improved the mood at the table. Mr. Goldson even allowed himself a small smile.

"Very well," said the king. "We shall wait until after the project to assess our tax situation."

"A wise choice, sire," said Mr. Baggs.

The king turned his eyes to Poldo. "I think I shall see those charts after all, if you please."

Poldo nodded and stepped forward.

"So … uh … the bandits were sighted north of Ebenmyre by …" Niln paused to scan a page from the Elven Embassy's dossier. "A ranger. Right? Yes."

Gorm rubbed his temples. He had hoped the high scribe might be better at strategy than at fighting, but watching Niln try to run a meeting was downright painful. The alleged Seventh Hero looked like he would rather be taking a sound beating from the training golems than mired in the Al'Matran temple's small conference room, floundering amid the papers and files he had scattered across the table.

"But the Myrewood is … I mean, if we didn't have to go there …"

"Of course we don't have to go there," snapped Heraldin impatiently. "In fact, assuming we like breathing, we probably shouldn't go there. We should look anywhere else."

"But the Myrewood is where the marbles probably are," said Laruna.

Gorm really didn't want to intervene. A party of heroes needed a clear voice of leadership; any sign of split authority or divided loyalties could send a quest spiraling into constant bickering about the best course of action, the best strategy for combat, or even the best tavern for the evening meal. That bickering could quickly descend into open fighting, and eventually inter-party violence. Gorm had seen it happen in too many parties.

No, the party needed to have one leader, and given that Niln held the purse strings, the contracts, and the backing of the Heroes' Guild, it was best for that leader to be the high scribe. Still, taking charge of a situation didn't seem to be Niln's strong suit.

"Um … there's also the tip about the Leviathan Project with the … the, uh, Orcs," said Niln.

"We don't want to spend a lot time on false leads," said Kaitha.

"I'd rather spend my time on any kind of lead than have it cut short in the Myrewood," said Jynn.

"Then go back to hiding in your tower, Rank One," sneered Laruna, prompting the meeting to degenerate into a shouting match.

"Uh … excuse me. If we could just …" Niln shot Gorm the desperate look of a drowning man.

Shaking his head, Gorm answered the scribe's unspoken plea. "All right! Enough," he barked.

The table fell into a sullen silence as Gorm glared at each of the other heroes in turn. "Now, the way I see it, we got three leads. The Elves think they know the marbles are a short ways into the Myrewood, where we may run into a fight we can't survive. Magrash thinks they might be with some Lizardmen in a tower by the Sudden River. Now, that's a fight for sure, but I'm hopin' we can at least handle a band of Lizardmen. And if those ain't good enough, we might get some insight about the marbles if we dig into this so-called Leviathan Project in Bloodroot. Most of the Orcs there are NPCs, so it's as safe as Orcs get — which still ain't that safe."

He pushed several of the papers aside and planted his finger firmly on a map of the Freedlands. "Our best chance of finding the marbles is our most dangerous. Our safest option probably won't get us much more than their backstory. But the middle option" — he plunked a finger down on the thin blue strip that represented the Sudden River — "only takes us a day or two off course if we're headed to either the Myrewood or Bloodroot."

"So we should go there," said Niln.

"If ye say so," said Gorm, sitting back and giving the priest an encouraging nod.

"Ah, right," said the high scribe. "So, we'll go to the tower, and then move on to the Myrewood, right? Right? So next … we should talk about …"

"Preparations," prompted Kaitha.

"Preparations! Right!" said the high scribe. "Er, how do you think we should prepare?"

All eyes turned to Gorm. He sighed, but split authority was better than no authority at all. "All right, here's what we need …"

Chapter 9

"Kaitha," Gorm said, knocking. "It's mornin'."

He knocked several more times before the oak door to Kaitha's bedchambers finally opened enough for the Elf to poke her bedraggled head out of the door. "Mrmhermm?" she asked.

"It's time to go."

"Hrmm?"

"To the Myrewood? On the quest?" exclaimed Gorm.

The ranger winced. "Shhh … jus' … shh."

"Are ye not ready? The whole caravan is waiting for—" Words failed Gorm as he pushed the door open. Kaitha was still wrapped in a bedsheet. The room was a wreck, littered with bottles and armor and debris. "What happened in here?"

"I needed li'l more … li'l more drink," slurred Kaitha. "I needed take th' edge off."

"Are ye still drunk? After all night?"

"Jus' a li'l more," Kaitha insisted. "'Sides, we don' leave 'fore sunup."

"The sun's been up an hour!"

"Then you're late." Kaitha burped. "Shoulda … shoulda got me an hour ago."

"What the burnin' hells happened? Ye were supposed to be keeping it together!"

"Hey! First've all, I'm up before noon," said Kaitha. "Point B, I woke up alone. An' number four, I'm still stand—oop." The ranger tripped over her blankets and toppled onto the bed.

Gorm rubbed his temples. The heroes were behind schedule; now it was doubtful they'd leave much before lunch.

"Okay, I admit I'm not standing," said Kaitha. "This is still going pretty good. For me."

"Well, ye need to do better!" barked Gorm. "This is the kind of stunt that gets heroes fired or killed. Or both."

Kaitha leaned over the side of her bed and heaved into an empty chamber pot.

"Bloody bones of thrice-cursed gods," swore Gorm. "Gleebek!"

"Gleebek?" The Goblin poked his head in the door.

"I need water here."

"Grot?"

"You know. Water? Drink? Water?" said Gorm, panto-miming with his free hand. "We need to clean her up."

"Dig ra'root zuggog …" The Goblin hurried away.

"I'm sorry," said Kaitha, in between violent fits of heaving. "I know it's bad. I know. I'll do better. I'm sorry."

"See that ye do," said Gorm. A part of him envied Kaitha, the part that still wanted to seek peace at the bottom of a bottle. The rest of him, however, needed to get this quest on track, and he was relying on the ranger to help it stay that way. It was too early for this.

Still, Gorm had been pulled from his fair share of gutters. Heaving something between a growl and a sigh, he hoisted Kaitha into a better position and started cleaning her off.

She scrutinized him through bleary eyes. "Your armor … your armor looks bad. Messy."

"I tried havin' Gleebek polish me gear."

"Really? It doesn't look like … did he shine any of it?"

"I ain't sure. Depends on how far he got before he drank the armor polish."

"Ah." Kaitha looked Gorm's outfit over with an appraising eye. "He's not a very good squire, is—?"

"Worst squire in history," said Gorm.

Gleebek returned a moment later. *"Da dibitz ska gluggoo,"* he said, presenting a bottle of wine.

"Good Goblin," said Kaitha. "Give it here."

"What the bloody bones are ye doing?" hollered Gorm. He snatched the bottle away and instructed Gleebek to watch Kaitha in his stead. "Here. Ye help her get clean. Lass, we leave in an hour if I have to tie ye to your horse. Understand?"

"Guz'pootig Hupsa!"

Kaitha nodded, and then bent over the bed for another round of hurling.

Gorm stormed down the hall. What kind of quest was this going to be if they couldn't get to the city walls without the party falling apart?

He stopped a passing acolyte, handed her the wine, and instructed her to bring a bowl of water to Kaitha's chambers. Then he headed back to the temple's stables to see how the others were progressing.

The Al'Matrans were holding a small ceremony for Niln in the courtyard, although few of the attendants and none of the heroes seemed to be paying attention to the affair. Most were preoccupied with getting the heroes' mounts and gear ready for the journey. Gaist sat perfectly still atop a rather unnerved-looking mare, all of his gear in place. The mages and Heraldin were still adjusting their equipment or seeing to the horses. Gorm's own horse was prepared, as was a mule for Gleebek to ride.

"Today is an auspicious occasion," High Scribe Pathalan announced loudly, waving a scepter with a falcon's head over Niln. "We celebrate the departure of Scribe Niln and his company of heroes."

"I think he meant that to sound differently," Laruna muttered to Gorm.

"I ain't sure he did," Gorm told her. "Come on. We've much to do."

And yea, the Heroes did set forth on their journey to retrieve yon Burial Stones of the Sons of Ogh Magerd, which the Orcs called Gargaist dur Garg, and the Elves called the Elven Marbles.

Niln wrote his latest scriptures by the light of a traveler's lantern, scrawling them in a small volume, a condensed copy of the *Second Book of Niln (A Worke in Progress)*. The high scribe had left his library at home, with the exceptions of the first and second Books of Niln and an old leather journal in which he had collected the prophecies of the Seventh Hero.

> *And for three days and three nights they did journey, and stay at heroes' inns and taverns along the way.*

It was initially surprising to Niln that there were inns and taverns that catered especially to professional heroes. Most of them just carried extra large stocks of ale, nailed down the bar stools, and fireproofed the rooms, although one of the more upscale establishments offered amenities such as masseuses, equipment repair and cleaning, workshops for skilled heroes to create and upkeep their own gear or potions, and more.

When they'd stayed in Vala's Song, a luxurious tavern complex with a fully stocked study and incredibly comfortable chairs, the goddess had been silent. Now that they were out on the open plain with nowhere to sit and write but a lumpy rock in his canvas tent, the scriptures flowed freely.

> *And on the fourth day, as the Heroes did cross yon Plains of Bahn they did encounter a Venomous Scarg.*

A Venomous Scarg, Niln learned, was a nasty sort of giant burrowing bat, with poisoned fangs and beady scarlet eyes. Jynn explained later that scargs are nocturnal scavengers that only attack solitary, helpless prey, and thus the specimen that had burst from the ground in front of Gorm's horse was most likely startled awake rather than springing an ambush. Whatever the scarg's intentions, the results were equally traumatic.

> *Gorm Son of Inger didst draw his axe, and set to smite yon Scarg a mighty blowe. But Laruna Trullon did loose a fiery Spelle at the Scarg at the same time, and Gorm did fall from his horse.*

It was more like the Dwarf dove to the ground, Niln noted. A split second later and Gorm would have been burned to a crisp.

144

The Scarg did fly 'twixt the Wizard Jynn and the Mage Laruna, and they did cast their Spelles Hastily, and each did blast the other from their steeds. And the Wizard Jynn did fly into the High Scribe Niln, who fell into the Bard Heraldin, who was holding a Grenade of Smoke, which he dropped upon the ground.

Niln nodded. He had been wondering what, exactly, had happened there. One moment, he had been shouting to Gorm, and the next moment he was on the ground in a cloud of blue-black smoke.

And yon fumes from the Bard's grenade didst choke Kaitha of House Tyrieth, so that her arrow flew wild. And it struck the Warrior Gaist upon the back of the thigh.

This was a slight discrepancy, but only because the scriptures generally didn't mention one's rear end.

And so Gaist did fall upon the Mage Laruna. Laruna was blinded by yon smoke, and did assume it was the Scarg atop her, and she did throwe many a mighty fireball in response. And the other Heroes did flee from her wrath.

Only Gleebek made it away unscathed, Niln recalled, and that was because Gorm had instructed the Goblin to avoid the fight. Most of the heroes had needed a healing potion. Kaitha had needed two.

Then the smoke was blown clear, and yon Scarg did fly away with much laughter. And the Heroes were greatly chafed. But Gorm Son of Inger was filled with great wrath, for the Heroes were Not Prepared. And he did decree that they would have Half Rations and Extra Training that night.

Niln acted as though he had agreed with the Dwarf's recommendation, and that it was a mutual decision to impose the rigorous regimen upon the others. In truth, he didn't know if he could have changed Gorm's mind, and he was sure that he didn't want to try.

Still, Niln knew, the Dwarf had more years of questing than Niln had years of living, and his experience was invaluable. There was nothing wrong with letting subordinates utilize their expertise, he told himself.

So the Heroes did train with much intensity that night. And there were No Exceptions, not even for the High Scribe to finish writing his—

"What are ye doing?" Gorm roared, sticking his head into the tent. "You're supposed to be training with Kaitha and Gleebek!"

"I … I needed to write in my scriptures."

"Do it when training's done, and not a moment sooner," barked the Dwarf. "Get out on the field!"

Niln set his book down. "I think that's a good idea," he said, because he wanted to be clear that he was still in charge of this party. Then he hurried from the tent, because he didn't want Gorm to yell again.

"You have to admit, she's pretty impressive," Laruna whispered.

Gorm gave an appreciative nod. Across the clearing, Kaitha moved along the perimeter of a squat, square tower as swiftly and as silently as a breeze. With her long emerald cloak flowing behind her as she darted from window to window, it was easy to see how she'd earned the name Jade Wind. Gorm whistled low as she scaled the exterior of the ruined tower, seemingly without effort, to peer through a third-story window.

"Very impressive," Laruna reiterated.

"When she's sober," Jynn added.

"Which hasn't been as often as one might have anticipated," Niln whispered.

"Well, at least not as often as one might like," said Heraldin.

Gorm nodded with considerably less appreciation. He'd been posting watches over Kaitha since lunch yesterday to make sure she didn't touch a bottle before the raid on the old tower. Still, it was worth it. Kaitha had finished scouting the ruins much faster than he had imagined, and she was already running back to the woods where the seven heroes were waiting.

Once they had huddled just inside the undergrowth, Kaitha began to deliver her findings. "All right. It's an old military tower. The main door to the tower opens into a small antechamber, twelve feet by eight feet. There's a door to the west and to the north. Inside the room are some ruined tables and a rusted suit of armor, but nothing of value."

"That's some really detailed information," Niln whispered to Gorm.

"Aye, a true professional." Gorm turned back to Kaitha. "What's through the west door?"

"A small, dark room with only one window. It smells like the Lizardmen have been using it as a latrine."

"Disgusting," said Laruna. "Okay, let's try the north door."

"It leads to a large room, a hundred feet by eighty feet. There's a staircase leading up near the eastern wall, and a staircase down near the—"

"Wait, wait. Let me get this straight." Gorm kicked the leaves from a patch of earth and began drawing a crude map in the dirt with a stick. "So there's an antechamber here …"

"Let me." Kaitha grabbed her own branch and filled out the rest of the map. "See? There's a door here, and these are windows. And here are the stairs down. There are painted stones and feathers all around it."

"That'd be where they're performin' the ritual," said Gorm.

"What ritual?" Niln asked. "Do you know what they're doing?"

"Oh, the gods alone know what they're doin'. But Lizardmen are always performin' rituals to something or another."

"Legends have it the lizardkin were bred by Noros back in the Third Age as commandos for Mannon in the War of Betrayal," said Heraldin. "To keep them fanatically loyal, even when far afield, Noros designed them to worship Mannon. But when Mannon fell, they still needed something to worship."

"So now the little buggers will bow down to anything," said Gorm. "Whenever a nest of them moves somewhere, they always find a weird-shaped rock or a cow with a funny marking or something and set it up as their god."

"Interesting," said Niln.

"It's all well and good until they start stealing things to offer to their newfound deity," said Laruna.

"Or making sacrifices to it," said Gorm. "Livestock, pets, even people. They keep on giving it bigger and more elaborate rituals. Whatever they've found to make a god of, I'm sure they're keeping it in that basement. And if they took the marbles, that's where they'll be. I'll wager it's well guarded."

Kaitha nodded. "There are four Lizardmen in the large room. Two by the stairs down, one by the north window—"

"Hang on," said Heraldin, and he ran off to the clearing where they had left the horses. He returned with his thrones set and placed four of the bannermen on Kaitha's map. "All right. Go on."

"Right. So there are Lizardmen here, here, and here," said Kaitha.

"So what do we do?" asked Niln.

"We'll assemble in the antechamber," said Gorm. "Warriors in the front, mages in the middle, bard and ranger at the back."

"Hang on," said Heraldin. More thrones pieces were added to the map, after a brief argument as to which piece would be used for each hero.

"Right," said Gorm. "So we burst through the door—"

"It's locked," said Kaitha.

"What? Ye sure? Lizardmen don't usually make use of anything more complicated than a spear, and even then they have trouble keepin' track of the pointy end."

"Oh yes. There's a giant iron padlock on the door."

"They may have accessed the basement through an underground passage," said Jynn.

"We could go searching for the secret tunnel," suggested Niln.

"No need," said Gorm. "Look, a lock ain't enough to stop us. We'll just move the mages to watch the back door, set Gaist and I up to support Heraldin, and we can get through it in no time." He shuffled the pieces around the map.

"I can't get off a good spell at that angle," said Laruna.

"And what about the secret passage?" said Heraldin.

"It could be miles from here," said Kaitha, setting off a wide-ranging argument that started at the average size of secret entrances, passed through mixed-unit tactics and proper ways of maintaining line of sight to a target, and wound up back at the best way to storm a tower.

"Look!" barked Gorm. "It's simple. We just need the bard to pick that lock, and then we move in like we planned!"

"Oh, I'm not picking that lock," said Heraldin, casually snacking from a parcel of crisped potatoes.

"Grongo da."

"What do ye mean ye ain't pickin' that lock? You're the closest we got to a thief!"

"Listen, friend, I know I was once a member of a less reputable profession—"

"I'm not sure that's possible," muttered Jynn.

"But my illicit ways are over. I've given them up for clean and simple living."

"All I seen ye do is drink and chase tavern maids!"

"Relatively clean and simple living," Heraldin amended.

"Grongo da!"

Gorm shook his head. "It's just a simple lock in an abandoned tower."

"Oh, it starts that way, yes. But once you've felt the click of the pins and tumblers, once you've seen a lock snap open, something stays with you. You'll have the itch again, and every locked door looks like a wrapped present, and every pocket holds a surprise just for you." Heraldin shook the wistful look from his eye. "Soon, you're stealing anything you take a shine to, and soon after that, you find yourself taking a shine to anything you don't already own. And then Benny Hookhand finds out you're back in town and kills you—if you're lucky."

"Enough!" said Gorm. "Spare me the excuses. You're pickin' that lock."

"I'm not. I don't even have lock picks with me," said Heraldin.

"Gleebek?"

"What kind of thief doesn't carry lock picks?" exclaimed Laruna.

"The kind that's actually a bard!" snapped Heraldin. "Why is this so difficult to understand?"

"Well, for starters, I've yet to hear you sing a song," said Laruna.

"And you can't really play the lute very well at all," added Jynn.

"And there's this general oily, sleaziness about you," said Kaitha.

"Hey!" said Heraldin.

"To be fair, a lot of bards have that too," Laruna said.

"*Ix'isst?*" said the Lizardman.

"Now listen, I'm sorry if I'm not your typical bard, but that doesn't—" Heraldin stopped short. The heroes stared at each other, communing in unpleasant realization before turning as one to the short, bipedal reptile leaning on a spear between Niln and Gleebek.

Gleebek threw his arms up in exasperation. "*Da spi'root ra!*"

"Bloody ashes," swore Gorm.

The Lizardman extended the vibrant crest on its scaly head, gave an open-mouthed hiss, and darted away.

"Don't let it warn the others!" cried Kaitha.

Gorm was already charging after the scout, the other heroes falling in behind him. Yet Lizardmen survived by compensating for their considerable shortcomings in stature, strength, and intelligence through sheer speed. The Lizardman had already reached the tower by the time the heroes emerged from the woods. With a weird, whistling cry, it scrabbled up the wall of the tower and slipped between the bars of the window.

"Guess there wasn't any thrice-cursed secret tunnel," sniped Laruna, as the heroes skidded to a halt.

"What now?" panted Niln, coming up behind them.

"Brace yourself," said Kaitha.

A chorus of reptilian shrieks rose from within the tower. As the cacophony reached its crescendo, the old building erupted with Lizardmen; they poured from every window, hissing and spitting and waving crude weapons.

"Stay together!" roared Gorm as the scaly tide rushed at them. The heroes pressed back to back into a tight ring, with Niln and Gleebek in the center. The oncoming Lizardmen parted and flowed around the heroes like a river around a stone, ringing them in but remaining an arm's length away.

"What's happening?" Niln shouted.

"Lizardmen may be fanatics, but they ain't particularly brave," Gorm hollered back. "If they can't separate one of us from the pack, they won't press in."

A Lizardman lunged forward, jabbing with a crude spear. Gorm easily deflected the blow, but he knew it wasn't the real assault. Lizardmen needed time to build up their courage. Every one that attacked and lived made the throng behind it that much bolder. Already, another warrior was darting forward to test Gorm. "Drive 'em back!" he shouted, dispatching the assailant with a quick blow from his axe. "Keep the fear in 'em!"

"What are you doing?" Kaitha shouted to Jynn as she nocked an arrow. Her shot took down a forward Lizardman and scattered its companions. "Cast a spell!"

"Sorry, but I'm n-not used to being jostled while trying to weave the raw energy of the universe!" snapped Jynn. Gorm had seen the noctomancer quickly erect a sorcerous shield in front of himself, but the wizard had not managed to cast a single spell afterwards. Heraldin's elbow caught the noctomancer's shoulder as the bard stabbed an encroaching Lizardman, and the weave Jynn was trying to craft melted away. "Watch yourself!"

"I just watched myself save your pale skin," snapped Heraldin, dodging a thrust from a stone spear. "Just throw some magic at them!"

With an indignant harrumph and a quick gesture, Jynn sent a burst of violet energy arcing at the nearest Lizardman. The creature shrieked and withered away like a flower in a desert wind. "Well, the weave was a little cruder than normal, but—"

All around the heroes, fountains of flame blasted skyward with a thunderous roar, sending spouts of charred and screaming Lizardmen high into the air. Gorm could feel his whiskers singeing as the front ranks of the Lizardmen were decimated. The surviving reptiles fell back from the sorcerous flame, shielding their eyes and gibbering in terror.

Laruna blew a wisp of smoke from her finger. "Nice kill, newblood," she called to Jynn. "See if you can get a second."

"Goddess above." Niln was slack-jawed as charred Lizardmen rained down around them.

Jynn only scowled and shriveled another unfortunate Lizardman with a blast of necrotic sorcery.

"Ha!" laughed Gorm. "Look at 'em scarper!" The tide of scales was receding as fast as it had flowed in. Every Lizardman who was still capable of running was darting back toward the tower.

"But what are they doing?" asked Niln. Instead of climbing back through the tower, the Lizardmen began running and dancing in rings about it; their whoops and cries fell into a unified rhythm.

"They're callin' to whatever god they found," said Gorm.

A deep bellow from beneath the tower answered the sibilant chant of the Lizardmen, like the rumblings of a distant-yet-not-distant-enough storm.

"What was that?" Panic rose in Niln's voice.

Gorm gritted his teeth. "Bone and ashes. Their god's answerin'."

A dark shape eclipsed the tower windows. The roaring from within was drowning out the ecstatic cries of the Lizardmen.

"I thought you said they worshipped rocks and cows!" said Jynn.

The Lizardmen's god slammed against the wall of the tower, shaking dust and mortar from the stones. The heroes took an instinctive step back in unison.

"Whatever it is, it's big," said Kaitha.

"How did it get into the tower in the first place?" Laruna said.

"A secret passage!" said Heraldin triumphantly, just as a mountain of muscle and scales tore a new—and far less secret—passage through the side of the tower. The beast's beady reptilian eyes found the heroes, and it let loose another ear-shattering roar.

"Stone Drake!" hollered Gorm.

Stone Drakes were among the basest of the dragon-kin, usually encountered in one of three conditions: eating, sleeping, or violently furious about whatever was impeding their eating or sleeping. Essentially a toothy mouth propelled by six legs and a voracious appetite, a Stone Drake was nothing if not straightforward—mostly because turning took so much effort.

The specimen standing in the rubble of the tower wall had been slathered in garish cobalt and lemon paints, with wooden totems and bunches of crimson feathers jutting from every ridge and crag in its scales. The makeup and accessories that the Lizardmen had bestowed upon the drake seemed to have done little to improve its mood. It opened its great maw and charged at the heroes, its throng of worshippers cheering the dragon-kin on.

"Scatter!" yelled Gorm, already in motion. The heroes broke apart and sprinted off in different directions.

Gorm quickly turned, arcing back toward the drake. The key to fighting a Stone Drake was to stay out of its path. Given how cumbersome a three-ton hybrid of stone and dragon could be, avoiding one was fairly easy, as long as you didn't run in a straight line directly away from it. He glanced back to check the position of the drake, and his heart dropped into his stomach.

The high scribe of Al'Matra was sprinting in a straight line, directly away from the Stone Drake. Niln held the hem of his robe up around his waist, his sandals flapped with the mad pumping of his bony legs, but he hadn't close to enough speed to outrun the engine of tooth and scale bearing down on him.

"Niln!" Gorm screamed. "Get out of its way!"

"Well, we all knew he'd wind up getting killed," said Heraldin, running up beside the Dwarf.

"If the high scribe dies, the guild will see us all hanged!" Gorm snarled.

"Niln! Dodge!" screamed Heraldin. The drake was closing in for the kill.

Then Gleebek was there. From nowhere, the tiny Goblin leaped and tackled the high scribe, sending them both flying out of the creature's path. The Stone Drake bellowed in angry confusion as momentum carried it past its prey.

"Run!" screamed Kaitha.

Goblins, however, need no prompting to flee; the only thing their race excels at is retreat. The Stone Drake hadn't finished skidding to a halt before Gleebek was on his feet, pulling Niln up. The pair was halfway back across the field, ducking projectiles hurled by the jeering Lizardmen, when the Stone Drake reoriented itself and started getting back up to speed.

Gorm was running back toward them. "Shoot it! Get it off Niln!"

The other heroes sprang into action. Gaist hurled throwing knives, and Kaitha fired arrows. Laruna unleashed another impressive blast of flame, and Jynn fired off a couple of relatively unimpressive magical missiles; yet projectiles bounced off the drake's scales, and sorcery washed over it like waves over a stone. The drake rushed forward, undeterred and gaining on its prey.

Gorm shook his head. "It's still after Niln."

"Of course," said Heraldin. "Why wouldn't it go for the easiest meal?"

"The easiest meal ..." A flash of inspiration struck Gorm. "Heraldin, ye and Gaist get in there and make Niln a bit harder to get hold of. I'll find our friend some easier targets."

"Got it!" said Heraldin, sharing a nod with Gaist. The bard charged to intercept the drake, drawing his dagger and rapier. "A bold offense distracts the foe while we launch a clever ploy. It's the Imperial Offense!"

"What's the Imperial Offense?" Jynn shouted.

"The most famous opening in thrones," Heraldin hollered back, running alongside the Stone Drake. His blades flashed in the sunlight as he slashed at the creature's legs. "I use it all the time."

"Don't you usually lose at thrones?" Laruna yelled.

"Huh. I suppose I do," said Heraldin, and then let out a startled cry as he dodged a swing from the Stone Drake's mace-like tail. The bard was too off-balance to totally avoid the backswing, and it was only through a feat of luck and dexterity that he managed to leap atop the tail and avoid being clubbed by it.

The Stone Drake skidded to a halt, its meaty legs churning up soil as they backpedaled. A growl rumbled in its throat as it turned a beady eye to the bard clinging to its tail.

"Perhaps it looks like I have this under control," said Heraldin as he tried to climb further up the drake's tail. "But some help wouldn't be amiss!"

Then Gaist was there, a black specter gliding over the battlefield. The weaponsmaster darted past the Stone Drake's face, lashing out with a pair of swords. Twin trails of black blood bloomed amid the yellow and blue paint on the drake's scales. The drake roared in pain.

Glancing back at the battle, Gorm gave a snort of satisfaction. The beast was well distracted, between the bard on its tail and the weaponsmaster dancing around it. Better still, the Lizardmen were wrapped up in the fight as well, cheering on their scaly deity and hurling unintelligible insults and small stones at its foes.

Gorm knew that the Lizardmen couldn't have trained the Stone Drake; the Empire of Man spent several centuries trying to tame dragon-kin, and they never managed better than teaching a Sand

Drake to sit and roll over before eating its handler. Yet, if the Lizardmen kept the Stone Drake well fed and comfortable, it was entirely possible it would start to see them more or less as scenery.

The trick was to readjust the drake's perspective.

He located a Lizardman who had strayed too far from the pack, likely distracted by the spectacle of the drake fighting the other heroes. Gorm quickly closed the gap between himself and the spectator and seized the surprised Lizardman's tail. The creature yipped and hissed in protest as Gorm lifted it above his head and swung it around and around like a bola until the perfect moment came, when he released his grip. The Lizardman sailed in a high arc through the air, screaming and tumbling, until it smacked against the side of the drake's head and flopped to the ground.

"Bones," Gorm swore beneath his breath. "Missed."

He launched another unsuspecting Lizardman, and then another. Both bounced off the distracted drake with no effect. By the fourth attempt, the Lizardmen around Gorm had noticed what was happening, so Gorm had to disarm his ammunition by giving them a good punch or two before hurling them toward the target. It took nine tries, but Gorm finally managed to get a perfect throw, over the protests and jabs of the nearby Lizardmen. His hapless missile flew like an arrow into the gaping maw of the Stone Drake.

A tense silence fell over the battlefield. The Lizardmen looked on in anxious confusion as the Stone Drake, initially confused by the assault with a long-range snack, thoughtfully champed on its victim before swallowing it. The dragon-kin cocked its head to the side, smacking its lips as it reflected, and then grabbed one of the dazed Lizardmen that Gorm had bounced off its face and ate that as well.

"What's happening?" shouted Heraldin, climbing down now that the drake's tail had fallen still.

"A taste test!" shouted Gorm.

Worried murmurs broke out among the Lizardmen, and a few started inching toward the woods. Perhaps sensing the shift in attitude, a Lizardman bedecked in a priestly array of chicken bones and feathers hopped from the crowd. Boldly scuttling across the tower grounds, the scaly shaman stood before the drake, raised a staff above its head, and launched into an impassioned speech. The drake considered its babbling priest with a lazy eye; then it snapped him up in one bite.

Gorm whooped, and the assembled Lizardmen shrieked, as the priest's tail slid down the drake's gullet.

"Reconsiderin' your religion, eh?" Gorm laughed at a nearby Lizardman. "I'd run if I was ye."

The Lizardman raised its crest and hissed at him, but it took his advice anyway and scampered off. Many of its companions were experiencing similar crises of faith. By the time the Stone Drake had finished off the last of the dazed Lizardmen Gorm had hurled at it, most of its worshippers had fled. With a hungry roar, the Stone Drake charged at the stragglers, sending them running in search of safer homes and more docile idols.

Kaitha trotted up to Gorm. "Well, that takes care of that," she said, watching the Stone Drake disappear into the woods.

"Now what?" said Laruna. She and Jynn held a panting Niln between them, Gleebek hopping along at their feet.

Gorm turned to the rubble that had been the tower's western wall. "Now we finally get to see what them lizards were keepin' in their tower."

"Nothing," said Jynn.

Gorm gave a grim nod. It wasn't that the tower was empty; it was actually difficult to maneuver through the heaps of offerings and tributes the Lizardmen had set before their god, but the Lizardmen failed to take current market trends into account when choosing their sacrifices. He'd often heard it said that one man's trash was another's treasure, but in his experience the opposite was more often the case.

"It's all garbage," Heraldin said, kicking at a rusted plow that had been decorated with chicken bones and rat pelts. Lizardmen had hoarded animal skeletons, wooden signs, wagon wheels, smithing tools, hunting knives, and many other mundane trinkets that, while undoubtedly valuable in the realm of reptile spirituality, were completely worthless to professional heroes.

"What's that?" shrieked Niln, pointing to an eerie amethyst glow near Jynn, emanating from a sphere about a hand's width in diameter, set atop a black iron frame.

"It's just an attunement orb," said Jynn, stepping closer to the sphere. The light grew slightly more intense. "It must have belonged to the omnimancers the Lizardmen displaced. They use it to see which side of magic they're attuned to."

The warp and the weft of high magic invisibly alter a person who channels their energies. The more noctomancy or solamancy a mage weaves, the more his or her flesh becomes attuned to that side of sorcery. A benefit of strong attunement is resistance to one's chosen discipline; Archmagi of the Moon are all but immune to noctomancy, just as solamancy can barely touch Archmagi of the Sun. The downside is a vulnerability to the opposing school of magic, and the fact that each order's greatest rival wielded their greatest weakness did little to improve relations between solamancers and noctomancers.

Most mages considered attunement spheres more of a nuisance than a tool; Solamancers, for example, don't need to be shown they're attuned to solamancy, nor does knowing how susceptible they are to noctomancy make the idea of getting hit by a death spell any more or less attractive. Omnimancers, however, could be ripped apart by the conflicting energies they channeled if too far attuned one way or another, and therefore took a much more active interest in their current level of attunement. The orbs were a telltale sign that the defunct Order of Twilight had found a space to convene.

Jynn gave the orb the derisive sneer that mages everywhere reserved for anything associated with omnimancy. "I'll find a blanket or something to cover it."

"Why?" asked Niln.

"What's the commotion?" asked Laruna, rushing into the basement from the upstairs, and the heroes were blinded as the attunement sphere flared with radiant golden light. Heraldin reeled and nearly fell into the deep tunnel the Stone Drake had burrowed into the cellar.

"It's an attunement sphere!" snarled Jynn, shielding his eyes.

"Thrice-cursed omnimancers!" cried Laruna, staggering back up the stairs.

Once the heroes could see again, they located an old rug and threw it over the sphere. Gorm took the opportunity to take Niln aside. "Are ye all right?" he asked the high scribe.

The high scribe glanced around the room. "W-why do you ask?" he whispered, when he was sure nobody was listening.

"Well, you're sweatin' like a Scribkin cook at an Ogre's grill, ye ain't said three sentences since we fought the Lizardmen, and one of the sentences ye did manage was screamin' in terror at a glass orb with an apprentice's cantrip. And trust me, I ain't the only one who's noticed it."

"I … I know," said Niln softly. He deflated as he let out a sigh. "I knew I wasn't the typical hero when we began this quest, but I always thought that conflict was the crucible of destiny. That once I was baptized in the fires of battle, something deep inside me would awaken."

"And it wasn't there."

Niln winced as though the words stung. "Maybe. The prophecy says an ancient power lies dormant within me, but it seems to be in a deeper sleep than I imagined. Instead of becoming the hero I'm meant to be, I was saved by a squire."

"Aye," said Gorm, giving an appreciative glance to where Gleebek lay. The Goblin had saved the other six heroes from the gallows when he pushed Niln out of the Stone Drake's path, and as a reward, Gorm had granted him all of the edible spoils from the tower. Unfortunately, the spoils lived up to their name, and worse still, Gleebek had a much more liberal definition of "edible" than Gorm had imagined possible. The squire's feast had been such a disgusting spectacle that the heroes had all made polite excuses and left the room. Now, however, Gleebek had finished his rotten reward, and he was dozing comfortably by a pile of dirty dishes and discarded bones.

"I wanted to fight. I wanted to rise up and lead us to glory. But … we came so close to death, and we sent so many Lizardmen to Mordo Ogg's gate …" Niln stared into space, watching the memory of flaming Lizardmen fall. "It was horrible."

"That's the job," said Gorm with a shrug. "Find foes, kill 'em, try not to die. Professional heroics in a nutshell. Take it or leave it, 'cause the guild ain't changin'."

The high scribe shook his head. "I cannot leave it, though the idea holds more appeal than I care to admit. What will it take to turn me into a hero? How many more horrors will I face before that finally happens?"

"I'd wager ye'll be seeing a lot more, and a lot worse than ye saw here today," said Gorm.

"R-really?"

"Aye. Because the Elven Marbles clearly ain't here." Gorm looked around the dank, cluttered cellar that was the ruined remains of the Temple of the Stone Drake. "We're headed to the Myrewood."

Chapter 10

The head landed in the dust in front of Kaitha, azure light fading from its eyes, its clockwork jaw hanging limp in an expression of shock and awe. "Well ... fought!" it said.

"Good, Gleebek," Kaitha said. She took a swig from her flask, grimaced, and kicked the head back to the Goblin.

"Good!" said the Goblin. He pulled his old dagger from the target point on the training golem's throat, one of several large red spheres sprouting from strategically vulnerable points on the automaton, like crimson fruit on a tree of iron and polished wood.

"You're almost done with your knife drills," she said, which meant she was another step closer to not having to play trainer. She took a celebratory drink from her flask.

"Good! Knaf!"

She watched the Goblin set the golem's head back in its socket and lock it into place. The golem's gemstone eyes lit up once more. "Hail ... mighty warrior!" it said in an ethereal, jilted stammer. "Shall ... we duel?"

Kaitha looked across the horizon. Stars lit up, one by one, in the deep blue sky above the orange horizon. Last light would fade soon. "No, we're done for the night," she told the golem. Another celebratory drink. "Let's pack up."

"Until ... next we ... meet!" declared the Golem. The automaton bent over, tucked its arms up behind its back, and neatly folded itself into a small box.

Kaitha instructed Gleebek to shove the compact golem into a large satchel. "Where's Niln?" she asked.

"*Kappo bop,*" said Gleebek, pointing back toward the campsite.

Kaitha looked. Niln cowered behind his tent, glancing around nervously. "What are you doing?" she hollered to him.

"No, don't—" the high scribe said, but it was too late.

Niln's training golem lunged from the other side of the tent, wooden blade in hand. "A-ha … knave! I have … you now," it intoned, and charged at Niln.

The high scribe raised his staff in feeble defense, but one blow from the golem's sword knocked the weapon from Niln's hands. The automaton thrust forward again, and while attempting a desperate dodge, Niln reached out and slapped the training golem across the face.

Whatever spells animated the golem had not prepared it for a slap to the face, and its assault halted in the confusion.

"Did I break it?" asked Niln.

The golem reached out and slapped him across the face as its mimicry enchantments activated.

Niln slapped it in return. Scribe and golem traded another round of smacks, gave each other an incredulous gasp, and launched into a vigorous slap-fight.

"By the gods," said Kaitha, holding her face in her palm.

"If I could … ack. If I might have some … arg … some assistance?" pleaded Niln, trying to land blows on the golem's head while craning his own face away from the automaton's relentless assault.

"Niln, what are you doing?" Kaitha strode into the melee and casually administered a couple of punches to the golem's weak points. Its left arm and head went sailing across the plains in a rush of steam and wind.

"I was defending myself," said Niln.

"You don't defend against training golems," said Kaitha. "They can't actually hurt you. They're for learning to kill."

The golem's head finally landed a few yards away. "Ha! A blow … well struck!" it said.

"I-I've heard it said that the best offense is a good defense," said Niln.

"You don't have a good defense," said Kaitha. "You can't use a shield. You can't deflect a blow. I'd swear you were trying to dodge into your opponent's strikes. And now you've lost a slap-fight to a training golem."

Niln retrieved the golem's arm. "I acknowledge that there's room for improvement," he said.

"There's just no foundation for it," said Kaitha. Gleebek handed her the construct's erstwhile head. "No training, no martial experience, no combat drills, and we're only days from the Myrewood. If you think you're going to be ready for that, then you really have been touched by the All Mother. I mean, not to be insensitive … my family used to say it about me all the time, when I was acting rebellious or … or …"

"Or crazy. Yes, I know," said Niln, sticking the arm back in its socket. He took the golem's head from Kaitha and set it in place.

"Hail … mighty warrior," it said.

"Pack yourself up, please," said Niln.

The golem cheerfully tucked itself away.

Kaitha couldn't find words, and given where she'd steered the conversation thus far, she surmised that was for the best. She caught herself scratching at her bracers. She always did that when she needed a potion or two. It'd been days since her last hit.

Niln hoisted the golem onto his shoulder, and would have fallen over backward had Kaitha not caught him. Together, they returned to their makeshift training circle and started packing the gear away for the night.

"People wonder why we follow a goddess who is so … eccentric," said Niln.

Kaitha maintained a diplomatic silence.

"The All Mother is lost," said the high scribe, looking up at the stars. "She yearns for something she cannot name, like a hunger for a food untasted, like a love for someone you've never met. She's been searching for so long that there's nothing to her but the want and the emptiness. That's what drove her mad."

Kaitha could identify with a deep and resonant longing, although she knew that five minutes alone with a knife and a vial of elixir would fix hers.

"We follow her because we feel the same hollowness, the need for something that we cannot name, the call of something we cannot hear. We see that the world is wrong, but we don't know the solution."

"And you think Al'Matra will find it?" Kaitha asked.

"She's the only god who's searching."

Kaitha nodded. "Fair enough."

"You do not seem so different from the All Mother. Not to me."

Kaitha interrupted him. "Look, a lesson on Al'Matran philosophy is well and good, but don't go passing judgment on me. You don't know me."

"I know you drink until you cannot walk, even when we are to leave early in the morning. I know that this isn't the first job like that."

"That's not … that's different!"

"Is it?" Niln asked. "Are you sure you don't miss what you never had, or search for something you cannot name?"

"I know exactly what I want," snapped Kaitha. "I want my career back."

"Then why did you take up drink when you had it?" said Niln, pointing at the flask in Kaitha's hand. "When you were at the pinnacle of the heroics industry, what did you hope to find at the bottom of a bottle?"

"I …" Words failed Kaitha. She wanted another hit of healing potion, but more than that, she wanted to not have another hit, and to not need it.

"Perhaps you were touched by the Lady after all," said Niln. "Goodnight, Kaitha. May you find what you are looking for."

Kaitha mumbled a good night, and then dismissed Gleebek as well. She packed away the folded golems and the rest of the training gear. Then she drained her flask, and upon finding it empty, promptly refilled it from the bottle of Marvelous Marvo's Famous Halfling Rum that she kept in her belt pouch. For a time, she drank in silence and watched the stars above the plains.

The flask was halfway empty again when Laruna stormed by, sparks flying from the solamancer's grinding teeth and flames writhing around her fists. The mage stalked past the ranger without so much as a glance. Kaitha watched her go, with another swig.

A moment later, Jynn followed the mage. Something about the man's walk annoyed Kaitha: his back always straight and rigid as a highbirch, his nose always held up and away, as though avoiding an unpleasant smell. He looked down at her with the serene condescension of an ancient statue. "I see you're drinking again, naturally."

"And I see your lesson went as well as ever," she shot back.

Jynn's lip curled slightly as he watched Laruna storm back to camp. "It's neither my fault nor my concern if she has no head for higher learning."

"Of course it is. If I can teach a Goblin to use a stave and knife properly, you should be able to teach one of the most gifted mages I've ever seen how to weave a better spell. Not that we need you to; she's outfighting you."

"You should focus less on the affairs of mages and more on sobering up enough to make yourself useful."

Kaitha took another swig of rum, stood up, and cracked her knuckles. Her earlier conversation with Niln still didn't sit well with her, and Marvelous Marvo's never sat well with anyone, so if the rank-one wizard wanted to lecture her on effectiveness, she wasn't going to take it sitting down. She stretched, stepped toward Jynn, and gave him a kidney punch that would put an Ogre on the floor. The wizard crumpled into her arms with a squeal.

"If you knew me half as well as you think you do, you'd know that I'm a violent drunk," she hissed into his ear. She grabbed the wizard's hand and twisted it behind his back.

"I … am the … high councilor of the Circle … of the Red Hawk," he spat through gritted teeth.

"And that plus a giltin will get you a fish on market day," growled Kaitha. "We're in the field, where the fights are to the death and nobody is going to challenge you to a duel and stand ten paces away before they try to kill you. What good is being a high councilor if you're so green that a few Lizardmen almost took you down?"

"I don't have to prove myself to you!" He snarled, struggling in her grip.

"Perhaps not. But until you do, you've got nothing to say to me about being useful, newblood. Understood?" Kaitha took a long, burning pull from her flask, daring the wizard to say something.

Jynn grimaced at the smell of the rum, but he remained silent in a rare display of wisdom. She could tell by his eyes, specifically in the way they never met her own, that'd she'd made her point. Some men were too proud to ever admit defeat; the closest they came to surrender was learning to keep their mouths shut.

"Good," she said, giving the wizard a shove, and left him without another word.

The satisfaction of putting Jynn in his place faded before she reached the campfire. It didn't change what had become of her career. It didn't make Niln any less right about the hunger, the emptiness that plagued her.

She exchanged halfhearted waves with the heroes around the fire as she made her way to her tent. Inside, she found her rucksack with the false bottom, and the vials of elixir secreted within. She didn't know what she was searching for, let alone how to find it, or if it existed at all. But she did have a private space, a sharp knife, and a bottle of blissful ignorance. For a short while, that was enough.

Ebenmyre was little more than a few farms scattered around an old inn, all within the shadow of Arth's most deadly swamp. The village was surrounded by overgrown foundations and rotting frames of buildings long gone, the skeletal remains of more prosperous times when the Myrewood's inhabitants were as wealthy as they were terrible. Lilacs grew around the ruins. Small baubles had been hung from every post; seashells and glass globes and beads dangled from every nail, all one shade of purple or another. Beyond the ruined town, the black trees of the Myrewood seethed.

After several days spent walking the empty road and several nights sleeping on the rocky plains, Ebenmyre looked like an oasis to Gorm.

"Please tell me they have heated baths," said Laruna, as the heroes rode toward the inn. "With lavender soaps."

"And spiced wine," said Jynn. "A good Elven vintage with Imperial spices."

"And a pretty barmaid," said Heraldin. "A cute and lonely thing with a set of —"

"Thank you, Heraldin," Niln interrupted.

"Don't set your hopes too high," said Gorm, eyeing the inn's rotting rooftop. As a general rule, the best inn in any given area was only ever slightly more comfortable than the best alternative sleeping arrangement, and this particular inn was competing with some ruins and a deadly swamp. "We'll be lucky for a hot meal and a bed without fleas."

"I'd settle for a wash bin by the fire," said Laruna, holding out hope.

"Anything that's not stale grog will do, really," said Jynn.

"Honestly, if she's got all her limbs and half her teeth—"

"Thank you, Heraldin!"

The Red Sow managed, somehow, to disappoint on every account. The only bath was a wooden basin in the barn. The bar served stale grog and cold sandwiches exclusively. The closest thing the inn had to a barmaid was the tavern keeper's ill-tempered wife. Heraldin was convinced the tavern was named for her. On a happier note, the innumerable fleas and midges that had taken up residence in the Sow's beds had starved to death long ago, and once their corpses were dusted away, the mattresses were serviceable.

It was getting late at that point, so Gorm and Kaitha went to settle the bill. "We'll be headed out at dawn, and we don't want to wake ye," Gorm told the tavern keeper.

"Oh, I'm up by then, for sure," said the tavern keeper.

"Well, then we don't want to wake your wife," said Gorm.

They all looked to the barkeep's wife. She glared up from sweeping the floor, made a sound like a gravelly retch at them, and shuffled into the back room.

"Fair enough," said the tavern keeper. "Forty two giltin, three shillings, and six cents." As Gorm counted out several ten-giltin notes and a handful of coins, the barkeep added, "Don't suppose you're going to the Myrewood."

"Don't suppose there's many other reasons to be in Ebenmyre," said Gorm.

"Have you got your purple?"

"I beg your pardon?" said Kaitha.

"Your purple. For the King in the Wood?" Sensing entrepreneurial opportunity, the tavern keeper lifted an old crate of seashells, painted beads, and handkerchiefs from beneath the bar. The crate said in thick, crude lettering, "PURPEL. 5S EACH."

"Five shillings for a string of beads?" said Gorm.

"And a bargain at that. It's the color that counts, you see. You know, like the kids used to sing: Carry purple, king to pay, a price to keep the dark away. No? Never heard it?"

"Can't say as I have," said Gorm.

"Well, it's a fairly simple transaction, really. People fall into peril in the Myrewood, the king saves them, and they leave him a bit of purple as thanks."

"Your king risks his life traveling the swamp in the hopes that people will tip him purple trinkets?" said Kaitha.

"It ain't like that. Probably not, anyways. Nobody's seen him, you see. Some say he's one of the old gods roaming far from the pantheon, or the spirit of the swamp, or an ancient Elven hero from the Fifth Age."

"Or an excuse to sell painted trash to passersby," said Gorm.

"Say what you will," sniffed the barkeep. "Gods know I've seen my share of cynics. And as many as not have come out of that wood swearin' they was saved by the king and thankin' us for making them take a simple scrap of purple. It's our civic duty."

"How benevolent of ye," said Gorm.

"Oh, not me," said the barkeep. "It's my wife. She just can't stand the idea of poor souls riskin' their lives in the swamp by going out without a scrap of purple to protect them. Can you, Burlinda?"

The backroom door burst open, the barkeep's wild-eyed wife—a rotund, grimacing apparition—rooted in the darkness beyond it. "Thar gone widdout parpel?" she shrieked.

The barkeep's smile oozed neighborly concern, but his eyes were the eyes of a salesman, predatory and calculating. "Why, my Burlinda could talk for hours about the dangers of going into the wood unprepared."

Gorm and Kaitha shared a look and found, unsurprisingly, that they had both reassessed the value of carrying a purple. Gorm slapped a five-giltin note on the bar. "We'll take eight," he said.

The barkeep gave Gorm a triumphant wink. "And a bargain at that," he repeated.

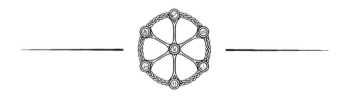

Sweat beaded on Laruna's brow. It took immense effort to restrain the flames that wanted to come roaring through her arms and out of her hands. A tiny plume of magic sprouted from the air an inch above her upturned palm, slowly spiraling into existence. It cast a warm glow onto the wooden posts and stone blocks that had once been an Ebenmyre home.

She bent her middle finger toward the strand of magic in her palm and shot a small stream of fire from it, bisecting the path the sorcery channeled through. The thread in her hand split into two streams, spiraling in opposite directions. She positioned her thumb and little finger to split the strands again, so that four threads of pyromancy danced in long, twirling arcs from her hand, like a glowing golden bloom.

She was startled to hear soft footsteps approaching, and as she jumped, her weave changed course again. The threads began to cross back and forth, taking on a new shape.

"Laruna?" Jynn called, and her concentration was shot. Flames surged through her, and the spell began to wobble and come apart as excess power coursed through it. She tried to correct the weave, but the spell twisted into a clumsy snarl of magic. Her spell wobbled uncertainly for a moment, then slid awkwardly from her palm and landed with a warm hiss on the floor of the ruined house just as the noctomancer stepped inside.

For a moment, both mages stared in silence at the dying glow of the failed spell. As it sizzled and sputtered out, anger and embarrassment flared within her. "What are you doing out here?" she demanded.

Jynn scratched at the patch of raven hair on his chin, clearly uncomfortable. "I … I see you're practicing your spells without me now."

"That's no concern of yours," she snapped. "It's bad enough the Dwarf sends me to your so-called lessons. What I do on my own time is my own business."

"You misunderstand," said the noctomancer, sitting atop a ruined bench with a heavy sigh. "When I was an apprentice, I had a … a cruel master whose lessons confused me, and he'd say that I … well, he didn't think much of me, and let's leave it at that. So I'd sneak away to practice spells on my own. And that's how I really learned, practicing my own magic, but I forgot that as I grew. All I remembered is how he taught me, and it became how I taught."

He gestured to the charred mark on the floor. "And now, I'm the cruel one, and you're sneaking off to practice. Perhaps we are not so different, you and I."

"Stop patronizing me," Laruna said. "You're not my master, cruel or thick-headed or otherwise, and I'm not your apprentice, nor am I a child. And don't fool yourself into thinking we're alike just because your private tutor made you cry when you were a boy. I'm nothing like you. I grew up eating dirt for dinner and getting beaten if I took too much sod. I've fought for everything I have.

"But you," she snarled, practically spitting the pronoun. "I know your type. You were some rich little brat under the tutelage of a powerful wizard because your father could buy you a spot at the academy. The whole world's been handed to you on a platter, and here you are moaning that the plate was tarnished!"

His jaw set, and she saw anger flash in his eyes and braced herself for a fight. Yet Jynn's retaliation never came. Instead, the wizard stared into the ruined house's fireplace and shook his head.

"Is that it?" she demanded. "Or do you have something else to say before you leave me in peace?"

His voice was softer than a whisper. "How do you do it?"

"What?"

"How do you fight when it's not a duel? When you don't know the rules—no, when there are no rules, and there's no academy to enforce them? When … when you're not fighting mages?"

"I don't see how it's any different," said Laruna, caught off guard. "You just fight."

"It's totally different," said Jynn. "I know magic. In a duel, I know what my opponent will do, what they should do. I can sense a spell coming. I've bested mages who outrank me, and those who have far more capacity to channel. But out here … I can't sense a knife coming, nor do I know when or how a Lizardman will strike. And so while I'm considering my next move, before I have time to even think of what to do, you step in and just … just …" His hand swept away an imaginary horde of foes.

Laruna tried to find the hidden insult, the slight she knew the wizard must have been trying to infer. "So, you're saying I don't think?"

He turned to look at her again, his blue eyes piercing. "On the contrary, I'm saying you think well on your feet. It's one of the things I … I admire about you."

Laruna took a step backwards, reeling from the compliment. Though perhaps that was his intention, she realized. If he wanted to put her off-guard, there probably wasn't any better way to do it. She recovered quickly and changed topics in a decisive counterattack. "Then give me your vote to make me a full mage."

His smile made it plain he had seen through her ploy. "You know as well as I do that magehood isn't about the power you wield but about the control you have over it."

"Control," she snorted. "You mean how fancy your weaves are. I'm sick of hearing about it, sick of seeing apprentices that couldn't hold a candle to me getting advanced just because they can stitch together a few threads of sorcery." Unpleasant memories of the academy surfaced in her mind, of long days wearing apprentice robes that were far too small, sitting in a classroom full of peers who weren't half her age. "I heard the other apprentices talking. Even though they were just children, they'd call me stupid and say I'd never learn to weave."

"And deep down, you wondered if they were right," said Jynn, watching the stars overhead. "And you couldn't help but think that if so many people thought that of you, if the whole world believed you incapable, then maybe you really were as worthless as they said." The wizard's words held no derision or mockery, just a wistful sadness, and something else — perhaps familiarity?

"Yes," said Laruna, watching the noctomancer's face carefully. "Has that ever happened to you?"

"Oh no, of course not," said Jynn. "But I did … I know the sting of harsh words. You must not listen to them. When people insult you, remember that they don't know you, not in your fathoms. Only you know what powers echo there."

"You called me an idiot."

"Prove me wrong, Laruna. Show the world the real strength inside you." The wizard stood. "I can help you with that. And you, in turn, can teach me to fight."

Laruna stared at him with open doubt. The man's words were well and good, but he was still Jynn. He was the councilor whose vote denied her full magehood, and who was indirectly responsible for her involvement in this sorry excuse for a quest.

Jynn seemed to sense her hesitation. "I've been tasked with teaching you to weave, and I want to learn how to fight," he said. "I cannot succeed in either if you fail. I'm not asking you to trust me, just to recognize that our interests are aligned." He extended a hand to her. "We have nothing to lose, and power to gain."

Laruna wasn't sure that was the case. Still, it wasn't like there was much of a choice; Gorm would insist she train with the noctomancer no matter what. If nothing else, Jynn's sudden change would make her mandated lessons a lot more tolerable. She took his hand and shook it.

Tuomas polished the blade of his shortsword vigorously. The enchanted blade crackled with sorcerous lightning that singed his knuckles, but he kept scrubbing long after he could see his reflection in the runesteel. He'd been cleaning his gear since the cart had rolled away, leaving his team to their task. His armor and shield were already polished to a mirror finish. His boots were immaculate, and his cloak, unsullied.

He told the others that his rigorous cleaning regimen was a mark of professionalism, but they just laughed and shook their heads. Everyone else in the company had been a licensed thug for years and recognized a nervous rookie when they saw one.

There was a lot to be nervous about. Tuomas had been a goon for his entire career, up until now. Gooning was good work, if a little dull. Easy. Simple. Low risk. Not like thuggery. Thugs had to deal with heroes, which never seemed to turn out well for the thugs in all the bards' stories. Sure, there were the great thug legends, mighty individuals who took down hundreds of heroes during their tenure with the Thugs' Union, but they were vastly outnumbered by the vast throng of thugs who had promising careers cut short: stabbed, incinerated, melted, or otherwise violently ended by professional heroes. Even with the venerable Damrod the Eye fighting by their side, and the fact that their marks were rumored to be a bunch of newbloods led by a few washed-up drunks, there was a good chance someone on the crew wasn't going to survive the ambush.

Of course, that assumed they survived *until* the ambush. Tuomas had been told it was at least a day away, which meant spending nights in the middle of the Myrewood. Nights waiting in dank caves while blackness closed in around them. Nights fighting whatever terrors skittered from the darkness. Nights spent sitting next to …

Tuomas shook his head and resumed polishing his blade with renewed vigor.

"Problem, kid?" Hogar asked him. The senior thug was a wiry man whose face boasted more scars than teeth.

"I just don't know why we had to do the ambush in the Myrewood."

"Same reason we do everything," laughed Hogar. "To avoid paperwork."

The death of any hero, even a rank-one fighter, prompted an automatic guild investigation to determine who was responsible. This was usually less a matter of blame than fiscal responsibility, but when thugs were involved, the Heroes' Guild went to extra lengths to investigate the killing of its members. The law left a gray area around thugs and heroes fighting or slaying each other, but every thug knew that some jobs were of a darker shade. In those cases, it was best to head off any inquiry by outside authorities.

The trick was that the degree of proof that guild coroners and medical investigators required was inversely proportional to the degree of risk in the investigation. When a hero was found dead in the street, a full forensic autopsy was usually needed to satisfy the guild's council, but proving that a party of heroes entered a Flame Drake lair and didn't exit again was usually enough to end any inquiry. Such a practice made deadly locales like the Myrewood, the Black Gorge, and the Ash Wastes the best places for thugs to handle any business they'd rather keep quiet; listing "the Myrewood" as the cause of a hero's death would settle any investigation.

The benefits of conducting the ambush in the middle of a deadly swamp had been explained to Tuomas several times over, and he understood the theory. Yet, sitting among the black trees, Tuomas was certain he'd have rather dealt with a mountain of paperwork than spend another hour in the swamp.

"Keep your eyes forward, Tuomas," barked Damrod.

"Aye, sir," said Tuomas, standing.

Damrod the Eye was called as much for the single leering eye that stared from his knobby, scarred face. The old mercenary stood in the entry to the cave, flanked by the other four veteran thugs, rain dripping from his crimson cloak. "And stop looking back at the stiffs."

"Yes, sir," said Tuomas, joining the others at the mouth of the cave. He pulled his cloak tighter around him, guarding against a chill from the enchanted bricks of ice sitting in the cave behind him. They stood and watched the darkness brood outside the torchlight.

"How come yous didn't bring the Mask along with yous?" said Big Blenny, who followed the ancient Thugs' Union tradition of adding an 's' to the end of every pronoun.

"He's on other business," said Damrod.

Something in the distant darkness roared, and then shrieked as it was eaten by something larger and more deadly. Tuomas was a little embarrassed to discover that he was subconsciously polishing his shield again.

"Hey, where's Davitt?" said Big Blenny.

Tuomas looked all around. Classy Davitt had been at the end of the line, sitting on a large stone that was now occupied by his ominously discarded top hat.

"Eyes forward, lads," Damrod said. He drew his sword, and the rest of the thugs readied their weapons.

Tuomas thought he heard something behind him—a wet slap, or a low shuffle. It was hard to tell, because things were definitely moving outside the cave as well.

"Eyes forward, thrice curse you, Tuomas!" roared Damrod.

Tuomas startled to attention. "Sorry, sir. I thought I heard something back by the—"

"Never you mind the cave! You keep your thrice-cursed eyes on the woods! Don't you worry about those bloody corpses. They've been dead for weeks—"

Damrod was cut off by a shriek. Dead green arms grabbed Vondo Tar-Mouth by the head and pulled him, screaming, back into the cave.

"That is not as much of an impediment as one might think," said a cold, hollow voice from the darkness.

"Weapons up," roared Damrod. "Ready yourselves, lads! Stay — aaarg!" Something seized the screaming mercenary and hauled him into the dark woods.

Tuomas readied his sword. He saw Hogar dragged into the shadows outside the cave, and Big Blenny fleeing into the woods. All around him, he heard shrieks and wails and inhuman growls.

"Stay back!" he shouted. "Stay back! I warn you!"

The shadows were unswayed by the mercenary's commands. Unnatural figures stalked toward him from the darkness.

"Please! Stay back!"

Classy Davitt stepped into the torchlight, his eyes dull and lifeless, his head hanging sideways from his thick, broken neck. The corpse jerked and lurched like a marionette at the mercy of a drunken puppeteer as he approached Tuomas.

"Davitt! Davitt, it's me! Tuomas!"

Davitt stopped.

"Yes! It's me! Remember? Remember how we talked about finding nice girls back home? You don't have to … to …"

Davitt's body bent down, picked up his fallen top hat, and placed it carefully atop the upturned side of his face.

"Oh, never mind the bloody hat," said the voice in the darkness. "Be quick about it."

Classy Davitt groaned something in response and staggered forward once more. The last thing Tuomas saw was the overdressed corpse staggering toward him with outstretched arms.

Chapter 11

"Do you see it?" said Heraldin.

"It's a weasel," said Laruna.

"And I'm a bejewled basilisk. It's a ravenous death machine," said Heraldin.

The heroes huddled in a line behind a fallen log, their eyes barely peeking over the mossy bark. Beyond the fallen log, a tiny ball of fur sat in the middle of the road, giving itself a vigorous tongue bath.

"Should we go around it?" said Niln.

"Ye think we should leave the road?" said Gorm.

The heroes looked. The Myrewood seethed around them. Its black, gnarled trees seemed to block out the sunlight just to spite whatever lived below them. The ground was thick with thorns and creeping nettles, but it still allowed for glimpses of rope-thick centipedes and hand-sized arachnids stalking each other through the undergrowth. Weird, bulbous fungi poked up through the leaf litter, occasionally rattling as some unknown creature slithered or skittered beneath them. Mysterious pools of muck periodically erupted with thick, greasy bubbles filled with noxious gasses.

"Good point," said Niln.

"We could have ridden past it, if we still had the horses," said Heraldin.

"Right into the jaws of something bigger 'n' nastier," said Gorm. "The smell of horseflesh brings trouble."

"Somebody just go over there and kill it," said Laruna.

"Sorry, I like my jugular," said Heraldin.

"You'll be fine."

"Have you noticed where we are?" whispered the bard harshly. "Everything here is man-eating or acid-spitting or spike-shooting!"

"It's smaller than a cat," said Jynn.

"So was that explosive firebeetle you sent me after."

"And you're fine."

"I barely got behind cover in time. Gaist here thought I was as good as dead."

Gaist nodded.

"Send the Goblin," said Heraldin.

"Nub nub," said Gleebek, shaking his head.

"We ain't sendin' anyone. The bard's right," said Gorm. "If we don't know what it is, we assume it wants to kill us."

"Gods, do we have to stop and hold a high council for every minor distraction we encounter?" said Laruna. "This quest is going to take forever."

"I prefer slow going to a sudden stop, if ye catch me drift."

"I could hit it with a subtle spell —" Jynn suggested.

"Oh no," said Heraldin. "Remember last time we tried magic."

"I didn't mean to attract those bloodsnakes!" said Laruna defensively.

"Well, I'm sure the two of ye won't mean to call over whatever your next spell attracts either," said Gorm. "No spellcastin' unless it's absolutely necessary."

"Shh! Shush! It's coming this way!" said Niln.

The heroes watched breathlessly as the creature ambled toward their log. It wiggled its ratty nose at them, forgot about whatever had brought it in their general direction, and resumed licking itself.

"Anybody have their copy of the *Heroes' Guild Handbook?*" said Gorm.

"I do," said Niln. He pulled the thick volume from his rucksack.

"Look it up," said Gorm.

Niln nodded and started flipping through the tome.

"Look," said Jynn. "One throwing dagger to the back of that thing's head and we're done. It's simple."

"Easy for you to say," said Heraldin. "It's always 'protect the mages.' 'Defend the mages.' I've been bitten and stabbed today more times than I care to remember just so you two can 'concentrate.'"

"The right spell can mean the difference between victory and defeat," said Jynn. "Protecting the spellcasters is a sound tactical decision."

"I don't see why Kaitha can't shoot the bloody thing with an arrow," said Laruna.

"Myrewood … Mire with a 'y.' Ah, all right. Fauna …" muttered Niln.

"Look under 'weasel,'" said Gorm. "And where is Kaitha anyway?"

"Protecting casters is well and good, but I prefer tactics that don't designate me as the meat shield," Heraldin told the mages.

"Why? You're quite suited for it," Jynn said.

"Kaitha?" whispered Gorm.

"She said she'd be right back," Niln said absently, flipping through his Handbook.

Heraldin shot Jynn a glare. "Look, wizard, you may think—"

Gaist interrupted the bard by seizing his collar and hauling the man up to look over the log.

"You … may … I …" Heraldin's voice fell away as he looked up.

"Bloody bones," swore Gorm. "She split the party?"

"Oh, here it is!" said Niln, examining an article next to a picture of the little creature. "It says here that … oh."

Jynn looked over the priest's shoulder at the entry. "Perhaps you were right, Heraldin."

"Perhaps," said the bard, craning his neck back.

"Of all the thrice-cursed stupid times to run off and split the bloody party!" Gorm snorted. "Who knows what trouble she's in?"

"Maybe she thought we could handle a little weasel," said Laruna.

"Burn what she thought!" barked Gorm. "We don't know what we're up against!"

"We do, unfortunately." Niln read from an entry in the Handbook. "It says here that the Northern Ragnaril, *Tyrannus incresco*, when enraged, will actually—"

"Grow to enormous size?" said Heraldin, looking higher.

"Why, yes. How … did … you—oh."

They stood just as the towering ragnaril roared.

Heraldin drew his rapier grimly. "Gods, I hate this place."

Kaitha crept through the malignant undergrowth of the Myrewood. Her hair had wound itself into an intricate web of knots and was cemented in place by some unidentifiable muck that one swamp denizen or another had spat on her in the heat of battle. Sweat and swamp grime were having a turf-war all over her body. Whichever won, her nose lost.

All she needed was a private space, Kaitha told herself. She just needed one potion to take the edge off, to make this nightmare of a quest a little more bearable. Getting a hit of elixir would take no more than five minutes; the others would hardly notice she was gone before she'd be back.

Something roared behind her, back where she'd left the other heroes. For a moment, she thought of turning back, but her wrists itched at the thought of not taking a potion. A fast one. She'd be back with the other heroes soon. No more than ten minutes.

She slipped around an ancient and gnarled oak, climbed over a stone wall overgrown with thick vines, and scurried down a gully choked with heavy brambles. There was a sheltered spot in the belly of the gulch, and Kaitha settled into it quickly. Her hands trembled as she pulled the healing potion and her hunting knife from her rucksack. Quickly, she removed her bracer and rolled up her sleeve.

The knife was almost to her wrist when the light caught her eye. It was just a faint glow under the brambles, as though the light wanted to look inconspicuous lest the huge shadows around it take notice and decide to snuff it out. But it was sunlight, and it carried with it the sweet scent of air unsullied by the Myrewood's foulness.

Something else carried on the fresh air as well—a sensation Kaitha couldn't identify but couldn't resist either. She slipped her rucksack back over her shoulder and put her knife to work cutting back the thick brambles. It took several minutes for her to thin the undergrowth enough to push through the briar. Kaitha stepped through the thorns.

The knife fell from her hands. Her breath caught in her throat.

Exquisite arrangements of wildflowers and emerald grasses spread before her. A few yards away, she found a stone path grown over with sugarmoss and mint-green lichens. Kaitha followed the path up a gentle slope, meandering under white trees that had been coaxed into natural arches. A cool stream of fresh, pure water bubbled alongside her. The branches overhead were sculpted such that brilliant sunlight cascaded into the glade and cast scintillating patterns over everything.

Questions flooded her mind as she crossed the garden, treading lightly on brilliant mosses. Where was she? How could such a garden, beautiful enough to rival the greatest of House Tyrieth's palatial grounds, be growing in the heart of the Myrewood? Who could conceive of a place like this, let alone grow and maintain it? Was it the work of a man, or a god? And if it was a man, was he single?

A song she didn't remember sprang to mind, and she couldn't hold it back. It had been decades since she'd lifted her voice, and her first notes wavered uneasily. She found the music soon enough, however, and filled the garden with her song.

There is a law to the universe, and among its many precepts is the certainty that when an Elven princess sings, small animals will be drawn to the song. Even if the princess was technically disowned centuries ago, and had since become a washed-up hero of somewhat ill-repute, and even if the only animals nearby were hardened and battle-scarred from a lifetime of fighting for survival in a death swamp, the law still held true. Ragged chipmunks and venomous snakes alike followed in Kaitha's footsteps, swaying with the melody of her song. She gently patted the nose of a savage-looking deer, the kind of grizzled doe that a soft puma from the foothills wouldn't stand a chance against.

For a time, she walked along the winding path, singing to the animals that flitted and skittered around her. In the inner parts of the garden, a song answered hers—a piping melody she hadn't heard for decades. An *aithanalasi* was perched high in the branches, sending its enchanting melody throughout the garden. Kaitha's smile widened as the tiny bird's music began to harmonize with her own, and soon she was in a duet with the most sacred of songbirds.

She began to dance, gracefully twirling through the trees with an imaginary partner. They danced beneath arches of lilacs, past fruit trees grown into exquisitely flowing shapes. She commented on the flowers as she passed, telling her nonexistent companion which blooms caught her fancy, or asking what his favorites were.

As Kaitha danced and spoke with her imagined partner, she felt a growing sensation he was actually there. Not in her arms, certainly, but just beyond the edge of her vision, like a spirit of the garden, moving along with her. It was like dancing with the memory of a lover, only one that she'd never known. She told him as much, but he remained silent.

Before she knew it, she was at the end of the path. Ivy and brilliant blooms spilled over the rocks like a lush, living river. Vibrant bushes and patches of wildflowers sprang from carefully arranged stones. Squarely in front of her, an ancient maple sat like a holy man atop a cluster of moss-covered boulders. The largest, clearest stream of sunlight poured down and bathed the maple and its stone circle in sacred light.

Kaitha stepped from the path and into the inner sanctum.

The garden's winding stream burbled from a spring beneath the stones. As Kaitha stole a sip of the cool spring water, she noticed a spot worn free of moss near the base of a large rock. Someone had moved the stone — recently, and often.

It took a surprising amount of effort to move the stone. Kaitha had to brace her back against it and use her legs to rock it from its place. It finally toppled with an explosion of vibrant color. Lavender beads, painted thrones pieces, mussel shells, scraps of velvet, violet figurines and decorations, grape quartz and amethysts — a spectrum of purple trinkets bled from a cleft in the stone. Kaitha watched the violet mass spill over the mossy ground and knew whose garden this was.

"Hello?" she said. "Are you the King in the Wood?"

The garden was silent.

"Are you there?"

As she recalled the innkeeper's tale of the Myrewood's mysterious monarch, it dawned on Kaitha that the King in the Wood was known primarily for protecting people from the perils of the swamp she was currently wandering through. It also occurred to her that, while the tales depicted the king as some sort of benevolent force, he might react differently to Elves who entered his sanctuary and vandalized his stash of brightly colored trinkets.

"I'm … I'm sorry about this … I … I really didn't mean to," said Kaitha. She drew the violet star-beads she had purchased from the innkeeper and placed them atop the pile of spilled trinkets in a feeble gesture.

And now the full weight of her folly was bearing down on her. She didn't know who the King in the Wood was, or what he was. The presence in the forest could have been a benevolent protector, but it could just as easily have been some loathsome denizen of the Myrewood luring her to a horrible doom, like some sort of botanical siren. The shadows were already starting to lengthen, and if she couldn't find the other heroes again before sunset, she'd be spending the night alone in the Myrewood.

Icy fear crept down her spine as she realized how vulnerable she had left herself. The last vestiges of the hero she had been echoed in the silence of her terrified paralysis, and the memories and experiences of the career that was drifting away from her could finally be heard. *Run, you fool,* said the remnants of the Jade Wind. *Get back to the party.*

"I'm sorry," she said again, and broke into a full sprint down the path. Dark shapes moved through the trees beyond the edge of the garden. She could hear the screeches and squeals of scargs and swamp-beasts and unnamed horrors ringing through the Myrewood around her.

She stopped when she reached the brambles and turned back to take in the sight of the wondrous garden one more time, a vision of paradise in the midst of a infernal swamp. For a moment, she stood torn between the feeling that she could stay forever and the knowledge that she had tarried too long.

Something howled in the distance. "Goodbye," she whispered to the garden, and pushed back into the brambles.

Gorm lodged his axe in the twisted trunk of a tree by the side of the road. Red sap bled from the gouge in the black bark.

"Do you think she'll see that?" Niln asked him.

"She's a ranger," said Gorm, wrenching the axe free. "And we're leavin' a trail so clear that a drunken Ogre could track us. If she has any of her senses left, she'll find our trail."

"Of course, if she had any of her senses left, she wouldn't have split the party in the Myrewood," said Heraldin.

"I'm still not sure why we didn't wait for her," said Niln.

"Because she didn't say to," said Gorm. "She could assume we've gone ahead and overshoot our position, and then how'd she find us? And how long will we sit in the middle of the Myrewood waitin' for her to show up? There's no good option when the party is split."

"I suppose you're right," said Niln.

"All we can do is keep movin' and hope for the best," said Gorm.

"And keep marking our path."

Gorm hacked at another tree by the side of the road. "That too," he said.

Kaitha saw another slash in the tree just ahead, red sap painting a crimson streak over the trunk. She was getting closer to the party; the sap was still fresh and oozing. The trail couldn't have been much more than an hour old.

Then again, an hour was a long time to survive alone. Dark shadows moved through the forest around her. Kaitha could make out the flowing reptilian shapes of swamp-threshers between the trees, running at a swift lope alongside her. She thought to ready her bow and take a stand against them, but a moment later, the great lizards veered away and left the road.

The swamp-threshers were only the latest threats to suddenly cease pursuing her. Kaitha had seen boggarts and swamp leeches that had seemed intent on fighting, only to flee at the last moment. At one point, a Tusked Muckbeast had actually charged her from the swamp, only to be seized by something even more terrible and yanked back into the undergrowth. Kaitha didn't wait around to see what could dispatch the creature so effortlessly; she was sprinting down the road again before the creature's death scream was cut short.

She had the sense of a presence keeping pace behind her, although she could never see it, and she wasn't sure it was actually in pursuit. It occurred to her that the phantom at her back could have been responsible for frightening off the Myrewood's other predators, but then, it could have done so to claim her as its own prey.

There wasn't time to think about it. She ran on, ignoring the fire in her lungs and the ache in her legs. The road turned to the right, and then hooked back to the left before curving around a festering pool. Then, two men were standing in front of her.

Kaitha skidded to a halt. The men in the middle of the road wore dark leathers and long scarlet cloaks over chain mail. Their swords looked sharp, their smiles looked cruel, and their eyes looked like they saw an opportunity.

"Well, what have we here?" said the first man.

"You must be who the others was leavin' a trail for, eh?" said the second.

"A good possibility," agreed the first man. "There was quite a few of them makin' that trail."

"But it looks likes there's only one of you, miss."

"Bandits," snarled Kaitha.

"Whoa, whoa, whoa," said the first man. "What's with the hostility and the labeling?"

"Don't be so eager to jump to conclusions," said the second. "Why, for all you know, I could be a druid concerned for the well-being of these precious, pretty trees that some uncouth cur has taken an axe to."

"And I could be a concerned citizen going to check on the well-being of those poor, unfortunate travelers."

"Get out of my way," Kaitha panted, hoping it sounded more like a warning than a plea.

"I would, I would," said the man who didn't seem very much like a druid. "But there are economic realities that we have to address."

"Most pressingly, we don't have enough money," added the man who was not acting like a concerned citizen.

"Or jobs," said the first man.

185

"Or jobs, yes, which is probably a big contributing factor to us not having any money."

"You, however, have the looks of someone with money."

"At least valuables that we could sell."

Kaitha reached for her bow, but the man who probably wasn't a druid raised his hand. "I wouldn't do that if I was you, miss. Something might happen."

Kaitha paused.

The three of them waited. As the men's patience faded away, so did their confident grins.

"I said, something might happen," repeated the man who almost certainly wasn't a druid.

"Like a warning shot could be fired from a crossbow," added the man who was definitely not a concerned citizen.

"You don't suppose—" said not-a-druid.

"He usually stays deeper in the swamp," said not-a-concerned-citizen.

Kaitha turned to look at the spot the bandits were staring at. A crossed pair of branches provided excellent cover for a crossbowman seeking to cover any highwaymen plying their trade below. There just wasn't a crossbowman in them.

Something fell from the branches above and landed on the road with a *clank.*

It was a crossbow.

"He's here," whimpered the man who wasn't a druid, drawing his sword.

"The King in the Wood," said the man who wasn't a concerned citizen. "What do we do?"

"Let's grab her and go," said the man who wasn't a druid. The bandit stepped toward Kaitha, although his eyes kept shifting to the dark swamp all around them. In his distraction, he had clearly forgotten he was not dealing with a helpless traveling merchant, but with a well-armed rank-ten ranger.

More importantly, he had failed to notice that Kaitha had drawn her bow while he and his partner were paying attention to the swamp. It only took one shot.

"Get out of my way," Kaitha repeated, training an arrow on the second bandit.

The man who wasn't a concerned citizen looked at the twitching body of the non-druid, and then at the Elf aiming at him, and, finally, at the swamp. Finding no good options, he chose the path of least visible resistance and fled into the woods.

Kaitha didn't lower her bow. She turned in circles, trying to find a target. Something out there had silently taken the crossbowman. Indeed, it seemed to be killing or chasing away everything that threatened her. And while her follower's activities had benefited her thus far, that didn't mean it was necessarily on her side. In the Myrewood, the enemy of your enemy might just be very hungry.

"Show yourself!" she demanded to the forest.

A short scream, perhaps from a citizen and certainly very concerned, rang out and was suddenly silenced by a sound that made Kaitha's stomach turn.

She pointed her arrow in the direction of the scream. "I know you're there!" she shouted.

The swamp quietly simmered all around her.

"Are you friend or foe?" she asked.

A sudden rush came from the bushes to her left. Kaitha shifted her aim quickly, but it was only a Bog Grouse flying from the undergrowth.

"Are you the King in the Wood?"

A hush fell over the swamp; even the insects and scrub-birds ceased their quiet chittering. Kaitha could feel the presence in the shadows growing near, but though she strained her eyes, she could see nothing in the Myrewood but trees and boulders and muck.

"Are you helping me?"

A new scent filled the air, like moss and earth, like the garden she'd left behind. The phantom was so close now it was almost palpable. She could feel its nearness in her bones. She could hear its heartbeat in her own.

It didn't feel like an enemy. After all, she reasoned, if it was hostile, why hadn't the phantom struck yet? Surely it had been presented with ample opportunities to end her; for all she knew, her back was to the creature right now.

Kaitha lowered her bow. "Was that your garden?"

There was no response.

She tried laying her bow on the ground and backing away from it. She sang as she had sung in the garden. She promised it that she was no enemy, pleaded that it accept her thanks, and begged it to come and show itself before she had to leave. But the phantom would not reply nor reveal itself, no matter what she did. It hovered at the edge of her perception, a hint of a companion, a whisper of a protector, and would come no closer.

The other heroes were drawing away from Kaitha with every passing moment, and there was no telling how long her invisible guardian would watch over her. She couldn't stay where she was, as much as she wanted to meet her savior. She surveyed the wood one last time. She didn't see anything. Perhaps the elixir was starting to get to her. Perhaps there was nothing to see.

"Thank you," Kaitha said to the phantom, just in case it existed and understood and cared. She retrieved her bow, slung it over her back, and resumed sprinting down the road. For another moment, the forest remained still.

Then, something followed her.

"Definitely male," said Jynn. "Look at the jaw bone."

"I would rather not, thank you," Niln managed.

The high scribe was doing his best to assist with the forensic investigation, but he didn't have the stomach for it. He'd been heaving his lunch into a ditch since the heroes had first stumbled across the body in the road. And in the ditch next to the road. And in the trees nearby.

Gorm surveyed the carnage. The dossier of intelligence provided by House Tyrieth indicated that the bandits who took the Elven Marbles were somewhere nearby. It was possible that the art thieves were all around them—or at least one of them was.

Jynn looked up from the collection of bones and scraps of clothing he'd meticulously arranged on the side of the road. "I'd say we're looking at a Human male, mid-fifties or older. Six foot tall. Has a physically demanding profession. Enjoyed tobacco and the odd spot of rum."

"You can't know all that from a pile of bones," said Laruna.

"Oh, but you can. Note the stained teeth …" The noctomancer launched into a lengthy explanation of his findings and methodology.

Gorm noticed something under the leaf litter. He picked up the smudged slip and examined it. "Male Human, forty-six years old. Six foot one. Weighed eighteen stone. Professional Thug."

"Now, how could you possibly know all that?" said Laruna.

"Found his Thugs' Union card." Gorm held it up. "Name's Blenford R. Curbonfert. Nicknamed Big Blenny."

"Well, that doesn't make any sense," said Jynn. "Why would a thug be a bandit?"

"He wouldn't. Thugs can make better money enforcing contracts or wrangling heroes," said Gorm.

"Maybe he was after the bandits?" suggested Niln.

"Maybe," said Gorm. "Maybe this has nothin' to do with the marbles." But he had a sense in his gut that the body and the artwork were connected. He just didn't know how. They needed more information. "We need to find where he was comin' from. And was he alone? And did he find our bandits?"

"Shebz cluggo Hupsa!"

Gleebek bounded exuberantly up the road. Relief washed over Gorm, who couldn't hold back his smile.

"What'd he say?" Niln asked.

"Still no idea," said Gorm. "But I'm betting they found her."

Gaist and Heraldin were already rounding the bend, supporting Kaitha between them.

"Ska dibi!" said Gleebek

The heroes gathered around the ranger and pelted her with questions. Where had she been? Did she encounter any trouble? How did she make it back? Why did she leave at all?

Gorm stood back and let them chatter. "Was she followed?" he asked Gaist.

The weaponsmaster shook his head.

"Good," said Gorm. "All right, that's enough!"

The reunion tapered to a couple of whispered conversations. All eyes turned to Gorm.

"I'm as happy to see the ranger as anybody, but we're still in the Myrewood, aye?" said Gorm. "And I, for one, would like not to be here any longer than necessary. So let's get in formation, figure out where our friend Big Blenny came from, and find them thrice-cursed marbles before nightfall. There'll be time for talk back at the inn."

He leveled his eyes directly at Kaitha, though leveling them was more like an upward incline. "And we will talk," he said. "At length."

Kaitha winced. "I'm sorry."

"Later," said Gorm. "This ain't the time or place for talkin' about it." Too many heroes met their end when a foe caught them settling interpersonal issues instead of scouting a dungeon or posting watch. Adventurers who lost their heads in a figurative sense often lost their heads in a more literal manner shortly thereafter.

The heroes formed a huddle around Big Blenny's discarded license.

"Right," said Gorm. "Here's what we know. This man was a licensed thug. He met Mordo Ogg earlier than he would have liked. And he was probably running from whatever sent him off."

"What makes you sure he was running?" asked Laruna.

"The expression on most of his face was pretty scared," offered Heraldin.

"Most of?" said Kaitha.

"Well, I doubt the rest of it is smiling either," said Heraldin.

Niln fell back to his knees and heaved up his breakfast.

Gorm sent Gleebek to attend to the nauseated high scribe. "A better clue," he said pointedly, "is that we don't see any traveling gear around. So either he was waltzing through the Myrewood without a care in the world, or he left his camp in a hurry. Which leaves us with two questions: why was he running, and where was he running from?"

"How can we know that?" said Niln.

Gorm grinned at Kaitha. "Luckily, we happen to have our ranger back."

Chapter 12

It turned out that Big Blenny had a horrible sense of direction. The trail the ex-thug left took a wide, meandering path that felt like a tour of some of the Myrewood's most treacherous terrain. The man had fled through sadistic briar bushes, a sucking swamp, and a thicket of bladewood trees on his last run, only to meet his end no more than a hundred yards from where he started. Kaitha and the heroes followed his trail to a small camp by the mouth of a cave, just off the main road.

Gorm kicked a charred iron cook pot off the ashes of a dead fire. A faint warmth still radiated from the deepest embers. "Ain't been more than a day," he said. "Whatever happened, it happened last night."

"Whatever it was, I'm glad I missed it," said Heraldin. The ground outside the cave had been tilled and churned and liberally sprinkled with blood and debris by some great battle.

"Something's not right here," said Kaitha, joining them.

"Well, grass shouldn't be red for starters," said Heraldin.

"Yes, thank you, Heraldin." Niln's skin had a green pallor.

"There's that. But where are the bodies?" said Kaitha. "What kind of fight leaves a battlefield looking this way and doesn't have a single casualty?"

"Or at least doesn't leave 'em behind," said Gorm. "Something could have ate 'em, or dragged them away."

"No," said Kaitha. "There's no sign the corpses were dragged. And I don't see any tracks big enough for a predator that large."

"Well, the bodies didn't just walk away," said Heraldin.

"Unless they did," said Kaitha.

There was an unpleasant pause while they collectively shuddered at the implications.

"Bloody necromancy," said Heraldin.

The line between necromancy and noctomancy was ill-defined and fuzzy, but walking corpses were a good indicator that some wizard or mage had violated the Order of the Moon's strict rules against the magic of undeath. Individually, a walking skeleton or a zombie was a nuisance on par with a door-to-door missionary from the Temple of Oppo; both had unnatural persistence, an unnerving grin, and a single-minded focus on making converts. Fortunately, zombies and skeletons tended to be rather feeble and slow, and so the odd undead was easy to get rid of—certainly easier than door-to-door priests.

The problem was that every couple of decades or so some wizard would notice that controlling people was enjoyable, and that controlling dead people was easy, and a kind of twisted algebra would lead him down a dark path. Given time, privacy, and a supply of cold bodies, a necromancer could raise a small army to rival that of the kings and queens of the Freedlands. The Heroes' Guild usually sent the best of the best to deal with such insurrections; inexperienced parties didn't fare well against the rotting armies of a dark wizard, and a hero lost to the undead was a foe gained.

"What's the best way to deal with a necromancer?" said Niln.

"You have to wait for the right moment to approach him," said Heraldin.

"How do you know the right moment?"

"It's any time after someone else has chopped the morbid bastard's head off," said Heraldin. "We don't want any part of this."

"If there is a necromancer threatening the countryside, we can't just leave," Niln said.

"And we ain't just leaving," Gorm interrupted. "We're also searching the area, and if the gods have any kindness, we're also finding them thrice-cursed Orc statues. And then we're leaving."

"But think of what a necromancer could do to people around here!"

"I will think about it. And then I'll write it down, and I'll put it in our reports to the guild, and then they'll deal with any overactive skeletons," said Gorm. "Not us. We're on a job."

"But—"

Gorm wanted to remind the high scribe that if he couldn't manage to stay on his feet after looking at the remains of Big Blenny, he wasn't going to do anything to a horde of zombies beyond ensuring that they were well fed. But you couldn't say as much to someone who believed in destiny. Lots of heroes started out like Niln, wide-eyed children who thought they knew the end to their story and just assumed that the middle would sort itself out. They all learned one way or another that life's tale doesn't work that way; many only learned as much when they met their end in an unfortunate plot twist.

"What if fightin' the necromancer means the Elven Marbles get whisked away while we're busy?" Gorm said, switching tactics. "What would the king say? Or, what if someone else owns the looting rights to the necromancer, and another party of heroes is on the way? We don't know the whole picture, lad. We only have a hint of a piece of it. So we stick to the job."

"It just doesn't feel right," said Niln. "It's not … heroic."

"No, it's professional," said Gorm. "We'll be sure to report that there may be a necromancer runnin' about when we get back to a city."

Niln sighed. "Very well."

"Hey, you may want to see this," Laruna called to them, waving from the mouth of the cave.

The solamancer and Jynn had searched a shallow cleft in the granite outcropping. A fine mist hovered around several huge slabs of ice a few yards inside the mouth of the cave. Jynn was sorting through shards and packing that was scattered around several broken wooden crates. One of the box's sides was stamped with the words RELIC INVESTMENT GROUP.

"Relic Investments? That sounds familiar," said Gorm.

"Isn't that the company that took the marbles?" said Niln. He rooted through his backpack and pulled out the maroon file Johan had given them. "Yes, Relic Investments was transporting the Elven Marbles from Scoria to Andarun."

"So, this could be the crate containing the marbles," said Gorm.

"Could have been," corrected Jynn. "Now it's more of a pile of debris with some packing under it. And this as well." Jynn pressed a necklace into Gorm's hand.

It was a string of wispy, scratchy twine threaded through colored beads and small, yellowing pearls. Pearls with sharp edges and small roots. Pearls that didn't actually look much like pearls, once Gorm examined them closely. "Teeth?" he said.

"Your squire found them behind the ice," said Jynn.

"Da shebz'a!"

"Jewelry made from teeth is a common practice among the Orcs," said Jynn.

"And we know that the Orcs have been after the Elven Marbles," said Laruna. "They must have gotten the Elves' intelligence as well and come in to take them."

"But what about the necromancer?" said Niln.

"Necromancer?" said Jynn.

"We found evidence of the undead," said Kaitha.

"What would the undead want with the stones?" said Laruna. "They don't show much interest in anything they can't eat."

"Why would Orcs drag away the corpses?" said Heraldin.

Kaitha shook her head. "Nobody dragged away any corpses."

"The Orcs could be the necromancer," suggested Niln.

"Or the undead?" said Heraldin.

Gorm rubbed his temples. The problem with the professional heroics industry, he had often said over one-too-many beers, was the title. The fame and the glory and even the very word 'hero' had a way of going straight to people's heads and convincing them there was more to their job than violence and wealth retrieval. Overconfident heroes often tried to act as army commanders or diplomats or, as in this case, detectives.

He watched the rest of his party wrestle with the clues like a litter of kittens attempting to take on a loom. They reviewed evidence and discussed possible scenarios as though they were town guards and thief-catchers, rather than a team of hired killers specializing in monster removal.

He looked over and saw that Gaist was watching him. The weaponsmaster tilted his head toward the arguing heroes, and then gave Gorm a nod that summed up the Dwarf's thoughts quite succinctly.

"Aye," Gorm said. "Amateurs."

Gaist nodded and resumed watching the squabble.

When they started discussing the possibility of thieves flying in and out of the swamp atop giant birds, Gorm couldn't hold back. "Stop overthinking this," he barked. "There's a time and a place to figure out who took the marbles and why, but it ain't when the Elven Marbles themselves are less than day's ride away and leavin' fast. The point is to get the marbles back."

"How are we to know where to find the marbles if we don't know who took them?" said Laruna.

"Somebody walked out of here, right? Orcs or walking dead or a troupe of mummers, but somebody carried the stones out through the woods," said Gorm.

"Unless they rode away on Great Eagles," said Heraldin, a vocal proponent of the theory.

"Shut up. If someone walked out, they left tracks. And if they left tracks, we can follow them. And if we follow them—"

"We could find the stones," said Kaitha.

"I suppose we could," said Niln.

"Yes, but do we really want to go chasing after an unknown threat?" said Jynn.

"We could face a necromancer with an undead army," said Laruna.

"Or Orc sky-knights," suggested Heraldin.

"Whoever has the marbles probably intends to keep them," said Kaitha. "If it's the undead or an Orc horde, what then?"

Gorm held up his axe. "We kill 'em all and let the guild sort it out."

Two things were quickly apparent when the Seven Heroes started tracking whomever had stolen the Elven Marbles (again).

The first was that the thieves had made for the road by the most direct route possible. There had been a good-sized group of them; Kaitha thought ten to twelve individuals creating a broad path of signs through the undergrowth straight to the dirt road that curved around the camp.

The second truth was that there was no use trying to track anything on the road. The gravel path saw too much use from the swamp's denizens and was crossed by too many shallow streams. Kaitha lost the trail almost immediately, and after a mile in either direction, she couldn't pick it up again.

The shadows were growing long by then, and it was a long hike back to Ebenmyre. Gorm didn't like the idea of leaving the trail to grow colder than it already was, but he preferred it to a night in the Myrewood. Reluctantly, he announced they should head back to the inn, as the road would soon become too dangerous to travel.

Except that it didn't.

For the entire journey back to town, Gorm didn't spot so much as a scargling. Even the murderous whipvines seemed to shrink back at their approach. There were no howls from the forest, no threatening growls, no magically empowered weasels scampering into the road. It was the kind of peace that made Gorm uneasy: quiet where there should be noise, respite that wasn't hard earned. In his experience, it was usually the calm before the storm.

The others felt it too, he saw. Gorm caught Kaitha staring into the woods at times. If he didn't know better, he would have sworn she looked wistful, almost yearning for something out among the black trees. It was hard to tell, though; the Elf always turned back to the task at hand whenever she noticed someone watching her.

The fallout Gorm anticipated never came, and they made good time back to town. They were still on the first torch when they saw the lights of Ebenmyre and the Red Sow through the trees.

The innkeeper welcomed them back with an easy smile. "Good journey?"

"Unproductive," said Gorm, stamping the dirt from his boots. The other heroes filed into the tavern behind him.

"And did you encounter much trouble on the road?"

"No, surprisingly," said Heraldin, hanging his cloak.

"Ah. See? That'd be the King in the Wood," said the innkeeper. "Did you leave him the purple?"

"I suppose we forgot," said Gorm.

"Oh, you'll have to leave it out on a post in town. He's taken them off the one behind the stables before."

Gorm was in no mood to settle a bill with a reclusive forest spirit that was fixated on a particular color. "Look, I—"

The innkeeper's wife burst through the back door and affixed her horrible, fishy eyes on him. "Y'ain't paid tha king?" she demanded.

"Was just steppin' out to do it now," Gorm finished. Cursing superstition under his breath, he hurried out into the night.

The horses whinnied and nickered as he walked around the decrepit stables. Thordin's month was well underway, and shrubs outside the inn were beginning to show hints of amber. Soon, the month of Fireleaf would earn its name, setting trees alight with brilliant reds, yellows, and hues of orange. Not long thereafter, the Festival of Orchids would start in the halls beneath the mountain of Khazad'im, and Gorm would be absent yet again—if he couldn't manage to find the thrice-cursed Elven Marbles.

He thought about the campsite in the Myrewood. He'd expected bandits to be there, but instead they'd found signs of almost everyone else. What were licensed thugs doing at the bandit camp? How could the Orcs have gotten wind of Elven intelligence on the marbles' whereabouts? And what would a necromancer want with old Orc statues?

Something skittered away into the shadows, and it reminded Gorm of Burt, the handbag performer who'd told him about the Leviathan Project. The exact nature of the project was unclear, but it must have been the reason an evil wizard wanted the marbles. Otherwise, Detarr Ur'Mayan and his cohorts never would have stamped the project's sigil on them.

Gorm placed the handful of purple baubles on an old post between the stables and the wood. As luck would have it, he knew where he could talk to someone about the Leviathan Project. And talk to some Orcs. And find at least one thug. All his best remaining leads pointed to Bloodroot, the Orc settlement One-of-Each Magrash had directed him to.

As he passed the stables again, he was surprised to see Mr. Flinn and Brunt leading their mounts from the pens. "What are ye doin' here?" he barked.

Mr. Flinn seemed equally surprised by the encounter. "Why, Mr. Ingerson," he said, attempting to recover with some measure of grace. "What a coincidence that we should meet here."

"Especially since ye was supposed to be on business elsewhere," said Gorm. "What are ye doing here?"

"I'm afraid the nature of the mercenary business means that Silver Talon assignments and the locations they take us to are highly confidential," said Flinn.

"Top … secret!" rumbled Brunt.

"Right you are, Mr. Brunt. But let us focus on the affairs we have in common. Have you found your marbles, Mr. Ingerson?"

"In the works," said Gorm.

"Ah," said Mr. Flinn. He added with calculated casualness, "It seems your best course of action would be to return to Andarun."

"'If'n I didn't know better, I'd say that sounded like someone attempting to interfere with Heroes' Guild business."

"Oh, certainly not! Mere speculation between professionals."

They exchanged smiles of cordial loathing.

"As a matter of curiosity, I would enjoy learning where your adventure will take you," added Mr. Flinn.

"I'm afraid the nature of professional heroics keeps our plans highly confidential," said Gorm. "And the nature of our relationship means I'd sooner knock your teeth out than tell you."

"Aha. Clever. Your intimidating nature is matched only by your subtlety, Mr. Ingerson. On a probably unrelated note, Mr. Brunt is in an unusually poor mood this evening."

"Out … of … chewing … gum!" rumbled Brunt, petting his ox.

"And not a confectioner for miles," lamented Mr. Flinn. "Ah well. Where did you say you were going again, Mr. Ingerson?"

"I didn't."

"I'm sure I misheard you."

"Do ye think ye scare me, Tinderkin?" Gorm asked. "Did ye really think it was ye and an Ogre made me join this outfit? Ye had the full force of the law behind ye then, remember? Contractually obligated death? Ain't that way anymore. The law is on my side."

"Ah, but law is an interesting thing," said Mr. Flinn. "It only works so long as people want it observed. Those regulations nobody wants have a habit of slipping, no? Nobody obeys the old statutes on not selling meat on temple days, you see, because people enjoy steak regardless of how holy a festival is."

The Tinderkin removed an apple from his pouch and started carving it with a long dagger. "It brings Shadowkin to mind, no? I mean, you can give a Goblin a job, let's say a squire, but just having a job doesn't mean that people want a greenskin around. How loudly would they protest if such a creature was snuffed out?"

Gorm's eyes narrowed.

"Makes you think," said Mr. Flinn, popping a slice of apple into his mouth. "What's to stop me from going out and just killing a Goblin? Can a few papers really protect it?"

"Oh, the law is way more than papers," growled Gorm. "Why, if the law didn't always matter, how could a shopkeeper put out his wares and know they wouldn't be stolen? How could men buy land if there was a chance the deed might not mean a thing? And if the law can't protect a Goblin from you, what on Arth could protect you from me?"

Mr. Flinn's grin grew wide and genuine. "I imagine that would be Mr. Brunt's job."

"Oh. Right." Gorm had gotten so caught up in defending the Goblin that he had forgotten about the Ogre behind Flinn. A great hand closed over his shoulders.

"'Nother ... day! 'Nother ... giltin!" rumbled Brunt.

It's remarkably unusual for anyone to be caught unaware by an Ogre, as they generally possess all the stealth and cunning of an avalanche. It's remarkably unpleasant as well, Gorm reflected as he was hoisted into the air.

"I'm afraid he tends to be overprotective," said Mr. Flinn. "Do try to remember that, when we meet again. And we will meet again. Good day, Mr. Ingerson."

With a flick of Brunt's wrist, Gorm sailed through the air, through the stable door, and through the stable's back wall. He blasted through the old building in a cloud of rotten splinters, and still had plenty of time to think up a witty retort to shout at Flinn before he hit the ground. The wind was knocked from his ribs when he came to a skidding, rolling landing. He probably would have rolled for another house length, had he not slammed into the old post where he'd balanced the trinkets for the King in the Wood.

Gorm opened his eyes, and the curses he planned to holler at the Gnome died on his lips. He was staring up into a pair of startled eyes. An apelike face with gray skin the complexion of granite and long, daggerlike teeth stared back down at him. He opened his mouth to shout a warning, but a massive hand closed over him and smothered the cry. In another instant, he was lifted into the air and carried back into the Myrewood.

Laruna asked the innkeeper. "What's taking Gorm?" Kaitha wondered aloud.

"He's probably seeing to the horses," said Jynn.

The heroes sat around one of the tavern's round tables, nursing bad grog and waiting for cold sandwiches.

"How is the bathwater coming?" Laruna asked the innkeeper.

"I've got swamp muck in places I'd forgotten I even had," said Heraldin. "I must smell worse than the Goblin."

"Grot?"

"Oh, my Burlinda is working on your bath," the innkeeper told them. "You're welcome to speak to her if you're in a hurry."

"It can wait," said Heraldin. He turned back to the heroes. "I'm fairly certain half of that man's business model is blaming his wife."

"It's surprisingly effective," said Niln.

Gaist tapped the bard on the shoulder and held up a box with a thrones board.

"Good idea," said Heraldin. "I think it's going to be a long night."

So they settled in. Heraldin and Gaist started a game. Jynn and Laruna reviewed magical theory. Niln quietly began cross-referencing his book of prophecy with the king's notes on the Elven Marbles.

Kaitha watched the door. She wondered where Gorm was, although truthfully she was almost as worried about his return. They had yet to discuss her foolishness in the Myrewood, and she was certain it wouldn't be a pleasant conversation. But it was getting long for him to tarry, and something might have followed them from the swamp.

Or someone.

She felt a clammy hand on her shoulder. *"Da wugga nip."*

Kaitha smiled at the little Goblin. "Thanks," she said. "If he's not back in a few minutes, we'll go and have a look, shall we?"

"Havva luk," Gleebek attempted. "Havva luk Gurm Ingerzon."

Kaitha smiled. "That's right. And in the meantime, we do the best we can."

"Bast weggan." Gleebek's smile was like that of a puppy: enthusiastic, clueless, and full of needle-like teeth.

"Very good," Kaitha said. She pushed her grog aside, along with her worries and daydreams of a gardener. "You know, we really should teach you Imperial."

The Myrewood slipped by in a blur of black and gray, leaving Gorm hopelessly disoriented. His mind raced as he was borne along an unseen path, into the swamp. He hadn't had long to look at the face of his captor, but he was fairly certain he was dealing with a Troll.

Gorm had never faced a Troll, but the evidence that he was being carried by one was compelling. The stony complexion and rough texture of the hand pressed over Gorm's mouth. The ragged fur, as clumped and bedraggled as swamp lichen. The unnatural speed and silence with which the beast moved through the wood. He recognized many of the traits from Heroes' Guild warnings, or from the post-mortem files of lost adventurers.

The histories of the Agekeepers said that Trolls, like all Shadowkin, were descended from the races of men that had been twisted by Stennish magic. Several ages and countless generations ago, the Orcs were once Elves, and Goblins had been Dwarves, and Gnolls, Gremlins, and Slaugh were all lost clans of Gnomes. The Trolls, however, weren't just twisted by the magic of the traitorous Sten; they were the last descendants of the Sten themselves.

Trolls' solitary nature and aversion to any sort of community meant they were rare, which was fortunate, because if they weren't, everything else would be. Legendarily cruel, unbelievably stealthy, and terrifyingly lethal, Trolls were one of only three types of monsters that the guild had no official classification for. Gorm recalled that the Troll entry within the *Heroes' Guild Handbook* merely showed a woodcut and read: "Flee and Praye."

They didn't go far before the creature propped Gorm against a tree, as though setting up a doll in a diorama. The Troll was like a mountain gorilla, but more mountain than gorilla. The fur covering his stony skin was charcoal with patterns of silver and steel blue and was covered only by a loincloth and a band of small pouches across the creature's chest. His broad, apish face was reminiscent of a skull, with wide nostrils and small eyes set in deep sockets. An array of twisted, mismatched fangs nearly bisected his face when he bared his teeth.

The Troll crouched down so low that its face was almost level with the Dwarf's. "I think we should have a talk," he said in a deep, grating voice, like granite on a grindstone.

It wasn't much of an opening, but Gorm didn't expect better. He drew his axe and swung it upward in a sudden strike that connected with the Troll's throat. He could feel the axe-head dig deep into the beast's jugular. Thick black blood poured out in spurts that matched the Troll's choking gasps. Seizing the chance, Gorm abandoned his old weapon and ran, bounding into the darkness as far as his legs would carry him.

Which, as it turned out, wasn't far at all.

The edge of the clearing was still far from reach when he was grabbed by the leg and hoisted into the air. The Troll's face swung into view, upside-down and decidedly unhappy. Gorm braced himself for the end.

The Troll reached up and, with pointed slowness, pulled the axe from his neck and offered it to Gorm.

Gorm took the axe. "Aha—yes, well, I was wonderin' where I'd misplaced that. Careless, really."

"Indeed," managed the Troll, his voice cracking as his vocal chords knit themselves back together. The wound in his neck had almost totally closed already. "And now, you and I are going to have a talk."

"Right," said Gorm. He launched a storm of axe blows that slashed across the Troll's face and arm, kicked his way free, and almost made it three steps before he was hauled into the air once more.

"Rrrg! Why do you keep doing that?" the Troll growled, once enough of his face had regrown.

"Pretty foolish of me," Gorm admitted.

"Can I trust you if I give your weapon back?"

"Aye."

"Good." The Troll handed Gorm his axe.

"But ye shouldn't," said Gorm, slamming the axe into the Troll's eye. Theoretically, Gorm reasoned, if he could blind the beast, he might buy enough time to get into the swamp.

It was, like many good theories, completely wrong.

"I suppose an abduction makes a poor start to building a foundation of trust," said the Troll, a few moments later.

"Probably," agreed Gorm.

"Then again, sticking an axe in someone's face doesn't help the situation much, does it?"

"Nor does pinning someone upside down to a tree," said Gorm. The blood was rushing to his head.

"Therein lies our problem. How can I be sure you won't run again if I put you down?"

"Don't know," said Gorm. He was starting to feel dizzy. "How do I know ye won't kill me if I don't run?"

"Master Dwarf, I can assure you that when I want to kill someone, they are well aware of it, though only for a very short period of time." The Troll twisted his wrist to right Gorm.

"Fair enough. Then what do you want?"

"I think I've been perfectly clear," said the Troll, furrowing his brow. "I want to talk. To parlay. To make a deal. It would also be nice to not get stabbed or hacked in the face while doing so, if that's not too much trouble."

"From what I hear, Trolls don't negotiate."

"And flying Dwarves don't burst through walls, but here we are," said the Troll, setting Gorm on the ground. "All I want is to talk."

"Ye dragged me from the inn all the way to the middle of the Myrewood just to talk?"

"Look, I'll acknowledge this wasn't terribly well thought-out." The Troll paused, struggling to find words. "It's just that, if you had screamed, she might have hear—anyone might have heard ... I ... we ... It's very difficult to explain."

"I can see that. How about ye take some time to think it over?" said Gorm. A few years would be ideal. "And I'll just head back to my friends at the inn."

"No!" shouted the Troll, and the trees shook with the force of his emphasis.

Gorm froze.

"No, I … look, sorry about that. Let's start over. My name is Thane," he said, extending a finger.

"Gorm Ingerson." He shook the Troll's finger as if it were a hand.

"Excellent. Mr. Ingerson, I noticed earlier that you have a Goblin with you."

"Aye," said Gorm slowly. "He's me squire."

"Ah. So you must be the same Gorm Ingerson who punched out the Elven Guard at—"

"Bloody bones, has anybody not heard about that?" Gorm was almost starting to regret giving the guard his comeuppance. A hero trying to revitalize his career needed to pay at least a little heed to his reputation, and at the rate things were going, Gorm's outburst at the embassy would probably be the talk of the Festival of Orchids.

The Troll bared his fangs again in what Gorm realized was actually a grotesque facsimile of a smile. "So you're at least somewhat receptive to the idea of working with Shadowkin?"

"Some Shadowkin," Gorm qualified. "Did ye bring me out here to ask for a job?"

"Technically, I was out there to collect payment," said the Troll. He reached into one of his pouches and held out a handful of trinkets and beads.

Gorm recognized the purple payment he'd left atop a post behind the stables. "You're the King in the Wood."

"Well, it's a bit much as titles go," said the Troll, with what could have been a hint of false modesty. It was hard to read the expression on a Troll's face; mostly, they just looked murderous.

"So ye followed us all the way back from the thugs' camp?" said Gorm.

"Right."

"And the swamp beasts stayed away because…"

"Exactly. Everything avoids me," beamed Thane. "It's natural instinct. And monsters and threats could avoid all of you, too, if I was traveling as your squire —"

"Slow down, slow down. It ain't so simple," said Gorm. "People see Goblins in town all the time, but a Troll's a different thing. There ain't any Troll NPCs. Imagine what unsuspecting folks would think if they saw ye walking us down the street. To say nothing of what they'd think of the Dwarf walking next to ye."

If he brought a Troll back, Gorm wouldn't have to worry about attending the Festival of Orchids anymore; the clan would reinstate him just so they could banish him again.

"I'm well aware of people's reactions, thank you," said the Troll, looking annoyed, or perhaps hurt. "But look!" He bounded back into the clearing and crouched low. His muscles and skin tensed and shifted. Some hairs retracted and others shifted into mossy patterns. Earthy patterns flickered over his skin. In less than a second, the Troll was indistinguishable from a mossy pile of granite boulders.

"Burn me," swore Gorm softly.

"See?" said the Troll, shifting from mineral to monster as he sprang to his feet. "They'll never see me."

"Maybe not a passerby, but what will I tell me party?" said Gorm.

"Nothing," said Thane. "You don't tell them a thing. It's our secret."

"I'd have to tell them," said Gorm.

"No," said the Troll. "That's the deal. I protect you, and you can't … you don't tell her about me. That's all I want."

"Who?"

"Her name is Kaitha," said the Troll.

"Why would ye — oh, no." There was no mistaking the enamored glint in the Troll's beady eyes.

"She came into my garden," said the Troll, looking wistfully into the distance. "She spoke to me."

"No. Nope," said Gorm, staring at his feet. Dwarves are reticent about almost any matters of the heart, but Gorm imagined most non-Dwarves would be equally uncomfortable at the thought of a Troll besotted with an Elf. "This ain't my business."

"We talked of life and dreams, of what we were and are and could be. And she sang to me, Mr. Ingerson."

"Ye don't have to tell me about it." Images were springing up in Gorm's mind, and he couldn't stamp them out fast enough.

"She sang a song so sweet that animals came into my garden. They weren't even scared!"

"It's just that it ain't proper to speak of such things."

"And her song — like the voice of a goddess. It's like I've lived my whole life just to hear that voice."

"So go and tell her that," said Gorm. "Or don't. So long as ye leave me out of it."

"Tell her?" Thane looked at Gorm incredulously.

"Aye. Ye talked, right? Just say hello. Or whatever it is ye tall folk do when you're … fond of each other."

"Well, yes. But to her, I was a spirit of the forest, a force of nature. If I just go and talk to her, I'd just be … this." The Troll gestured helplessly at himself. "This is what makes people who see me run screaming, or try to put an axe through my face. What if she did that?" He shuddered visibly at the thought. "I couldn't endure it. Not from her."

"Sorry," said Gorm. "But I've a job to do, and I don't need some tragic, unrequited love interferin' with it."

While the *Heroes' Guild Handbook* couldn't forbid anything, it recommended against any sort of romantic involvement on the job. To a professional hero, any sort of distraction could be deadly — for the lovers and others — so the guild frowned on budding romances, passionate interludes, or even unseen pining. While the guild wasn't specific on fraternizing with Trolls or other monsters, Gorm was confident it would be universally frowned upon. The only thing more distracting than an inter-species relationship among the party would be the inevitable torch-waving mobs that came to end the abomination.

"I'm not asking you to get involved," pleaded the Troll. "I'm asking for the exact opposite. Keep my secret. Let me stay by her side as she'd prefer me, as the faceless king."

Gorm shook his head. "It's just … ye don't keep a secret this big from your party."

Thane seemed to wither like a flower in frost. "I see," he said. "I suppose it's for the best. If I can't sway the Dwarf who defended a Goblin, what hope could I have with her?"

Gorm let out a long, weary sigh and tried to convince himself that fame and fortune and the Festival of Orchids were all overrated.

"You won't regret this," said Thane.

"I regretted it the moment I agreed to it," said Gorm, allowing the Troll to gently set him down a few yards behind the tavern.

"You won't regret this any more than you already do."

"I've said as much about a lot recently, and I'm always wrong." An autumn evening was falling on the Red Sow, and Gorm could see concerned figures peering through the glowing amber windows. Soon, the heroes would send out searches. "Now, if ye'll excuse me, I've got to run to the stables."

"The stables?"

"Aye. A piece of straw or two in me beard and some muck on me boots, and everyone will think I spent too long groomin' the horses."

Bidding farewell to Thane was more involved than he expected, as the Troll required several reassurances that his secret was safe. After several grumbled promises, Gorm managed to extricate himself and start for the stables. He glanced back over his shoulder when he had crossed half the distance. The ruins of Ebenmyre were empty, save for a pile of boulders that briefly flashed him a thumbs-up.

Gorm's explanation of his prolonged absence, which included his encounter with Flinn and Brunt and his trip to the stables but omitted any reference to the Troll encounter, was to everyone's satisfaction, save the innkeeper and Niln. The innkeeper was unhappy about the hole in his stables. Niln was unhappy that he had to pay for it.

There was just one piece of unfinished business left for the evening.

Gorm held off until after he'd laid the case for going to Bloodroot, after Niln and the others had reluctantly agreed, after the food had been served and eaten and complained about, and after the other heroes had grown weary, one by one, and headed upstairs to bed. It wasn't until he and Kaitha were the only two left at the table that he started the conversation they'd both been dreading.

"Ye split the party, Kaitha."

The Elf wilted a little. "I know."

"Ye never split the party."

"I know."

"Ye had me chewin' my whiskers with worry. If ye'd fallen out there, or gotten lost, what could we do? Ye might have died. Ye might not have been the only one."

"I know."

It hadn't been the only time she'd slipped, Gorm told her, but she knew that as well. Her late-night drinking binges were making them depart late and compromising combat readiness. She knew that, too. People were starting to think she was in the midst of another of her famous meltdowns, and to worry they would soon be at the center of another story for the more salacious town criers. Kaitha was well aware. The unspoken issue sitting between them wasn't that Kaitha didn't know she was in another spiral, but that she didn't know any way out, except the spot at the bottom.

Gorm sighed. "So why did ye split the party?"

"I … I needed a drink," said the Elf reluctantly.

"Right in the middle of the swamp?"

"I think we've made it clear that I have a problem."

"So how do we fix it?" said Gorm.

"Here." Kaitha pushed her grog away. She rummaged through her rucksack, produced a silver flask, and dropped it on the table. "I'll have no more drink. Not another drop."

"Ye think it's that simple?"

Kaitha shook her head. "Gorm, when I was in the wood, I felt like … like something followed me, keeping me safe. A protector. And when it was there, I wasn't so … thirsty."

She looked out the window wistfully, and Gorm felt a chill run up his spine. The ranger was looking directly at the spot where he had left Thane.

"And I know he likely isn't there, that this King in the Wood is probably a superstition wrapped in a marketing ploy, but thinking he is there, that he might really be watching over me, it helps, you know? I don't want to ... drink as much. I'm more myself. The me I used to be, when I was the Jade Wind."

She turned back to Gorm. "It's a useful lie, so I believe it. It's better than reality. Like telling yourself there's justice in the world, or that we can make a difference. They're probably not true, but we'll be better people if we pretend they are.

"I don't know if I can fix everything about myself by giving up drinking and handing you the flask, or even fix anything. But I'll come closer if I trust it will work, so what choice do I have but to believe? We need the lie."

Gorm looked out the window and saw the silhouette of a pile of boulders that was not a pile of boulders. "Aye," was all he could say.

Kaitha followed his gaze. "I still dream that the King in the Wood is more than a spirit, and perhaps even a man, an Elf. And that he made the garden I found in the Myrewood, and I could join him there again someday, after all of this."

"It's possible," Gorm lied. His heart was heavy as he bade her goodnight.

Chapter 13

"And so we can see that loot yields have dropped another thirteen percent." Poldo pointed to a chart that looked like a crimson ski slope. "It's starting to have an adverse effect on some of our other holdings. Adventure Capital is down four percent. Vorpal Corp. dropped six."

"Indeed," said Baggs, without looking up from his ledger. Neither he nor Goldson seemed particularly interested in Poldo's report, despite the extra red ink and very large print Poldo had used to try to attract their attention. Poldo had tried many things to get his superiors to notice his findings, from big graphs to long reports to props and visual aids. He'd even hired a painter to do an emotive rendition of the recent profit reports, but the resulting work was too horrible to display. He'd had the thing burned. He still had nightmares about it.

Yet Mr. Goldson and Mr. Baggs seemed wholly unconcerned by the dismal figures. If anything, they were more boisterous than normal, and they were definitely becoming more aggressive in their stock purchases. The whole world screamed that financial calamity was almost upon them, and yet Goldson and Baggs acted as if it were the golden era of the empire. As a general rule, Poldo always assumed they knew something he didn't, but he'd be burned for a Sten if he wasn't really bloody curious what it was this time.

A chime rang out from the back of the room. One of the small crystals in the back wall was glowing with a faint ruby light.

Goldson frowned. "Mr. Poldo, if you could do me the favor."

"Yes, sir," said Poldo. He hurried back and read the small plaque under the lit crystal. "It says Damrod the Eye, sir."

The ancient Dwarf and the nearly-as-ancient Halfling looked up from their respective ledgers, suddenly concerned.

"It appears it shall be the contingency after all," said Mr. Baggs.

"Let's hope so," said Mr. Goldson. "We shall have to call upon the Mask." He rang a small silver bell on the side of his desk.

A smartly dressed Halfling opened the great black doors and ducked her head in. "Sirs?" she asked, peering over her horn-rimmed glasses.

"Miss Lobelia, send a message to the Elven Embassy," said Mr. Baggs. "Memo: Damrod the Eye has died."

"And whom shall I address it to?"

"Damrod the Eye," said Mr. Baggs.

"Yes, sir." Miss Lobelia shut the door behind her, leaving Mr. Goldson and Mr. Baggs to their ledgers and Poldo to his confusion.

"But he … why would you …?" Mr. Poldo looked from the door back to the great black desks of Goldson and Baggs, and back to the door again. "Wasn't Damrod the Eye—?"

"Mr. Poldo, are your reports quite finished?" said Mr. Baggs.

Poldo collected himself. "I did have several more key points, sir."

"What's the market doing with the Dragon of Wynspar?" asked Mr. Goldson.

"It's up four and a half giltin, sir."

"Tell the men in the brokerage to buy ten thousand shares," said Mr. Goldson.

"Thank you, Poldo," said Mr. Baggs.

Poldo felt a twinge of despair. "It's just that I did have several more reports to review."

"That won't be necessary, thank you," said Mr. Baggs.

"We will offset our risk by investing in the Dragon of Wynspar," said Mr. Goldson.

"I even had a bit to do with some props and, ahem, visual aids," said Poldo, losing his nerve as Mr. Goldson and Mr. Baggs looked up from their work and directly at him.

"Your reports have been noted," said Mr. Baggs coldly. "Investing in the DOW will help rebalance and stabilize our portfolio."

"Thank you, Mr. Poldo," repeated Mr. Goldson, with deliberate finality.

"Yes, sirs," said Poldo. He felt a twinge of regret as he hurriedly packed up his charts and visual aids. He'd been very much looking forward to the bit with the toy dagger and the inflated rubber bladder.

The road between Ebenmyre and Bloodroot was flat and barren, with nothing to be seen but oceans of tall grasses and the same mountains in the misty distance. There was nothing to do either, except swat at the midgeflies and count the dirt-pig nests for three days.

The evenings were different, Laruna reflected, as she rushed to finish her dinner. It wasn't easy to hurry through the meal; dirt-pig was tough and gamey enough to gag a Dire Wolf, and Dwarven hardtack managed to be even less edible. The only diversion Laruna found to distract her from the monotony of the ride and her saddle sores was her nightly training with Jynn.

"Shall we begin?" Jynn asked, walking to the campfire.

"Mpph," she replied through a piece of dirt-pork. After considerable effort, Laruna managed to force down the bite of gnarled meat and tell Jynn that she would need a couple of minutes. He offered to set up the training area while she finished, and she gave him a smile and a grateful nod while trying to take a bite of hardtack.

After dinner, she returned to her tent for some quick preparations. She cleaned the grease off her hands and the crumbs off her robe. She glanced over the reading she'd been doing in *Thurmon's Guide To Magic*. A dash of vanilla oil on her wrists helped mask the persistent odor of sweat and horse that followed traveling heroes everywhere. She ran her hands through her hair and, after a moment of consideration, decided to tie it up with a long ribbon. Finally ready, she left the tent.

Heraldin lounged on a pile of saddlebags next to the campfire and plucked idly at a lute. Gaist stood a short distance away, arms crossed in the usual fashion, but somehow looking more relaxed than normal. They watched Laruna with lazy eyes as she crossed the campsite. "Well, don't you look nice this evening," Heraldin called to her. "Look, Gaist, she's put her hair up."

Laruna grit her teeth as she felt a blush rising in her cheeks. "Shouldn't you be playing your board game?"

"In time, in time," the bard assured her. "I find it best to let the hardtack settle. Besides, not all of us are so eager for our lessons." There was a barb in the bard's voice and a smug twinkle in his eye.

"And just what are you getting at?" Laruna demanded, planting her feet in front of the bard and her hands on her hips.

"Oh, come now," laughed Heraldin. "We all see it. You and the noctomancer have been closer than a Kobold tribe since the Myrewood. The whispered conversations you hold. The secret smiles you share. The lessons that last far longer than they need to."

Laruna stiffened. "We're sharing arcane knowledge," she snapped. "It's to improve our spell casting."

"Typical mages," Heraldin said to Gaist. "So busy unlocking the mysteries of the universe that they can't see what's right in front of their noses."

Gaist nodded.

"Don't encourage him," said Laruna, jabbing a finger at the weaponsmaster.

"Listen, friend, it's not our fault that a lifetime of study at the academy has left you two blind to what's happening here."

"And what exactly do you think is happening here?" she hissed.

"Oh, they met as foes, but their animosity is a facade to mask their hearts," said the bard airily, playing a slow melody on his lute. "And now that fate has brought them together, they can't hide their true feelings. Like a flower blooming within the harshest desert, love finds a way."

"Ridiculous," snorted Laruna.

"If you say so," said the bard, sharing a knowing glance and a disaffected shrug with Gaist. "But if there was a chance for such love, it would be a shame to miss out, would it not? Romance between former rivals is passionate and wonderful. Truly, it is the best kind of love."

Laruna hesitated. Jynn had been much more personable lately, she had to admit. She couldn't deny a certain anticipation of her nightly training with the wizard. The last lesson hadn't even involved that much sorcery; they had spent most of their evening talking.

She shook the bard's fantasies from her head. "You know nothing," she snarled.

"On the contrary, if there is one thing I know, it is the heart of a woman," said the bard. "Though I'm familiar with the rest of her body as well," he told Gaist with a sly wink.

The weaponsmaster scowled.

"Killjoy," said Heraldin. "Still, I know what I see, and I see a noctomancer and solamancer spending a lot of time together."

"And? The two orders work together all the time," Laruna shot back, though she knew collaborations between solamancers and noctomancers were usually far more terse and involved much less laughter than her last few sessions with Jynn.

"Do they? A pity. Forbidden love is the best kind of love."

"You throw that word around too freely."

"And you hide from it like a schoolgirl," said Heraldin. "Still, your business is your own, and I'll leave you to it. I won't tell the others of our chat, and I'm sure it's safe to assume that Gaist won't say anything."

Gaist nodded.

"Why should I care who you tell your inane theories to?" Laruna waved a dismissive hand.

Heraldin strummed his lute with a wistful sigh. "Because a secret love, a romance known only by the lovers who hide it, is the very best kind of love."

"You say every kind of love is the best kind."

"Yes," said Heraldin, wearing an infuriating grin.

"Fine. Think what you please," said Laruna, throwing her hands up and leaving the obnoxious duo to their games and their lute music. She had better things to do than listen to the bard's ramblings. Besides, she didn't want to be late for her session with Jynn.

"He's getting better," Kaitha offered.

Gorm snorted. "Well, he sure as flame couldn't get any worse."

"No, really. A week ago Niln was running from the training golem."

They watched as the high scribe furiously dueled the training golem in the center of a dusty ring situated off the side of the old dirt road. Niln made a couple of simple jabs at the dummy, feinted in the wrong direction, and was knocked off his feet by a clumsy blow upside the head.

"Now he's just getting beat by it."

"We'll call it progress," Kaitha repeated.

"And what of Gleebek?" They turned to another dusty ring, where the Goblin squared off against the other training golem.

"He's a star pupil," said Kaitha. "That's on the expert setting."

"Have at … you!" The golem made an aggressive lunge for the Goblin, but Gleebek quickly sidestepped the blow and jabbed his dagger into the target spot beneath the left shoulder. The golem's arm blew off with a loud rush, and its fate was sealed. A couple of moments later, Gleebek struck the heart target and sent the golem's head rocketing out across the plain. Its cry of, "Well … met!" faded as it flew into the distance.

"Bones," said Gorm. "That's pretty good."

"And he's starting to pick up a little Imperial as well," said Kaitha.

"Oh?"

When Kaitha nodded, he hollered to the distant Goblin. "Hello! Ye speakin' Imperial with everybody but me now?"

Gleebek waved furiously. "Hallo, Gurm Ingerzon! Hallo!"

Gorm couldn't help but laugh at his squire's vigorous enthusiasm. "Aye. Hello, Gleebek."

"No! No hallo Gleebek! *Tib'rin!* Gleebek is hallo!"

"We'll call it progress," Gorm muttered to Kaitha. Waving his goodbyes, he resumed his rounds. Ostensibly, he was on guard duty, but that job had been outsourced.

As dusk fell, he headed out into the field, away from the other heroes, and located a likely looking pile of rocks. "Troll," he said, giving the stones a tap with the toe of his boot. "Aye, Troll, is that ye?"

"No," said a voice behind him, sending Gorm into the air and his heart into his throat.

He tried not to jump whenever Thane appeared, but natural selection had not been kind to those who weren't terrified by the approach of a Troll. Thane always looked hurt by Gorm's reaction.

Rather than dwell on it, Gorm asked if Thane had anything to report.

"A groundshark around noon," said Thane. "A pack of dust-scargs not two hours ago. They all kept a wide berth."

"Good."

"I told you this would work, didn't I?" prompted the Troll. "You have yet to see a single roaming monster. I heard the bard tell the wizard that's almost unheard of this far out in the wilderness."

"Aye, but it's gettin' to be a lot of work keepin' them from seeing the one monster who's roaming next to us all day long. The Elf keeps lookin' directly at wherever ye are. It's almost eerie."

Thane looked at the firelight flickering in the distance. "Our depths echo with the same song," he said wistfully.

Gorm suppressed a shudder. "So go talk to her if ye've such a connection."

"Well, it's not that much of a connection."

"Right."

"I've kept my part of the bargain," said the Troll. "All you need to do is let me pretend I'm one of you — the ninth in your party."

"It's a mummer's farce."

"No, it's my farce," growled the Troll. He turned back to the distant camp. "I sit close enough to smell the fire, to hear your voices, and it's like I'm among friends. And we laugh and talk, and I belong. I'm where I should be. Even if it's just a daydream, it's mine."

"But it ain't really there."

"It's still more than I had a week ago." Thane jabbed a finger like a sapling at Gorm's chest. "And it's my price for keeping watch over your party. I think it more than fair."

Gorm shrugged and dropped the matter. The business of tall-folk was their own. He thanked the Troll for the report and headed back to camp.

Heraldin and Gaist sat next to the fire, as they did every night, with a game of thrones balanced on a rock between them. Each had taken to carving notches on his side of the board to mark his victories. Gaist's edge was covered with nicks and scars, while Heraldin's remained pristine.

Gorm retrieved the maroon file on the Elven Marbles and sat down next to the game.

"What are you reading, my friend?" asked Heraldin.

"I'm looking through the king's file. There may be some mention of the Leviathan Project."

"Do you suppose the project has any relation to the Leviathan of legend?" The bard advanced a priest, and Gaist quickly knocked it down with a knight.

"Can't say I recall that one," said Gorm.

"It's in the old sagas, the songs that all the bards know and nobody cares to hear." Heraldin took the knight with a bannerman.

"What's it about?"

Heraldin began to sing:

> *In the lost age of Fables*
> *in the high reign of the Sten,*
> *When Al'Thadan was noble,*
> *And Shadowkin were still men –*

Gorm cut him off. "Give me the short version."

"See? Nobody wants to hear the old sagas," Heraldin said to Gaist.

The weaponsmaster nodded and knocked over Heraldin's bannerman.

"The story is a strange one. It takes place back in the Second Age, when Mannon, King of Shadows, roams the world freely and Al'Thadan has not yet turned to serve him," said Heraldin. "The people who are now the Shadowkin had just joined sides with Mannon, as did some of their gods, splitting the pantheon. Al'Thadan sets out to reunite them." He knocked over Gaist's last knight.

"So he challenges Mannon to a fight, Al'Thadan with his holy sword, and Mannon with his dark claws. And it's a big battle."

Gaist killed Heraldin's bannerman.

"Their duel lasts for days. The ballad has over thirty-six verses of them fighting." Heraldin took a lord, unanswered.

"No wonder nobody listens to these songs."

Gaist advanced a priest and lost it.

"In the end, Al'Thadan prevails, and he casts Mannon from the heavens out into the nothing." Heraldin grinned as he took Gaist's final lord, leaving the weaponsmaster with a king and a couple of bannermen. "But Mannon does something unexpected."

Hints of a smirk rippled the crimson scarf Gaist wore over his face. He moved his king back, pinning Heraldin's knight and making it his own.

Heraldin frowned and advanced a lord. "A fish dies at the same moment as Mannon, and he uses low magic, the old magic of blood and stone and prophecy, to bind his spirit to that of the dead fish."

"A fish?" Gorm sounded dubious.

"I said it was a strange tale."

Gaist advanced his new knight, pinning a bannerman.

"Mannon cannot go wherever it is that fish go when they die, but the fish is bound to the great weave of reality, and so Mannon cannot leave it." Heraldin advanced a bannerman, and his priest was pinned. "Bound together by curse or prophecy, there's nowhere for Mannon and the fish to go but Arth, where they share one life, one body. The Leviathan."

Heraldin lost another knight. Now his forces were evenly matched with Gaist's.

"The gods think Mannon is dead, and so does everyone else. But years later, in the Third Age, this great fish shows up in the Teagem Sea, massive and deadly. It sinks ships. It wipes out an entire coastal city."

The bard and the weaponsmaster exchanged a quick flurry of moves that left Heraldin with only a pair of bannermen to protect his king. The weaponsmaster was definitely smirking now.

Heraldin scowled. "So the people of the world send out a great fleet of warships to hunt down the Leviathan. The greatest heroes of the age are on the expedition; the ballad has another twenty-seven verses just describing the captains of the various vessels."

"Who would have ever listened to this stuff?"

"Bard apprentices," said Heraldin. "Trust me, it's awful."

"I'm surprised ye went to the Bards' College at all," said Gorm. "I thought ye was always a thie—"

"I was a bard long ago, when I was running from a past life," Heraldin interrupted loudly. "But singing for my supper didn't suit me, nor did the Heroes' Guild, and so I pursued an alternative career."

Gaist took one of Heraldin's last bannermen.

"As a thie—"

"As a hoard adjuster. But then word got out that I was, aha, adjusting the value of the hoards in too literal a sense."

"You were steal—"

"I was exercising lifelong skills in creative acquisitions," said Heraldin. "But the guild did not see it that way, and as our mutual friend Mr. Flinn was quick to point out, Benny Hookhand likely won't see it that way either. And one does not practice certain illicit skills in the Freedlands without the approval of the Hookhand, especially not if you have a history with him. And so here we are."

Gaist took the final bannerman, leaving Heraldin with a lone king.

"Trapped," muttered the bard.

"So what happened with the Leviathan?" asked Gorm.

"What? Oh. When the warships killed it, Mannon and his host were separated. The fish swam away or died or something, but Mannon ascended to the heavens and gathered the lost gods back to him. It's the start of the War of Betrayal, where Mannon is almost victorious until Tandos strikes him down, and Al'Thadan and the Sten turn traitor and are wiped from the great weave."

Gaist knocked Heraldin's king over with an air of finality.

"Is there no way to defeat this man?" fumed the bard. "I was within an inch of victory. Come on, set up the board again."

Gorm thanked the bard and sat back to think about the story. It explained the symbol of Project Leviathan—the monstrous, tentacled fish that Gorm had seen stamped on the bottom of the Elven Marble. Perhaps more telling, the Leviathan's story was about a power that returned from beyond the grave, and such legends drew necromancers like moths to a flame. Yet if there was more than a connection, Gorm couldn't see it.

He turned back to reading the file on the Elven Marbles, and continued to study them until an inferno exploded in the night sky. The giant ball of flame cast a light as bright as midday, so that Gorm could clearly see the fireball's blast wave rippling across the camp. Niln, Gleebek, and Kaitha were lifted into the air by the shockwave.

The training golems cried out as every target joint on their wooden bodies triggered simultaneously and blew them apart. Gaist and Heraldin dove for cover as their game of thrones flew away in a cloud of dust and ornately carved pieces. Then a wall of force and heat washed over Gorm, drowning his curses and throwing him back into the dust.

"Beautiful," gasped Laruna, staring into the sky. All that remained of the fireball was a cloud of golden embers drifting across the stars above where the mages lay on their backs, side by side.

"That was amazing," said Jynn, his voice breathless and full of awe.

"I never thought I could ... I mean, I just didn't think it could be so ... so ..." Words failed Laruna.

"I know," said Jynn.

Angry shouts rang out from the direction of the campsite. She could hear Gorm and Kaitha hollering to each other and recognized Gleebek's terrified babbling.

"I'll see to them," said the noctomancer, standing. Getting up took considerable effort; Jynn struggled to extract himself from the wizard-shaped crater created when the concussive wave from Laruna's fireball had blasted the mages from their feet and driven them into the loose earth of the plains. He hollered an apology to the campsite, and was answered by a stream of distant, shouted curses.

Laruna paid them little mind as she gazed up at the cinders dancing in the wind. She remembered the feeling of the magic channeling down her arms. Her fingers still felt the tiny currents of air Jynn had sent to guide her, as gentle as a whisper, as firm as a touch. Her hands had danced in the breeze he conjured, and under his guidance, she wove sorcery into forms she had never imagined. When she finally released the spell, it flew up to the heavens and unleashed an explosion that dwarfed anything she had ever conjured, anything she had ever seen. It was a power beyond her wildest dreams, and she already possessed it. All she needed to do was learn how to take it.

"I think I've smoothed things over," Jynn told her.

From the distant campsite, Gorm roared another torrent of profanity.

"Mostly," the noctomancer added, lying back down next to Laruna. "Still, we should probably stay out here a while longer."

For a while, they silently watched the sky. Laruna found herself tracing her hands with her fingertips, remembering the caress of the wind. "I burned down my village when I was a girl," she said softly.

"I read that in your file when you were before the council for full magehood," said Jynn. "Nobody blames you. It can be confusing or terrifying to discover the sorcerous gift."

"Terrifying? Try wonderful," said Laruna. "My father used to beat me every night with a reed for being a dolt. The other villagers used to mock me, day in and day out. Everywhere I went, they called me stupid and ugly, always telling me I'd never amount to anything. Do you have any idea what it's like hearing that day after day?"

"I can imagine," said Jynn.

"Finding my gift was the second-greatest thing ever to happen to me. The best was my father's face when I burned his hovel to the ground." She could still feel the rage and exultation of that moment; just the memory of it was enough to send errant sparks from her clenched fists. She opened her hand reluctantly. "Call it blame or call it credit, but I'm the one who torched every single building and left those buck-toothed cow-herds behind with the ashes. But…" She trailed off.

"But their words always haunt you," Jynn said.

"Yes," said Laruna. "I guess I always just assumed the townspeople, my father, all of them were right: that I didn't have what it took be a real mage. That the gift was all I had. But now, that fireball … I can weave."

"You can weave," said Jynn. She couldn't see his face, but she could hear the smile in his voice.

"This is why you didn't vote for my ascension, isn't it?" she asked him, pointing to the last embers drifting across the stars. "This is why you kept me an apprentice."

"It certainly wasn't because you burned down some shacks and frightened a bunch of farmers," said Jynn. "You could have stumbled upon such a spell by yourself. You might have discovered how to start a powerful weave, but not how to tie it off. A mage must have power and control. You had one."

"I don't think I'll ever have control like you do," she told him. "I mean, you practically wove that spell for me using my own hands. Bones, Jynn, where did you learn to weave like that?"

"When I was a boy, I had to weave well to please … to please my master," he said. "As I got older, I realized I needed to weave twice as well as most mages if I wanted to succeed, because I can channel half as much. I learned to compensate. But you, you don't need to control magic as well as I do. With the power you wield, you'll be besting Archmages in duels before you have half my skill. You will be a greater mage than I."

She reached across the space between them and touched his hand. "I may be more powerful someday, but I will never be greater."

He took her hand in his own. Together, they stared up at the ash cloud swirling in front of the moon. Laruna took the chance to silently revise the list of the best things ever to happen to her.

Niln sat in his small tent, holding his quill above a page as he waited for scripture to appear. The lantern was dry and dark. Flecks of ash and sear marks on his sacred stone were the only remnants of his consecrated incense. He was on his last candle; the rest had been reduced to dribbly piles of wax over the course of the night. Now, in the early hours just before dawn, even the crickets and nightfrogs were silent.

The page beneath his quill was blank.

Sweat beaded the high scribe's brow. He had prayed tirelessly. He had imbibed holy tea and inhaled the fumes of consecrated incense until his head spun. He had meditated, chanted, sung, studied the scriptures, and prayed some more. Muttered prayers, silent prayers, spoken prayers, sung prayers.

The goddess was silent. There were no words from her, no sense at all of her presence. It was just him, sitting alone in the cold darkness of the plains, surrounded by heroes who had put aside their skepticism to join him out here, with their lives on the line, because of his words, his prophecy, his faith.

The same faith that had brought him to the middle of nowhere.

Niln had experienced silent stretches before, of course. Even a prolific high scribe still had more nights without divine intervention than with it. The problem was the final line of the *Second Book of Niln*, which was relayed to him the evening after their day in the Myrewood. It sat at the bottom of his last page.

And the work of High Scribe Niln was complete.

Years of training to be a priest and then an acolyte. Countless hours of prayers and study. A massive initiative and campaign within the temple, diplomacy and bartering with the Temple of Tandos, two failed recruiting efforts before the current strategy. He had spent all of his life in preparation for this quest, this work.

And the work of High Scribe Niln was complete.

He'd had doubts about his capability, to be sure. There wasn't a single aspect of professional heroics that Niln could perform with a shred of confidence. The other heroes looked to the Dwarf for leadership. The wizard was more knowledgeable. The training dummy could still best him in a duel. Yet in the face of all this adversity, Niln had always had his faith to guide him. He'd known that he was the Seventh Hero, even if all of the facts said otherwise.

And the work of High Scribe Niln was complete.

He pulled his robe tighter around him, trying to ward off a chill that bit deeper than the deepest winter. Had he misinterpreted the scriptures, or were they wrong—the madness of Al'Matra as so many contended? Had the scriptures been the words of Al'Matra at all?

Dawn's light crept beneath the flaps of his tent. After a long night wrestling with the silence, he still had nothing but a blank page and a pain in his head that made it throb like a beating drum. Niln put his paper and quill away and stepped out of the tent. Gorm was tending the cookfire. Heraldin was attempting to toast hardtack over it. Neither noticed the scribe slip to where the horses were tied and grab a satchel from the bags of gear.

Taking his staff in one hand and the bag in the other, Niln made his way out into the field, well past where he and the Goblin had sparred the night before. When he found a suitable spot, he opened the satchel and removed a wood and iron box. He placed it carefully on the ground, took a step back, and rapped his staff on the ground. "Let us begin," he said.

The training golem unfolded like a clockwork blossom and drew itself to its full height. "Greetings … honored foe! Command?"

"Duel mode. Easy—no, medium difficulty."

"A fight … then!" said the golem, jerking into a combat stance. "Well … then! Have … at ye knave!"

Niln lunged, and got a blow to the ear that knocked him to the ground. The golem's sword was a wooden dowel, but Niln could already feel the welt forming along the side of his face. He stood again and resumed his attack with all the desperation of a man with nothing left to lose.

The first three blows never even touched the golem. But on the fourth try, his staff landed on the automaton's right arm. Soon, his strikes were reliably connecting, and he even managed to parry a few of the golem's counterstrikes.

"A worthy … foe!" said the golem.

Niln grinned. "I think I'm starting to get the hang of this."

Something breezed past the high scribe's ear. The golem jerked to a halt as its wooden face was split down the middle by a hefty axe. "Well … fought …" the golem said, its voice warped as it fell to its knees and slumped forward into the dust.

Niln turned, trembling, to face a band of hulking figures, their faces ranging from a mottled olive color to bright emerald. They wore leather armor and sharp-tusked grins, and carried an assortment of axes, cleavers, and long, cruel knives. Orcs.

The Orc in the lead stepped forward. "I am Char, of the Guz'Varda Tribe. You will come with us," he said.

"I'd rather not, if it's all the same to—"

"Your wooden stick is feeble and tiny," roared the Orc, pointing at Niln's staff. "My blood-brothers have many blades, sharp and deadly. You would do well to consider this!"

Niln considered it, and dropped his staff. "Where shall we go?"

The life of an NPC was more difficult for Orcs than for most other Shadowkin. Andarun, indeed much of the Freedlands, was like a great cultural melting pot, but Shadowkin had a tendency to sink to the bottom. Gremlins and Goblins and Kobolds had no qualms about eking out a meager existence on the margins of society; long histories of serving as cannon fodder in the armies of darkness had bred them for a life underfoot. Orcs, however, were once the most elite warriors of Mannon, and Orcish pride could seldom tolerate the jobs and stations afforded an NPC.

Instead, Orc NPCs tended to form their own communities. They traditionally lived in an honor society, and as is often the case with honor societies, their tradition had less to do with noble codes of chivalry and more to do with chopping people's body parts off for perceived insults. The blend of Freedlands law and Orc custom that governed NPC Orc settlements usually meant they paid taxes but kept the public maiming, frequent duels to the death, and remarkably common executions that were the hallmarks of Orcish society. Worse, from the outside, these NPC communities were virtually indistinguishable from the tribes of Orc foes, wherein not being an Orc was a capital offense. So it was always wise to view an approaching mob of fifty or more Orc warriors with a healthy degree of caution. Gorm found that the healthiest degree was to draw his weapon and shout for the other heroes when he saw the warband marching down the road.

"I am Char of the Guz'Varda Tribe," announced the foremost Orc as the warband drew close. Beads and teeth, many more than those worn by the others, dangled from his long chin-curtain beard. "You will come with us."

"We're on our way to Bloodroot," said Gorm. "One-of-Each Magrash sent us."

"Excellent," said the Orc. "And we will take you. Cast aside your weapons."

"And why would we do that?" asked Gorm, as the other heroes assembled behind him.

"Your axe is small and dull!" roared Char. "Your feeble weapons are worthless. You will come with us. I have many men, with many sharp and mighty axes and blades! And in my fortress there are hundreds more with even greater weapons!" The Orcs behind him brandished an impressive array of implements.

Gorm's grin was more snarl than smile. He didn't want a fight, but not as much as he didn't want a public beheading. "I'll take me chances with this old axe. Move along if ye don't want trouble." Behind him, the other heroes displayed their own weapons.

The Orcs began to mutter to each other in the low, guttural dialect of the Shadowkin tongue. Char seemed taken aback by the Dwarf's defiance, but he recovered and tried a different tack. "Ah, but your friend here has already agreed to join us," he said. The mob of Orcs parted behind him, revealing a slight figure in formerly white robes.

"Hello, fellows," said Niln sheepishly.

"What say you now?" asked the Orc.

Gorm maintained a stoic silence. Inside, he was a storm of creative and energetic cursing.

Kaitha leaned close and whispered in Gorm's ear. "Even if we could take on the whole warband, we couldn't stop them from slitting his throat."

"I know," hissed Gorm.

"They might kill him anyway. Look at the bruises on him," Heraldin whispered, nodding to the welts on the high scribe's face. "We'd be surrendering for nothing."

"Even if we could leave Niln, the guild will hang us all if we return to civilization without him," Laruna countered.

"Well," Char said. "You made your choice?"

Gorm gritted his teeth. There wasn't really a choice at all.

Chapter 14

Dwarves' starchy standards of decency and their belief that baths are best saved for special occasions prevent them from disrobing often. Even in those rare moments when a Dwarf is nude, however, he usually carries an axe or small hammer with him, just in case. So when the Orcs took Gorm's axe, with grinned assurances that he wouldn't be needing it anymore, he felt more vulnerable and exposed than he had in his entire life.

They were separated and marched in single file down the road. The Orcs hounded them constantly, boasting about the deadly nature of the various weapons they carried, or hewing tree stumps and rotting logs in two to prove their worth. They walked for the entire morning and past lunchtime.

Gorm's mind raced as he and his handlers plodded along, but his handlers left no chance for escape. There was no sign of Thane swooping in to save them either; the Troll seemed to have vanished into the night. Some good the deal had done him. Gorm had half a mind to tell Kaitha the whole story of the Troll as soon as they made it out of this.

If they made it out of this.

The fortress that was Bloodroot sat just off the road, like a great beast lurking in the tall grass. A ring of sharpened pine trunks formed its walls, divided by four watchtowers and split by a massive, well-guarded gate. Beyond the wall, a sprawling assortment of mud and wood huts spilled onto the landscape. Orcs hustled and hollered through the dirt streets, carrying baskets of food, dragging racks of weapons and armor, herding disagreeable-looking pigs around, and baring their teeth at the heroes as they paraded down Bloodroot's thoroughfare. Deep chanting reverberated through the village, rising and falling with the rhythm of a distant drum.

Gorm had been through Orcish settlements before, though he had always been pillaging or torching them at the time. There was something different about Bloodroot. Orcs and Orcesses alike moved with industrious purpose. They manned long stone factories that belched violet smoke into the air. Some smithed and wove and butchered in shops and shacks along the streets, but others carried briefcases and folios to and from some meeting or another. Gorm saw one Orc before a gathering of blacksmiths and tanners, pointing to a graph painted in crude slashes on an animal hide.

The Orcs also tended kennels full of huge wargs; the great wolves barked and slavered as they beat themselves against the wooden posts of their pens. "Don't worry," Char told the wargs, as the heroes marched past them. He shot Gorm a fanged smile. "You'll have a turn with them after the chief."

At the center of Bloodroot, they reached a squat, round tower draped in crimson and emerald banners decorated with crude skulls, axes, and wolves. Guards nodded to Char as he, and a select few of his retinue, led the heroes up the steps inside the tower.

The hall at the top of the tower smelled of pine and musk. Animal furs and vivid tapestries hung from the walls. Strings of hanging beads shaded windows that overlooked Bloodroot in all directions. Opposite the top of the tower steps sat a great throne of ivory and stone, flanked by a motley assembly of Orcish guards and dignitaries. Atop the throne sat the largest Orc that Gorm had ever seen—more like a lime-skinned war elephant than a man.

He had tusks like daggers. He wore a set of banded mail armor studded with a small armory's worth of blades and spikes. He shifted on his throne as the heroes were assembled before him and rattled the myriad beads and teeth that dangled from his chin-strap, which hung down to his waist. When he spoke, he did so in voice like distant thunder: low and promising coming fury. "I am Zurthraka daz'Guz'Varda, chief of the Guz'Varda Tribe and ruler of Bloodroot," he announced. "See? You are honored by my presence."

"Don't let them see weakness," Jynn muttered to Gorm. "They go for the throat when they sense weakness."

"Are you not pleased?" rumbled the great Orc. "Perhaps I shall honor you with my axe instead."

"Give me my old axe and I'll honor ye with a few new orifices," snarled Gorm. "Just say what ye want with us!"

The assembled Orcs collectively gasped; several rattled their weapons and muttered darkly. Looking unhappy, Zurthraka turned to consult with a thin specimen in long violet robes.

"What do we do now?" Heraldin asked.

"Keep your heads about ye."

"That is the goal, yes," said the bard, eyeing a guard with a wickedly bladed halberd.

"Perhaps they would be willing to parlay," said Kaitha.

"Just don't say anything," hissed Gorm.

"You may want to tell that to your Goblin," said Laruna.

"Yuggo grong, zug Poobah. Been da'pog'ti da'agga root ra'eddi."

"What? Gleebek! Gleebek, get back here!" But by the time Gorm saw Gleebek, it was too late. The tiny Goblin was marching across the floor, the eyes of the assembled Orcs trained upon him.

"Why do they scowl so, Dengark?" Zurthraka asked his wise-one.

"I know not, Lord," said Dengark the Venerable. The wise-one stroked his luxuriant white mustache — the longest in Bloodroot — as he pondered. *"Perhaps the weapons should be sharper?"*

"Sharper?" said Zurthraka. *"How could such a weapon be? We have sharpened them as the gods must sharpen their own blades. They would cut through the earth when set on the ground if we sharpened them more."* It couldn't possibly be the weapons. Nor could it be the assembly; the chief had brought all of his family, his most trusted advisors, even his High Council to stand beside him. He'd even offered his axe to the Son-of-Fire. How could he further honor their guests?

Yet the assembled Lightlings scowled and muttered as if asked to muck the pigsties. The Dwarf was making threats.

"What is our next step, Lord?" Dengark asked.

"I was about to ask my wise-one exactly that," said Zurthraka.

"A thousand pardons, Great Chieftain," interrupted a small voice. A Goblin in a white tunic stepped from the ranks of heroes. *"Honor me with the chance to speak in your presence."*

"Hello!" cried the Dwarf. *"Hello!* Get back here!"

"You speak out of turn and upset your comrades," said Zurthraka. *"Why should I honor you so?"*

The Goblin tapped his fist to his chest in salute. *"Hello, Chief Zurthraka. I am Tib'rin, once of the River Turtle Clan. I fear that your problems with the Lightlings are rooted in misunderstanding, as so often happens."*

"Hello? What are ye sayin' to them, *Hello?"* said the Dwarf.

Zurthraka considered the Goblin. *"Why does the Son-of-Fire keep calling you 'Hello'?"*

"Alas, Great Chief, as I said before, misunderstandings are common between us and the Lightlings."

"Ha!" Zurthraka grinned. *"That they are, Tib'rin River Turtle. Very well. I honor you by hearing. First, tell me how it is that you travel among the Pink-skins."*

"The Son-of-Fire is called Gurm Ingerzon, Lord. He is a gold-hound that saved me from a gold-hound, and got me my life-papers. Now I am honored to be his blade steward."

Whispers ran through the assembly as Zurthraka turned to the Dwarf. "Gorm Ingerson?"

"Aye, what of it?" said the Dwarf.

"Was it you who struck an Elven guard for offending this Goblin?"

The question seemed to greatly agitate the Dwarf, who began to curse in the tongue of the Old Empire.

"He has saved me many times," said Tib'rin, looking fondly at the Dwarf. *"But he is loath to boast."*

"Very loath indeed," said Zurthraka, watching Gorm tug on his beard and swear. *"But tell me, Tib'rin, how have I offended the honor of these mercenary-dogs. I have made every effort to please them. See, I sent them my own son to assist with their satisfaction."*

"Indeed, Lord Father," said Char, stepping forward. *"And I have followed the way of aggressive sales, just as you have commanded."*

"And how did you open?" Zurthraka asked him.

"I showed them our fine assortments of weapons for sale."

"A thousand pardons," said the Goblin. "But it could also be said that you waved your axes at the Lightlings, and took their own weapons from them."

"I contrasted our product and disparaged the competition," said Char. "It is the way of the aggressive seller."

"And then we were commanded to follow you," continued the Goblin.

"I would not take no for an answer!" Char was becoming agitated.

"And we were separated from each other – "

"You were given service at a personal level!"

"Then were paraded through town – "

"I showed off our impressive facilities and shopping centers!"

"Wait a moment," said Zurthraka, pointing to the Goblin. "Do you suggest that our guests felt too much sales pressure?"

"No, Lord. I suggest that they think we are prisoners."

"What!" Orcs and Lightlings alike stepped back as Zurthraka leaped to his feet.

"Impossible!" bellowed Char. "I wore green beads over orange, and my beard – "

"But surely," growled Zurthraka, "you remembered that Lightlings do not read the beads, and green over orange beads would mean nothing to them."

Char faltered. "I … uh … I was true to the path of the aggressive seller."

"You failed to establish your value proposition!" Zurthraka roared, shaking his mighty fists in the air. "You have fallen from the way of aggressive selling! One must always announce one's purpose in the market to the potential customer!"

"I … I am …" Confusion turned to frustration on the warrior's face. "And what if I did fail this path? I tire of this folly! Day after day I am forced to read your Pink-skin books, and for what? A chance to act as a simpering Halfling for a handful of their gold. In days of honor, I would take all of their gold and keep it in a purse of their scalps!" Char stared daggers at the assembly around him.

Zurthraka stared broadswords back at his son. "And then you would have a purse full of gold until the gold-hounds came and took it from your corpse. If we follow the ways of commerce, we have our life-papers to ward off the gold-hounds, and we collect a handful of gold from the same Lightlings again and again. It is the path of prosperity."

"It is the path of cowards."

"*It is the path of my tribe!*" roared Zurthraka. "*And as long as my beard is longest, I will brook no more slight from my own whelp!*"

"*Then perhaps it is time for me to grow my beard into that of a chief,*" shouted Char. "*Perhaps a return to the old days of —*"

Zurthraka didn't give Char the chance to finish. With an angry roar, he pounced upon his son. The boy barely had time to cry out before he was knocked to the ground and pinned under his father's massive boot. "*I am not so far from your old days that I will not defend my throne. Do not mention your axe unless you mean to draw it,*" he growled, drawing his great knife. "*And do not draw it until you are fit to rule.*"

"*I did not mean —*"

"*Silence!*" Zurthraka grabbed a fistful of his squealing son's beard and cleft it from his chin with a few swift strokes. He threw the hair and beads on the floor next to Char as he walked back to the throne. "*You will go and shave your face clean. Your duty is to muck the pigs and walk the wargs until it grows back.*"

Char managed to muster the wisdom to say nothing as he stood, head bowed.

"*In your days of honor, your head would be decorating a pike on my ramparts and I would have one less son,*" Zurthraka said, sitting. "*Leave, and speak no more of your foolishness.*"

"*Your mercy is as endless as legends say,*" Dengark told him.

"*It is tried to its very limits,*" Zurthraka grumbled, watching Char scurry from the room. He turned back to the Goblin. "*You have done us a great service, Tib'rin of the River Turtle. I will grant to you a boon. Think on it, and ask when you are ready.*"

"*It was my honor, Great Lord,*" said Tib'rin.

Zurthraka nodded and turned back to the Lightlings. They stood rigid with awe and uncertainty, and wore the expression of those who have escaped the frying pan and now wonder whether the cookfire has been left lit. "And now, my friends," he said. "It is time to, as you say, clear things up."

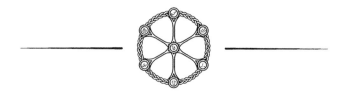

As the heroes followed the chieftain down the thoroughfare, Gorm was reminded of the days when Gnomish eyeglasses had been a favorite toy for all the lads in his mine. His father had given him a pair for his eighth name-day, a tiny pair of handcrafted goggles with cheap leather straps. When young Gorm had put them on, the mine suddenly became a fragmented swirl of sapphire, topaz, and emerald — an entirely new world of wonder and color.

In a similar way, a cordial discussion with Chief Zurthraka had let Gorm see their circumstances through a different lens, and now the heroes were walking through an entirely new Bloodroot, although it was still predominantly brown and green. The bustling Orcs put Gorm in mind of the industrious Scribkin villages of the Ironbreakers. Shopkeepers smiled from every stall, silently inviting them to view their wares. The Orcs sang as they worked, chanting to the beat of a musician's drums, and the song seemed familiar to Gorm in a way he couldn't describe.

"The chief tells us we have ye to thank for this," Gorm told Gleebek — no, Tib'rin — as they walked down the street.

"*Grot?*" said the Goblin.

One of the Orcs in Zurthraka's retinue kindly translated. When Tib'rin chittered something back, the Orc told Gorm, "He says he owed you a blood debt. You saved his life."

"Do me a favor and tell him we're even," said Gorm.

The wargs were loosed when the heroes passed their cages. The massive wolves ran barking and baying from their pens, only to flop down in front of the heroes and refuse to move until their bellies had been sufficiently scratched. Given the quantity of wargs in the pack and the impressive size of an average warg belly, it took the heroes considerable time and effort to extricate themselves and continue on their royal tour.

Zurthraka's tour continued with a walkthrough of one of several factories in Bloodroot. A sign outside identified it as a sword smithery for the Vorpal Corp., a well-known manufacturer of exceptionally sharp blades.

"I didn't think Vorpal swords were made in a factory," said Laruna, as the heroes and Zurthraka's retinue crammed into factory's entryway. "I always assumed they were crafted by that smith who's pictured on the crates they come in."

"Right, the one with the picturesque mountain village behind him," said Kaitha. "Everyone wants a sword crafted by an old master."

"Marketing is its own kind of magic, is it not?" said Zurthraka. "An illusion that men pay to be fooled by."

He pushed the doors open and showed them a nightmare.

Waves of heat and choking smog washed over the heroes. The factory was a termite mound of steel and stone, swarming with bare-chested Orcs. Some worked over pools of molten slag, standing tenuously close to the edge and stirring it with long metal rods. Others stood along glowing tracks, crammed shoulder to shoulder, their hands gliding faster than sight over streams of weapon parts that bobbed down the line on currents of magic. Swords were assembled from their base components: gems and pommels, crossbars and grips. The Orcs went about their work with dull eyes and blank expressions.

"Bloody ashes," whispered Gorm.

"But … but how can this be?" Heraldin asked. "Every Vorpal sword is crafted from rare ingredients. They're made with the blood of a Flame Drake and the teeth of a Diamondfang Skarg."

Zurthraka pointed to an emaciated figure in a suspended cage near the upper catwalks. "They are." Through the smog, Gorm could just make out the crimson-scaled body of a Flame Drake; its breathing was slow and labored, and thick tubes were stitched through its body.

"They are forced to drink your elixir to keep them alive, but their bodies are ever harvested for the components to craft the blades," said Zurthraka. "And my tribe is not treated so much better. Daily my tribesmen lose hands and fingers to the river of blades, but they are given a potion and told to get back to work. Day in and day out, they bleed and drink the potions and bleed again."

"Are you all right?" said Laruna.

"Hmm?" said Kaitha.

"It almost sounded like you said that sounds nice."

"What? No! Ha ha! That's funny. No. I said that's not right."

"It is not right," agreed Zurthraka. "It is an abomination. But it is what the Vorpal Corporation demands." He nodded to a small group of Humans and Gnomes in smart suits, who supervised the factory from the top of the catwalk.

"So why do ye do it?"

"It is better to bleed than to die, is it not? These factories gave us life-papers and jobs when we had no other path. Our wages let us build this city. It was a high price to pay, but now we have a foundation to build a dream."

"I suppose," said Gorm.

"Come," said Zurthraka. "I will show you a dream that is worth our blood."

He led them from the factory, through the streets, to a small alley littered with anvils and forges. Amid the orange glow of the coals, blacksmiths hammered glowing metal to the rhythm of their ancient chant. Around them, Orcs carefully polished and packaged the product of the blacksmith's labors: weapons and armor, but also plowshares and farming tools, candelabras, ornate gates, and even an angular sculpture of a dancing Orc.

"This is the future of the Guz'Varda Tribe," Zurthraka told the heroes. "My kin craft weapons and armor of the finest quality, in the old ways of my people."

"And they're as good as Vorpal blades?" Jynn sounded doubtful, and Gorm was inclined to share his skepticism. Everyone knew Vorpal made the sharpest, finest blades possible.

"As good?" snorted Zurthraka. "They're better! Corporations like Vorpal or Plus-Five know nothing of the proper heft of a blade or the right curve of a crossguard. They talk only of sharpness and magical flame on the blade or the gems on the hilt. What good is a blade that shoots lightning if you cannot strike your foe with it?

"We shape the steel as our ancestors did, when every Orc smithed his own blade, and our greatest craftsmen were our greatest warriors. Our weapons are balanced by hands that know how they should swing. Our ancestors lived and fought and died for ages of unceasing war, and we fold their knowledge, their curses, their spirit, into our steel. Our blades are forged in the fires of our history. They are peerless."

"The secret ingredient is bloodlust," said Heraldin.

"Here," said Zurthraka. He selected an axe from a weapons rack and handed it to Gorm.

"Oh, I couldn't—oh." The weight of the weapon surprised Gorm; he could feel the heft of its head, but somehow it seemed easier than lifting his own. His old weapon was well-balanced and sufficient, but this was perfect: an extension of his arm from the moment it dropped into his hand.

"It's ... it's amazing," said Gorm, giving the axe a test swing.

"It is, and what is more, it is an opportunity," said Zurthraka. "Asherzu, present the opportunity!"

An Orcess in harvest gold and lilac wrappings stepped forward holding up a set of charts painted on a lambskin. "I am Asherzu Guz'Varda, second daughter and fourth child of Zurthraka Guz'Varda! Our research makes clear that Lightlings want handcrafted traditional goods and perceive their superior quality. If we strike now, we can establish a brand to rival the Vorpal Corp. Our product lines shall have much glory and honor, and also a premium price."

"Once we have built our brand, that is. For now, we sell them cheaper than a sword by Plus-Five," said Zurthraka. And then, in the manner of his so-called Path of the Aggressive Seller, he added, "How many shall I package up for you?"

Gorm bought the axe; it would have been foolish not to, at that price. Kaitha found a hunting knife that suited her. Heraldin picked up a pair of daggers. The Orcs were pleased with those sales, but they were unabashedly thrilled with Gaist. The weaponsmaster bought a small battalion's worth of concealable weapons as well as a great two-handed sword to strap across his back. He also proved an excellent haggler; Gaist placed a bag of giltin on the table and stared straight ahead, unflinching at the exhortations and gyrations of the desperate sales Orcs around him, until they finally, brokenly, scooped up his offered price and limped away.

Niln alone was unhappy about the transactions, although that was entirely because he was bankrolling them.

"The temple has already spent incredible amounts of money on weapons and armor for the party," he argued. "Don't you think we should save some of the quest's budget for other things?"

"I don't understand your question," Gorm told him.

"What else would we spend the money on?" asked Kaitha.

"Lots," said Asherzu with a smile.

They toured several more shops offering exotic treasures. Clothiers offered them brightly colored shawls and strings of intricately carved beads. Furriers hawked coats and gloves and bedrolls made from the furs of yaks and wargs. Steaming legs of yak and ram drizzled with spiced honey sizzled over fire pits, and for tuppence, a wiry Orc shaved several thick, juicy strips off any meat the heroes wanted. There were tools and toys, produce and pottery, cheeses and wines — a wider array of products than Gorm had imagined any Orc would use, let alone create.

He was still licking spiced yak from his fingers when they arrived at a small stone hut near the center of Bloodroot. From the outside, it resembled most of the huts in the town, but inside, it had the musty, lovingly worn air of a shrine. Silence rang like a call to worship.

Zurthraka led them through the small antechamber to rooms built of oak and pine. Treasure gleamed everywhere: masks and weapons hung from the walls; gems and ceremonial relics sat atop pedestals and benches; suits of armor and great war drums stood in the corners. Gorm recognized plundered Dwarven burial masks, Elven shields, and gold and jewelry from the bygone Empire of Man.

"This," said the chieftain softly, "is the *Zuggo'lobgar,* the High Vault. The greatest treasures of our tribe are stored within these walls."

"What's with the pile of rocks?" asked Laruna.

"Ah," said Zurthraka, striding to a pile of crude granite stones somebody had carelessly left amid a collection of priceless artworks and heirlooms. "These are heartseeker beads. In the days before we had our life-papers, every member of the tribe carried one at all times."

"Why?" asked Kaitha.

The Orc lifted a stone the size of a Halfling's fist and carved with crude, jagged designs. "When the ... heroes of the Lightlings come to make war on Shadowkin, they cannot be stopped, only delayed. If we hold out against one warband, another is behind them, and another behind that. No matter how mighty a clan is, they will fall to the Lightlings eventually.

"And the houses will be looted and burned, and the livestock slaughtered, and the treasures taken away, until the village is ashes and rubble. Nothing can stand. Nothing is left behind. As locusts are to wheat, so are heroes to my people. When we had no life-papers, we knew that if they came we would have but one option: to flee.

"And so we planned that if the heroes should come, every Orc and Orcess would take a heartseeker bead. Half would stay to fight for the honor of the clan. Half would take the children and flee. And one would take the Heartstone." He held up the stone and squeezed it. A sibilant *shushing* rippled through the silent shrine as every bead in the great pile reoriented itself to point toward the stone clenched in Zurthraka's fist. "And so we would find each other, led by the beads."

"It's horrible that you should live in such fear," said Niln.

Zurthraka smiled. "It is passed. Now the beads remind us of the hope we held, even in the darkness. Come. I must show you something."

They passed through a second chamber of treasures and weapons into a small back room lit by ornate paper lanterns. The walls were lined with metal masks, or perhaps helmets that completely encased the head in iron. Their faceplates were carved into jagged skulls, each lower jaw piece giving the impression of a ferocious underbite. The masks that hung from the walls were black and charred, but at the back of the room, one of the largest was pristine. White and red paint splattered over it in clear, if rough, patterns. Several smaller masks, no bigger than a hand, sat on a smaller dais behind it.

"These," said Zurthraka, "are the *gaists* of my line. A *gaist* is the death mask of a chieftain or a champion — the last face a great warrior wants his foes to see. It is the face they will be remembered by."

"Is that what it means?" said Gorm, shooting a sidelong glance at Gaist.

"Did you not know?" said Asherzu with a wry smile. "We assumed his name was part of your brand, your … uh … as you say 'image,' no? To be so dark and brooding."

Gaist casually glanced at Gorm, and then looked back to the great death masks of the Orcs without so much as uncrossing his arms.

"You said you have one of our ancestor stones. May I see it?" Zurthraka extended a hand to Niln.

The high scribe looked uncertain, but when Gorm nodded, Niln carefully pulled the marble from its velvet pouch and handed it over.

"Burks, the third son of Ogh Magerd," said Zurthraka, reverently holding the stone. "He slew the entire Doz'narad Tribe for the insult they paid to his father. Truly, he was among the greatest warriors of all time."

He set the marble atop the third pedestal along the back wall. "It is said that the Elves let the original gaists rust and rot from the stones. We made these, so that the ancestors may have their true faces back,"

Zurthraka said, carefully placing the small death mask over the statue. The gaist fit perfectly, encasing the marble head in a leering iron skull.

"He is whole again," the chef said, reverently lifting the completed statue. "Promise me one thing, Niln of the Al'Matrans. You said that you have the power to give the stones to whomever you choose. I will leave you your decision."

Gently, Zurthraka handed the statue back to Niln, complete with its new gaist. "But if you do decide to deliver them back to the Elves, say you will put their gaists back on them first. Let the ancestors be who they chose to be, wherever they are."

"I will," Niln promised. "I swear it by the All Mother."

"Thank you. If the Guz'Varda can provide you with aid in your journey, we shall do so."

Gorm smiled. He'd been waiting for the offer. "Well, there is one thing."

Gorm, flanked by Heraldin and Gaist, hurried down a dingy alley. Orcish children fought mock wars and pillaged imaginary villages throughout the dirt streets. Laundry hung between the buildings to dry, and scrawny wargs napped in dusty yards. Orcesses lounged on almost every doorstep, watching them with heavy-lidded eyes.

A wiry Orc in amethyst robes, Dengark the Venerable, traveled with them to act as a translator and guide. "Perhaps it would be best if we just fetched Ghabrang for you, Master Dwarf. You three could join the other heroes as we prepare the feast of honor."

"No thanks," said Gorm. "I've a pretty good idea of what type of Orc our friend Ghabrang is. The kind who'll be half a league away if he gets word we're looking for him."

Dengark clicked his fangs and looked around uncomfortably. "Perhaps. I cannot say; I've never met him myself. But as for the company he keeps … this not a good place. There are many *Threk'gongurdin*."

"I can't say we're familiar with the term," said Heraldin.

"Ah. No, I suppose you would not be," said the Orc.

"What does it mean?" asked Heraldin.

Dengark blushed a deep pine color. "Well, sometimes, when an Orc and his woman find each other suitably mighty, they go to their hut and —"

"Right, right," Gorm cut him off. "Get to the point."

"And when an Orc isn't suitably mighty and has no lady, he goes to a *Threk'gongurdin* with a fistful of gold and —"

Gorm shook his head. "Enough said."

Heraldin looked thoughtful. "I wonder how much? — ow!"

"Either invest in some shinguards, or learn to keep your trap shut," Gorm grumbled.

Dengark led them into a dilapidated hut. Thick smoke with the herby, umbral scent of opiates choked the cramped chambers of the hut. Semiconscious Orcs were strewn about the floor and the furniture, some taking drags from long wooden pipes and riding the fumes to the gates of oblivion. Aetherbloom was the preferred drug of the poor, being cheaper than elixir and almost as safe. When questioned, a couple of the more responsive smokers indicated that Ghabrang could be found in the back room.

Gorm stepped through a doorway of hanging beads into a sparse room containing a table, three chairs, and three hulking Orcs who were carving doses of opium from thick brown bricks and wrapping them in wax paper. They didn't look happy to see unexpected guests. "What do you want, Lightlings?" snarled the largest.

"Looking for Ghabrang," said Gorm. "Got a couple of fast questions."

"Get lost before I have your beard for boot-linings," said the Orc.

"It's just a few questions, Ghabrang," said Gorm.

Ghabrang glared at Gorm through narrowed eyes. "You're the one everybody's talking about. The one who punched out an Elf because he talked bad about some Goblin."

"I am."

"And I'm supposed to care? I've killed Point-ears for less. I'm not going to fall at your feet like a lonely warg for the favors you've done a Goblin."

"You will watch your tongue around our honored guests!" snapped Dengark. "And you will answer their questions!"

"Or else what? Will I wind up telling everybody who's been fawning over the good and noble Goblin-friend how he came into my home with demands and threats of violence?" grinned Ghabrang. "Will the Orcs of Bloodroot think he's just another gold-hound who is strong-arming Zurthraka into doing his bidding?"

"Can't have that," said Gorm. "I got a reputation to protect. Come on, Dengark, let's step outside."

"But—"

"I think Heraldin and Gaist might have a bit more luck talkin' to our friend here than we will," Gorm told the wise-one.

Ghabrang and his cohorts laughed. "Oh? And who are they?"

"What? Ye ain't heard of them?"

"Of course not."

Gorm grinned wolfishly. "Well, I guess they don't have much of a reputation."

Gaist cracked his knuckles. The Orcs blanched.

Gorm and Dengark didn't even make it to the front door before Heraldin called them back with a proclamation that Ghabrang was suddenly feeling much more hospitable and talkative. "But he said he wants to speak to the Dwarf alone," Heraldin added.

The courtyard behind the drug den was crammed between several windowless huts. A small table amid the potted aetherbloom plants afforded Gorm and Ghabrang a measure of privacy. The Orc slouched on his stool and shot Gorm a sullen look. "You've got my ear, Longbeard."

"I want to know about the Leviathan Project."

Panic flashed across Ghabrang's face. "I … I know nothing about that."

"I have it on good word that ye do. Or, at least, better word than yours."

"I … I can't say anything about it."

Gorm leaned in. "Try."

"Do you know what could happen to me if anybody working on the project found out I talked?" Sweat beaded on Ghabrang's brow.

"Working on it?" Gorm's brow furrowed. "I thought the project ended when Johann took Detarr Ur'Mayan's head."

Ghabrang wiped his forehead as he realized he'd loosed more information than intended. "I-I will say nothing more."

"Are ye workin' on the project?" Gorm pressed.

"I will say nothing more," Ghabrang repeated forcefully. "Your bard and the psychopath can do their worst. I will not speak."

"The bard and the weaponsmaster? Did ye think they're my threat? Lad, they ain't my leverage. They're here for your protection."

Ghabrang harrumphed. "Tell that to Burthak. It will take a couple of moons for his face to heal."

"Aye, but it will heal. And now your Wise-one Dengark thinks you're speaking to me because me lads roughed ye up, and not because I know ye've been workin' as a henchman on the side."

"By Razar's flame …" Ghabrang wore the panicked look of one who has seen his own future and discovered there was distressingly little left.

"Aye, now ye see how bad a day you're actually havin'," said Gorm. "What do ye suppose the tribe would do if they found out there was a villain's minion living among them, eh? I suppose nobody outside of Bloodroot would ever hear of it. But inside the town, they'd have to make an example of ye, right? And if I remember my history correctly, your people have ways of makin' an execution … memorable."

"I don't know much about … about the project itself, all right?"

"I can go and have a talk with Dengark, if ye like," said Gorm.

"No! No …" Ghabrang's shoulders fell. "Look, I used to run in a mob of Orcs for Aya of Blades, back when she was working with the big noctomancers. Detarr Ur'Mayan, Teldir of Umbrax, Win Cinder, Az'Anon the Black, and Lady Aya, they were all working on something huge. The other henchmen called it Project Leviathan, and they'd send us to get whatever it was the wizards needed.

"Usually, we were hauling old statues or Stennish charms or other creepy bits of art, and always in crates with a weird stamp on it, like a fish with a long mustache. We'd just move the goods from one tower or dungeon to another. I don't know what they wanted it for. They don't pay us to ask questions, right? We just moved the crates."

"So, what's happening with it now?"

Ghabrang rubbed the sweat from his brow. "Somebody's started the project up again. I don't know who, or why, but they're paying good money for the loot that came out of the old noctomancers' dungeons. Guy I knew got fifteen thousand giltin for a sword that Win Cinder carried. Fifteen thousand! You know that statue of that Sten king, or whatever, they got up at the top of Andarun?"

Gorm felt a chill run up his spine. "Aye."

"A chip from that statue will get you a hundred thousand—just a chip the size of a pebble! Nobody has figured out how to get it yet, but still ... think about all that money."

Gorm was too busy thinking about the statue itself. The idea that anyone besides Niln had taken an interest in the Dark Prince was troubling. "Who's the buyer?" he asked.

"I don't know. It's someone with deep pockets and a desire for old art. I swear on Gathra's blade that is all I know! Everyone just calls him the Master!"

"And what's your part in all of this?"

Ghabrang licked his lips and looked to the door, before whispering, "The Master routes his treasures through Bloodroot. I help his henchmen move the shipments through. Helped. I'm done. I swear it."

"Why Bloodroot?"

"Because it is so close to the border with Ruskan, and to the Master's lair. Do not make me say more, Dwarf."

"Ye know what I need. Tell me."

"Men have died for less," protested the Orc.

"Where is the lair of the Master?" demanded Gorm.

Ghabrang slumped back into his chair, defeated. "Just over the border in the Ashen Tower," he said. "The old lair of Detarr Ur'Mayan."

Chapter 15

"Going to the Ashen Tower is folly," Jynn hollered, slamming his palm down on the table. There was a brief lull in the raucous commotion of Bloodroot's Longhouse, but once the Orcish patrons realized it wasn't the sound of a bar brawl starting, they quickly returned to bar brawls already in progress.

An Orcish Longhouse, Gorm decided, was much like any other tavern, except that it was long instead of tall and everything was stronger: the beer stung like Dwarven whiskey; the food was spiced with pungent peppers that burned Gorm's tongue; the Orcs that lined the long tables were quick to prove their might with boisterous, almost jovial, fights; and the bartender keeping the chaos in check was almost as big as Chief Zurthraka.

"We don't even know the stones are there," hissed Jynn.

"Aye, but we don't have a better lead, do we?" asked Gorm.

"It's barely a lead!" said the noctomancer. "It's the word of a known smuggler, desperate to have you out of his hut. For all we know he's sending us into a trap."

"Still the best lead we have," said Gorm.

"How far is it?" asked Niln.

"No more than two days ride to the northeast, if the maps are right," Kaitha said. "It's close enough, to be sure. The question is whether we're ready to go riding into the lair of a potential necromancer."

"The answer, by the way, is no, not at all," said Heraldin.

Gaist nodded in agreement.

"If there's a necromancer there with half as much gold as Ghabrang said, we won't have any problem getting reinforcements," said Gorm.

"You're not seriously considering this, are you?" said Jynn.

All eyes turned to Niln. Niln's eyes turned to Gorm. "I … excuse me." The high scribe slipped from the bench and ran from the longhouse.

The other heroes stared after him, perplexed. "Did he just run away from us?" Laruna asked.

"I should probably check on him, Gleeb — er — Tib'rin." His squire's new name — which was to say, his old name — was proving a difficult adjustment.

"*Zugzug.*"

Fortunately, a Human in white robes attracted a lot of attention in an Orc village, so it was easy to find Orcs who could direct Gorm to Niln. The high scribe was sitting on a boulder a little way beyond the town gate, looking up at the stars.

"Do you know what the Shadowkin call professional heroes?" Niln asked, as Gorm sat down beside him. "In their own tongue."

"My Shadowtongue ain't so good."

"Gold-hounds," said Niln. "Chief Zurthraka told me. It's because they hunt Orcs down and kill them once they get the scent of gold."

"That's clever."

"And accurate, by the stories they tell."

Gorm couldn't deny it. He couldn't even deny being a part of it.

For a time, they sat and watched the stars come out. Fulgen's Light flared brightest of them all, an azure lantern shining across the heavens.

Niln eventually broke the silence. "I always thought of heroes as these paragons, archetypes of man," he said. "The best we had to offer. That's what the stories and ballads tell us. They're just average people with pure hearts and righteous intentions, and then … I don't know … things work out for them. They save the day. And it's not because they're strong or skilled or have ridiculously sharp flaming swords. I mean, maybe they have strength and skill and weapons, but the villain has those things too. They're not the reason the heroes win. In the legends, the heroes win because they're good."

Gorm sighed. "But those are just stories. The truth is that mankind needs to be defended from monsters, and doing as much takes stone-hearted killers. There ain't no honor in it. It's a job. Sometimes, the ones who are best at it ain't much better than the monsters themselves."

"I knew we were hired swords. I just thought we could still be something more. I thought we had purpose."

"If the common folk didn't believe in the cause, how could they stand to have us among them? And if professional heroes didn't believe in it, how much worse off would we be? The stories of good and noble heroes may be a facade, but when we believe it, it gets a little closer to becoming reality. It's the lie we need to believe."

Niln had the mournful eyes of a dog in a downpour. "So, that's it? We run around killing and looting just to line our pockets and marginally improve people's disposition."

Gorm shrugged. "It beats accounting."

"But didn't you ever think there was something more? Destiny? A reason for all of this?"

"I did," Gorm said softly. "And then I learned better."

"As have I," said Niln. He wiped a tear from his eye. "And now the party expects me to know what to do. They're asking me where to go, or what's next. I couldn't … I can't face them and say I've no idea what we should be doing. Before, I was following the All Mother, seeking our destiny, but now I'm not sure we have a purpose, and I don't know what the goddess is doing anymore."

"She's giving me and all them other heroes another chance," said Gorm. "Kaitha, Heraldin, Jynn, Laruna, even Gaist, we all had careers in the gutter before ye came along. If we finish this quest, we have our careers again. I can go home to me old clan, Niln. Kaitha can be the Jade Wind again. Heraldin … Heraldin probably won't change much, but at least he'll be gainfully employed. And ye'll have helped your temple in the eyes of the people."

"Those may be nice things, but I have dedicated most of my life to this quest, Gorm," sighed the priest. "I didn't give all of that up to provide employment opportunities, nor for public relations. It was … it was to bring the Seventh Hero."

"Jobs and goodwill are more than nice things, lad. And we may not believe everything ye say, but you … you're good, Niln. The way heroes are supposed to be good."

"Don't flatter me."

"I ain't in the habit of flattering anybody. People think I'm special because I punched an Elf for Tib'rin, but I treated that Goblin like the dirt on me boots when first we met. It took me days before I'd look him in the eye. And the first time ye met him, ye were as kind to him as ye'd be to anybody. Ye may not be a better hero than me, Niln, but I'll have Baedrun's boots if ye ain't a better person. In the end, maybe that's worth more than all me strength."

The high scribe met Gorm's gaze. "Or maybe that's the lie you need me to believe."

Gorm looked away.

"We will go to the Ashen Tower," said Niln, hopping down off the rock. "I trust you in this."

"Niln—"

"Please allow me the small dignity of walking back on my own," said Niln. "I'd not have the others thinking you've fetched me."

"Aye," Gorm said. "I'll catch up with ye later."

The high scribe thanked him softly and walked back to the town gates, leaving Gorm to ponder their exchange. He leaned back on the rock and watched Fulgen's Light glow in the night sky.

"So was it true?" asked the rock.

Gorm startled and fell, cursing and sputtering, into the dusty road.

"Sorry," said Thane, mid-shift from stone to troll. "I forget."

"Where have ye been, anyway?" Gorm hissed. "Ye were supposed to be keepin' watch."

The Troll's spine and shoulders cracked as he stretched. "I have been keeping watch."

"Well, you're doing a fine job of it. A whole troop of Orcs marched into our camp!"

"Yes, but they were only selling things. Good things, too. Look at this! New outfit!" The Troll gestured at the bandolier and loincloth he wore. They looked exactly like his old outfit, except cleaner and dyed in the bright colors Orcs favored.

"Aye, but how could ye have been sure those Orcs weren't going to attack?"

"They were wearing green beads over orange," Thane said, in a manner that suggested it was obvious.

"What does that even—never mind that. The point is that ye let intruders into the camp without so much as a warning."

"Fair enough. It won't happen again. Perhaps we need a signal that there's something amiss. Like, I could throw a rock to get your attention." Thane casually picked up a head-sized chunk of granite.

"Don't ye think that would get a lot more attention than just mine?"

"Well, you have to make sure it hits out of sight and lands somewhere soft," Thane said. "But don't worry. I'm very good at throwing rocks."

Gorm had a vision of a small boulder crashing through his tent in the pre-dawn hours. "Why don't ye whistle instead?"

"If you like." The Troll set down the stone, clearly disappointed. "I just think a rock would be harder to miss."

"Not missing is what I'm afraid of," said Gorm. "Regardless, we leave at dawn. I should probably be gettin' back to the longhouse to hit the hay."

"Where are we going next?" Thane asked.

"We head to the Ashen Tower."

"What's in the Ashen Tower?"

Gorm turned his eyes to the northeast, where Fulgen's Light glittered over the pines of western Ruskan. "That's what I aim to find out."

"This is a fool's errand," Jynn muttered.

"No, Heraldin is keeping watch," said Laruna, clambering over a fallen stone. "Finding a magically concealed door is a mage's errand."

"Ha. I spoke of the entire expedition," said Jynn. "There clearly isn't anything in the Ashen Tower. We would have seen some sign of activity, would we not?"

Laruna had to admit that the ruined tower certainly seemed empty. They hadn't encountered a single soul around the courtyard, nor any soulless corpses. There were no coils of celadon mist emanating from its high windows, no violet flames in the baroque braziers that ringed the grounds, no apocalyptic clouds swirling ominously above its ruined spire. If a necromancer was plying his foul trade here, he had forgotten to hang his metaphorical slate above the door.

"Still, all the better to search the place and be done with it," said Laruna. "Come on."

Like any good wizard's stronghold, the Ashen Tower had been designed to be accessed exclusively by the magically gifted. It had no door, nor any windows at the base, nor any seams to use as a hand or foothold. Gorm had tasked the mages with finding an entrance, while the other heroes searched for signs of activity around the tower grounds. After a full walk of the perimeter, however, the mages had yet to see any switches, statues, or similarly promising concealed mechanisms for gaining entry.

Laruna pressed her hands to the wall and was surprised to find her skin blackened when she pulled away. "Is this … soot?"

Jynn nodded. "The tower is said to be white marble under the ash. The pine forests around us are bound to an eternal cycle; they burn down every few decades and grow up again. The tower always stands, either surrounded by a forest or a field of ashes, stained with the smoke of an age's fires."

"How do you know all this?"

"I read it on the commemorative plaque," said Jynn, pointing to a small granite and brass monument. "I think they put it up after Johan's … adventure here."

"When he killed the necromancer."

Jynn pursed his lips and nodded. Many noctomancers were reluctant to speak of necromancers, in the way that templegoers avoided talking about crazed zealots, or kings seldom spoke of past tyrants. The Order of the Moon's reputation was constantly tainted by those few who had crossed the line between speaking with the dead and inviting them back for a spell.

There had been a time when Laruna had been inclined to join in the disparagement of noctomancers, but lately she found many reasons to reconsider her old prejudices. Of course, she'd gained a better understanding of the Order of the Moon's philosophy through long talks after training, and her lessons had shown her the skill and dedication of noctomancers, but she'd also gained an appreciation for the fine cut of Jynn's jaw and the sparkle in his cool blue eyes.

"What's that look for?" Jynn asked, smiling.

"Nothing." Laruna blushed and turned her attention back to the tower. She tried running her hands over another section of the wall and gasped. Beneath layers of ancient ash, currents of magic ran along the stone. "Wherever it is, the door's still working. I can feel the conduits."

"The conduits might be there, even if the enchantments have failed."

Laruna concentrated a moment. "No. They're active. Currents are flowing in them. They're all over the tower, even up to the top."

"When did you become so skilled with weaves that you could sense working conduits?" Jynn marveled.

"I had a good teacher."

Jynn looked doubtful. "Perhaps."

"I can follow the currents," Laruna added, walking along the walls, her fingers drawing faint lines in the ash. The sorcerous conduits ran over ornate stonework and beveled arches to a nondescript wall, where they changed course and joined new flows. "There's something here. Didn't you already search this area?"

"I must have missed it," said Jynn. "Still, the spell could be decades old, and there's no telling how they're configured."

"True," Laruna said. "But I don't need to."

"Wait—"

Jynn's caution was too late; Laruna was already channeling. Glowing, ethereal strands wrapped in serpentine spirals down her arms, spread out from her fingers, and drew a glowing sigil of rings and jagged lines across the wall as her weave flowed into the conduits that ran along the tower.

"Laruna, you don't know what you're doing," Jynn cautioned.

"That's the thing," said Laruna. "I know exactly what I'm doing." Channeling magic through anything, be it an enchantment or a wand or even a mage, strained and weakened the channeler. Too much channeling would break enchantments, melt wands, or cause an overzealous mage to pass out. The amount of magic a channeler could handle before failing varied, but two things were certain: a channeler could handle only a finite amount of magic in any given timeframe, and that finite amount was less than Laruna could manage.

She poured more magic through the conduits. Her weaves were simple compared to the intricate enchantment they were illuminating, but they were also more powerful. The glowing lines along the tower began to wobble and heave under the stress. Safeguards and control mechanisms in the enchantment began to fail under the pressure of

Laruna's magic. She didn't stop channeling until the enchantment gave a final, tortured shudder and dissipated in a burst of golden light. Patterns of warm luminescence rippled over the stone beneath Laruna's hands, and then the wall partially crumbled inward.

"These stones were probably supposed to swing open like a door, or fly out in some fancy pattern," she said, kicking in the masonry. "But this works."

The Ashen Tower was open.

Jynn stepped up to the ruined door, staring in awe at the portal hewn into the side. "You're ready," he said softly. "No apprentice would think to overload the enchantment. Most mages couldn't do it, even if they had the idea. You aren't an apprentice anymore. You … you have my vote."

As he spoke, Laruna's robes began to change.

A mage's clothing is not chosen for its appearance; instead, its appearance depends upon the stature of the mage who wears it. A wizard who advances within his order finds that his robes grow more in finery, while a wizard who falls in rank may find his robe's gems receding back into the fabric. Each mage's attire is attuned to his or her sorcerous abilities and to the order to which he or she belongs.

With Jynn's proclamation, Laruna finally had all of the votes needed to advance in her magical career. Gold and royal purple threads grew from the cuffs of her sunrise-orange robe, embroidering flaming designs around the trim and hem. Ruby buttons and golden tassels sprouted. Laruna knew that distant enchanted ledgers were rewriting themselves to include her new rank.

The sudden praise, the advancement, the change in her attire, everything caught Laruna off guard. The surge of emotions caught in her throat. "I … I had a good teacher."

The wizard seemed troubled. "No. I have not been fair to you … I have … I was not—"

Laruna struggled to speak, and her words were barely a whisper. "You were right to hold me back. I wasn't ready. Now I am."

The wizard was too wrapped up in his own apology to see the joy behind her tears. "You just have to know that I'm sorry, and I never meant to hurt you. I've never meant anything to hurt—"

Laruna cut him off by pulling him into a kiss. His apologies and protests melted under the press of her lips.

"No more apologies," she whispered, when she eventually loosed him from her embrace. "The past is behind us."

The wizard's expression fell somewhere between elation and slack-jawed zombie. "Gah …" he managed.

"We can talk more when we're done in the tower," Laruna told him. "For now, let's go tell Gorm."

"Gahaha."

"Or, why don't you stand watch over the door instead?" Laruna told Jynn with a quick peck on his cheek before making her way to the spot where she'd last seen the other heroes. She tried to hold back a wide grin as she walked, and couldn't bring herself to care when she failed.

"*Poot spug*," said Tib'rin, waving a claw in front of his nose as he stepped through the doorway. "Bad smell."

"Aye, it stinks of a tomb," agreed Gorm. The base room of the Ashen Tower was stale and cool, but there were acrid hints in the musty air. "One with recent arrivals."

"And a lot of visitors," Kaitha added, pointing to the floor. Innumerable tracks had been stamped and dragged through the thick dust. "Somebody has been here recently."

"They don't seem to be here now," said Laruna.

"Well, then, let's search the place as fast as we can," said Gorm. "I want to leave it far behind before dusk."

The Ashen Tower's interior was granite and ash-gray limestone, built in the stark, angular motif favored by dungeon architects everywhere. The furnishings were likely sparse and functional before Johan's triumph over Detarr Ur'Mayan, but now the rooms were bare. Everything left was broken and rotting; anything of value had been carted off twenty years ago as Johan's spoils. Even the wall sconces were missing. "I'm surprised they left the door hinges," sneered Jynn.

The first floor of the tower contained just a couple of rooms filled with dust and cobwebs. The second floor held more promise; one of its chambers was filled with discarded crates, several bearing the piscine sigil of the Leviathan Project.

"Ghabrang's story checks out," said Gorm, searching through the empty crates. "Somebody's definitely been through here recently."

"It doesn't make any sense," said Jynn. "Why would this … Master come back here? Why go to the effort of bringing this back?"

"Perhaps it is Detarr Ur'Mayan's son, come back for revenge," said Laruna. Gorm saw her give Jynn a strange smile.

He didn't return it. "Doubtful," he said.

"We should be so lucky," said Kaitha. "If the songs are half accurate, he's the kind of villain you'd want to face."

"Yes, the kind that would soil his pants and flee when we arrived," said Heraldin, laughing.

"Indeed," said Jynn humorlessly. "But barring that hilarious possibility, I wonder who actually did this."

"Only one way to find out," said Gorm. "Let's head upstairs. Stay close, Tib'rin."

"Stah close!"

The third floor was made up of long empty larders and servants' quarters built around a small kitchen. The fourth was an old laboratory filled with broken glass and bloody stains and rows and rows of cages of various sizes. The fifth floor was the old living quarters, with ruined beds still rotting in two large bedrooms. The stairs to the sixth floor arrived at the remnants of a large door. Beyond the splintered oak, the entire floor was one ballroom, featureless aside from an old pedestal and a back staircase that led straight to the servants' quarters.

"I didn't think there would be much call for a ballroom out here," said Kaitha.

"It probably doubles as a space for dark rituals," said Heraldin.

"Or weddings," said Laruna.

"Weddings?" asked Niln.

"Detarr Ur'Mayan was trying to wed his son to Princess Marja when Johan killed him." The solamancer pointed to a claret-colored stain on the stone by the altar. "I bet this is where Johan beheaded the wizard."

"It's like we're standing on history," said Kaitha.

"Or stepping in it," said Heraldin, checking his boots.

"What we're doing is wasting time," Jynn barked from the staircase. "Whatever happened in this room, it didn't include the storage of the Elven Marbles."

"He's right," said Niln, already shuffling for the stairway.

Gorm chewed the edges of his beard as watched the high scribe head for the stairs. The apathy in the young high scribe's eyes, combined with his gait, put Gorm in mind of a Scribkin walking engine: a slow, purposeless plodding. He'd seen young heroes get distracted and hopeless before, and much like a Scribkin walking engine, they almost always ended in calamitous tragedy.

"Something wrong with Niln?" asked Kaitha.

"I think he's learned the difference between being a hero and being a professional."

"Ah."

"He's also probably figured out that he ain't either of them."

"That's harsh. Not untrue, but harsh," said Kaitha. "No wonder he looks so out of sorts."

"The problem is that ye can't last long in the field if you're half as distracted as he is."

"The bigger problem will be if he goes from demoralized to desperate," said Kaitha. "He might actually try something heroic."

Gorm cringed at the thought. Just a few months ago, the well-regarded Silver Slayers were rumored to have met an unlikely end when their junior member broke rank and charged through a hatchery with an ill-advised war cry, awakening several Acid Drakes and their hungry progeny. "Let's hope not, aye? Come on."

The stairs to the seventh floor were covered in dust like fresh-fallen snow, and the only tracks Gorm could see were those of the heroes who went up before him. "Maybe Jynn's got a point," Gorm said, arriving at the top of the staircase. "Don't seem likely anything's up here when nobody's using these stairs."

Jynn nodded, but said nothing.

"On the other hand," said Laruna, "there's the door." She pointed to a massive set of oak doors, bound with black iron and a massive padlock. Faint enchantments of strengthening hummed in the air around the lock. Delicate yet sinister-looking devices lurked within the keyhole.

The heroes quickly formed a huddle around the padlock. "That looks promisin'," Gorm said.

"How so?" asked Niln.

"A big lock means big treasures," said Gorm.

"Also, big traps," said Kaitha. "What's the plan?"

"Simple," said Gorm. "We need a thief. Or an acquisitions expert."

All eyes swiveled to Heraldin.

"Aha, yes, I can see why this situation warrants a specialist," said the bard reluctantly. "However, you'll recall that, as a simple musician, I have left a certain lifestyle in my past."

"What's the harm in temporarily coming out of retirement?" said Gorm.

"I think I made it very clear at the tower that I don't—"

"But that was just a little lock," said Kaitha. "This one is so big, and full of traps and enchantments."

"Aha, yes, I know, but—"

"It's the kind of lock people talk about," said Laruna. "The kind you hear about in legends."

"Yes, and as tempting as a once-in-a-lifetime lock such as this is, that kind of talk is exactly the problem. If it were to get back to certain individuals that I had picked such an amazing lock—"

"It's only this once," said Gorm.

"I'd like to think that, I really would, but the life of an … acquisitions specialist has a certain addictive nature." Heraldin's throat seemed to be drying up. "It was very, very hard to stop, you see, although Benny Hookhand does offer a very motivating recovery program."

"Well, I understand if ye don't want to take on the challenge," said Gorm. "It's a very big lock."

"Don't misunderstand me," protested Heraldin. "I can absolutely pick that lock. I mean, I could, if I did that sort of thing. If I had the tools. Which I don't."

"Oh?" Gorm snapped his fingers, and Gaist pulled a long leather folio from his cloak. Opening it revealed an extensive set of delicate picks and oddly shaped tension wrenches.

"And you, too, Gaist?" Heraldin said. He hung his head. "You've forced my hand. I would truly hate you, Dwarf, if you weren't bloody magnificent."

"So ye'll do it?"

"If I must!" The bard snapped into exuberant motion, plucking the lock picks from Gaist's hands as he practically skipped to the giant lock. "I might as well enjoy it, no?"

"That ye might," said Gorm. Seeing the bard kneel before the lock was like watching the old master smiths at their craft. He could see the same care in Heraldin's gleaming eyes, the attention to detail, the joy of an artist at work as he inspected the padlock from every angle. The bard caressed each tool gently as he considered them, feeling the weight of each piece in his hand.

"Are you quite ready?" said Jynn.

"Hush," said Heraldin. "Selecting the proper tools is the second-most important aspect of a entry engineer's work. The most important being a high degree of dexterity."

"Dexterity?" asked Gorm.

"The agility of the fingers, the delicate skill of the hands," said Heraldin. He pulled an odd-shaped pick from the toolkit and flicked it with his finger, striking an odd chime that grew in intensity and caused the tip of the pick to glow. At the zenith of the glow, he plunged it into the lock and made a series of quick, precise motions.

"Magical lightning trap." A small burst of electricity fizzled harmlessly over the lock as Heraldin removed the glowing lock pick.

"Well done," said Laruna.

"It's all in the wrist," replied the relapsed thief. His hands darted over the picks and selected another to thrust into the lock. "Picking locks is all about deft hands." He paused in his work long enough to turn and waggle his brows at Kaitha. "And I am very good with my hands."

"It'd be a shame to have to break them again," said the ranger.

"You can't ruin this for me," said Heraldin, happily returning to his work. "Do watch yourselves. Nightshade needle trap."

Heraldin twisted his pick, and a thin steel spike dripping with ominous purple fluid snapped from the lock hole. He inserted another strange tool, twisted them both counterclockwise, and caught the needle as it fell harmlessly from the lock.

"Two traps on the same lock?" asked Niln.

"No," said Heraldin, working several picks simultaneously in and out of the lock. "Three. Acid gas trap." With a coppery, tinkling sound, several small mechanical parts poured out of the keyhole. A moment later, the bard extracted a small glass globe filled with viridescent liquid.

"And now, the defenses are down," said Heraldin. He attacked the lock with manifold tools and renewed vigor, his picks probing and plucking, twisting and clicking.

"Can you hurry this up?" said Jynn.

"Not at all," said Heraldin, inserting another pick. "I'm going to savor every last moment." He chose one last pick—a large, ornate-looking tool—and delicately inserted it into a keyhole that was already sprouting a thick bouquet of picks and torsion wrenches. "And, there you are," said the bard, leaping to his feet.

"It's unlocked?" asked Gorm.

"Unlocked?" smirked Heraldin. "Don't be pedestrian." He twisted the largest pick half a twist to the left. The padlock shuddered for a couple of seconds, shedding bits of machinery as it spasmed, and then the lock fell apart and rained down on the floor.

"Shall we?" asked the bard. He took a bow, to light applause, then slipped the lock's dangling shackle from the doorway.

A warmth spread over Gorm as the heavy doors swung open, and his grin spread with it. Old feelings were stirring within him, long forgotten thrills shared by every veteran hero. "Looks like we found us some loot," he said, rubbing his hands together.

The great study was filled to the brim with strange treasures and arcane equipment. Books and scrolls spilled out of overstuffed shelves. Paintings and icons and charms hung from the walls. Statues cast long shadows in the cobalt and crimson light of massive stained-glass windows. Strange crystals perched on a contraption of great brass and steel rings that hung from the ceiling, spinning slowly on several different orbits. Everything looked old, and powerful, and—best of all—exceedingly valuable.

"These … these are priceless artifacts," breathed Niln.

"First rule of professional heroics, lad. Nothing's priceless," said Gorm, giving an antiquated shield an appraising look. "Perhaps there's some money to be made on this job after all."

"But what is all of this doing back here?" said Jynn, staring in wonder and confusion. "It was all hauled away after Johan…"

"And the Master hauled it back," said Kaitha. "Whoever he is."

"Come on," said Gorm. "Let's find them statues."

They split up and attacked the room with merciless efficiency. Safes were cracked. Chests were broken open. Drawers were forced. Shelves were stripped and lockboxes pilfered as the heroes swept through the study.

"It just doesn't make sense," said Jynn, his voice sounding almost distraught as he stared at the artifacts. "Why is all this here?"

"Don't turn up your nose at good fortune," Kaitha advised him.

"Yes. Just take what you can carry," said Heraldin, his pockets bulging with treasures.

"I've found them!" cried Niln. "The Elven Marbles!"

Gorm let out a small whoop as he and the other heroes rushed to the table Niln had uncovered. The high scribe pulled back a heavy blanket to reveal the remaining burial stones. Gorm couldn't hold back a whoop of joy when he saw the four smooth, milky-white sculptures almost glowing in the cool light. "Well done, lad! Well done!" he shouted, grabbing Niln by the shoulders and shaking vigorously.

The high scribe allowed himself a slight smile and gave a small nod of appreciation. "We should probably get these out of here."

"Yes," said Jynn, absently. "Yes, let's get out of here."

"Did anyone hear a whistling?" asked Kaitha.

"A what?" asked Gorm.

The heroes stopped and listened.

"It's more like a wet blowing noise, like a child spitting loudly," said Heraldin.

"Or like someone is trying to whistle," said Kaitha, cupping a hand to her pointed ear. "And there!"

"I didn't hear anything," said Gorm.

"I very distinctly heard someone mutter 'sod this.'"

Gorm was about to ask for more information, when something crashed through the largest of the stained-glass windows and tumbled to the floor. The heroes dove for cover under the assault.

"What is it?" hollered Kaitha.

"It's a large rock," Laruna shouted.

"No …" Gorm breathed. It was more than just a stone. It was a signal. "Trouble's comin'!" he cried, already sprinting for the doorway. "Shut the door!"

Gaist had just pushed the great doors closed when something cried out at the base of the tower, a long, horrible howl that sent spiders creeping down Gorm's spine. "Intruders," said a voice as cold and dry as a tomb.

"Build a barricade!" shouted Gorm, pushing an empty bookshelf against the door. Gaist and Kaitha joined him, while Heraldin and Niln grabbed an old table. Tib'rin struggled to push a heavy chair into place.

"What is it?" asked Niln.

"It's comin' back to a necromancer's tower, and it's got a shout like a banshee's ballad," said Gorm. "Whatever it is, I don't want to meet with it. And why aren't ye helping?" he shouted at the mages.

Jynn was standing transfixed, his face paler than the Elven Marbles. "It … it can't be," he said.

"Snap out of it," Gorm told him. "Help us with the barricade!"

"N-no good!" wailed Jynn. "No … no!" He lurched into motion and grabbed a bench, but instead of throwing it atop the barricade, the noctomancer began his own stack of furnishings against the back wall.

"What are ye—what is he doing?" Gorm shouted to Laruna.

The solamancer wasn't any more helpful. She was totally engrossed, even perplexed, by a large painting set on the back wall.

"Look," Laruna said.

It depicted a man in royal purple robes standing next to a boy in a skull-themed sailor suit. Someone had slashed the painting about the wizard's head, obscuring everything between his thin beard and cruel eyes.

"Aye, it's Detarr Ur'Mayan," said Gorm.

"Nobody used the stairs up here!" wailed Jynn, pushing a bookshelf onto his pile. "He never used the stairs!"

"No, not Detarr!" said Laruna. "Look!"

"What are you gaping at?" hollered Kaitha, throwing an ancient statue on the makeshift barricade.

"It's just a painting of the necromancer and his…" Gorm lost his words. The boy in the painting looked every bit as dull and spineless as the ballads made him out to be, with a feckless face and a mop of shaggy, raven hair. Yet there was something undeniably familiar in the way his heavy-lidded eyes regarded the viewer, a subtle strength in his jaw, an arrogance in his tiny smile.

"Is that—?"

Sorcerous light flared on the wall behind Jynn's haphazard stack. A thousand pinpoints of magic raced through ancient paths to form the frame of a great doorway. The wall behind the furnishings parted like a sliding Elven door, and the feeble barricade the noctomancer had erected was blown inward with a crack of thunder. Jynn himself was thrown to the floor in the blast.

"Who dares enter the Ashen Tower?" intoned the cold, hollow voice. A figure floated through the doorway in the wall, its feet hovering inches above the floor. It was like a tall man clad in dark, ornate robes, yet its hands were nothing but bone, and where its head should have been there was a pillar of amethyst flame surrounding, or perhaps suspending, a bleached skull. Orange pinpricks of light blazed from the eye sockets. "Who would face the wrath of Detarr Ur'Mayan in his own—oh, by the gods, it's you."

The heroes followed the undead wizard's gaze to their own noctomancer, sitting up amid the rubble of his barricade.

"F-father?" said Jynn.

Chapter 16

"I should have known it was you," sighed Detarr Ur'Mayan, rubbing the bony ridges where his temples used to be. "If there's a problem with my plans, it's always safe to assume you're near the center of it."

"Y-y-you … I thought y-you were d-d-dead," stammered Jynn, groping his way to his feet. The noctomancer was shaking and seemed unable to stand upright, as if his spine had been pulled from his body.

"I am dead, you yammering fool," said Detarr, floating into the study. "Use your eyes. My head is a flaming skull, by the gods. I have made myself into a liche."

All necromancers courted death, but only the most potent among their number had ever approached the mastery required to make a return trip from the other side. When such wizards rose again as liches, they were free to pursue their dark craft unfettered by the frailties of a mortal body or the constraints of a sane mind.

Gorm felt the bottom drop out of his stomach. He looked to Kaitha. The color had drained from her face, and sweat was already beading on her brow. Necromancers were hard enough to kill the first time around; liches were foes of legend.

Jynn tried to recover. "I-I meant that—"

"We all know what you meant," said the liche, looking around the study. "But why wouldn't I let you think I was destroyed? You knew utterly nothing of my plans, and it only took you twenty years to come blundering in here and destroy half of my work. Imagine how quickly you could have ruined everything with a clue as to my whereabouts."

"B-but—"

"Stop stuttering," snapped Detarr. "And stand up straight. You look like a buffoon. If people must know that you're an Ur'Mayan, at least try not to embarrass the family name."

The wizard stood rigid upon command, and collected himself enough to say, "What are you doing here?"

"I'm continuing my research, of course. I thought that was clear. The better question would be: what are you doing here? How did you find out about my plans?"

Niln straightened, his face rigid with impetuous determination. "We serve as protectors of the people of light, vile necromancer!"

The liche's skeletal grin seemed more of a smirk as he contemplated the high scribe. "People of light? Vile necromancer?" he asked, amusement plain in his hollow voice. "Are we still hung up on branding people as good or evil? Why, little priest, you travel with a Goblin; surely you've seen the good in the 'barbaric' Shadowkin. And I'll tell you I've found no greater example of the depravity of the world than the olive markets of Kesh. My work has nothing to do with your outmoded labels of morality. It's about research and progress."

"We're here for the Elven Marbles," said Gorm, trying to steer the conversation away from the grand conflict between light and darkness, or any conflict, really.

"What? The Orcish sculptures?" said Detarr. "You came all this way for a few carved heads? I had hoped they had some traces of Stennish enchantments in them, but they're not even the least bit magical. Believe me, I've done the tests. They're just worthless stones."

"Then … you'll let us have the marbles?" asked Jynn.

"Oh, don't be stupid," said the liche. "I can't have my research exposed prematurely. You'll all have to die. Though, if it's any consolation, I'll bring you all back to join my project. Except the Elf," he added, looking at Kaitha. "I'm afraid raising Elves is technically impossible. Most inconvenient for us both, I assure you."

"N-no!" said Jynn.

"Oh, don't fuss about it," said Detarr. "Undeath is like so many things: it only seems horrible until you've tried it. Trust me, you'll hardly even miss having flesh."

"You're an abomination!" said the high scribe.

"Am I? I couldn't say," said Detarr with a shrug. "As I said, your labels are of no concern to me. Progress marches on, and you are but a bump in its path."

A casual wave of the liche's hand sent a burst of violet electricity arcing from his skeletal fingers toward Niln's heart. The priest looked shocked, and all the more so when a tiny green body knocked him from harm's way. Tib'rin let out a garbled shriek as the spell struck him in the back.

"No!" shouted Gorm, already running across the room.

"That was unexpected," said the liche, energy still arcing from his hand to the screaming Goblin. "But it doesn't matter what order I finish—" A lance of violet lightning struck Detarr's skeletal hand, blasting it apart. The bones slowed to a halt in mid-air before drifting back into place and reforming the liche's hand, but his spell was already broken. Tib'rin slumped to the floor.

The pinpricks of light in Detarr's eye sockets seemed to narrow as he glared at Jynn. "So," he said, "my son has finally learned to weave a half-competent spell."

"B-better than h-half!" stuttered Jynn. "Y-y-you don't g-get to—"

A wall of nether energy washed over the noctomancer. He barely erected a shield in time to prevent the flesh from melting off his bones.

The liche stalked across the room. "If you are to fight, son, then fight! Don't make some foolish speech about—" Jynn's blast of sorcery forced Detarr to raise his own shield. An arrow from Kaitha's bow bounced off it as well, followed closely by a dagger from Heraldin, which nearly made it through the liche's defenses. The liche prepared to retaliate, but had to dodge a sudden slash from Gaist's broadsword.

"So it is to be something of a fight after all," said Detarr. With one hand he erected a shield of violet flame around him, and with the other he flung bolts of black energy at the heroes.

Gorm reached Tib'rin's side and found Niln already checking the Goblin for a pulse. "He's not long without healing," the priest told him.

"Get him elixir," said Gorm. "Keep him alive."

"What will you do?"

"Me job," said Gorm.

In the seconds it took to ready his axe and shield, Gorm made a quick survey of the battlefield, which only confirmed his suspicions: the heroes were going to lose. Behind his shield of amethyst flame,

Detarr was impervious to everything the heroes could throw at him. His spare hand cast spells that wreaked havoc on the heroes running around him. The liche flung Gaist against the eastern wall with a gust of enchanted wind. He conjured a series of bolts that struck at Kaitha's feet, forcing her to dance away from the study's western hemisphere. An arc of lightning chased Heraldin to the spot where Gaist had landed, and finally blasted the bard from his feet.

Gorm froze. The liche was herding them, guiding the heroes toward the leftmost point in the room. No, not toward anything, but *away* from something on the far side of the chamber: a large desk overflowing with scrolls and books.

"Laruna!" Gorm shouted. "His research!"

"What?" Laruna screamed, narrowly dodging a blast of arcane energy.

"The papers!" He pointed to the desk. "He's protectin' his papers!"

Understanding flashed on Laruna's face as Detarr let out a cry of despair. She leveled a blast of white hot flame that likely would have incinerated the papers, the desk, and the floor beneath it were it not for a shield of violet energy that suddenly crackled to life around the research.

"Do you have any idea what is in that desk?" shrieked Detarr.

"Nope," said Gorm. "And neither will anyone else if ye drop that shield."

"It's more than twenty-five years of painstaking work!"

"Then I wouldn't drop the shield," said Gorm.

Detarr didn't drop the shield that protected the papers, nor did he lower his own defenses, but maintaining both defensive spells left the liche without a hand free to mount an effective offense. Laruna's relentless streams of fire aimed at the research, and the other heroes' combined assault, denied him the opportunity to cast spells in retaliation.

"It seems we're at an impasse," said Detarr, deflecting a blow from Gorm's axe, even as he dodged a strike from Heraldin at his back.

"It's whoever's magic dries up first," said Gorm. "And I'd not bet on Laruna running out."

"You're a fool if you think I will let myself be destroyed before I let the research burn," said the liche, catching an arrow from Kaitha in his shield.

"But would ye rather us die or flee with the research?" said Gorm. "Ye leave the stones, we don't burn the papers. In a way, everybody wins."

"Or, I kill you all and win in a much more satisfying way," said Detarr. "Come, Bonereaper."

The terrifying howl rang out again, but it was much closer now. Something massive banged against the barricaded door.

"Bonereaper?" asked Gorm.

"Does that sound gauche?" asked Detarr, deflecting a blow from Gaist. "It seems heavy-handed, but I need it to be instantly recognizable. And its not like I have anyone else to bounce ideas off; zombies are efficient shock troops, but they have no sense for this sort of thing—"

"What's a Bonereaper?" The door shook on its hinges with the rhythmic pounding of a battering ram.

"The name may not be elegant, Master Dwarf, but I feel it gets the point across sufficiently," said the liche. "All you really need to know is that my sorcery can hold out against your attacks far longer than your barricade can hold against the Bonereaper. Or you can, for that matter. I'm afraid this is the end for your little—"

A new voice roared behind the door, a bellow deeper and more gravelly than that of Detarr's Bonereaper.

"What was that?" asked Detarr.

The door began to shake again, but rather than the slow thudding of a siege, it sounded like a frantic battle was raging outside. The Bonereaper's howl rose in pitch and intensity, and then cut off in a series of loud, grisly thuds.

Detarr seemed perplexed. "Is there another—?"

The shrieking resumed, with a mad scrabbling at the door. A great tusk, thick with black blood, punched through the doorway, only to be hauled back a moment later. Silhouettes of struggling titans locked in mortal combat flashed through the hole, and then the melee could clearly be heard descending the stairs and spilling into the ballroom below. With another shriek, the Bonereaper fell silent once more.

Detarr paused for a moment. "What in the hells would—?"

The Bonereaper howled again, and a brief struggle erupted beneath them. A few bone-crunching thuds rang out before the howl faded.

Heroes and liche alike waited in silence. "Well, I built the thing to be resilient," said Detarr eventually, "but this is getting—"

Another chilling shriek rang out below, along with the crash of shattering glass. Screams and bellows echoed through the pine forest as the unseen combatants fell from the tower and struck the ground below. Sounds of battle rang out again, although slower and less vigorous, and then a sickening snap prompted a final, charnel wail from the Bonereaper. Silence descended once more.

Detarr looked around. "Is that it? Do we think this is done? Yes?" The liche backed over to the enchanted doorway in the wall and stared down into the tower's courtyard. "By the gods, how did you manage to get a Tr—?"

But Gorm had seen the liche's surprise coming, and he took it as the only opening he was going to get. Launching into the air, into the amethyst flames of Detarr's shield, he swung his axe in a desperate strike that, against all odds, connected. Detarr's head bounced on the floorboards.

"Oh, flaming ashes, not again!" said the liche. His hand slapped the air where his forehead had been moments ago. "Do you know what a pain it is to align that properly? If it's a fraction of an inch off, I can't walk in a straight line!"

"Won't be a problem for long!" said Gorm, lunging for the skull. He swung his axe for the killing blow, but the liche's skull flitted away like a flaming gnat.

"Very well. Keep your burial stones, or Elven Marbles, or whatever you call them," said Detarr's head, hovering above the heroes. The liche's body clenched its fist and gestured firmly, and the entire desk of research lifted unsteadily into the air and bobbed toward the doorway in the wall. "Should we meet again, I won't underestimate your strength. I should endeavor to avoid such an encounter, were I you. Jynn, stop slouching. You look like a peasant." With that parting admonition, the liche, his research, and his head, glided out the door and into the air.

Gorm rushed to the doorway and watched Detarr's aerial retreat. The liche descended to hover above a mob of shambling corpses and skeletal warriors as they shuffled dutifully to the north. As Gorm watched, the last zombie in the group stopped at the tree line and tipped a large top hat to the tower before disappearing into the forest.

"We did it," said Gorm, awe and relief washing over him. They'd beat back a liche—and with a party that'd been shamed by a lowly scarg just weeks before! It was an achievement bards would be singing about for years to come.

His elation subsided as he was reminded of the subject of some other popular ballads. He turned back to the study. The other heroes were all wounded, weary, and staring at Jynn with varying degrees of shock and confusion.

"I … I can explain this," said the noctomancer, his expression that of a hunted animal.

"And ye will," said Gorm, unable to keep the menace from his voice. "At great length. But not until we're well on our way. Everybody, take salve as ye need it, and then load up all the treasure ye can carry."

Jynn tried to protest. "I really do think I should …"

"If I were ye, I wouldn't be in any rush to have me find out how much ye've been holding out on us," barked Gorm. "Gaist, help me get the Elven Marbles. This quest is almost done. And good bloody riddance."

"What will you do when it is over?" Thane asked, sitting amid the ferns and needles that carpeted the pine forest floor.

"I ain't sure. It depends," said Gorm. "Hold still."

Gorm knew of little that could inflict lasting harm on a Troll, but he was forced to add the Bonereaper to the list. Tusks and shards of bone protruded from Thane's back and shoulders. Gorm grabbed a great tusk jutting from the Troll's shoulder and wrenched it free, with some difficulty because the Troll's flesh had regenerated around it. A gout of thick, black blood poured out after the tusk, stopping when the puncture wound closed and healed. Seconds later, hair sprouted from the new skin, and within moments there was no sign there had ever been a wound.

"What does it depend on?"

"Well, a lot of it depends on how the public sees us. Image and all that. It's the third-biggest part of heroics, after the killing and the looting. This quest was supposed to get us back on the guild's good side, but now ... who knows? We've been traveling with the bloody Ur'Mayan boy the whole time."

"Ah yes, the wizard—*hurk!*" The Troll grimaced as Gorm ripped a claw from its lower back. "Where is he now?"

"Skulking in his tent, I'd imagine."

"What did you think of his side of the—*ooh!* – story?"

"I ain't got the stomach to hear it. Not yet, anyway. This one'll hurt."

Thane growled something unintelligible as Gorm ripped a jagged bone from his back.

"Besides, I already know what he'll say. That he didn't know. That he left that life behind. That he was scared that we'd ... we'd..."

"That you'd shun him and leave him to skulk in his tent?" The Troll spoke softly, with notes of melancholy among the gravel of his voice. "I can understand the fear."

"I'm sure ye can, but now ye see the problem too, aye? Secrets come out, and they damage the party. Trust is broken, and there may not be time to recover from the surprise. Another big tusk here."

"Some risks are worth—*rrrrrgh* – taking."

Gorm shook his head. "Ye don't keep secrets from the party."

"Don't tell me you're reconsidering our arrangement." Desperation twanged in the Troll's voice. "It's worked out well so far, hasn't it? I mean, I know I slipped up with the Orcs, but I killed this bone monster."

Gorm shook his head. "And I'm grateful, but that's beside the point."

"I'd never let any harm come to her, to any of you. And if anything threatens you—"

"This agreement ye and I have is the threat, lad. Secrets hurt. Look at the noctomancer."

"Yes, look at him! None of you will give him more than dirty looks. The woman-mage won't even look in his direction. And from what I can see, he's just a Human with a bad childhood. What will they do to a Troll?"

"A bad childhood? Detarr Ur'Mayan was a necromancer, now a liche. He's the son of a monster!"

"So am I." The Troll jerked to attention, looking back toward the heroes' camp. "Did you hear that?"

A voice rang out, soft and musical, calling for Gorm.

"She's coming!" The Troll seemed on the verge of panic. "She'll come and—do not tell her, Master Dwarf! Please! I beg you. Do not tell her!"

"All right, all right. Quiet," hissed Gorm. "I ain't decided anything yet. I just have to think about it."

"Very well," Thane conceded. "I will wait on your decision." The Troll's shoulders slumped, and then continued sliding as the Troll transformed into a pile of mossy granite.

Thane had barely settled into place when Kaitha stepped into the small clearing. Gorm threw himself atop the Troll-turned-stones and attempted to look casual.

It didn't work; Dwarves never look casual, especially not when they want to.

"There you are," said the Elf. "Niln wishes to speak with you tonight."

He jumped back to his feet. "Why? Is it Tib'rin?" The Goblin's wounds had healed with the first drops of salve, but he had yet to regain consciousness.

"No, no, Tib'rin hasn't changed."

"Ah. Well, thank ye. I'll talk to the scribe before bed. Let's get back to camp."

"Just a few weeks ago, we were on Andarun's pinnacle, commiserating about how we'd been dragged into this Al'Matran business," said Kaitha. Gorm cringed as she sat down atop Thane. "And now? Now we've raided a liche's tower. We're going to expose the return of Detarr Ur'Mayan. We recovered the Elven Marbles."

"We aren't done yet," he said. "We should probably be at the camp, guardin' them."

The ranger looked up at the sky beyond the treetops, painted a lurid orange by the dwindling sun. "Well, yes, there's more to go, but this is big, Gorm. This isn't just a fetch quest anymore. This is break-out career type adventure."

"Aye." Gorm couldn't decide whether it was better to stand or sit. He opted for setting one boot atop a rock, and then nearly fell over when the stones shifted uncomfortably.

"I mean, Leiry will probably want me back," said Kaitha. "And then I'll tell that fat hack where to stuff his offer, because he'll be in line behind ten better agents."

Gorm allowed himself a small smile. "Aye."

"You could be the Pyrebeard once more."

"Let's not get ahead of ourselves, Kaitha." Gorm shot her a wink. "Or should I say, Jade Wind?"

"I could get used to that. Again." The ranger wore a wide grin.

"Ye've earned it. Ye really turned the quest around."

"I had help," said Kaitha softly. "It's been good, not drinking. Helpful. I feel like I used to. Or, at least, like I think I did. So, thank you for that."

"T'wasn't anything. Ye did it."

Kaitha nodded and looked back to the treetops. "What do you think killed the Bonereaper?"

Gorm slipped and nearly fell off the stones again. "Ah, I … I thought maybe … Detarr lost control of it, on account of being so distracted. It could have been fightin' the other undead."

"That's what Laruna said," said Kaitha. "And Heraldin thought there could have been two of them, and one destroyed the other. But I think it was the King in the Wood."

"Oh?" said Gorm. He tried to keep his eyes away from Thane and simultaneously maintain an air of indifference, but he didn't manage to do either.

Fortunately, Kaitha's attention was elsewhere. "I keep finding the tracks of monsters that should have found us, but instead turned tail and ran. We haven't encountered a single foe since the Myrewood, save for the Orcs, and they weren't really hostile."

The rocks beneath his feet twitched in a manner not unlike a knowing elbow to the arm. Gorm grimaced down at the rocky outcropping, which looked as smug as a pile of granite could. "Aye, but it's best not to turn up your nose at good fortune, right?"

"It's more than good fortune. I see shadows within shadows, movements from the corner of my eye. I've seen something—

someone—out there, through the trees. But he only moves when he believes I don't see him, and I can never get a good look."

"Well, the forest can play tricks."

"Oh, tell me about the forest, Sir Dwarf," laughed the ranger. "I know what I see. I know what I sense. I feel the same spirit that I felt in the Myrewood." She leaned back, into a comfortable recess in the stone. "He is here. Either that, or I'm touched by the All Mother after all."

"Or maybe both," muttered Gorm. He didn't know if it was stranger that a Troll was smitten with an Elf, or that she seemed to be just as lovelorn. "Come on. Let's get back to camp."

"You go on ahead," Kaitha told him. "I'm going to rest here for a while."

"Oh, I couldn't leave ye alone in the woods—*whup!*" Gorm nearly fell on his face as the stone beneath his feet shifted and jostled.

"Watch your step," said Kaitha. "And don't worry about me. I'm not alone, remember?"

"Or maybe you're just crazy," muttered Gorm. Yet Thane didn't seem to want Gorm to stay, and the Elf was clearly comfortable, so he bade her goodbye and headed back to camp.

Kaitha smiled as she watched Gorm trundle off through the pines in the last of the day's fading light. Beneath his curmudgeonly facade was, well, yes, a genuine curmudgeon, but a curmudgeon who clearly cared for her. A famous heroine would see multitudes of agents and groupies and would-be lovers come and go over a career, but true friends, friends who offered as much help and support as they needed, were rarer and more precious than any loot. Even the persistently grouchy ones.

It made her feel all the worse for deceiving Gorm.

"I meant it," she told the forest, after the Dwarf was well out of earshot. "I know you're out there."

That much had been the truth. Sometimes, she would speak to the watcher in the forest, and she would swear she heard answers whispered on the wind. She could feel the presence from the Myrewood as surely as she felt her own heartbeat, just not as pressingly as she felt the itch in her wrists.

She slipped the elixir and the hunting knife from her belt pouch.

The idea of the King in the Wood made her want to be a better person, but if he was anything more than an idea, he was content not to show it. Every night that she spent imploring him to show himself, the vials in her pack implored her to come and float away on streams of blood and elixir. The man and the bottle, her ideal and her obsession, were pulling her in opposite directions, but only one of them had decided to show up tonight.

"It won't be often," she told herself as she slipped off her bracers. Just a dose now and then. She could spread them out. Maybe stop altogether someday — some distant day, to be more specific.

"For once, I hope you're not there," she whispered to the woods. She must have cut deeper than she thought; the very rocks beneath her seemed to jerk as the knife bit into her wrist. She let the blood pour down her hand and onto the stone for as long as she could stand, and then eagerly sucked the elixir from the bottle and drifted away on a cloud of dreams.

Gorm found Niln in his tent, still at the side of Tib'rin's cot, washing the sleeping Goblin's face with a cool cloth. The patient's breathing was slow and regular, his eyes sunken in their gigantic sockets.

"Any change?" Gorm asked.

"Not yet. But don't worry. He will awaken," Niln said. He dunked his cloth into a bowl of cool water and pressed it to the Goblin's head again. "He just needs time to fight off the corruption. Dark magic bites deeper than flesh."

"Ye've seen this before, then?"

"Several times," said Niln. "I worked with the temple healers during my days as an acolyte, and I know the malady. Tib'rin will be fine."

"Good." Gorm sat down on a stump next to the Goblin. "Kaitha said ye wanted to see me."

"I wished to ask whom you plan to give the Elven Marbles to," said Niln.

It caught Gorm completely off guard. "I … I didn't … I'd assumed you'd decided the Elves," he told Niln.

"I had," said Niln. "And now, I would not be so sure. But in truth, it isn't my decision. The other heroes follow you, Gorm. They tolerate me, insofar as it benefits them. If you and I disagree where to take the marbles, I have no doubts as to who they'll side with."

"But we won't disagree," Gorm protested. "How could we? The king gave ye the power, and I don't have an opinion."

"Then you must find one. The mantle of leadership is like destiny, Mr. Ingerson. It chooses whom it will, regardless of the wishes of kings or men, and you cannot give it away should you be chosen." The high scribe gave a resigned sigh. "No more than you can seize it for your own should you be passed over."

"Don't go blaming destiny again. You're passing leadership off to me right now."

"Am I?" The high scribe's smile was small and waning. "Have I led up until now? Is the party looking to me for wisdom? Am I letting them down?"

Gorm thought about it. "No," he admitted eventually.

"I wish I was wrong in this," said Niln. "But you and I both know otherwise. I have many things to decide before we reach Andarun, but the fate of the Elven Marbles is not one of them."

"Aye," said Gorm. His mind was racing; he'd sworn to carefully consider who should have the Elven Marbles, but he'd made those promises secure in the knowledge that his opinion didn't matter. "I'll … I'll think on it."

"Good." Niln took the cold cloth from Tib'rin's brow and replaced it with a fresh one. "I've heard you plan to interrogate Jynn about his past."

"Once I can bring myself to look at him," said Gorm, "and do it without breaking his teeth."

"Let me save you the trouble. I'll provide you with a dossier on Jynn Ur'Mayan's history."

Gorm leaped up so fast he nearly jostled Tib'rin off his cot. "Ye knew? And ye kept it secret from the party?"

"Secrecy was exactly why Jynn joined our party. You weren't the only hero who was brought into our company under duress, if you'll recall."

"So ye blackmailed him, just like ye blackmailed me."

"No, Mr. Ingerson. It's very different. You were a criminal with a respectable past. Jynn was the opposite. You gave up a life on the highway for a chance at redemption. He was forced to give up his redeemed life to join the guild that killed his father. I have never felt a shred of guilt, not even a moment of hesitation, for the manner in which you had to be recruited. But for Jynn … yes, I regret that." Niln gazed through Gorm, staring at something that only he could see. "I told myself it had to be done, but then, I did it for the sake of many things that did not come to pass.

"If you must be angry at someone for the secrecy, let it be me." Niln stood. "Forgive Jynn. The questions he faces tonight will be penance enough for him."

"No," said Gorm. "No, ye talked me out of it. I'll spare him my questions. Reading his file will be enough."

Niln stopped in the tent's doorway. "I'm glad, Mr. Ingerson, but I wasn't referring to your questions."

Laruna's knuckles were white as her fists reflexively clenched and unclenched. Her arms were crossed over her chest so tightly that they ached, straining against the fury that she was barely containing. "I'm here." Her words scraped out between grinding teeth. "What do you want?"

"I feel like I owe you an explanation," Jynn said. He looked small and frail, like a frightened animal in the middle of the clearing he'd led her to. Well, that fit the story.

"There's no need. I've heard the ballads."

"Oh, we've all heard the ballads." The noctomancer's lips twisted, as though he tasted the bitterness in his words. "They don't tell the whole story."

"You kidnapped a princess. You tried to force her to marry you," said Laruna. "I'd say that's enough to know."

"We d-didn't k-k-kidnap. Arrgh!" He stopped and collected himself. "All right, look, believe what you will about F-f-father. I was a boy, Laruna, not yet ten years old. What makes you think I'd want to marry anyone? F-father told me I was to be married, and that he had found a princess for me, and I was to be a prince."

Laruna faltered. "Well, maybe you could have reasoned —"

"I'd been on half rations for two years because I kept failing in my studies. I hadn't spoken to a soul outside of that tower for even longer than that, and then F-f-father was telling me I could have a new life in a new castle. He said he'd be proud of me. Even if I could have seen a reason to tell him no, and even if I wasn't scared to death of the man, I wouldn't have refused him.

"And yes, I was at the wedding. I won't deny it. But Marja thought even less of me than F-father did. So when Johan came, I took my chance and ran away. Can you say you would have done any different?"

"I don't know," said Laruna. "It's a sad story, and if it's true, I'm very sorry for you."

"Please believe me. Why would I lie to you?"

"That's my question!" she screamed. Her resolve cracked as reservoirs of pain and fury overflowed. "'Have you ever felt alone?' I asked. 'Do you know what it's like to feel stupid?' I said. No! Not Jynn!"

"Laruna, I —"

The dam had burst. Her rage was rushing out now, and a simple protest would not stop it. Laruna could feel wisps of flame writhing around her fists. "I poured out my heart to you! I told you my secrets, secrets the academy doesn't know! And all I got was this stone wall, this facade you show everyone else!"

"I'm sorry," said Jynn. "I really am. Of course I've felt that way. But … there are men who would see me dead just for my heritage. The most popular ballads in the land feature me as a fool. There are drinking songs about how I wet myself on my wedding day."

"What?"

"I believe it's called 'Cold Feet, Warm Pants.' They say it's very catchy. I spent two decades building a new life separate from my past. I can't go around sharing my story with just anybody who tells me theirs."

The words shocked her for a moment, but shock was quickly vaporized by white-hot wrath. She saw the flash of fear in Jynn's eyes, saw him quickly raise an intricate magical shield. But she was not the apprentice she had been, and though the noctomancer's weaves were far more complex than Laruna could hope to create, she knew enough to destroy them. A quick burst of fire bored through his barrier and blew it apart, leaving him open and defenseless.

As the remnants of his shield burned away, she slapped him so hard he almost fell. "You weren't just anybody to me!" she sobbed. "And you made me think I wasn't just anybody to you!"

He stared at her with piercing blue eyes, ignoring the red welt rising on his cheek. "You're not just … you're very special to me. If you forgive me, I can show you that."

"Can you?" she said. "Can you tell me there are no more secrets? Can you say that I know you as well as you know me?"

He winced at her question but recovered quickly. Some of his old self returned as he straightened, and he gave her a small, brave smile. "Could you believe me if I did?" he asked.

They both knew the answer, and so they both walked away.

The sun had long set before the Elf stood again, wobbling and giddy. She cleaned her hands and wrists with an old rag before she fumbled her bracers into place. The warm glow of the distant campfire guided her as she staggered back to camp, leaving behind a blood-spattered pile of rocks that waited until she was well out of earshot before transforming into a blood-spattered Troll.

A tear ran down Thane's face as he watched her go. He looked around the clearing, as though dazed, and his eyes locked upon something that gleamed in the faint moonlight.

He picked up the small, empty vial etched with an ornate spiral pattern. He considered the bottle sitting in his palm, a tiny drop of glowing amber swirling around its base. And the longer he considered the bottle, the more ragged his breath became, and the more his face hardened into a determined grimace.

His hand closed around the bottle. With a trembling fist, Thane slowly, deliberately ground the vial into crystalline dust.

One by one, the heroes shuffled off to their tents for the night. The moon rose high above the pine tops, washing the forest in pale azure. The fire died to a few glowing embers that sparked in the cool night. Gorm remained by Tib'rin's side, lost in thought.

Of course he should give the Elven Marbles to the Elves. It had been all but a foregone conclusion a few days ago. The gratitude of House Tyrieth could prove invaluable to Gorm's professional comeback, and their spite could be damaging in equal measure. If he thought at all about his career, there wasn't really even a choice.

Besides, there was a long tradition of looting for all the races of Man. Orc fortresses had been built with plunder from Elven cities; in the old days, powerful Orcs had worn necklaces of Elven teeth and ears to prove their might. Likewise, the Elves took the marbles, or the burial stones, or whatever they were, and carted them off to display them as a source of national pride. That was how everything had always worked. Loot was the prize, the goal was to take it, and the Elves won. It wasn't fair for Shadowkin to fault the Elves for playing the game just because the Orcs lost.

Burt's tiny canine voice rang out in Gorm's memory. *"Shadowkin never win, Lightling. We can't win."*

Gorm remembered the Orcs of the Guz'Varda Tribe, toiling every day for the dream of a life that he had taken for granted. The return of their sacred burial stones would be more than a gift to Bloodroot; they would be a beacon of hope for Shadowkin everywhere.

The smart thing to do wasn't the right thing to do. If he did the right thing, he'd probably be laughed right back into the gutter, and there'd be no returning to the glory days. If he played it smart, he could have his old career back. But he'd never be the same Dwarf he was twenty years ago.

"I guess ye really can't go back," he whispered to himself.

"Gurm Ingerzon?" said a weak voice.

"I'm here," said Gorm, relief washing over him.

The Goblin tried to push himself to his elbows. *"Grot? Whut?"*

"Nay, nay, lie down. Niln is fine. He's good, see? Sleeping in his tent. Sleep, aye?" Gorm pantomimed a person sleeping, unsure how much Imperial the Goblin had actually picked up.

Tib'rin nodded with an awkward "Ayiee," and fell back on his cot.

"Ye saved the high scribe again," Gorm told his bedridden squire. "And all of us, really. If Niln died, we'd all be for the hangman's noose."

Tib'rin managed a wan smile. "Gurm Ingerzon … frand."

"Aye, we're fast friends," said Gorm. And he knew then that he'd always known, deep in his bones, what he was going to do with the Elven Marbles. It just took the friendship of a Goblin for him to accept it.

"Gurm Ingerzon?"

"Aye?"

"Hangry." The Goblin pointed a spindly claw at his open mouth.

"Aye, of course ye are," laughed Gorm. "Never change, lad."

Chapter 17

A flash flood of celebration rolled through the streets of Bloodroot. The streets filled with thousands of Orcs of all shapes and sizes, bedecked in ceremonial paints and teal and sunglow beads. Spontaneous choruses formed in the streets and burst into song. The factory floors emptied, the shouts of the workers drowning out the protests of their managers. Warriors delivered great ululating cries that rose above the roar of the crowd.

Gorm caught only flashes of the festival erupting around him. He remembered Zurthraka announcing that the burial stones of Ogh Magerd had returned home, and a great blast of drake-horn trumpets announcing the decree. He recalled carrying one of the stones through the dirty streets, Orcs cheering and jostling for a better view of the sculptures and the heroes who had saved them. Vendors pressed through the crowds to press gifts into the heroes' hands: braised meats, strings of beads, intricate knives, and other trinkets.

They were led atop a great platform at the center of town, where Chief Zurthraka placed the miniature death masks on each of the marble heads. One by one, the names of the ancestral warriors were read aloud by Zurthraka's children, and the entire city roared the names in reply. Then the ceremony ended, and the celebration began in earnest.

At the festival's zenith, Gorm stood with the other heroes in the chieftain's tower, watching a tide of green flow to the rhythm of the band's frenetic drumming.

"Tomorrow will be a new day," Zurthraka told them.

"What will happen tomorrow?" Gorm asked.

"We will go to work."

"That sounds a lot like yesterday, actually," said Heraldin.

"But tomorrow we will have the stones. We'll be that much closer to the dream."

"I don't mean to be rude," ventured Heraldin, "but I'm still not seeing much difference."

"The change we seek will not come all at once," Zurthraka reflected. "It may not come in my lifetime. But when I was a whelp, our tribe was starving, and today, I bounce fat grandchildren on my knee; tomorrow — who can say? My grandchildren's grandchildren will have riches that my people can only dream of, and they will know that we built their inheritance slowly, day by day, brick by brick."

The chieftain nodded at the raucous crowd in the streets below. "The stones are a very big brick."

"I suppose they are, my friend," said Heraldin.

Zurthraka turned to Gorm. "A bigger question is: what will you do tomorrow?"

"The guild has an office in Haertswood, not three days west of here," said Gorm. "We'll go to turn in the quest there. And after that, well …"

Niln seemed far less insistent that the heroes track down a long-dead Sten, and Johan had seemed certain there wouldn't be any more assignments coming from the Temple of Tandos. It was likely that the Heroes of Destiny would take a hiatus. Perhaps he could make the Festival of Orchids after all.

"Who can say?" said Zurthraka.

Gorm smiled. "Who can say?"

Yet regardless of how long the party would stay together, one member wouldn't be joining them.

A crowd of admirers parted as Gorm approached the table where Tib'rin was attacking a pile of spiced meats and roasted tubers. "Well, seems like ye've done pretty well here for yourself," he said.

"Aiyee," said Tib'rin, grinning up from a half-eaten pig haunch.

Gorm requested a word alone with his squire. The Orcs reluctantly left them, save for a wise-one in crimson robes, who had been designated as Tib'rin's translator.

"Tib'rin, you're a great friend, and we owe our success to ye. But I've been wanting to tell ye something for a while now."

"Yas?"

"You're absolutely rubbish as a squire."

"Grot?"

"He say, 'What?'" said the Orcish translator.

"My gear would fall apart if it wasn't for me taking care of it. Ye ate half me supplies, and I wish I were talking about me rations. You're too short to saddle the horses, and they're frightened of ye anyway. I've never heard of a squire half so bad as ye. And I thought ye'd improve, but if anything, you're getting worse. I don't even know how that's possible."

The Goblin looked crestfallen as the translator conveyed Gorm's message. "Tib'rin Fa-eet?"

"Aye, ye can fight better than some, but a squire ain't supposed to fight. Ye keep on running into trouble and saving our lives." *And miraculously surviving certain death,* Gorm mentally added. The problem was that you might get a miracle one time for every twenty desperate situations. A professional hero couldn't rely on luck alone to survive, or to keep a friend alive.

"You're fired, Tib'rin." Gorm dropped a pouch of giltin on the table. "Here's your back pay. Plus severance. And, coincidentally, a job offer from Chief Zurthraka." He presented a piece of paper covered in jagged glyphs.

"Zuggog?" The Goblin grabbed the paper and read eagerly.

"He say, 'Is it truth?'" added the translator.

"Aye. Apparently Zurthraka needs more guards for the burial stones. He figured having one of the heroes who retrieved the stones on the brigade would be inspiring to them."

"Nub'gub dibarg'hest."

"He say, 'I not a professional hero.'"

"Aye, lad. Not a professional. Just a hero."

The Goblin's giant amber eyes misted up. He choked out a speech in hurried Shadowtongue.

"He say that he very grateful—"

"Ye don't have to tell me," said Gorm. "I know what he's sayin'."

It would be an understatement to say that the Heroes' Guild was important to Haertswood. It would be far more accurate to say that Haertswood was important to the guild; the entire town was more like an extended campus for the massive guildhall at its center. The houses and shops clumped around the great stone building like toadstools around an old stump. The streets were filled with arbiters, clerks, and assistants, all wearing smart navy-blue suits and lapel pins that bore the guild's sword and sorcery insignia.

There were also heroes—hordes of them. Crowds of warriors in ornate armor languidly patrolled the streets, glowing blades slung over their shoulders. Shadowy assassins and mysterious rogues lurked in every alley. The shrines overflowed with clerics and paladins, meditating over flaming warhammers and other instruments of divine wrath. Enough mages to fill a small academy sat in the taverns and teahouses, poring over spell books and scrolls. The air thrummed with the magic of countless enchanted armaments.

"Must be a big job comin' through here soon," said Gorm.

"Or the rumor of one," said Kaitha. "Good quests are scarce these days."

"Well then, we'd best put in our claim fast," Gorm muttered. The Ashen Tower was still filled with the loot the heroes couldn't carry, and until they filed the hoard with the guild, it was still technically up for grabs.

The Heroes' Guild crouched at the center of Haertswood, a massive spider among a web of roads that drew in visitors. Underneath the towering spires and flapping sapphire banners, beyond the granite façade carved with images of heroic battles, paper pumped through its red-tape veins. It inhaled unknown men and breathed out heroes with the documents to prove it.

Gorm and the heroes waited in a long line of heroes and prospective clients for their turn at one of the tiny windows at the back of the main hall. Behind the glass sat a thin, balding, and slightly unhappy-looking clerk, the Human equivalent of mashed porridge. When he smiled at them for a fraction of a second, it was the kind of smile that says, *regulation dictates that I must smile at you now.*

"Greetings," said Niln. "My party and I—"

"Names!" demanded the clerk. A glimmer of recognition lit up his beady eyes as Niln introduced the party, and he was already leafing through a stack of paperwork before the high scribe finished. "You were expected," the clerk told them, peering at a memo through his thick bifocals. "You are to meet with Arbiter Thorpe. Office three-seventeen. Third floor, on the left after the stairs. Next!"

"How did they expect us?" Heraldin wondered aloud as they made their way up the stairs.

"Must have got word from Bloodroot," said Gorm.

Arbiter Thorpe reminded Gorm of the deadly Dire Walruses of the Icegale Sea, though more pink and shriveled, and far more docile. The old man was slumped behind the mahogany desk at the back of his spacious office, his mustache swaying gently as he snored. He burst into a fit of snorting and coughing when Niln gently prodded him awake.

"Hey, yes! Who? What? Hey?" said the arbiter, his spectacles dangling from his face as he peered wildly about the room.

"Niln of the Al'Matrans, sir. And these are Gorm Ingerson, Kaitha of House Tyrieth, Heraldin—"

"All right, all right, I know who you are," grumbled Arbiter Thorpe. "The Al'Matrans, right? Mission for King Handor, long live His Majesty, yes? Hey? Hey."

"Yes," said Niln.

"Good! Good! And I am Arbiter Thorpe, hey. Now, you were after the wossnames … the Goblin stones. The Gnome rocks."

"The Elven Marbles," said Gorm.

"That's the one. I would have got there eventually, hey?" The old man cleaned his spectacles. "Good. And you have them with you?"

"No, sir."

"What? What are you doing here then, hey?"

Niln relayed the story of their adventure, with occasional interjections from the other heroes.

"What? The Orcs?" said Arbiter Thorpe. "Most irregular! Most irregular! Loot must be processed. It must be divided by an arbiter of the Heroes' Guild. And we don't just go handing national treasures to Shadowkin, believe you me. Hey? On what authority—hey!—on whose authority did you think you were acting?"

"King Handor's," said Niln, holding up the King's Commission.

"What? Hey? And you have proof? Let me see that."

Arbiter Thorpe reviewed the documents carefully, his mustache bobbing up and down as he scanned every page of the King's Commission and the Al'Matran Contract, and even the maroon binder on the Elven Marbles. "Very well then," he said eventually. "Highly irregular, but in order."

"So, are we done now?" asked Niln.

"Good heavens, no. Ha ha! Now we're ready to start."

Gorm had always found tallying the loot and points to be the most tedious part of professional heroics. Thorpe personally counted, catalogued, and indexed every piece of loot down to the last copper before placing them in a great iron strongbox. Niln filled out a claim on the remaining loot within Ashen Tower, while the heroes filed kill reports to account for every creature and foe dispatched.

"I've got enough points on my license to gain a rank," said Laruna, as she finished tallying her points.

"That you have, hey!" said the arbiter, taking a momentary break from counting to look over the forms. "And, it looks like your wizard has gained three. Congratulations, m'boy!"

Jynn forced a polite smile and resumed his paperwork.

Gorm resumed his own paperwork. He had an extra file to complete, as he was requesting the restoration of his old ranks and certifications. His hands shook as he wrote out the request: ten ranks of warrior, a certificate of master axe proficiency, ten ranks of berserker … The tally of his old qualifications was long, but if facing a liche in the direct service of the king of Andarun wasn't enough to get his ranks back, he didn't know what would be.

The sun was casting long shadows through the office windows when the last of the paperwork was finally settled. Arbiter Thorpe collected the loot catalogues, kill reports, the rank requests, the King's Commission, the folio on the Elven Marbles, and every other scrap associated with the quest and assembled them in a thick manila envelope. "The papers will remain in my office until arbitration," he said, sealing the envelope with a dribble of wax. "All loot will remain in the strongbox until said appointment, at which point we'll dispense it according to all applicable claims and contracts, hey?"

"When will that be?" Gorm asked.

"Oh, not long. Not long. Two, three days at the most," Arbiter Thorpe assured them. "Just enough time for representatives of the Temple of Tandos and the Crown to come in from Aberreth."

He handed Niln a small slip of paper. "The guild has arranged for your stay at Kaedna's Rest, hey! Fine little inn. You'll be comfortable there. I'll send word when we can start arbitration."

"And our ranks?" asked Gorm.

"Hey? Should be processed by then, yes. Can't see why not. Maybe a day or two more."

A few days. Less than a week from regaining his lost status. He'd send a petition to the Dwarven Embassy at Andarun first thing. He could be back within the halls of Khazad'im within a month. They'd call him Pyrebeard once more.

"We did it," Kaitha whispered to him as they walked from the Arbiter's office.

"Aye," said Gorm. "Soon, everything's going to be different."

The man introduced as Arbiter Thorpe watched the Seven Heroes of Destiny leave the office. His smile disappeared the moment the door shut behind them, and he sprang into motion at a decidedly un-Thorpe like speed.

He took a thin black case from a drawer and placed it on his desk. It snapped open when he touched a silver latch, revealing several pairs of tiny crystals arranged in neat rows. Each pair had a small silver plaque between it, engraved with a name or location. As he pressed the crystals with a fingertip, they illuminated with a faint emerald light from within if they were above the plaque, and a warm ruby glow if below. Niln of the Al'Matrans, green. Haertswood, green. The Elven Marbles, red. The Baetwolds, green. The Mask, green.

The man snapped the case shut. He opened the door of a small closet at the back of his office and wheeled out a maid's cart, a dress draped across its top. He placed the black case on the second shelf of the cart, and then hefted the strongbox of loot onto the shelf next to it. It took only a quick reshuffling of the towels, doilies, and dusters on the cart to effectively conceal its illicit cargo.

Working with methodical efficiency, he selected a small carmine vial from the various cleaning solutions and soaps on top of the cart. He grabbed the manila envelope that contained the Seven Heroes' paperwork from the desk as he passed. His mustache twitched upward with an elusive smile as he dropped the envelope into the metal waste bin.

"Tell Damrod I said hello," he muttered. Squeezing his eyes shut, he poured a single drop of red liquid into the bin.

With a blinding flash and a whiff of sulfur, the sealed envelope—along with its contracts, commissions, and other pieces of crucial paperwork—was reduced to a sad pile of ashes around a few drops of hissing wax, which the man emptied into a larger trash can on the cart. A dirty teacup, still laced with traces of sleeproot, was tossed into the trash as well.

The man's leathery skin rippled and smoothed. His rolls of fat wobbled and receded back into his body, so that his clothes slid from him as he walked across the office. His mustache receded into his lip, and his complexion shifted from a rosy pink to ash gray as he opened the door to the water closet. By the time he had dragged the nude, but otherwise comfortably dozing, Arbiter Thorpe from the water closet, the Mask had returned to his original form. The doppelganger re-dressed the prone Arbiter, with considerable effort, and then rolled him back into position behind the desk.

A short time later, a maid walked out of Arbiter Thorpe's office, leaving the old man comfortably napping. She pushed her cart out of the servant's entrance, turned down a side alley, and was never seen again.

Kaedna's Rest was a small, pleasant inn just outside Haertswood's walls. A stocky house covered in forest-green shingles, the slate above the door depicted the Wandering Goddess relaxing by a peaceful stream. The beer was cold, and the meat still pink in the middle, and the beds were free of lice. It was everything a Dwarf could want in a tall-folk inn.

Gorm awoke from the best night of sleep he'd enjoyed in a long while, looking forward to a few days of relative peace before the loot was divided and points were awarded. The best start to any day was a plate of runny eggs and chewy bacon with a slab of oat bread and a pot of coffee to wash it down. He was halfway through the greasy, glistening platter of breakfast when Niln found him.

The high scribe bade him good morning as he took the seat Gorm offered, but politely declined to order breakfast. "I've packed some biscuits for the road," Niln explained.

"The road?" Gorm looked up fast enough to launch tiny globules of egg from the tips of his whiskers. "Where are ye going?"

"I have decided to return to Andarun as soon as possible. Back to the temple."

Gorm's mind raced. He wasn't sure he could technically complete the quest without Niln, and he didn't wish to find out. They'd come too far to lose everything on a technicality. "But the loot?"

"I've taken vows of poverty, Mr. Ingerson. The Temple of Al'Matra was always to have my share."

"But you're the Seventh—"

"You have never humored me before," said Niln. "Don't start now that I can finally admit the truth. I am not the Seventh Hero."

Gorm grunted, but nodded in assent.

The high scribe seemed to sense the source of the Dwarf's anxiety. "I will talk to the Temple of Tandos about how best to release you from service, but you have fulfilled your contract. I will see that all of you are compensated."

"And what will ye do?"

"I will resume my life as a scribe. And I will be available to advise you on the prophecy as you strive to fulfill it."

"But ye just said ye were through with this prophecy nonsense."

"No!" said Niln with sudden urgency. He gripped Gorm's arm with a strength he didn't look capable of and stared into the Dwarf's eyes with uncharacteristic fierceness. "I said that I am not the Seventh Hero. I was to gather the Heroes of Destiny, and I assumed that made me the Seventh. I wanted to be, Gorm. I wanted it to the point of blindness.

"But even if I failed to see my role for what it was, that doesn't change your part to play. You have been chosen, Gorm. As have Kaitha, Laruna and Jynn, Gaist, and even Heraldin, though the goddess alone knows why. You are the Heroes of Destiny."

"Niln—"

"Please, Gorm." Niln pulled a bundle wrapped in heavy leather from his satchel and pressed it into Gorm's hands. "Look. These are the *Books of Niln*—all of my scriptures—and collected notes on the prophets who came before me. You must take the prophecy and learn the signs, so that you can find the Seventh Hero and stop the Dark Prince."

Gorm tried to extricate himself from Niln's prophecy as gently as possible. "Lad, I don't think any of that is going to happen," he said, pushing the books back to the high scribe. "I don't know who your books are talking about, but it ain't me. Probably ain't any of us. It definitely ain't Heraldin," he added.

"Just take them." The priest begged. "Take them, and pretend you'll read them. Say you'll study them and learn your destiny. For me. Tell yourself it's the lie that I need to believe."

Gorm was skeptical. "And that will satisfy ye, even if ye know I'm just going to shove them into me rucksack and never think of them again?"

"Yes, because I don't think you'll do that. That's the lie you need to believe."

"Perhaps," Gorm allowed, his lip twitching into a hint of a smile. "Have it your way, lad. I'll take your books and read about what to do."

"It's what to look for," Niln corrected. "The signs will tell you that your destiny is coming. When it comes, you'll already know what to do."

"If ye say so," said Gorm, stuffing the satchel into his pack. "So, when do ye plan to leave?"

"Now." Niln stood and lifted his own pack. "I sent a falcon to the Silver Talons yesterday afternoon. A contingent is on its way from their base in Aberreth, and I shall meet them at an inn a day's ride to the west."

"Have ye said goodbye to the others?"

The high scribe smiled wistfully at the window. "Last night we drank and laughed and talked about the quest and the future," he said. "Everybody was happy to see me, and everyone had nothing but kind words. And it was almost like I was the hero I always wanted to be. And perhaps, if you come and ask me for help with the prophecy, it will feel that way again. But until that day, last night is how I'd like to remember you all, and all the more how I'd have you remember me."

"It was a good night," said Gorm.

Niln gave him a small smile, but his mismatched eyes were filled with melancholy. "It was a good adventure."

"A grand one."

"And when you think about it, it was remarkably smooth for a quest everyone predicted to be a disaster."

It suddenly struck Gorm that, all things considered, the boy was right. "Aye …"

"It's almost enough to make one believe in destiny," quipped the high scribe, already on his way to the door.

"Don't push it," smirked Gorm. "Goodbye, Niln."

"Goodbye, Gorm." With a nod and a wave, Niln was gone.

The high scribe's parting jest about the ease of the quest was meant to be funny, but the fact of it was like an itch that Gorm's mind couldn't scratch.

He was reminded of the joke again when he told the other heroes about Niln's departure, even as they solemnly agreed that Niln's decision was probably for the best. The remark flitted to mind again as, during a light lunch at a street side cafe, Jynn pointed out that the streets of Haertswood had become conspicuously empty of adventurers. A thoroughfare that had been mobbed with professional heroes the day before was now empty. There wasn't so much as an idealistic farmhand with his father's sword.

By the time dinner was served at Kaedna's Rest, Gorm was still pondering. Why had the quest been so easy? Something in his bones screamed that this was wrong; it just wouldn't say what.

"Are you all right?" Kaitha asked.

"Just … just thinkin'."

"It's just that you've still got most of your steak left," said Laruna. "It isn't like you."

"I'm lettin' it cool before I eat it."

"Right. It's not like you at all."

"Got me there," said Gorm. He shoved a bite of beef into his mouth for show, but he took no pleasure from it, or not much, anyway.

"So what rank will you be after your paperwork goes through?" Kaitha asked Laruna.

The solamancer broke into a wide grin. "Ninth."

"Ooh! One more and it's time to specialize. And I'm sure you're going to choose pyromancer."

"That's a safe bet for anyone who's seen me trying to weave water or light," laughed the mage. "Still, I expected it would take at least another five years of adventuring before I could wear the red robes. And that was before I got recruited by the Al'Matrans."

"Gods. I assumed my career was over when I got tricked into signing on with Niln," Kaitha said.

"Well, that was optimistic of you," laughed Laruna. "I thought we were all going to die."

"And look at us now," said Kaitha. "This was the best thing that could have happened to our careers." She held up her glass of wine. "To Niln, and to crazy Al'Matra as well, and to whatever god of fortune sent us such an easy and profitable quest while we're at it."

Gorm's brow furrowed as the women laughed and toasted. It was beyond good fortune. A few weeks ago, he'd been trying to survive the adventure, and now he was waiting to split up one of the top ten hauls he'd ever taken in. They'd had more than one spot of trouble, and having a Troll for a bodyguard had made things smoother, but, all told, the quest had been easy. The first interview at the Elven Embassy had given them a tip that pointed them to where Detarr had hidden the Elven Marbles. By the odds, they should still be searching for leads as to the marbles' whereabouts.

He was still lost in thought late that evening, while Heraldin and Gaist were engaged in their nightly games of thrones.

"You know, my friend," said the bard, "the key to victory is to know your opponent, to understand how your adversary works. And all these weeks that we've been playing this game, every game that you've defeated me, I've watched for the pattern in how you play. And I think I've found it."

The other heroes watched the game with renewed interest. Gaist didn't move.

"Your pattern is that there is no pattern. As soon as I figure out how you're moving, the instant I see what strategy you are employing, you shift to another tactic. You are always where I'd least expect it."

Gaist looked almost amused as he advanced a bannerman.

"But there is a limit to how long you can hide yourself, my friend." Heraldin advanced a knight. "No matter what strategies or maneuvers your adversary cloaks himself in, you cannot face him for so long without growing to know the man behind the mask."

Gaist's amusement faded. Gorm saw the weaponsmaster hesitate as he moved his king.

"It has been a pleasure getting to know you," said Heraldin, his eyes sparkling, his grin triumphant. He moved a knight. "I think you'll find I just won."

The weaponsmaster stared at the board in front of him. He reached out and stoically toppled his king.

"Oh, come now. Don't be such a sore sport," said Heraldin.

"He doesn't seem upset," Laruna said from her seat by the fire.

"Clearly, you don't know him as I do," said the bard. "Play a couple hundred matches of thrones with him and you'll recognize a tantrum well enough. I've lost two hundred and fourteen times to you, my friend. Don't begrudge me my first win."

Gaist said nothing, but he flipped his king back up to standing position. With a slight nod, he began to set the board up again.

"A rematch?" said Heraldin, setting up his own pieces. "You'll regret it. I'm only down by two hundred and thirteen, and my comeback is on a hot streak. Remember, I know you now."

The exchange reminded Gorm of something else that didn't sit well. He knew the Heroes' Guild well; he'd been their favored son for twenty years and had then spent more than another twenty exiled from them. In all his decades of service, he'd never seen the guild treat unproven heroes with such respect. A free mercenary escort. A pre-arranged meeting with an arbiter on their return. Deferring to Niln on the distribution of the Elven Marbles.

It wasn't the Heroes' Guild he knew.

He brooded until long after the other heroes had gone to their rooms for the night. His bed brought him no comfort, and he spent a sleepless night tossing and turning. The truth seemed like a whisper too low to hear, or a shadow forever in the corner of his eye.

The rest of the party was halfway through breakfast by the time he stamped down to the dining room and slumped into his chair.

"Rough night?" Heraldin asked.

Gorm grunted and quaffed the bard's coffee in reply.

"Rough night," said Kaitha, waving to the wait staff.

A pretty barmaid in a plain russet dress brought Gorm his customary pile of bacon and eggs, and a tin carafe of coffee for the whole table. The maid filled Jynn's mug last, and shot him a wink as she did so.

"Ah, it seems you've attracted the attention of one of the tavern's fine serving girls," Heraldin told the noctomancer.

"It seems as much," said Jynn. He quietly attended to his own breakfast of dry toast and poached eggs.

"Don't pass up an opportunity to enjoy the finer things in life, my friend," said Heraldin. "And I can say from experience that the barmaids here are—"

"Thank you, Heraldin!" chorused the table.

"I'm merely suggesting that you introduce yourself to her during our stay," Heraldin said.

"I appreciate that, but I'd rather not," said Jynn.

"Perhaps you'd prefer to kidnap her instead," suggested Laruna.

The expectant hush of a crowd before a fight fell over the table.

"I've put up with a lot these past few days, and I imagine I shall be forced to endure much more before we can finally disband." Jynn spoke softly, his voice shaking with restraint. "But I'm not going to sit here and take false accusations. I never kidnapped anyone, nor did my f-father."

"Don't be ridiculous," said Laruna. "Everyone knows that the Ur'Mayans kidnapped Princess Marja to—"

"Bloody ashes to what everyone knows," snapped Jynn. "If I traded three whiskers for common knowledge, I'd be cheated. Marja was sent by her father, the king of Ruskan. He was the one who proposed the marriage."

"Why would the king propose a marriage to the son of a necromancer?" asked Kaitha.

"Oh, everyone hates necromancy, except when shrines must be erected or elixir must be brewed, or the dearly departed must be consulted to get the combination for the family safe. Necromancy is half of vitamancy, and we use it every day."

"Well, yes, but there's a line that shouldn't be crossed," said Laruna.

"And I'd say Project Leviathan crossed it," said Heraldin.

"Project Leviathan wasn't even necromancy," said Jynn. "Necromancy is still weaving High Magic, the warp and weft of noctomancy and solamancy. My father and his peers were searching for Low Magic, the loom that High Magic is woven upon."

"The magic of the Sten," sneered Laruna. "Magic that changes destinies and levels kingdoms and brings the dead back. Magic that no mortal should have."

"Magic that kings and queens cannot resist," said Jynn. "Who do you think funded Project Leviathan? How do you think my father and his compatriots gained so many artifacts in so short a time? It was secret, yes, but not from the kings of Ruskan or Andarun. They bankrolled the work until Az'Anon grew too powerful, too ambitious, and turned to darker magics. Once the project went sour, the kings sought to bury it."

"That still doesn't explain why they would marry Marja to you."

"Obviously, they never intended us to marry," said Jynn. "The princess was a false peace offering, a death sentence disguised as a gesture of goodwill. Perhaps Father saw through it, and that's what turned him to the dark arts. But, at least in appearance, he accepted it. And once she was in our tower, the Kings spread word that my f-father had carried out the kidnapping."

Gorm jolted so hard that he spilled his coffee. "So the guild could declare him a foe."

"Exactly," said Jynn. "All you need is a perceived threat sitting atop something of great value, and the guild will send in the heroes to wipe out the enemy and loot everything worth a copper from the corpses. Why not send in a false offering? They'll get it all back with interest."

And finally, Gorm knew the truth, and saw what had been gnawing at him. His stomach felt like lead. "Get to the horses," he gasped.

"What?"

"Now!" roared Gorm. "We need to get to Bloodroot!"

Poldo was surprised to find that Mr. Goldson and Mr. Baggs weren't behind their desks. The offices had been a maelstrom of frantic activity since yesterday, when the opening of a new dungeon sent the brokers and traders into a frenzy. Poldo had left his own office looking like a blizzard had swept through, with papers piled like snowdrifts in the corners around his desk. It was going to take his staff a week to sort out everything the firm had bought and sold. Yet Mr. Goldson and Mr. Baggs were relaxing in front of their great panel windows, sipping brandywine from crystal snifters and watching the traders and merchants along the Wall clamor in the street below.

"You wanted to see me, sirs?"

"Ah, Poldo, do come in," said Mr. Baggs, without looking away from the window.

"Pour yourself a glass," said Mr. Goldson, nodding to the bar.

Poldo measured out two fingers of brandywine, and then added enough to make it an even fist. He gulped half of it down before joining his bosses at the window.

"Look down there, Poldo," said Mr. Baggs. "What do you see?"

Poldo peered down at the Wall. "It looks to be stock traders, sir."

"It's the free market," said Mr. Goldson, watching the commotion below. "It's commerce unleashed, shaping the world more than any war ever has."

"It's the way of the world," said Mr. Baggs. "Pure, unbridled competition. The strong rise to the top, and the rest sink."

"And do you know how we stay there?" Mr. Goldson asked.

"I couldn't say, sir."

"Aggression," said Mr. Goldson. "Bold, decisive action against those who stand in our way."

"Quite," agreed Mr. Baggs. "Take, for example, the matter in the Baetwolds."

"Sir?"

"An old beet-farming community," said Mr. Baggs. "Or it was, until it was overrun by Orcs carrying those silly NPC papers. Now Vorpal Corp. has a couple of factories there."

"And we have a majority interest in Vorpal Corp.," said Mr. Goldson.

"Did you know that the pig-nosed blighters had the gall to start a competing company?" said Mr. Baggs. "They were even trying to undercut us! What gives greenskins such gumption?"

Poldo shifted uncomfortably. "Well, sir, they do say that all men are equal in the Creator's eyes."

"Do they now?" said Mr. Baggs. "That doesn't sound right to me."

"Total nonsense," agreed Mr. Goldson. He looked down at the brokers and the merchants churning several stories beneath his feet. "If all men are created equal, how can the best man win?"

"I couldn't say," said Mr. Poldo.

"Of course you couldn't, Poldo," said Mr. Baggs. "That's what's wrong with you. You only see problems, never solutions."

"The field of professional heroics is about to change," said Mr. Goldson. "There are going to be a lot more foes about for adventurers to slay and loot. But you've been too busy making dour predictions to foresee it."

"Let alone to help us make the change happen," said Baggs.

Poldo felt like he'd been punched in the gut. "Sirs, I've only endeavored to do what is best for the company."

"Perhaps, Mr. Poldo," said Mr. Goldson, stroking his thinning snow-white beard. "But Goldson Baggs measures results, not endeavor; there is no reward for effort here."

"Well, maybe a small one," said Mr. Baggs. "Unfortunately, it comes in the form of a severance package. You will put in your notice and letter of resignation by the end of business today."

"But, sirs," protested Poldo, panic rising in his voice. "I was only doing my job! Goldson Baggs faces a serious problem with its portfolio!"

"No, we recently faced a serious problem," said Mr. Baggs.

"Indeed," said Mr. Goldson, grinning at the city sprawling before him. "But we solved it."

"Lord, we are betrayed," said Dengark, his long mustache blowing in the ill wind that swept over Bloodroot's ramparts.

Zurthraka grimaced. Below him, the gates rumbled and clanked as the party of professional heroes attempted to batter them down. The bodies of the Orcs' advanced guard were strewn around the road. A few corpses of gold-hounds lay with them as well; three guild parties had been cut down by the honor guard as they tried to storm the gatehouse. The fourth group of gold-hounds, however, had slaughtered his exhausted men with little trouble, and were now pounding at the city's great doors.

The gold-hounds at the gates would fall. Zurthraka had many more troops inside the walls. But a fifth party of hired heroes was already polishing their arms a few paces back from the gates, and a sixth and a seventh and an eighth just behind them. And beyond them, the road was crammed with heroes, all armed to the teeth, all waiting to take the city of Bloodroot and its treasures. As numerous as locusts. As certain as the grave.

"Bring me my gaist," Zurthraka said.

Chapter 18

Gorm spurred his stallion up Haertswood's main thoroughfare with reckless speed, ignoring the clerks and merchants scrambling to get off the street. It was all the other heroes could do to keep up.

"What about the loot?" Heraldin shouted from somewhere behind Gorm.

"Burn the bloody loot!" Gorm shouted back to them. "They'll take it and your head as well!"

"But the quest?" hollered Laruna.

"The quest was a sham! Why do ye think it was so easy for us to find the thugs who stole the stones? We were *meant* to find them!"

Startled bannermen dove from the street as the heroes sped through Haertswood's north gate. The open road lay ahead of them.

"Why have the quest at all, then?" shouted Kaitha.

"We were meant to die in the Myrewood! The mercenaries were there to kill us and pin our deaths on the Orcs as a pretense for declarin' 'em foes. Detarr must have foiled their plot, but it don't matter anyway because we went and gave the Guz'Varda Tribe the marbles," spat Gorm, the words tasting bitter in his mouth. "Now they're a perceived threat sitting on top of something of great value."

There was an unsettled pause in the conversation as the grim truth settled in.

"King Handor gave us the quest," said Laruna.

"He told us what a bloody headache the Orcs were for him. Here's his solution, may he burn to bloody ashes!"

"That means Johan the Mighty was in on it," said Kaitha.

"Always hated that smarmy bastard," said Gorm.

"I know the feeling," said Jynn.

"You don't … you don't suppose Niln knew?"

"No. Niln ain't the sort for deception. He's the type to fall for—" Sudden realization struck Gorm, and his heart dropped into his stomach. "Oh no."

Niln looked down at the dagger. It was a fine weapon, with a silver grip studded with small gemstones. The pommel was wrought into the shape of a dragon's claw wrapped around a ruby. The blade was hard to see, but Niln was certain it was very sharp, because it was buried to the handle in his chest.

"I don't understand," he said. "You … you were supposed to protect me."

"Indeed we were," said Mr. Flinn. "Right until your work was completed."

His work was completed—just as the final words of his scripture had said. Niln had to smile at that, despite himself. He stumbled in the loose gravel of the road, clutching the dagger. His lifeblood ran over his hands.

"And now, I'm afraid, our time together must end," said Mr. Flinn.

"The … the Seven Heroes …" said Niln. Perhaps he shouldn't have split the party after all. The thought made him smirk.

"Total nonsense, it seems. But on the bright side, you and your companions can say you were spared Al'Matra's madness before your deaths."

"Madness?" The whole world had gone mad, and sanity looked insane. He could see that now. He could see a lot that he had missed, ever-present signs that had nonetheless escaped the notice of a prophet. It was ironic. Funny. Despite himself, Niln started to laugh as he dropped to his knees.

"Or perhaps not," said Flinn.

"Wasn't … nonsense …" Niln gasped, although he couldn't tell if his difficulty speaking stemmed from the laughter or the blood loss.

"The Al'Matran prophecy?" queried Mr. Flinn. "I'm afraid evidence suggests otherwise."

Niln's laughter twisted his mouth until it hurt. A fog was drifting over his vision, yet he saw more now than he had in all his life; revelations he would never have dreamed of as a scribe. He'd been so wrong. So wrong about everything, but just not in the ways that mattered. He grinned at his killer, tears of laughter in his eyes.

"Wasn't … Al'Matra …" he managed, before he pitched forward and finally, mercifully, fell silent. It was just like Gorm had warned him.

Professional heroics is all a laugh, until it isn't anymore.

The eyes of Andarun's shrine to Mordo Ogg flared with crimson light. Ignatius Wythelm, Priest of Mordo Ogg, watched the light with some interest. It wasn't fading fast enough.

"A fighter, eh?" the old man cackled. "Master hates fighters."

The light in the skeletal shrine's eyes grew in intensity and shifted in hue from crimson to purple, and then to a vibrant blue. The air smelled of ozone and ash, and the shrine trembled at a distant roaring sound that was just on the edge of Ignatius' hearing. The mad priest jumped back to escape any sudden blasts, but nothing happened. A moment later, the azure light suddenly winked out.

"Well, that was strange," said Ignatius. Given that he was living in a pile of crates next to a shrine to the god of death, his accusations of strangeness carried a lot of weight.

The shrine's eyes returned to their standard red flicker, and Ignatius cautiously settled back down to enjoy the show. The lights had been coming fast and steady all day. A lot of people were dying, somewhere.

There is a critical distinction between fear and desperation. Fear is the knowledge that something dreadful might be, the awareness of a horrible possibility. Desperation is the knowledge that something dreadful isn't just possible but probable, and that escaping misfortune is becoming increasingly unlikely. Gorm felt the difference acutely when he saw the first professional heroes riding toward him on the road to Bloodroot.

"That's a bad omen," said Kaitha.

"Heroes don't leave a quest unfinished," agreed Jynn.

"Keep movin'," said Gorm.

Any faint flicker of hope faded as the day wore on. They passed more and more heroes returning empty-handed: a likely indicator that a job had ended before their team had a shot at it. About midday, they started to see wagons loaded with treasures: sacks and chests of giltin, cartloads of Vorpal Blades packed in branded cases, fine silks and bejeweled beads, pots and pans and armor scraps, and anything and everything of value that one could imagine coming from an Orc village.

Behind the last of the wagons came a party of four heroes, their weapons and armor still stained blood red. They laughed with each other and talked about loot and career advancement the way Gorm and his friends had done not three days ago.

Kaitha and the others watched the bloody heroes until they were nothing but a laughing dot on the horizon behind them. "Gorm, I'm not sure ..."

"Ride on," he said.

"We know what happened."

"We do." The certainty was like a lead ball in Gorm's stomach. He squared his jaw and turned back to the road ahead. "And we'll see it through."

They saw smoke on the horizon an hour's ride from Bloodroot. They could see the fires smoldering from well outside the gate. Yet the full extent of the desolation didn't dawn on them until they were in Bloodroot's streets, walking among the ruined huts.

"My gods," breathed Laruna.

Ash fell on Bloodroot like a dusting of snow, leaving the city gray and still. Fire had gutted and blackened the huts until they resembled strange outcroppings in a bleak landscape. Fires still burned in the larger buildings, and thick clouds billowed from the windows of the factories.

Still, silent forms lay amid the ruins, petrified under the thin layer of ash and soot, like reposing sculptures strewn about the streets. Anything of value had been stripped away: the warriors' weapons and armor, the women's jewelry, even the wargs' pelts had all been torn off and hauled away.

Gorm walked aimlessly through the ruined city, his arms hanging at his sides. His mouth was dry and his eyes burning, but the pain was separate from himself somehow, the message coming from someone else's body. The voices of the other heroes sounded distant and muffled, and the images he saw blurred together in one gray, dead miasma. Every sensation was muted and distant, drowned out by the agony roaring in his heart.

His eyes fell on a tiny doll sitting forlornly in the middle of what had been Bloodroot's main street. Her skin was burlap dyed olive; her hair, an unruly mop of black yarn; and her eyes were cherry-colored beads stitched on with thick twine. She wore a burlap dress and a red-twine smile, complete with a tiny pair of wooden fangs jutting up from the corners of her mouth. Some young Orcess had loved that doll, had carried it into the streets, had dropped it in front of the oncoming killers as she fled. How far had she made it?

He lifted the doll slowly, tenderly, and tucked it into his belt as he started down the road. He heard the other heroes call after him, asking him what he was looking for. He couldn't bring himself to say. They knew the answer anyway.

The chieftain's tower had been looted of every last item, but the marauders had otherwise left it untouched. They found Zurthraka a short way from the tower's base, slumped against a building that was ringed with the corpses of fallen professional heroes. He still wore his gaist; the ancestral iron skull mask was caked with blood and ash. Enchanted weapons had cut deep furrows through his flesh, and arrows protruded from him like strange blossoms. Gorm nodded solemnly, apologetically, to the fallen chieftain as he passed.

Near the High Vault, the shrine of treasures at the center of town, the fallen guards were thickest, having died to protect the treasures within. Their efforts were in vain. The vault was bare; every treasure, plundered. The pedestals in the back room, set aside for the burial stones, were empty and smashed. Lying among their wreckage was the small, broken form that Gorm had been searching for and yet dreading to find.

"We honor the dead," he said plainly as he stepped out of the High Vault, Tib'rin's broken body cradled in his arms.

"I know your heart must ache, my friend," said Heraldin, "but we should not tarry here."

"We burn the Orcs on pyres," said Gorm. "That's their way. Every last one ye can find, drag 'em onto some wreckage. Laruna can start the fires."

"Heraldin is right, Gorm," Kaitha tried. "Whoever set us up will send —"

"We honor the dead," he said again. It wasn't a request. It wasn't even an order. It was a fact.

"I'm not sure we should do that," said Jynn.

"Who else should? Who else will?" asked Gorm, laying Tib'rin's body next to Zurthraka's. The Goblin's knife had been looted, as had any armor he might have worn. All he had was a loincloth and a few stray beads clutched in his hand. "Can ye leave them here to rot after what they did for us? After what … after what we did to them?"

The other heroes looked away. "No," said Kaitha.

"Then come on," said Gorm, feeling more world-weary than ever before. "We've much to do."

Laruna set another makeshift pyre alight, wreathing the charred wooden frame and figures stacked within it in a burst of sorcerous flame. She adjusted the silken scarf she wore over her nose and mouth to ward off the soot and stench as she watched the fire burn. When she was satisfied that the fire would eventually burn itself out, she went in search of the next grave.

A couple of streets over, Jynn and Heraldin were setting up another heap of bodies in the ruins of a hut. It was smaller than many of the pyres she'd cremated earlier in the day. "Do you think we'll finish soon?" she asked, a twinge of hope in her voice.

"I believe we're nearing the end," said Jynn.

The noctomancer was the key to finishing the cremations quickly; Laruna remained uneasy about necromancy, but she had to concede that Jynn's magic made locating the fallen much easier. "We should be done by tonight."

Laruna nodded. She'd been sending off the dead since the evening before. She'd mourned for the Orcs at first, stealing moments, when there was nobody looking, to silently weep. But hours and hours of gathering the bodies to the incineration pits, seeing so many people go up in smoke, had leeched away her capacity for emotion. Coupled with the exhaustion of a sleepless night, the task left Laruna numb and aching. She wanted to honor the dead, but she wanted to be finished even more.

"Have you seen Gorm?" Heraldin asked.

"He's still by the tower," Laruna told him. She hadn't seen Gorm come back to camp the night before, and his tent and bedroll were still rolled neatly when she awoke. He'd built the first pyre—the one they laid Zurthraka on—and as far as anyone could tell, the Dwarf had been working straight through.

A sudden cry came from near the campsite.

"That sounded like Kaitha," said Jynn.

They rushed to find the Elf in the middle of the campsite, or rather, the remnants thereof. At first glance, it looked like a bear had rampaged through the small square by Bloodroot's burned-out gatehouse that they'd used as a base of operations, flattening tents, and dragging bags out and emptying them all over the ground. Then again, bears weren't so meticulous. Whatever marauder had struck their camp had unpacked their gear and placed the contents of each rucksack and parcel in neat rows. In fact, it was Kaitha herself who was making the mess, searching through the rows with frenzied desperation.

"The elixir!" the ranger gasped as the other heroes approached. "Someone has stolen the healing potions!"

"What?"

"They're all gone! Even the backup stash! Every one!"

"Do you need one right now?" asked Jynn.

"You keep a backup stash?" said Laruna.

Kaitha stopped searching long enough to catch her breath, glancing back and forth at the other heroes. "I don't … need one right now," she conceded eventually. "But we're in a dangerous situation here. We don't know who the guild will send after us. And if we're going to be fighting, or even traveling in the wilds for long, a dose of elixir can mean the difference between life and death. We need to find it."

"This is true," said Heraldin. "We won't last long without healing potions."

"Now, wait a moment," suggested Jynn. "We don't have to rely on elixir for healing. We have a solamancer with us."

The other heroes paused to consider the solamancer for a moment.

"Right," said Heraldin. "We're dead without those potions."

"Sorry," Kaitha said to Laruna. "I forget that you have healing magic."

"No, I'm with Heraldin on this one," she replied. The only part of healing Laruna excelled at was cauterizing things. She wasn't sure she could heal a serious wound if her life depended on it, so she preferred that nobody else's did either. "We need to find those potions."

She turned to search the campsite and was surprised to find herself staring into Gaist's eyes. "Er—where did you come from?"

Gaist stared down at her dispassionately.

"Is there something you need?" Laruna asked.

"What's wrong?" asked Heraldin. "Is there danger? There's danger."

Gaist glanced at the bard.

"He didn't say—"

"To the battlements!" shouted Heraldin, already running for the gatehouse.

"How can he understand Gaist?" Kaitha asked, as they ran after the unlikely pair.

"I'm not even sure that he did," said Jynn.

"Then why are we running after them?" asked Kaitha.

"Perhaps to find out if he was right," said Jynn. "When the whole world goes crazy, what can you do but try to keep up?"

Heraldin, as it turned out, was correct: there was danger. "Silver talon thugs," he said, looking out at a black- and silver-clad army.

Career thugs had relatively short life expectancies, as their duties often brought them into contact with members of the Heroes' Guild. Such match-ups invariably favored heroes; many highly skilled, lethally trained thugs with top-end gear met their ends at the hands of one plucky young hero or another who beat the odds in a narratively expedient blaze of glory. Thugs used an array of tools to compensate: intimidation, subterfuge, appeals to the law, and, most crucially, numbers.

Veteran heroes had been known to single-handedly eradicate entire platoons of mercenaries. A well-coordinated party could take down several companies of men. Yet no hero can fight forever; eventually, their magic runs out, their weapons break, their strength fails. With strength of numbers, thugs and mercenaries can take down any hero eventually. It's not uncommon for an entire battalion of mercenary thugs to mobilize when combat with heroes is inevitable.

The Silver Talons brought at least two battalions.

They marched in neat formations, the sunlight glinting off their weapons as they fanned out around the walls. Laruna could see companies of Silver Talons moving into place along the eastern wall, and more at the west. At the head of the southern force, closest to Bloodroot's gatehouse, a familiar pair stepped forward.

"Flinn and Brunt," said Kaitha.

"Hello!" called Mr. Flinn across the distance. "I see we've been spotted."

"Have you come to see your handiwork?" Laruna shouted back.

"Actually, I'm here to tie up a few loose ends," Mr. Flinn hollered back. "In this business, it pays to be thorough."

"Come out … hands up!" rumbled Brunt.

"Ha ha! I was just getting to that, Mr. Brunt! You see, by order of the Heroes' Guild I have come to notify you that, for your crimes against the Freedlands, your Heroes' licenses have been revoked! I am authorized to try you as enemies of the city-states and carry out your sentence."

"What kind of corrupt institution makes the same man prosecutor, judge, and executioner!" exclaimed Jynn.

"The efficient kind," shouted Mr. Flinn. "I think you'll find that the ruins you inhabit are very effectively surrounded. I'll spare you the empty rhetoric about nobody coming to harm if you surrender peaceably, but I can promise that the harm you come to out here will be much swifter and less painful than what awaits you if we have to scour the city."

The heroes nodded to each other.

"Laruna, answer the man," said Kaitha.

Her reply was a fiery blast as wide as the road, aimed directly at Mr. Flinn. A pair of Silver Talon mages leaped from the squad behind the Tinderkin and the Ogre and erected a hasty shield, but the barrier collapsed under the fiery onslaught. Mr. Flinn and Mr. Brunt barely had time to dive out of the way, and the unfortunate mages behind them didn't even have that.

"I'll spare you the empty rhetoric of promising to let you live if you leave now," shouted Heraldin. "But I can promise that if you and your army disperse, we probably won't kill you today."

"I find it's best not to taunt your foes when you're outnumbered by at least a hundred to one," hissed Jynn.

The bard shrugged. "Life is better with bravado."

"I was hoping for a cleaner resolution to this situation," yelled Mr. Flinn, dusting himself off as he eyed the black smears on the road that had been a pair of Silver Talon mages until quite recently. "But it seems that Mr. Brunt shall have his way after all. He usually does."

Brunt raised a meaty fist above his hand and gave a guttural cry. The front ranks began to rush forward as magical shields wove into existence ahead of them. From the back of his company, a line of crossbow bolts whistled into the air.

"This is a poor spot to mount a last stand," Jynn observed, blowing a crossbow bolt off course with a wave of his hands.

"I really wish you didn't say it that way," said Heraldin.

"I really wish there was a reason not to," said Jynn, ducking another volley of bolts.

"Fall back!" Kaitha shouted.

Laruna loosed a fireball at the oncoming soldiers before running down the burned-out stairs after the other heroes. She glanced out the windows, and through the smoke and ash that still clogged the air, she could see the dark shapes of Silver Talons pouring into the city.

They made for the tower as swiftly and silently as they could, but mercenaries infested the streets, and dispatching them complicated their efforts to go undetected. Thugs gave small screams and gurgles whenever Kaitha's arrows or Jynn's lances of lightning caught them. Silver Talons choked on the colorful clouds that burst from Heraldin's smoke bombs, and screamed a moment later when Gaist's blades found them. Laruna incinerated an entire squad of Silver Talons with a tower of fire, which erupted around them, painting the smoky sky golden.

"Impressive," Heraldin said to Laruna, shielding his eyes from the heat and glare of the flames. "But perhaps we could fight without letting the entire enemy force know where we are."

"I don't really do stealth," Laruna told him.

Laruna quickly found herself wishing she was a bit better at subtlety; it didn't take long before half a battalion of mercenaries was running at their heels. A burst of sorcerous acid nearly took Gaist's head off. A moment later, a crossbow bolt grazed her arm. She grunted in pain and threw a spell back at her pursuers, but her eyes stayed focused on the road ahead.

Down a ruined street, through a side alley, and they were on the thoroughfare again. The tower was in sight, but she could hear the rumble of the Silver Talons charging through the streets behind her. Bolts, arrows, and caustic spells rained down around them, sending up plumes of dust and ash wherever they landed. Gaist was already at the base of the tower, hurrying the other heroes up the ladder.

Laruna saw something out of the corner of her eye. She gasped as a Silver Talon leaped from the top of a ruined hut, twin blades flashing in the air. There wasn't enough time to get a spell up, and she instinctively braced for the attack.

It never landed. An enchanted arrow slammed into the assassin halfway through his flight, and he finished his final descent with an ungainly roll into a burning hut. Kaitha waved to her from the window of the tower.

"Thanks!" Laruna shouted to the ranger.

"Thank me once you're inside," Kaitha hollered back.

Laruna was already in motion, crossbow bolts pelting the ground around her. Another near miss tore the hem of her robes as she raced up the tower's rickety steps.

Behind her, Gaist stepped in front of the ladder and squared himself for the oncoming assault.

"No!" shouted Heraldin, bounding back down the stairs. The bard grabbed the weaponsmaster by the collar and attempted to pull him down to his eye level. Instead, Heraldin pulled himself up to Gaist's face, his feet dangling in the air. "No, my friend! Not now! Death is the one wish that you can be certain will be granted someday. If you must seek your end, don't make it today. Not when we need your help."

Gaist didn't seem to react until suddenly, silently, he glided up the stairs into the tower, dragging the bard along. A moment later, Jynn and Kaitha pushed the heavy trapdoor shut behind them.

"Make a barricade," Kaitha said.

They piled what ruined furniture and heavy detritus they could find before the door, but it was already shaking with the pounding of the Silver Talons below.

"It won't hold them for long," Jynn said.

"What do we do?" asked Laruna.

"Excuse me!" called Mr. Flinn's voice. "I'd like to parley!"

Cautiously, they peered out the tower windows. Mr. Flinn stood just below the window, smiling up at them. Brunt loomed behind him, and behind Brunt were Silver Talons as far as the eye could see.

"Hello!" said Mr. Flinn. "I'm sure you're aware by now that the outcome of this charade is really quite certain. But sieges take time, and assaults cost men and arrows, and I'm loath to waste any of the three. So, I'm willing to overlook the considerable inconvenience you've caused, to say nothing of the men you killed, and re-extend my earlier offer. Surrender now, and I'll grant you a swift and mostly painless execution."

Laruna shot a burst of flame at the Tinderkin, but the Silver Talons' mages were ready this time and her spell rippled harmlessly across the surface of a much stronger shield.

"Have … your way!" rumbled Brunt.

"Indeed they shall, Mr. Brunt!" said Mr. Flinn. The pounding on the door resumed.

"Spread out," said Kaitha. "Look out the windows for some roof we can leap onto, some alley they've left unguarded, anything that can get us out of this situation."

"And if we can't find one?" asked Heraldin.

"Then we won't be getting out of this situation," Kaitha said grimly.

Laruna checked the back window, opposite Mr. Flinn and Mr. Brunt. Directly below the tower, the Silver Talons were beginning to surround them, all of them watching the windows with drawn crossbows. But beyond the mercenaries, in the clearing where they'd laid Zurthraka to rest, she spotted a forlorn figure, oblivious to chaos around him, stacking stones upon a cairn.

"Gorm!" she screamed.

Gorm had burned the Orcs on great pyres, in accordance with the Orcish customs that he could recall. Yet he didn't know any Goblin rites or ceremonies, so he buried Tib'rin as a Dwarf, deep in the earth with a suitable cairn above the chest. Technically, the cairn should have been decorated with the Goblin's weapons and armor, but Tib'rin's had all been looted. Instead, Gorm decorated it with the doll from the street, and Zurthraka's gaist, and the handful of beads that his friend had clutched in death.

Sweat rolled from his brow, and the smoke and ash and stench of death burned his throat and his lungs. A numbness he had never known before dulled his core, a weariness that bit to his marrow. All of his work, all of his efforts, had gained him nothing and had cost his friends everything; no, he'd cost an entire people their lives. He'd always known the system was rigged; he'd have told anyone the system was rigged a few months ago. Yet all they had to do was wave a pardon and some gold in his face, and he'd jumped in feet-first. The guild had used him, because he'd let them. And now that they'd won, and the Guz'Varda Tribe was gone, he'd outlived his purpose to anyone. There was nothing left to do but die.

"I knew ye'd come," he said.

Mr. Flinn paused. "Well done, Mr. Ingerson. I must say, most people can't hear me approaching when I don't wish to be heard."

"I said ye were expected." Gorm didn't even look at the mercenary; he just stared into the empty eyes of Zurthraka's iron death mask. "I'd imagined you'd wanted to finish me yerself."

"Well, rank has its privilege," said Mr. Flinn. "As much as I've enjoyed our rivalry these past few weeks, I confess I'll enjoy ending it much more."

"I suppose Niln's dead."

"Officially, he was killed by the Orcs during the theft of the Elven Marbles."

Gorm nodded. He'd already mourned the high scribe, along with all the rest, back when his heart still ached, before the numbness set in. "I imagine we were officially killed at the same time."

"That will be the story, once we've rooted your friends out of their tower and I've finished with you. I'm afraid you're much more valuable as victims than heroes," said Mr. Flinn. The assassin was circling warily, looking for an opening in the defenses that Gorm wouldn't bother to raise. "Though, I must admit, you played your part admirably here."

Gorm shut his eyes. "Ye knew I'd bring the stones here?"

"Sir Johan did, yes." Mr. Flinn beamed, the glee evident in his voice. "He was certain that you'd bring the marbles to the Orcs once he heard you were traveling with a Goblin. It's why he insisted that you be recruited. And when you punched the Elven captain for insulting a greenskin, we all knew that he'd been right."

"He could always count on me to do the right thing," said Gorm, recalling Johan's last words to him. "But why bother with all that if ye planned to kill the party in the Myrewood?"

"Heroes have a habit of ruining the best of plans, and your party was no exception. You were our contingency plan, Mr. Ingerson," laughed Mr. Flinn. "We would have preferred that a Guild Inspector find your bodies alongside some Orc corpses in the Myrewood. You escaped our ambush, but then you found the stones and gave them to the Orcs of Bloodroot. You slipped out of Haertswood before my forces could apprehend you there, yet you brought your party straight back here. Whenever your team escaped our grasp, you immediately brought them back into our hands. I've never met so predictable a rebel."

Gorm shook his head. He was a rebel no more; the fight had left him. His last failure was his greatest shame, but at least he wouldn't have to suffer it long.

"You've made all of this possible, Mr. Ingerson. I truly mean it when I say that we couldn't have done it without you. And as your thanks, I'll make your end swift."

He could see Mr. Flinn tensing for the final strike, a shortsword readied in each hand. Behind him, snickering Silver Talons watched and waited for their leader to deliver the final blow. In truth, Gorm was waiting for the same thing.

He turned back to the cairn he'd built for Tib'rin. Zurthraka's gaist. The forgotten doll. The nondescript granite beads. Though, now that he thought of it, the pattern he'd arranged the beads in had broken somehow. He stared at the pile quizzically.

The beads moved.

Gorm's breath caught in his throat as the heartseeker beads rotated in unison to point northeast. Somewhere across the Ruskan landscape, an Orc was pressing the Heartstone, calling to his brothers and sisters. There could be hundreds, no, even thousands of them out there, trying to connect again.

A spark of something long forgotten awoke in Gorm. They could rebuild the tribe. They could start anew. Yet the Orcs would be branded as foes. They'd be hunted by the guild and its heroes. They'd be pariahs, with nobody to stand up for them. No one to fight with them. Nobody to take their side.

Gorm reached out and seized the spark. "Me," he whispered.

Mr. Flinn must have seen the change in Gorm, noticed the sudden glint in the Dwarf's eye, and thought better of a frontal assault. The Gnome deftly changed course mid-charge, which was the only reason Gorm's sudden punch didn't break his jaw. It was still enough to send him reeling into the dust.

"Well," said the assassin, pushing himself to his feet. "It seems that we shall—"

"Shut your trap," said Gorm, retrieving his axe and shield. He felt the spark growing, burning, fanning flames within him that he hadn't thought he'd ever feel again. "You're right. I did this. I was so eager for a bloody title and some thrice-cursed loot that I let myself be blinded to the ways of the world. The blood of the Guz'Varda Tribe is on my hands."

He pointed his Orc-crafted axe squarely at the Tinderkin. "And I'm gonna wash it off with yours."

Mr. Flinn's smirk gleamed like his blades. "I think you'll find otherwise," he said, and he lunged forward again.

The assassin moved with a fluid grace, almost gliding through the air as he swept toward his target. His swords seemed to dance in his hands as he moved, weaving hypnotic patterns of steel and death.

Gorm held nothing but contempt for such fancy shenanigans. A quick jab from his shield put the prancing Gnome off balance, and the following blow from Gorm's axe forced an awkward dodge. Another punch with his shield caught Flinn directly in the face with a satisfying crunch. The reeling Gnome stumbled back, onto the ground.

"Did ye think I was scared of ye?" yelled Gorm, the fire growing within him. "Did ye think I joined the quest because ye've got a pair of short swords and ye murdered your mum? I played along because I didn't want to pit meself against the full force of the thrice-cursed Heroes' Guild and spend the rest of my life fighting their thugs and enforcers."

"They'll still come for you," said Mr. Flinn, trying to scramble to his feet.

"Aye! Let them come!" Gorm delivered an overhand chop that would have cloven the assassin's head in two, had he not managed a feeble parry. He swept the Gnome's sword aside with another shield bash. "I want to fight! I want them to know my name, and to know I'm comin' for them!"

Mr. Flinn dove to the side and scrambled for his swords. With a guttural roar, Gorm leaped upon the Gnome, bringing his axe down with the full force of his rising fury. Flinn tried to roll out of the way, but the axe caught his hand, lopping half of it off, from the edge of his wrist to just above his thumb.

The assassin sprang to his feet and tried to run, clutching his mangled hand. "Mr. Brunt, some assistance!" he screamed.

"Burn your bloody guild!" Gorm roared, charging after the fleeing Gnome. The fire within had become a roaring inferno. The rest of the world melted away, leaving only Gorm and his axe and the objects of his vengeance. "Burn your markets, and hang your king! Johan the Mighty is going to taste my axe! You're all on borrowed time!"

"Mr. Brunt!" screeched Mr. Flinn.

Suddenly, Brunt charged onto the battlefield, roaring with a volume to match Gorm's. The Dwarf got his shield up in time, but the force of the Ogre's punch still lifted him high into the air and sent him flying over the burning rubble. He felt a crack as he hit the wall, and then the world went crimson.

Chapter 19

Kaitha watched Brunt hit Gorm like a runaway carriage. The mercenaries below laughed and hooted as the Dwarf flew through the air, tumbling head over feet. The heroes collectively winced as he slammed into the wall of a burned-out factory with an unpleasant crunching noise. Their spirits sank as the warrior slid down the wall, a cloud of ash billowing from the flaming ruins where he landed.

Mr. Flinn turned back to the cheering Silver Talons, his face locked in a determined sneer as he clutched the stub of his hand. "One down, as they say. Right, Mr. Brunt?"

Then they heard the laughter, a rib-rattling cackle that echoed from the depths of the grave. All eyes turned to the ruins where Gorm had landed. A figure was emerging from the ash and flames: a Dwarf-shaped apparition that barely resembled the warrior Kaitha knew. He seemed a demon wrought from soot and sweat, his beard glowing blood red in the firelight, his eyes like burning coals. With every step, he banged his axe on his shield, a slow and purposeful rhythm beneath the horrible laughter.

Several of the Silver Talons backed away from the advancing Dwarf. Mr. Flinn took a cautious step behind Mr. Brunt, although the Ogre seemed just as unsettled. Even the flames around the warrior writhed and parted as he walked, as if trying to get out of his way.

"What's happening right now?" asked Heraldin.

Kaitha knew. The handful of berserkers she had encountered throughout her career were impressive and terrifying all at once, and they'd never achieved anywhere near the level of renown that Gorm Ingerson had once commanded.

"Pyrebeard," Kaitha whispered.

He ran toward the Ogre now, his axe hammering on his shield with every step, a bestial roar in his throat. Brunt responded with a bellow of his own and lumbered forward.

"This is madness," said Jynn.

"Yes," agreed Kaitha as the combatants met. "Brunt should have run."

Gorm was a whirlwind with a manic grin, ducking and weaving and striking around the bellowing Ogre. Kaitha couldn't actually see the Dwarf moving, but Brunt jerked and shuddered like a broken marionette under the onslaught. He staggered from an axe blow to the shoulder, reeled from a shield bash to the nose, doubled over at a strike to the kidneys, and was knocked back by a steel-toed boot to the face.

The assembled mercenaries fell silent when Gorm finally landed, still howling like a madman. A moment later, Brunt toppled into the dust behind him.

"That was unexpected," said Jynn.

"Flinn seems to have predicted it well enough," said Heraldin. "Look."

Gaist pointed. Kaitha saw the Gnome pressing through the lines of Silver Talons, headed for the city gates. A moment later, Gorm hit the ranks of mercenaries like a cannonball, sending men and their dismembered components scattering into the air. The impact signaled the start of a race; Flinn pushed through the panicked crowd of soldiers, and Gorm carved a path in hot pursuit.

"He's winning a brawl with an army," said Laruna.

"For now," said Jynn. "But it's only a matter of time before the Silver Talons collect themselves, or he slips."

Kaitha sent an arrow out the window and into the throat of a Silver Talon. "Well then," she said with a determined grin. "Let's go even the odds."

It was as smooth and professional an operation as Kaitha had ever participated in. A sudden eruption of sorcerous flame blew the trap door off the tower and onto the unfortunate soldiers below. The heroes rolled down the steps and across the courtyard. Laruna dispersed crowds of mercenaries with great spouts of flame. Kaitha and Jynn covered her flanks, sending arrows or blasts of magic to put down any resistance the Silver Talons mustered. Heraldin and Gaist ran around the group, striking at groups of archers as they attempted to rally. They scythed through the crowd of soldiers with mechanical precision, like a Gnomish harvest engine through a field of wheat.

The problem with mercenaries, from an employer's perspective anyway, is that while it is relatively easy to find a man who will fight for money, it's much less common to find those willing to die for a paycheck. Seeing Brunt fall diminished the resolve of the soldiers; getting caught between five heroes and a Dwarf-shaped ball of rage and death demolished it. The rank and file began to evaporate. A few self-preserving individuals broke away from the rear of the battalion, and the formations nearest the heroes began to fall apart as mercenaries scrambled to avoid them. Soon, almost the entire army was running for one gate or another.

There were still pockets of resistance amid the chaos. A squad of dagger-wielding assassins rushed to attack the heroes' rear, but stopped short when their leader began to bubble and smoke. The man twitched and shrieked as his skin burned away, his body shriveled and black beneath it.

"Do you have to kill them so … messily?" Kaitha said, making a face.

"Noctomancy is effective, not aesthetic," said Jynn, deftly weaving a death spell around the mercenary. "Besides, I think fear is a more efficient way to win the day." He nodded to the rest of the squad, who were backing away from the withered husk of their squad leader.

"Fair enough," said Kaitha, dropping another assassin with an arrow to the eye. The rest of the squad turned and fled.

"Magic shield," said Laruna.

Ahead of them, a group of mages had conjured a sorcerous barrier, shimmering in the hazy air, and ranks of archers were gathering behind it. The archers wound their crossbows, took aim at the advancing heroes, and shrieked in dismay as several clouds of greenish smoke engulfed the squad of mercenaries.

"The bannerman's gambit!" Heraldin called, bounding into the cloud from the mage's right flank as Gaist sprang into the opposite side of the cloud.

Kaitha couldn't see into the noxious cloud, but if the screams and cringe-inducing crunches that emanated from it were any indication, the bannerman's gambit was decidedly unpleasant. The bard and weaponsmaster bounded back into view a moment later.

"Let's choose another route," said Heraldin, directing them down a different street. "When that smoke clears, it's not going to be pretty in there. Even Gaist wouldn't want to see it."

Gaist nodded.

As they fought, they caught only glimpses of Gorm—a murderous, screaming phantom amid the destruction. Kaitha saw him burst through the wall of a charred hut to pounce on a terrified mage. Heraldin pointed out the Dwarf chasing a pack of mercenaries atop the roof of one of the ruined factories; Gorm caught them as they all went over the edge. Jynn swore he saw the berserker riding on the shoulders of a fleeing Silver Talon, laughing and waving his axe as he went.

Despite herself, Kaitha was smiling as well. On the one hand, her career was officially dead, and the guild would prefer it if she was as well; on the other hand, the exhausting pursuit of success had ended. She'd caught it once, it got away, and now she was free. There would be no more loot, no ranks, no agents, no vying to get into the most prestigious parties or the biggest jobs.

She felt like a new Elf. On this side of the guild, being a ranger meant what it was always supposed to: self-sufficiency, defending the weak, and the pursuit of justice. There was a purity, a simplicity, to the idea. It was like being in the garden in the Myrewood, or sitting with the King in the Wood, as she imagined him anyway. She couldn't be sure if she was regaining some part of herself that she had lost, or finding the person she always wished to be, but it was what she had always yearned for.

"Perhaps I missed what I never had," she said.

"What?" asked Laruna.

"Nothing," said Kaitha, and she put an arrow through a charging mercenary's throat. It did sound a little mad when she said it aloud. Perhaps she was touched by the All Mother after all.

She didn't care if she was.

Garold Flinn, as a rule, never fled. He was not fleeing as he dashed northward, clutching the remnants of his ruined hand; he was making a tactical retreat, which stood in contrast to the common soldiers desperately running through the streets. Flinn had a plan, and a destination, whereas the rabble making a mass exit around him had no goals beyond existing another hour or so. Flinn paid them no mind. Silver Talon deserters were dead to him, and they'd be dead to everyone else as well shortly after this business with the heroes was settled.

The thrice-cursed heroes! He could still hear the Dwarf's roaring laughter echoing through the city. Johan predicted that Gorm Ingerson would lie down and die after the Orcs were dead, just like he tried to drink himself to death after being shamed at the dungeon of Az'Anon. The paladin's theory had held true, right up until Gorm gave Flinn a punch the Gnome could still feel.

Flinn shook off the thought. It was of no matter. There was a contingency in place, of course. There were always contingencies; that was the hallmark of good planning, after all. And the latest contingency was the greatest yet: a third battalion lying in wait just beyond the north gate. The heroes thought they had broken Flinn's forces, but when several hundred men marched into the chaos of Bloodroot, the element of surprise would belong to the Silver Talons again.

The heroes who had ransacked Bloodroot came from the south and left south again, so the north gate was still closed and barred when Flinn reached it. It took considerable effort for the Tinderkin to lift the heavy bar, using his back to spare his mangled hand. He used his good arm and shoulder to push the door open, heaving with everything he had. When he finally stumbled through to the road beyond the gate, he stopped short.

The road and field were empty. Nothing was in place.

On second glance, parts of the army were in place. They were just in more places than they should have been, and decidedly sticky. Weapons had been dropped in the field.

Flinn stepped through the gate. "What the flaming—?"

A pile of stones shifted, and then began to stand. Lichens grew into hair, rocks became hands and fingers, and a large boulder near the front became an unpleasant-looking face that curled into a snarl. The

Troll drew itself to its full height and stared at Flinn with undisguised hostility.

The situation warranted a moment of reflection. Flinn had no army, no Ogre, and crucially, no more contingencies. He was unarmed, wounded, and face-to-face with one of the most deadly beasts on Arth, a specimen that appeared to have a predilection for killing Silver Talons, no less.

As a rule, Garold Flinn never fled.

His tactical retreat back to Aberreth, however, was much more frantic than normal.

When the crimson fog finally lifted, the world was dark and wet. A quick inventory told him that he still had all of his limbs and digits, his beard was intact, and, miraculously, nothing felt worse for wear. He could have sworn he remembered cracking a rib.

Gorm Ingerson was lying in a ditch, covered in sooty mud, staring into a smoke-filled sky that was suddenly eclipsed by a pair of beady red eyes and a set of long fangs.

"Hello, Thane," he said.

"I was wondering when you'd wake up," said the Troll, taking a step back.

"I'd say a few more minutes yet." Gorm winced as he laboriously pulled himself to a sitting position. His mouth tasted of soot and … something metallic. Copper, perhaps. "What happened?"

"We broke the army of the men in black armor," said Thane, "and chased the remnants from the city."

Gorm nodded. Scenes of the fight flitted before his eyes, flickers of memories cast in shades of crimson. "I remember the battle, I think."

"I would hope so. From what I could hear you sounded very … enthusiastic about it."

"I felled Brunt," said Gorm, clutching his head as he tried to remember. "What happened to Flinn?"

"Who?"

"The Gnomish snake that always stuck by that Ogre's side."

Thane considered it. "A little man with a topknot and a thin beard? I saw him flee."

"Ah, should have been the other way around, if one of them had to live. I don't think Brunt was as bad as he was loyal. I'd be surprised if he was smart enough to understand what he was fightin' for, anyway. But Garold Flinn helped orchestrate this whole thing. He's a big part of the reason Bloodroot and Tib'rin …" Gorm stopped himself. The thought of the Silver Talons' leader was enough to have him balling his hands into a fist so tight it hurt. Much more talk of him and the crimson mist would descend again.

"Where are the others?" Gorm asked.

"They're searching the ruins for you."

"Oh? Then what are you doing here? Won't ye be seen?"

"They're searching the other side of the city," said Thane, jabbing a thumb over his shoulder.

There wasn't much Gorm could remember about the other heroes in the fight, although he had a vague recollection they'd watched him fall from a roof. Still, Gorm was a veteran of waking up in a strange place with a surplus of questions and a shortfall of memories. He wasn't even hungover this time.

"Right." Getting to his feet took considerable effort. "We'd best be making our way over there."

Thane lumbered alongside him. "What happens now?" he asked.

"Still figuring that out," said Gorm. He mulled over his options as they walked through the city. Oddly enough, being marked for death by the Heroes' Guild didn't trouble him. If anything, there was a comfortable familiarity about it; the guild had wanted him tried and hanged well before he'd ever heard of this quest. The only difference now was that the guild would be actively seeking his downfall, and that the feeling was mutual.

"So did ye fight the mercenaries?" Gorm asked as they neared Bloodroot's central square.

"They had a force of many men hiding to the north," said the Troll. "I ambushed them in their hiding spot."

"Ye took out a third battalion?"

"I felled some of them. Most ran away when they saw me." The Troll smiled and shrugged. "I have that effect on people."

"Some people. I find it's handy having a Troll around. Thank ye, Thane."

Thane's grin was like a motley set of daggers. "I'd say our arrangement is working out rather well."

Gorm stopped in front of the cairn he'd built, now covered in ash and dust and spattered with blood. "There ain't no more arrangement," he said. "I'm dissolving it."

Panic flashed across the Troll's face. "But, you said—"

"Your secret's safe. I won't tell anyone about ye until you're ready, no matter how much I think ye should step forward and be seen for what ye are. And if ye want to continue to fight alongside us, it's an honor and a great help. But I'll not have your aid because you're in my debt, or because I'm holdin' your secrets ransom." He lifted the heartseeker beads from Tib'rin's grave. "And I'll not have ye pretending to be me squire, or taking orders from me neither. I ain't better than nobody. And I'll not have ye act like it."

Thane wore a small smile as he shook his head. "Gorm, I never thought you acted like you were—"

"Never again!" shouted Gorm. His eyes stung, and it wasn't just the ash in the air. "I'll never again have a better man than I actin' like it's the other way around, be they pink or green or brown or gray. You're not me squire, me debtor, or me victim. You're me friend, and that's the only arrangement we'll ever have from here on out. Understand?"

The Troll replied with a burly hug that crushed the air from Gorm's lungs.

Duine Poldo placed his platinum pen in its small mahogany case. He snapped the lid shut and read the message engraved upon the top in bright golden letters: "Duine Poldo—100 Years of Fyne Service—

Goldson Baggs." With a sigh, he placed it atop his other belongings in the box. Then he squared away his blotter, refilled the inkwell for his successor, and carried his box down the steps from his high desk.

The other employees avoided eye contact with Poldo in the hallway. Avoiding eye contact with a Scribkin is easy for most, as simple as not looking down. His old staff gave him apologetic nods as he passed through the room, but nobody actually dared to say goodbye. Poldo couldn't blame them; it was best not to be any more associated with someone on the way out than you needed to be.

Laughter rang out from the executive lounge. Through the steel and glass doors, Poldo could see Mr. Goldson and Mr. Baggs having a drink with Grandmaster Weaver Ortson of the Heroes' Guild and Johan the Mighty. They toasted each other in celebration and laughed raucously at each other's jokes. Poldo was staring when Johan the Mighty noticed and gave him a wink. Mr. Goldson noticed and gave Poldo a glare that sent the Scribkin scurrying on his way.

He clutched his box to his chest as he waited for the lift in the lobby. The smooth black doors opened, revealing an Elf in a scarlet and gold uniform.

Poldo sighed as the lift began to descend. He'd never thought he'd miss a Gnoll, but he had quite liked Hrurk. The old lift attendant had been loyal, easy to please, and didn't shed much. But on the day that Poldo was given notice, Hrurk had told Poldo, in a nervous whisper, that rumors were spreading among the Shadowkin, rumors that the Orcs of Bloodroot had been framed, that no papers could really be trusted anymore. The Gnoll quit and went missing before word that the Bloodroot quest was complete even reached the top offices. Poldo could only assume the Gnoll had taken his family and fled, as had most of the NPCs Poldo knew.

The lobby, all smooth steel and black marble, bustled with activity. Shouts of traders and plunder-fund managers washed over Poldo as he stepped out the doors of Goldson Baggs. Poldo held his box tightly, gaping at the spectacle. Up and down the Wall, everyone was in a frenzy of buying and selling. The exodus of NPCs had turned an entire class of citizens into a commodity. Wherever the fleeing Shadowkin were found holed-up could be declared a new dungeon, a new quest, a new cache of loot for the Heroes' Guild to harvest. As the sun set on the NPC program, a golden age of professional heroics was dawning. It was a whole new world.

A terrible new world.

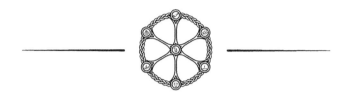

The bead pivoted in Gorm's palm, reorienting its tapered end to point north by northwest. He closed his fist around it and looked toward the northern pine forests, black against the late-afternoon sky. The sun would set soon. "They're in the Pinefells," he said. "They've started to head west."

Kaitha followed his gaze. "Are we going to follow them?"

"If ye was an Orc of Bloodroot and we came knocking on your doorstep, what would ye do?"

"I'd have our heads on pikes," said Laruna.

"Aye. Far as they can see, we're probably the worst professional heroes of the lot."

"So what will we do?" asked Jynn.

"We're alone out here, with limited gear and no healing potions," said Kaitha.

"Yes, we know the healing potions went missing," said Heraldin.

"Well, it's important!" snapped the Elf.

"We'll reach out to other Shadowkin, make our case to them," said Gorm. "Gather evidence against the guild. Whatever we can to convince the Guz'Varda that we aren't who they think we are. Then we'll find them."

"I don't know about you," said Heraldin. "But I'm hearing a lot of 'we' here. Some of us might prefer to return to Andarun and straighten this out with the guild."

"Don't be daft. The guild's way of straightening this out would be to put a sword through you and dump your corpse in the river," said Jynn.

"Ah. Good point," said the bard. "Then we could petition King Handor for a pardon."

"The same king who set us up on this phony quest?" said Kaitha. "Do you think an army of Silver Talons killed poor Niln and tried to do the same to us without Handor's blessing?"

"Well, then, we could seek sanctuary at a temple." Heraldin was starting to sound desperate.

"What temple will shelter you from the Champion of Tandos?" asked Laruna. "Johan the Mighty had his hand in the scheme."

"But … but …" Heraldin looked around for some hope of escape, some alternate path. A heavy hand fell on his shoulder, and he looked up to see the weaponsmaster.

Gaist shook his head.

"You're right, my friend," sighed Heraldin. "I'm sorry."

"Look around ye," Gorm told the other adventurers. "We're all we got. So we stick together. There's no guild, no kingdom, no temple for us. This is as much home as ye'll have until this ends, one way or another, because as far as Andarun is concerned, we're foes. Villains. Outlaws."

"A criminal after all," sighed Heraldin. "Benny Hookhand will be wearing my skin for this."

"I'd say you've got bigger problems than Benny Hookhand," said Jynn.

"Then I'd say you've clearly never crossed paths with Benny Hookhand."

"The sun is setting," said Laruna.

Gorm nodded. "It's time."

The heroes gathered around a small triangle made from three pine branches set atop a stone cairn, just outside the gates of Bloodroot. The memorial was covered in small tokens. Falcon feathers were holy to Al'Matra, but as no falcons could be found, a few hawk feathers had to suffice. Kaitha had contributed one of her arrows. The mages had each dropped off arcane-looking gems, and Heraldin and Gaist had found some torn silks to hang from the triangle's peak.

Gorm had found a silver and gold icon of a glowmoth amid the charred rubble, an emblem of Fulgen, the Silent God. Why the Orcs had an icon of the Dwarven God of Light remained a mystery. Still, a holy symbol was a holy symbol, and it seemed appropriate that a high scribe's memorial would have some sacred object or another. Besides,

Fulgen was said to be a friend to anyone in need. Perhaps the Light in the Darkness would guide Niln's spirit wherever it was meant to go.

Heraldin sang. Kaitha blessed the high scribe's spirit. The mages conjured globes of light to dance over the ceremony. Gaist put his hand upon the memorial, eyes closed, reverent. Tears were shed and memories shared.

"Ye were the least hero among us, and yet ye were the best of us," Gorm told Niln's memorial. "And ye accomplished something. Ye mattered, and not just to those of us that loved ye. Ye changed our world, Niln. And we're going to change everybody else's, for ye."

Then the heroes said their goodbyes and headed off.

Gorm lingered for a moment. "And I'll read your books," he whispered to Niln, patting the satchel that held Niln's scriptures and notes. "Not because I believe in the Dark Prince or the Seventh Hero or any of that nonsense, but just because I'm your friend, and I need to believe ye still know that somehow."

"Come on, Gorm!" shouted Laruna.

"Aye!" He hurried after them and caught up at the first bend in the road.

"It's going to feel strange," Kaitha said. "Not being heroes anymore."

"What are ye talkin' about. I'm still a hero," said Gorm.

"Not as far as the Heroes' Guild is concerned," said Jynn.

"Burn the guild. Everybody's hero is someone else's villain, aye? And the other way around. We'll be a hero to those who don't have many of them."

Gaist nodded.

"Right," said Heraldin. "But we're no longer professionals."

"Why? Ye get another job?" asked Gorm. "Is this a hobby now?"

"I suppose we didn't really lose our jobs at all," said Kaitha. "We're just working pro bono now."

"That's even worse," said Heraldin.

Gaist patted him on the back.

"No, my friend, don't try to cheer me up. Look at me. A traveling bard siding with the Orcs, working for free. Who would have thought I'd wind up this way?"

"We'll call it progress," said Gorm.

The heroes laughed together as they made their way down the road.

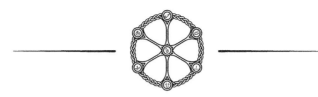

The fires of Bloodroot had all but burned out. Hissing coals lingered here and there, glowing orange in the cool twilight, but the smoke was clearing and the ash had settled. The rats and crows had yet to brave the ruins and partake of their morbid buffet of strewn Silver Talons. The city was empty.

Almost.

The Ogre's breathing was slow and labored. Blood and ash caked his skin. His eyes were glazed and vacant, much more so than normal.

He didn't even look at the figure approaching him. "Getting … old … for this … stuff …" Brunt rumbled weakly.

"I heard you only fought because it was your job," said the Troll.

"Was gonna … retire … two weeks," lamented the Ogre. Every word took intense concentration and fortitude, much more so than normal.

"But why did you fight with the mercenaries? Why did you help kill all of these Orcs?" asked Thane.

"Brunt … fight … for justice …"

"And is this justice?"

Brunt said nothing.

"Is it?" the Troll asked.

"No," whispered the Ogre. He closed his eyes, and the fight drained out of him.

Thane reached into his pouches. "I didn't steal these," he said. "I'm just watching them for … for my friends. So they don't get misused." He produced a small amber vial. "I'm like the party healer, if you really think about it. After all, I healed Gorm when I found him in the ditch."

Brunt opened one eye, but said nothing.

"The point is that having these potions is a big responsibility. But I don't think the others would mind giving one helping to a good man."

"Brunt … bad."

"You were," said the Troll, unstoppering the vial. The amber liquid sparkled in the twilight as the Troll poured it into the prone Ogre's mouth. "But you don't have to be." And he walked away, following the path the heroes had left in the fallen ash.

Brunt lay in ponderous silence for a long time. Then he sat up, heaved himself to his feet, and shuffled into the night.

Epilogue

The carriage rumbled through the woods, kicking up mud and splashing through puddles as it went. Jalana watched the trees fly by the window with little interest; she'd seen nothing but verdant forest since the carriage had entered the Green Span early that morning. As a Wood Elf—and Wood Elf nobility, no less—Jalana was expected to have a certain affinity for the trees. Perhaps she had, once, but she'd found the woods remarkably dull for at least three centuries. It was the primary reason she'd originally requested to be House Tyrieth's ambassador to Andarun.

Jalana smoothed the folds of her long violet gown and turned back to the other passenger in the wagon, an attendant sitting primly, quietly, on the velvet seats with a leather briefcase on her lap. She looked vaguely familiar, but as ambassador, Jalana had never paid much attention to the staff.

"Looking forward to our arrival in Tyrieth?"

"Yes, ma'am."

"Good. Though I'm surprised they let you on the carriage. I arranged for this trip in the utmost secrecy."

"Sorry, ma'am. I'm on top-secret business."

Jalana sighed. There was always something secret or classified going on in the embassy. She wanted no part of it. An ambassador, she liked to say, was like a local queen; her job was to be beautiful and attend galas and make everybody love House Tyrieth. The paperwork and debating was for her expansive staff and their underlings. "Well, so long as you keep this a secret. Who knows what they'd do to poor Boots if they knew I still had him?"

She nodded to the gently snoring handbag on the seat next to her. Boots's NPC papers had been revoked — almost all Shadowkin's had — in the wake of the mishap in the Baetwolds with the Elven Marbles. Andarun's Shadowkin started a mass exodus, and soon people started saying you couldn't trust the ones who stayed behind.

"Yes, ma'am."

"Why, he'd probably be hanged by a mob, the brutes. I mean, you can't trust most Shadowkin, certainly, but my Bootsy couldn't do a cantrip's harm. Why, he wouldn't hurt a fly."

"Yes, ma'am."

"I had to pull quite a few strings to get a secret carriage for him and I, you know." And Jalana didn't have many strings left to pull. House Tyrieth's influence wasn't what it had been after the shameful incident with the Elven Marbles. Kaitha — a former princess of the house! — was said to be among the villains who had betrayed and murdered the Al'Matrans' high scribe and tried to give the Elven Marbles to the Orcs. And now Jalana's sister and her fellow vagrants were said to be roaming the countryside like common bandits. It was disgraceful.

She eyed the attendant nervously. Something about the woman seemed untrustworthy. "You won't tell anyone about our Boots, will you?" she demanded.

"No, ma—"

The carriage jerked to a halt, flinging baggage and women alike around the cabin. Jalana was thrown to the floor, and something heavy landed on top of her. She heard a loud commotion outside. Steel rang on steel. Her guards screamed. There was a blast of heat and light from somewhere. Then everything fell silent.

"Boots?" Jalana pushed herself to her knees and started to ask the attendant what happened but cut her words off with a gasp. The attendant was gone, and in her place was a mirror image of Jalana. The impostor wore a malicious sneer and pointed a silver dagger at Jalana's throat.

"A doppelganger?" Jalana asked, just as the door burst open.

A ruddy face with a hawkish nose and a scar over the right eye poked through the entryway. "Hello there!" said the Dwarf, the same Dwarf who had visited Jalana's offices a few months back.

"You—!" said Jalana.

"You're Gorm Ingerson," said the impostor, hiding the dagger. "You're with—"

"My sister," said Jalana.

"Hey, Jalana," said Kaitha, poking her head in beside Gorm. "Whoa."

"Aye, suppose we should have seen it comin'," said Gorm. "Now, which one of ye fine ladies would be me old friend the Mask?"

"I'm Jalana," said her impostor. "This … this doppelganger turned into me!"

"Kaitha, what are you doing?" said Jalana, panic rising. "And I'm Jalana."

"She turned into me!" exclaimed her double. "I wouldn't be caught dead in an outfit like that!"

"I … how dare you?" gasped Jalana.

"Burt," barked Gorm, "care to settle this?"

Boots popped out of his purse, grinning widely and, Jalana was shocked to see, lighting a cigar.

"Boots?" she said.

"Not my real name, thanks," said Boots, or Burt, or whatever. He gave Jalana a curious sniff. "This is the real one," he told the Dwarf.

"I'm in your debt again." Gorm turned his attention to Jalana's snarling double. "Hello, Mask."

"I'm Jala—"

"Don't," said the Dwarf. "After all these years, I think we owe each other the truth, aye?"

Jalana's double was breathing heavily, her eyes searching for some avenue of escape.

"I'll be straight with ye, and maybe ye can do the same. We know ye tipped Johan off about me squire, and that's what got me recruited. And we're pretty sure it was ye who delivered the false evidence at the embassy, leadin' us to the Myrewood. Unless I miss my guess, ye were the arbiter who took our paperwork in Haertswood."

"I guess you've got this all figured out," snarled Jalana's double.

"Almost. We still don't know who's paying ye. The king and the Temple of Tandos would never dirty their hands. But I know someone is, and I'm bettin' the secret's in that briefcase of yours."

The doppelganger reflexively tightened its grip on the case.

"There's where our offer comes in," continued the Dwarf. "After what ye've done, I'd be in the right takin' yer head off here and now. But if ye hand over the case and come quietly, we'll take ye to the Shadowkin, and they'll try ye fairly. More fairly than I would, anyway. But I'm only givin' ye this—"

With a feral hiss, the doppelganger leaped for Jalana, raising its silver dagger. Before Jalana could scream, a massive fist in a black leather glove punched through the window opposite the Dwarf and caught her assailant by the throat. The false Jalana choked and clutched at the hand, her eyeballs bulging and then shifting as her face began to fluctuate between a myriad of different people.

"I was hopin' ye'd pick this way," said Gorm. "Much more expedient. Gaist."

The doppelganger was hauled back through the window by the massive weaponsmaster and dragged out of view. His brief scream cut off abruptly with grim certitude.

Jalana paled. "Gods above," she whispered.

"Ah, lady Jalana." A man in a bard's costume, complete with a wide-brimmed hat, leered through the hole in the carriage. "It's been a pleasure saving you today, but I understand that such unpleasantness can be unsettling to a lady of your delicate sensibilities."

"Thank ye, Heraldin," said Gorm.

"If you need anything after this traumatic experience, any comfort whatsoever, I'm willing—"

"Thank you, Heraldin," said Kaitha, much more firmly.

"As you say," sighed the bard. "Another time, my sweet," he told Jalana as he left.

Gorm reached into the wagon and grabbed the briefcase the doppelganger had been holding. He handed it back to the pair of mages, who popped it open and ruffled through the papers inside.

"Receipts, contracts, purchase orders," said the noctomancer. "We should be able to find what we need."

"Including an invoice made out for Goldson Baggs," said the solamancer.

"Well, fortune must have taken a shine to us. So the only question is, how much did ye know?"

Jalana startled as the Dwarf's gaze fell back on her. "What?"

"Ye knew we was on the quest. Flinn arranged our meeting with ye. It was the Mask who fed us the tip about the Myrewood, but he did it in your office, without ye knowin'. Leaves a man wondering if ye were in on the scheme."

"I didn't … I didn't know anything!" Jalana felt the panic rising again.

"Oh? Nobody told ye a thing?" said the Dwarf, leaning in.

Tears welled in Jalana's eyes. "Johan said you might talk of giving the marbles to the Orcs, but to just ignore it. They said we'd definitely get the marbles back. I swear."

"And I'm supposed to believe that?"

"I swear!" sobbed Jalana.

"Good!" beamed Gorm. "I thought as much. Kaitha told me ye wasn't in on it."

"You never had the inclination for intrigue," Kaitha told her.

"Never had the brains for it either," said Boots, taking a long drag of his cigar. "You got what you wanted, Dwarf? I kept up my end of the bargain."

"That ye did," said Gorm. "Come on, Burt. Let's go."

The Kobold grabbed a small pouch from the seat and hopped down. "Seeya, Lightling. It's been fun."

Jalana could barely comprehend what she was seeing. "Boots? You know these people?"

"Course he does," said Gorm. "How do ye think we tracked the Mask down?"

"You … you betrayed me?"

"That's nothing," called the Kobold, sauntering off. "Wait till you see what I did in your purse." The mages, the weaponsmaster, and the bard followed the diminutive Shadowkin into the woods.

Jalana's lip quivered uncontrollably. "But … where will I go?"

"House Tyrieth, I'd imagine," said Gorm. "Your driver and guards are bound up in the front. Ye should still make it by nightfall."

"Goodbye, Jalana," said Kaitha. "Give Mother my regards."

"Good travels," said Gorm with a friendly wave. He and Kaitha started after the other adventurers.

A sudden rush of anger welled in Jalana. "Enjoy your victory while you can!" she hollered after them. "Johan the Mighty is coming for you, and the king and the Heroes' Guild as well. Soon enough you'll pay for everything you've done!"

She regretted her outburst almost immediately. Gorm stopped and turned back to the wagon, wearing a strange grin, or perhaps baring his teeth. "What we've done?" he asked softly, walking back to the wagon. "Raiding a wagon here and there? Stopping a professional hero from slaughtering some Shadowkin now and then? Ye think Johan's worried about that?"

Jalana leaned back in her seat as he approached.

"Ye go back to Andarun," the Dwarf snarled, fire blazing in his eyes, "and ye tell Johan not to pay any mind to what we've done, 'cause it's a drop in the bucket, ye hear? We're coming for justice, even if we have to burn the world to get it. And as sure as the north wind blows cold in the winter, nothin' will stand in our way."

TO BE CONTINUED IN
THE DARK PROFIT SAGA BOOK II:
SON OF A LICHE

About the Author

J. Zachary Pike was once a basement-dwelling fantasy gamer, but over time he metamorphosed into a basement-dwelling fantasy writer. His animations, films, and books meld fantasy elements with offbeat humor. A New Englander by birth and by temperament, he writes strangely funny fiction on the seacoast of New Hampshire. Find him online at **www.jzacharypike.com**.

Read more books of Arth by J. Zachary Pike:

Son of a Liche
A Song of Three Spirits

Glossary

Agekeepers: A sect of esoteric historians who keep and update the official records of Arth. It is the Agekeepers who define when an age begins and ends.

Al'Matra: Technically, the highest-ranked Elven god, as the queen of the pantheon, the All Mother and her followers are really impoverished outcasts. The scriptures say that she went mad after the All Father's betrayal.

Al'Thadan: Once called the All Father, the high god was once the king of the pantheon. He is said to have been Arth's greatest defender against the forces of Mannon until he colluded with the Dark Lord during the War of Betrayal in the Third Age. According to the Agekeepers, Al'Thadan was struck down along with all the Sten at the end of the war.

Andarun: Capital of the Freedlands, built in a cleft of Mount Wynspar between the Ridge and the Wall.

Arth: A world much like Earth, but with more magic and fewer vowels.

Bannerman: The bannermen are the town guard, armies, and other armed officials of the Freedlands. Every branch of every civic organization within the Freedlands is required to maintain some number of armed men who may be called to arms when fealty demands it. Each bannerman is loyal to such a company, which is loyal to a city, which is loyal to Andarun, which is loyal to the Freedlands. In this way, each bannerman serves his country as well as his city-state.

Bugbear: Neither a bug nor a bear, but instead a rather large breed of Demi-gnoll.

Class: Professional Heroes fall into a variety of classes (e.g. warrior, mage) and sub-classes (e.g. swordsman, pyromancer), largely distinguished by the methods they use to kill monsters.

Doppelganger: A widely distrusted race of shapeshifters, commonly believed to have been created as infiltrators for Mannon's armies in the War of Betrayal. Doppelgangers would make ideal diplomats, were they not such ideal spies, double agents, and assassins as well.

Dragon: Great reptiles that command the elements, most famously fire. It is well known that dragons slumber deep beneath the ground atop great mounds of treasure, and it is universally agreed that it's always best to let sleeping dragons lie.

Drakes: Dragon-kin that are much like full dragons, except smaller, weaker, and nowhere near as smart. Drakes still pose a significant threat, however, especially when encountered in their native element.

Dwarf: Dwarves are shorter than Elves and Humans, but as Dwarves stand almost twice as wide at the shoulder and are famous for violent grudges, it's generally best not to mention that. Rigid, industrious, and usually stoic, Dwarves live in massive clanhomes dug under the mountains. To the puzzlement of many of the other races, there are no Dwarven women.

Elf: The most enigmatic of the Children of Light have sharp, angular features but flowing, graceful movements. They live in tree huts, and many of them have accumulated untold wealth. They are immortal and yet innocent, playful yet powerful, whimsical yet wise. Above all, they are infuriating to almost everyone who is not an Elf. Elves all belong to houses, each of which swears fealty to a Great House. Of course, Elven fealty shifts frequently, and so the Elven houses are forever in flux, playing games of intrigue and power.

Elixir: A miraculous healing potion brewed by magical means, elixir or salve can close wounds, restore organs, and even regrow lost limbs if consumed soon enough after an injury. It's nearly as effective as it is addictive.

The Empire: Usually referred to as the southern Empire or the Desert Empire, the Empire is the remnant of the Empire of Man.

The Empire of Man: An ancient nation that once ruled most of Arth, but was dismantled when the Freedlands and other provinces rose against it.

The Freedlands: The most powerful nation on Arth, the Freedlands is a federation of semi-autonomous city-states. The Freedlands has a small centralized government, ruled by a king set in Andarun, that regulates the powerful guilds, associations, and corporations that do business in the Freedlands and beyond.

Fulgen: Fulgen, also called the Underglow or Father Tinderhope, is the Dwarven god of light. He rules over candles in the darkness, purity among corruption, and truth amid lies. Among the Dwarves, he is a favorite of miners and heroes.

Giltin: The currency of the Freedlands, long considered the standard for all of Arth. The common symbol for giltin is G, as in 5G. One giltin is ten silver shillings. One shilling is ten copper cents.

Gnoll: A race of Shadowkin with canine traits, once known as Clan Galden, or the Golden Gnomes. Gnolls were bred for a variety of purposes in the War of Betrayal, and many of these breeds (technically known as Demi-gnolls) are still around today.

Gnome: Gnomes take as many shapes and sizes as the clouds in the sky. While their legends hold that all Gnomes once shared a common ancestor, the great Gnomish clans have all become their own sub-races. Be that as it may, it's proper to refer to any of them as a Gnome, be they a Halfling to a Tinderkin to a Deep Gnome. Said sub-races are often used interchangeably with clan names. All Gnomes stand shorter than most Humans, and most are shorter than Dwarves.

Goblin: A race of Shadowkin that descended from the lost clans of the Dwarves. Goblins are short, scrawny, potbellied creatures. Their skin is green, their limbs are spindly. Stereotypes say that Goblins excel at little except breeding, at which they are amazing. It's true that a handful of Goblins can become a tribe in just a few years.

Golem: Enchanted automatons created by the Scribkin, golems serve many useful purposes across Arth.

Griffin: It is said that a griffin is a lion with the head, talons, and wings of an eagle, but the Zoological Society of Monchester has determined that a griffin is, in actuality, a giant eagle with a lion's butt.

Gremlins: A race of Shadowkin with both feline and lizard-like qualities, once known as Clan Remlon, or Moon Gnomes. Gremlins are known for their inquisitive nature, their mastery of bioengineering, and their tenuous grasp of ethics. Over the centuries, they've created a multitude of Gremlin variants, from the acid-spitting Bilebelly Gremlins, to hulking Brute Gremlins, to spry and acrobatic Stablins, and so on. While some scholars have meticulously documented these variants over the years, most people recognize them all as "Gremlins," and accept a wide degree of "surprises" when dealing with them.

Halfling: Halflings are Gnomes of Clan Haughlin. They have round features, pot bellies, and curly brown hair (even on the tops of their feet.) While generally good-natured, Halflings are averse to manual labor, or indeed anything that isn't comfortable. Unfortunately, they're often very comfortable with petty theft.

Heroes' Guild: An international organization of professional adventurers who specialize in monster slaying, treasure acquisition, hostage retrieval, and more. The Heroes' Guild is among the largest and most powerful organizations on Arth. Its wealth rivals that of the city-states of the Freelands, and even some small countries.

High Magic: The elemental energy woven through the universe, high magic is called the great weave. High magic is divided into two distinct orders—solamancy and noctomancy.

Human: Y'know. Humans. Originally mixed-race men, the first Humans were children of Gnomes and Elves and Sten. In time, they became so common that they married among themselves and spread throughout Arth. Now they are the most populous race of man, outnumbering all of the old races combined.

Kobold: Kobolds are a diminutive breed of Demi-gnoll, standing just below a man's knee in height. They have big eyes, a short muzzle, thin limbs, and a severe case of small dog syndrome.

Lawyer-monks of Adchul: A reclusive sect of monks who believe that discipline, law, and study represent a non-exclusive method to obtain enlightenment, with no guarantee of enlightenment or of any other goods and services made by said monks.

Lizardman: One of the monstrous races, Lizardmen are small bipedal lizards that are surprisingly social given their reptilian origins.

Leviathan: A legendary sea monster said to be born of the ultimate evil.

Low Magic: The oldest laws of the universe, the rules of life and death, love and hatred, blood and bone.

Mankind, Man, Races of Man: Legends say the Creator made the four races of Man—the Dwarves, Elves, Gnomes, and Sten—to make Arth more interesting, and has regretted it ever since.

Mannon: Malice incarnate, the ancient foe of the Creator deceived mankind, created the Shadowkin, and even corrupted some of the gods in ages past. Depending on the temple one visits, it is said that Mannon is either dead, in hiding, or a little bit of him lives in all of our hearts.

Magic: The essential forces of the universe, as understood by those who fiddle with them. Magic is divided into high and low magic.

Mage: A person able to see and weave high magic, usually through years of dedicated study and social isolation.

Mercenary: Killers for hire. Specifically, mercenaries are the killers for hire that are not professional heroes. Assassins, soldiers, thugs, goons: they all fall under the general headline of "mercenary." While more common than professional heroes, mercenaries are less regulated. With some assassins and thugs aside, they're generally thought to be weaker as well.

Monstrous Races: Humanoids bred for various combat roles by Mannon and Noros to fight in the War of Betrayal, the monstrous races are

Continued next page

Continued from previous page

distinguished from Shadowkin in that they didn't descend from the races of Man.

Naga: A race of Shadowkin with serpentine traits, Naga were once Clan Nagata, the Iron Gnomes. They resemble green-skinned, scaled men and women from the waist up, but their lower halves are those of serpents.

Necromancer: While all noctomancers can touch the shadowy side of high magic that binds the dead, the word necromancer is reserved for those who have created undead for nefarious purposes.

Noctomancer: A member of the second great order of mages, the Order of the Moon. Noctomancers are Humans and Gnomes that can weave the elements of air, earth, and shadow.

Noros: Once the Gnomish god of dreams, Noros became Mannon's greatest lieutenant.

Orc: A race of Shadowkin, Orcs were once Elves that sided with Mannon. Hulking, bucket-jawed, green-skinned barbarians, Orcs have a war-torn history and a legacy of brutality.

Order of the Moon: See Noctomancer.

Order of the Sun: See Solamancer.

Owlverine: All the deadly ferocity of an owlbear, packed into a beast no bigger than an owlhound.

Ogre: One of the monstrous races, Ogres are like clubs: big, simple, and made for violence.

Rank (Heroes' Guild): There's no way to measure the value of a life, except the life of a professional hero, in which case their rank is an effective metric. As a hero attains ranks in different classes by killing things, it's essentially a measure of how deadly, and therefore how valuable, a hero is.

Scarg: A vaguely humanoid bat-like creature, the origins of scargs are unknown. Some say they're naturally occurring monsters, while others say scargs are a monstrous race or a Gremlin experiment gone wrong.

They come in many varieties and breeds, most of which are more annoying than threatening to a professional hero.

Scribkin: The Gnomes of Clan Tinkrin, or Scribkin, stand half as tall as most Humans, with stocky builds, bulbous noses, and thick, bushy hair. Industrious and curious, Scribkin are Arth's most innovative inventors, enchanters, and engineers.

Shadowkin: Legends hold that by the Third Age, many of Arth's people followed Mannon or the gods loyal to him. Before launching the War of Betrayal, Mannon and Noros corrupted these lost people into more aggressive, poetically ironic shadows of their former selves.

Slaugh: Imagine a Gnome-sized frog walking on its haunches. Now imagine it has a foul temperament and a fouler odor. Now you know why almost everybody hates Slaugh. Technically, they're Shadowkin descended from the Gnomes of Clan Slaughin, but other Shadowkin are loath to admit as much.

Solamancer: A member of the first great order of mages, the Order of the Sun. Solamancers are Humans and Elves that can weave the elements of fire, water, and light.

Sten: The great traitors. Legends say that members of the fourth race of man were long considered aloof and enigmatic before they followed the traitor god Al'Thadan and colluded with Mannon. Gray-skinned, as tall as Elves, and as broad as Dwarves, Sten were masters of low magic. The Agekeepers confirm that they were wiped out in the War of Betrayal.

Tandos: The Elven god of war and glory, Tandos is the greatest son of Al'Thadan and Al'Matra. It was he who finally struck down his traitorous father, and it was Tandos's servants who defeated the Sten. Today, he rules over the pantheon as the divine regent in the place of his mother, who is unfit for rule.

Tinderkin: The Gnomes of Clan Kaedrin, Tinderkin are taller than any other Gnomes, standing a little taller than even a Dwarf. They are lithe, graceful figures with sharp, slender features. Tinderkin are nomadic, traveling in small, familial bands. They take their name from the fires they build for nightly gatherings, which are often elaborate visual spectacles.

Troll: Trolls are massive, ape-like creatures, the corrupted remnants of the now-extinct Sten. A Troll is a gray-skinned Shadowkin with a flat, broad-nostrilled face and a shaggy coat of thick fur. They have peerless regenerative abilities and can shrug off mortal blows or regrow limbs within minutes. Originally bred for war and killing, they are regarded as good for little else.

Wizard: A title given to male mages. Its counterpart, witch, fell into disuse during the Age of Darkness.

Wynspar: The mighty mountain that Andarun is set inside is riddled with caves, tunnels, dungeons, and various other dark places for monstrous horrors to lurk.

Wyvern: A variety of drake with leathery wings instead of forelegs, much akin to a bat, and a barbed, venomous tail, much akin to a scorpion. It is every bit as unpleasant as it sounds.

It was an unusual rat, and not just for its extraordinary size and exaggerated features but also for the vermilion twinges in its coat, like flame dancing in its fur when it moved; the eyes that burned with an otherworldly malevolence; and the unnatural death scream it gave when a dagger pinned it to the bottom of its cage.

For a time, they sat and watched the dead rat.

"And you're sure where you got this?"

They were.

A moment later, the rat began to hiss like a teakettle that had been left on too long. The air around it thrummed to a climax, and the cage exploded in a flash of light and smoke.

"Interesting."

An imp leaped from the wreckage with a burst of minuscule pyrotechnics. The tiny demon cackled falsetto and whisked itself away in a burst of sulfur, presumably to wreak some tiny evil upon the world. Moments later, a rat, bewildered but otherwise unremarkable, crawled from the ruins of the cage, sniffed the air, and skittered away.

Detarr Ur'Mayan sat back to consider the specimen, clasping his skeletal hands in front of a lipless grin. "Very interesting," he said

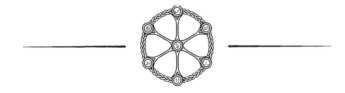

Printed in Great Britain
by Amazon